Dream a Little Dream

Dream a Little Dream

Susan Elizabeth Phillips

ISIS
LARGE PRINT
Oxford

First published in Great Britain 2006
by
Piatkus Books Ltd

Published in Large Print 2006 by ISIS Publishing Ltd.,
7 Centremead, Osney Mead, Oxford OX2 0ES
by arrangement with
Piatkus Books Ltd

British Library Cataloguing in Publication Data
Phillips, Susan Elizabeth
    Dream a little dream. – Large print ed.
    1. Single mothers – Fiction
    2. Widowers – Fiction
    3. Love stories
    4. Large type books
    I. Title
    813.5'4 [F]

ISBN-10 0–7531–7736–6 (hb)
ISBN-13 978-0-7531-7736-5 (hb)
ISBN 978-0-7531-7737-2 (pb)

Printed and bound in Great Britain by
T. J. International Ltd., Padstow, Cornwall

To Tillie and her sons.
And in memory of Dad and Bob.

CHAPTER
ONE

The last of Rachel Stone's luck ran out in front of the Pride of Carolina Drive-In. There on a mountainous two-lane blacktop road shimmering from the heat of the June afternoon, her old Chevy Impala gave its final death rattle.

She barely managed to pull off onto the shoulder before a plume of dark smoke rose from beneath the hood and obscured her vision. The car died right beneath the drive-in theater's yellow and purple starburst-shaped sign.

This final disaster was overwhelming. She folded her hands on top of the steering wheel, dropped her forehead on them, and gave in to the despair that had been nipping at her heels for three long years. Here on this two-lane highway, just outside the ironically named Salvation, North Carolina, she'd finally reached the end of her personal road to hell.

"Mommy?"

She wiped her eyes on her knuckles and lifted her head. "I thought you were asleep, honey."

"I was. But that bad sound waked me up."

She turned and gazed at her son, who had recently celebrated his fifth birthday, sitting in the backseat amidst the shabby bundles and boxes that held all their worldly possessions. The Impala's trunk was empty simply because it had been smashed in years ago and couldn't be opened.

Edward's cheek was creased where he'd been lying on it, and his light-brown hair stuck up at his cowlick. He was small for his age, too thin, and still pale from the recent bout with pneumonia that had threatened his life. She loved him with all her heart.

Now his solemn brown eyes regarded her over the head of Horse, the bedraggled stuffed lop-eared rabbit that had been his constant companion since he was a toddler. "Did something bad happen again?"

Her lips felt stiff as she formed them into a reassuring smile. "A little car trouble, that's all."

"Are we gonna die?"

"No, honey. Of course we're not. Now why don't you get out and stretch your legs a little bit while I take a look. Just stay back from the road."

He clamped Horse's threadbare rabbit's ear between his teeth and climbed over a laundry basket filled with secondhand play clothes and a few old towels. His legs were thin, pale little sticks hinged with bony knees, and he had a small port-wine mark at the nape of his neck. It was one of her favorite places to kiss. She leaned over the back of the seat and helped him with the door, which functioned only a little better than the broken trunk.

Are we gonna die? How many times had he asked her that question recently? Never an outgoing child, these last few months had made him even more fearful, guarded, and old beyond his years.

She suspected he was hungry. The last filling meal she'd given him had been four hours ago: a withered orange, a carton of milk, and a jelly sandwich eaten at a roadside picnic table near Winston-Salem. What kind of mother couldn't feed her child better than that?

One who only had nine dollars and change left in her wallet. Nine dollars and change separating her from the end of the world.

She caught a glimpse of herself in the rearview mirror and remembered that she'd once been considered pretty. Now lines of strain bracketed her mouth and fanned out from the corners of green eyes that seemed to eat up her face. The freckled skin over her cheekbones was so pale and tightly stretched it looked as if it might split. She had no money for beauty salons, and her wild mane of curly auburn hair swirled like a tattered autumn leaf around her too-thin face. The only cosmetic she had left was the stub of a mocha-colored lipstick that lay at the bottom of her purse, and she hadn't bothered to use it in weeks. What was the point? Though she was twenty-seven, she felt like an old woman.

She glanced down at the sleeveless blue chambray dress that hung from her bony shoulders. The dress was faded, much too big, and she'd had to replace one of its six red buttons with a brown button after the original cracked. She'd told Edward she was making a fashion statement.

3

The Impala's door squealed in protest as she opened it, and when she stepped out onto the blacktop, she felt the heat radiating through the paper-thin soles of her worn white sandals. One of the straps had broken. She'd done her best to sew it back together, but the result had left a rough place that had rubbed the side of her big toe raw. It was a small pain compared with the larger one of trying to survive.

A pickup truck whizzed by but didn't stop. Her wild hair slapped her cheeks, and she used her forearm to push away the tangled strands, as well as to shield her eyes from the billow of dust the truck kicked up. She glanced over at Edward. He was standing beside the bushes with Horse tucked under his armpit and his head bent at a sharp angle so he could stare up at the yellow and purple star-burst-shaped sign that soared above him like an exploding galaxy. Outlined in lightbulbs, it contained the words *Pride of Carolina*.

With a feeling of inevitability, she lifted the hood, then stepped back from the gust of black smoke billowing from the engine. The mechanic in Norfolk had warned her the engine was going to blow, and she knew this wasn't anything that could be fixed with duct tape or a junkyard part. Her head dipped. Not only had she lost a car, but she had also lost her home, since she and Edward had been living in the Impala for nearly a week. She'd told Edward they were lucky to be able to take their house with them, just like turtles.

She sat back on her heels and tried to accept the newest in a long string of calamities that had brought her back to this town she'd sworn she'd never return to.

4

"Get out of there, kid."

The threatening sound of a deep male voice cut through her misery. She stood so fast it made her woozy, and she had to grab the hood of the car for support. When her head cleared, she saw her son standing frozen before a menacing-looking stranger in jeans, an old blue work shirt, and mirrored sunglasses.

Her sandals slipped in the gravel as she flew around the rear of the car. Edward was too frightened to move. The man reached for him.

Once she'd been sweet-tongued and gentle, a dreamy country girl with a poet's soul, but life had toughened her, and her temper flared. "Don't you touch him, you son of a bitch!"

His arm dropped slowly to his side. "This your kid?"

"Yes. And get away from him."

"He was peein' in my bushes." The man's rough, flat voice held a distinct Carolina drawl, but not the smallest trace of emotion. "Get him out of here."

She noticed for the first time that Edward's jeans were unfastened, making her already vulnerable little boy look even more defenseless. He stood frozen in fear, the rabbit tucked under his arm, as he stared up at the man who towered over him.

The stranger was tall and lean, with straight dark hair and a bitter mouth. His face was long and narrow — handsome, she supposed, but too cruelly formed with its sharp cheekbones and hard planes to appeal to her. She felt a momentary gratitude for his mirrored sunglasses. Something told her she didn't want to look into his eyes.

5

She grabbed Edward and hugged him to her body. Painful experience had taught her not to let anyone push her around, and she sneered at him. "Are those your personal peeing bushes? Is that the problem? You wanted to use them yourself?"

His lips barely moved. "This is my property. Get off it."

"I'd love to, but my car has other ideas."

The drive-in's owner glanced without interest at the corpse of her Impala. "There's a phone in the ticket booth, and the number for Dealy's Garage. While you're waiting for a tow, stay off my land."

He turned on his heel and walked away. Only when he had disappeared behind the trees that grew around the base of the giant movie screen did she let go of her child.

"It's all right, sweetie. Don't pay any attention to him. You didn't do anything wrong."

Edward's face was pale; his bottom lip trembled. "The m-man scared me."

She combed her fingers through his light-brown hair, smoothed down a cowlick, brushed his bangs off his forehead. "I know he did, but he's just an old butthead, and I was here to protect you."

"You told me not to say *butthead*."

"These are extenuating circumstances."

"What are tenuating circustands?"

"It means he really *is* a butthead."

"Oh."

She glanced toward the small wooden ticket booth that held the phone. The booth had been freshly painted in mustard and purple, the same garish colors as the sign, but she made no move toward it. She didn't have the money for either a tow or repairs, and her credit cards had been revoked long ago. Unwilling to subject Edward to another confrontation with the drive-in's unpleasant owner, she drew him toward the road. "My legs are stiff from being in the car so long, and I could use a little walk. How about you?"

"Okay."

He dragged his sneakers in the dirt, and she knew he was still frightened. Her resentment against Butthead grew. What kind of jerk acted like that in front of a child?

She reached through the open window of the car and withdrew a blue plastic water jug, along with the last of the withered oranges she'd found on a produce markdown table. As she directed her child across the highway toward a small grove of trees, she once again cursed herself for not giving in to Clyde Rorsch, who'd been her boss until six days ago. Instead, she'd struck him in the side of the head to keep him from raping her, then she'd grabbed Edward and fled Richmond forever.

Now she wished she'd given in. If she'd agreed to have sex with him, she and Edward would be living in a rent-free room in Rorsch's motel where she'd been working as a maid. Why hadn't she shut her eyes and let him do what he wanted? What was the point of being fastidious when her child was hungry and homeless?

She'd made it as far as Norfolk where she'd used up too much of her small reserve of cash to have the

Impala's water pump fixed. She knew other women in her position would have applied for public aid, but welfare wasn't an option for her. She'd been forced to apply two years ago, when she and Edward were living in Baltimore. At the time, a social worker had stunned Rachel by questioning her ability to care for Edward. The woman had mentioned the possibility of putting him in foster care until Rachel could get on her feet. Her words might have been well-intentioned, but they had terrified Rachel. Until that moment, she had never considered that someone might try to take Edward away from her. She'd fled Baltimore that same day and vowed never again to approach a government office for help.

Since then she'd been supporting the two of them by working several minimum-wage jobs at a time, earning just enough to keep a roof over their heads, but not enough to be able to set anything aside so she could go back to school and improve her job skills. The battle for decent child care devoured her meager paychecks and made her sick with worry — one of the sitters kept Edward propped in front of a television all day, another disappeared and left him with a boyfriend. Then Edward had gotten sick with pneumonia.

By the time he was released from the hospital, she'd been fired from her fast-food job for absenteeism. Edward's expenses had eaten up everything she had, including her pitifully small savings, and left her with a staggering bill she had no way of paying. She also had a sick child who needed to be carefully watched while he recuperated and an eviction notice for nonpayment of rent on her shabby apartment.

She'd begged Clyde Rorsch to let her have one of the smaller motel rooms rent-free, promising to double her hours in exchange. But he'd wanted something more — sex on demand. When she'd refused, he'd gotten mean, and she'd struck him in the head with the office telephone.

She remembered the blood trickling down the side of his face and the venom in his eyes as he'd vowed to have her arrested for assault. "Let's see how you take care of that precious kid of yours when you're in jail!"

If only she'd stopped resisting and simply let him do what he wanted. What had been unthinkable only a week before didn't seem so inconceivable now. She was tough. She could have survived it. Since the beginning of time, desperate women had used sex for barter, and it was hard to believe she might once have condemned them for it.

She settled Edward next to her beneath a buckeye tree, unscrewed the lid of the water bottle, and handed it to him. As she peeled the orange, she could no longer ignore the compulsion to lift her eyes toward the mountains.

Sun shimmered on a wall of glass, testifying that the Temple of Salvation still stood, although she'd heard it had been taken over by a corrugated-box factory. Five years ago it had been the headquarters and broadcasting studio for G. Dwayne Snopes, one of the wealthiest and most famous televangelists in the country. Rachel pushed away the unpleasant memories and began handing Edward the orange segments. He savored each one as if it were a piece of candy instead of a tough, dried-out segment of fruit that belonged in the garbage.

As he polished off the last one, her gaze moved idly to the drive-in's marquee.

GRAND REOPENING SOON
HELP WANTED NOW

She grew instantly alert. Why hadn't she noticed that earlier? A job! Maybe her luck was finally going to turn.

She refused to think about the drive-in's surly owner. Selectivity was a luxury she hadn't been able to afford in years. With her eyes still fixed on the sign, she patted Edward's knee. It was warm from the sun.

"Sweetheart, I need to go talk to that man again."

"Don't want you to."

She gazed down into his small, worried face. "He's nothing but a big bully. Don't be afraid. I can beat him up with one hand tied behind my back."

"Stay here."

"I can't, pug. I need a job."

He didn't argue further, and she considered what to do with him while she sought out Butthead. Edward wasn't the kind of child who roamed, and she momentarily contemplated leaving him in the car, but it was parked too close to the road. She would have to take him with her.

Giving him a reassuring smile, she tugged him to his feet. As she led him back across the highway, she didn't bother sending up a prayer for divine intervention. Rachel no longer prayed. Her store of faith had been eaten up long ago by G. Dwayne Snopes, and now, not even a mustard seed remained.

The patched strap of her sandal dug into her big toe as she led Edward down the rutted lane past the ticket booth. The drive-in must have been built in these mountains decades earlier and, most likely, abandoned for another decade. Now the freshly painted ticket booth and new chain-link fence that enclosed the property testified to its renovation, but it looked as if there was still a lot of work to be done.

The projection screen had been repaired, but the lot, with its concentric rows of empty metal speaker polls, was overgrown with weeds. In the middle, she spotted a two-story concrete block building, the drive-in's original snack bar and projection booth. Its exterior had once been white, but was now streaked with dirt and mildew. The wide-open doors on the side emitted a blare of acid rock.

She spotted a shabby play area under the screen. It held an empty sandbox, along with half a dozen fiberglass dolphins mounted on heavy springs. She guessed the dolphins had originally been bright blue, but the passing years had faded their color to powder. A rusty jungle gym, the frame of a swing set, a broken merry-go-round, and a concrete turtle completed the pathetic cluster of equipment.

"Go play on that turtle while I talk to the man, Edward. I won't be long."

His eyes silently pleaded with her not to leave him alone. She smiled and gestured toward the playground.

Other children might have thrown a temper tantrum when they realized they weren't going to get their way, but the normal feistiness of childhood had been leeched out of her son. He worried his bottom lip, ducked his head, and tore her insides into a million tiny pieces so that she couldn't let him go.

"Never mind. You can come with me and sit by the door."

His small fingers clutched hers as she drew him toward the concrete building. She could feel the dust invading her lungs. The sun pounded down on her head while the music wailed like a death scream.

She dropped Edward's hand at the door and leaned down so he could hear her over the poisonous guitars and feral drums. "Stay here, punkin."

He clutched at her skirt. With a smile of reassurance, she gently disentangled his fingers and stepped into the concrete building.

The snack bar's counter area and appliances were new, although the dirty concrete-block walls still held a decade-old assortment of ragged flyers and posters. A pair of mirrored sunglasses lay on one section of the new white countertop next to an unopened bag of potato chips, a sandwich wrapped in plastic, and a radio that blasted out its violent music like lethal gas being pumped into an execution chamber.

The drive-in's owner stood on a ladder mounting a fluorescent light fixture to the ceiling. He had his back to her, which gave her a moment to observe this latest mountain standing in the path of her survival.

She saw a pair of paint-splattered brown work boots and frayed jeans that revealed long, powerful legs. His hips were lean, and the muscles of his back bunched under his shirt as he braced the base of the light fixture with one hand and twisted a screwdriver with the other. The rolled cuffs of his shirt revealed deeply tanned forearms, strong wrists, and broad hands with surprisingly elegant fingers. His dark-brown hair, cut a bit unevenly, fell over his collar in the back. It was straight and showed a few threads of gray, although the man didn't seem much older than his early- to mid-thirties.

She walked to the radio and turned down the volume. Someone with less steady nerves might have been startled into dropping the screwdriver or making an exclamation of surprise, but this man did neither. He simply turned his head and stared at her.

She gazed into a pair of pale-silver eyes and wished he were still wearing his mirrored sunglasses. His eyes held no life. They were hard and dead. Even now, when she was most desperate, she didn't want to believe her eyes looked like that — so unfeeling, so empty of hope.

"What do you want?"

The sound of that flat, emotionless voice chilled her, but she forced her lips into a carefree smile. "Nice to meet you, too. I'm Rachel Stone. That five-year-old you terrorized is my son Edward, and the rabbit he carries around is named Horse. Don't ask."

If she'd hoped to draw a smile from him, she failed miserably. It was hard to imagine that mouth ever smiling. "I thought I told you to stay off my property."

Everything about him irritated her, a fact she did her best to conceal behind an innocent expression. "Did you? I guess I forgot."

"Look, lady —"

"Rachel. Or Ms. Stone, if you want to be formal. As it happens, this is your lucky day. Fortunately for you, I have a forgiving nature, and I'm prepared to overlook your giant case of male PMS. Where do I start?"

"What are you talking about?"

"That sign I saw on the marquee. I'm your help wanted. Personally, I think we should get that playground cleaned up right away. Do you know what kind of lawsuits you're setting yourself up for with all that broken-down equipment?"

"I'm not hiring you."

"Of course you are."

"Now why's that?" he asked with no particular interest.

"Because you're obviously an intelligent man, despite your surly manner, and anyone with intelligence can see that I'm a terrific worker."

"What I see is that I need a man."

She smiled sweetly. "Don't we all."

He wasn't amused, but neither did he seem annoyed by her flippancy. There was simply nothing there. "I'm only going to hire a man."

"I'll just pretend I didn't hear that, since sexual discrimination is illegal in this country."

14

"So sue me."

Another woman might have given up, but Rachel had less than ten dollars in her wallet, a hungry child, and a car that wouldn't run.

"You're making a big mistake. An opportunity like me doesn't come along every day."

"I don't know how to say it any plainer, lady. I'm not going to hire you." He set the screwdriver on the counter, then reached into his rear pocket and pulled out a wallet that had molded to the shape of his hip. "Here's twenty bucks. Take it and get out."

She needed the twenty dollars, but she needed a job more, and she shook her head. "Keep your charity, Mr. Rockefeller. I want steady work."

"Look for it someplace else. What I have is hard manual labor. The lot has to be cleared, the building needs paint, the roof repaired. It'll take a man to do that kind of work."

"I'm stronger than I look, and I'll work harder than any man you'll ever find. Besides, I can also provide psychiatric counseling for that troublesome personality disorder of yours."

The moment the words were out, she could have bitten her tongue because his expression seemed to grow even emptier.

His lips barely moved, and she thought of a flat-eyed gunslinger with a mile-deep grudge against life. "Anybody ever tell you that you've got a smart mouth?"

"It goes with my brain."

"Mommy?"

The drive-in's owner stiffened. She turned to see Edward standing in the doorway, Horse dangling from his hand and lines of worry etched in his face. He kept his eyes on the man while he spoke. "Mommy, I got to ask you something."

She moved to his side. "What's wrong?"

He lowered his voice into a child's whisper, which she knew the man could hear clearly. "Are you sure we're not gonna die?"

Her heart twisted. "I'm sure."

The foolishness of coming here on this wild-goose chase once again hit her. How would she support them until she found what she was looking for? No one who knew who she was would give her a job, which meant her only chance lay in finding someone who'd moved here recently. That brought her full circle to the owner of the Pride of Carolina Drive-In.

He stalked to the old black wall phone. As she turned to see what he was going to do, she spotted a tattered purple flyer hanging nearby. Its curled edges didn't conceal the handsome face of G. Dwayne Snopes, the dead televangelist.

Join the Faithful at the Temple of Salvation as We Broadcast God's Message to the World!

"Dealy, it's Gabe Bonner. A woman's car broke down out here, and she needs a tow."

Two things hit her at once — the fact that she didn't want a tow and the man's name. Gabriel Bonner. What was a member of Salvation's most prominent family doing running a drive-in?

As she remembered, there were three Bonner brothers, but only the youngest, the Reverend Ethan Bonner, had lived in Salvation when she'd been here. Cal, the oldest brother, had been a professional football player. Although she understood he'd visited frequently, she'd never met him, but she knew what he looked like from photographs. Their father, Dr. Jim Bonner, was the county's most respected physician, and their mother, Lynn, its social leader. Her fingers tightened on Edward's shoulders as she reminded herself that she had come to the land of her enemies.

". . . then send the bill to me. And Dealy, take the woman and her son over to Ethan's. Tell him to find them a place to stay for the night."

After a few more terse words, he hung up and returned his attention to Rachel. "Wait by your car. Dealy'll send somebody out as soon as his truck gets back."

He walked over to stand by the door, one hand on the handle, his responsibility clearly discharged. She hated everything about him: his aloofness, his indifference, and she especially hated the strong male body that gave him a survival advantage she didn't possess. She hadn't asked for charity. All she wanted was a job. And his presumption in ordering her car towed threatened more than her transportation. The Impala was their home.

She snatched up the sandwich and bag of potato chips he'd left on the counter and grabbed Edward's hand. "Thanks for lunch, Bonner." She swept past him without giving him another glance.

Edward trotted at her side all the way down the rutted gravel lane. She held his hand crossing the highway. As they once again sat down under the buckeye tree, she fought against her despair. She wasn't going to give up yet.

They'd barely gotten settled before a dusty black pickup with Gabriel Bonner at the wheel shot out of the drive-in's entrance, turned onto the highway, and disappeared. She unwrapped the sandwich and investigated its contents for Edward: turkey breast, Swiss cheese, and mustard. He didn't like mustard, and she wiped off as much as she could before she handed it to him. He began to eat with only the slightest hesitation. He was too hungry to be fussy.

The tow truck arrived before he finished, and a short, stocky teenager got out. She left Edward under the tree and crossed the road to greet him with a cheery wave.

"As it turns out, I don't need a tow. Just give me a push, will you? Gabe wants me to put the car behind those trees over there."

She pointed to a grove not far from where Edward was sitting. The teenager was clearly dubious, but he also wasn't very bright, and it didn't take her long to convince him to help her. By the time he left, her Impala was hidden.

For now, it was the best she could do. They needed the Impala to sleep in, and they couldn't do that if it had been towed to a junkyard. The fact that the car couldn't be driven made it even more imperative that she convince Gabe Bonner to give her a job. But how? It occurred to her that someone so devoid of emotion might better be convinced with results.

She returned to Edward and pulled him to his feet. "Bring along that bag of chips, partner. We're going back to the drive-in. It's time for me to get to work."

"Did you get a job?"

"Let's just say I'm going to audition." She led him to the highway.

"What's that mean?"

"It's sort of like showing off what I can do. And while I work, you can finish your lunch on that playground, you lucky dog."

"You eat with me."

"I'm not hungry right now." It was almost true. It had been so long since she'd eaten a full meal that she'd passed the point of feeling hunger.

While she settled Edward by the concrete turtle, she studied her surroundings and tried to see what chore wouldn't require any special tools but would still make an impression. Clearing the lot of some of its weeds seemed like the best option. She decided to start in the middle, where her efforts would be most conspicuous.

As she began to work, the sun beat down on her, and the skirt of her blue chambray dress snagged her legs, while dirt sifted through the straps of her battered sandals and turned her feet brown. Her toe began to bleed beneath the makeshift patch.

She wished she were wearing her jeans. She only had one pair left, and they were old and frayed with a gaping hole in the knee and a smaller one in the threadbare seat.

The bodice of her dress was soon soaked with sweat. Her damp hair lay in wet ribbons against her cheeks and neck. She pricked her finger on the spine of a thistle, but her hands were too grubby to suck the wound.

When she had a large pile, she threw everything into an empty garbage can, then dragged it to the dumpster behind the snack bar. She returned to her weeding with grim determination. The Pride of Carolina represented her last chance, and she had to show Bonner that she could work harder than a dozen men.

As the afternoon grew hotter, she became increasingly light-headed, but she didn't let dizziness slow her down. She hauled another load to the dumpster, then bent back to her task. Silvery dots swirled before her eyes as she pulled up ragweed and goldenrod. Her hands and arms bled from deep scratches made by blackberry brambles. Rivulets of sweat ran between her breasts.

She realized that Edward had begun pulling up weeds at her side, and once again, she cursed herself for not giving in to Clyde Rorsch. Her head felt as if it were on fire, and the silver dots raced faster. She needed to sit down and rest, but there was no time.

The silvery dots turned into an explosion of fireworks, and the ground began to shift beneath her. She tried to keep her balance, but it was too much. Her head spun, and her knees gave way. The fireworks passed into inky blackness.

Ten minutes later when Gabe Bonner returned to the drive-in, he found the boy huddled on the ground, guarding the motionless body of his mother.

CHAPTER
TWO

"Wake up."

Something wet splashed on Rachel's face. Her eyes flickered open, and she saw bars of blue-white light shining above her. She tried to blink them away, then panicked. "Edward?"

"Mommy?"

Everything came back to her. The car. The drive-in. She forced her eyes to focus. The bars of light were coming from the fluorescent fixture in the snack bar. She was lying on the concrete floor.

Gabe Bonner crouched on one knee at her side, and Edward stood just behind him, his little boy's face old with worry. "Oh, baby, I'm sorry . . ." She tried to struggle into a sitting position. Her stomach heaved, and she knew she was going to throw up.

Bonner pushed a plastic cup against her lips, and water trickled over her tongue. Fighting the nausea, she tried to turn away from it, but he wouldn't let her. The water splashed over her chin and ran down her neck. She swallowed some of it, and her stomach steadied. She swallowed more and noticed a faint aftertaste of stale coffee.

She barely managed to sit up the rest of the way, and her hands shook as she tried to take the thermos cup from his hand. He let go the moment their fingers touched.

"How long since you've had anything to eat?" He uttered the question without much show of interest and rose to his feet.

Several more swallows of water and a few deep breaths let her recuperate enough to manage a smart-ass response. "Prime rib just last night."

Without comment, he thrust some kind of snack cake into her hand, chocolate with a creamy-white center. She took a bite, then automatically held it out toward Edward. "You eat the rest, honey. I'm not hungry."

"Eat it." An order. Curt, flat, impossible to disobey.

She wanted to shove the snack cake in his face, but she didn't have the strength. Instead, she forced it down between sips of water and found that she felt better. "This'll teach me not to stay out dancing all night," she managed. "That last tango must have done me in."

He wasn't buying her act for a minute. "Why are you still here?"

She hated having him loom over her and forced herself to her feet, only to realize her legs weren't working all that well. She settled into a paint-splattered metal folding chair. "Did you happen to notice . . . how much work I got done before my . . . unfortunate lapse of consciousness?"

"I noticed. And I told you I wouldn't hire you."

"But I want to work here."

"Too bad." With no particular haste, he ripped open a snack-sized bag of tortilla chips and handed it to her.

"I *have* to work here."

"I doubt that."

"No, it's true. I'm a disciple of Joseph Campbell. I'm following my bliss." She pushed a tortilla chip into her mouth, then winced as the salt stung the cuts on her fingers.

Bonner didn't miss a thing. He caught her by the wrists, then turned her dirty hands upward to study her thorn-slashed palms and the long, bloody scratches on the undersides of her arms. The wounds didn't seem to bother him much. "I'm surprised a smart-ass like you doesn't know enough to wear gloves."

"I left them at my beach house." She rose. "I'll just slip into the ladies' room and wash off some of this dirt."

She wasn't surprised when he didn't try to stop her. Edward followed her to the back of the building where she found the ladies' room locked, but the door to the men's room open. The plumbing was old and unsightly, but she spotted a pile of paper towels and a fresh bar of Dial soap.

She washed as much of herself as she could reach, and, between the cold water and the food, felt better. But she still looked like a train wreck. Her dress was filthy, her face ashen. She combed the snarls out of her hair with her fingers and pinched her cheeks while she tried to figure out how she could possibly recover from

24

this latest disaster. The Impala wasn't going anywhere, and she couldn't give up.

By the time she returned to the snack bar, Bonner had finished putting the plastic cover over the fluorescent light. She summoned a bright smile as she watched him lean the folded ladder against the wall.

"How about if I start scraping these walls down so I can paint them. This place won't look half bad when I'm done."

Her heart sank as he turned to her with his flat, empty expression. "Give it up, Rachel. I'm not going to hire you. Since you wouldn't leave with the tow truck, I've called somebody to come get you. Go wait by the road."

Fighting despair, she gave a saucy toss to her head. "Can't do it, Bonner. You forgot about the bliss thing. Drive-ins are my destiny."

"Not this one."

He didn't care that she was desperate. He wasn't even human.

Edward stood at her side with her skirt crumpled in his fist and that old-man worried look on his face. Something inside her felt as if it were breaking. She would sacrifice anything, everything, to keep him safe.

Her voice sounded as old and rusty as her Impala. "Please, Bonner. I need a break." She paused, hating herself for begging. "I'll do anything."

He slowly lifted his head, and as those pale-silver eyes flicked over her, she was conscious of her wild hair and dirty dress. She experienced something else — an intense awareness of him as a man. She felt as if she'd come full circle right back to the Dominion Motel. Right back to six days ago.

His voice was low-pitched, almost inaudible. "I seriously doubt that."

He was a man who cared about nothing, yet something hot and dangerous filled the air. There was no lechery in his gaze as he studied her, but at the same time, a primal alertness in the way he was watching her told her she was wrong. There was, indeed, at least one thing that he cared about.

A feeling of inevitability came over her, a sense that all the battles she had fought had led to this moment. Her heart slammed into her ribs, and her mouth felt like cotton. She had fought destiny long enough. It was time she gave up the struggle.

She drew her tongue over her dry lips and kept her eyes nailed to Gabriel Bonner. "Edward, sweetie, I have to talk to Mr. Bonner in private. You go over and play on that turtle."

"Don't want to."

"No arguments." She turned away from Bonner long enough to lead Edward toward the door. When he was outside, she gave him a shaky smile. "Go on, pug. I'll be over to get you before long."

He moved away reluctantly. Her eyes began to sting with tears, but she wouldn't let a single one fall. No time. No point.

She drew the doors of the snack shop closed, twisted the lock, and turned to face Bonner. She forced her chin high. Fierce. Haughty. Let him know she wasn't anybody's victim. "I need a regular paycheck, and I'll do whatever it takes to get it."

The sound he made might have been a laugh, except it was as devoid of amusement as a scream. "You don't mean that."

"Oh, I mean it." Her voice cracked. "Scout's honor."

She lifted her fingers to the buttons on the front of her dress, even though she had nothing on beneath but a pair of blue nylon panties. Her small breasts didn't justify the expense of a bra.

One by one, she opened the buttons while he watched.

She wondered if he was married. Considering his age and overwhelming masculinity, the odds were strong. She could only breathe a silent apology to the faceless woman she was injuring.

Although he'd been working, there were no dark rings under his fingernails, no half-moons of sweat staining his shirt, and she tried to feel grateful that he was clean. His breath wouldn't reek of greasy onions and bad teeth. Still, an inner alarm warned her she would have been safer with Clyde Rorsch.

His lips barely moved. "Where's your pride?"

"I'm fresh out." The last of the buttons gave way. She slipped the soft blue chambray dress from her shoulders. With a soft whish, it dropped around her ankles.

His empty silver eyes took in her small, high breasts and the ribs that showed so plainly beneath. Her low-cut panties didn't conceal either the sharpness of her hipbones or the faint stretch marks that showed above the elastic.

"Put your clothes back on."

She stepped out of the dress and made herself walk toward him, clad only in her panties and sandals. She held her head high, determined to keep her dignity intact.

"I'm willing to work a double shift, Bonner. Days and nights. No man you hire is going to do that."

With grim resolve, she reached out and cupped his arm.

"Don't touch me!"

He jerked away as if she'd struck him, and his eyes were no longer empty. Instead, they darkened with a rage so profound that she took a quick step backward.

He snatched up her dress and shoved it at her. "Put it on."

Defeat curled her shoulders. She had lost. As her hand caught the soft blue fabric, her eyes found the photo of G. Dwayne Snopes staring at her from the purple flyer curling on the wall.

Sinner! Harlot!

She slipped into her dress while Bonner made his way to the doors and unlocked them. But he didn't push them open. Instead, he planted his hands on his hips and bent his head. His shoulders rose and fell as if he were breathing hard.

Her stiff, cumbersome fingers had just managed to fasten the last button when the snack shop's doors swung open.

"Hey, Gabe, I got your call. Where —"

The Reverend Ethan Bonner froze in place as he saw her. He was blond and breathtakingly handsome, with finely shaped features and gentle eyes; he was the complete opposite of his brother.

She saw the exact moment when he recognized her. His soft mouth thinned and those gentle eyes glazed with contempt. "Well, well. If it isn't the Widow Snopes come back to haunt us."

CHAPTER
THREE

Gabe turned at Ethan's words. "What are you talking about?"

Rachel sensed something protective in the way Ethan looked at Gabe. He moved closer, as if he were guarding him, a ridiculous notion since Gabe was larger than Ethan and more muscular.

"Didn't she tell you who she is?" He studied her with open condemnation. "I guess the Snopes family hasn't ever been known for truthfulness."

"I'm not a Snopes," Rachel replied woodenly.

"All those downtrodden people who sent money to keep you in sequins would be surprised to hear that."

Gabe's gaze moved from her to his brother. "She said her name was Rachel Stone."

"Don't believe anything she says." Ethan addressed Gabe in the gentle tones people usually reserved for the sick. "She's the widow of the late, but hardly lamented, G. Dwayne Snopes."

"Is she now."

Ethan walked farther into the snack shop. He wore a neatly pressed blue oxford shirt, khakis that held a sharp crease, and a pair of polished loafers. His blond hair, blue eyes, and even features formed a marked contrast with his rugged brother's more brutal good looks. Ethan could have been one of heaven's chosen angels, while Gabriel, despite his name, could only have ruled a darker kingdom.

"G. Dwayne died about three years ago," Ethan explained, again using that solicitous sickbed voice. "You were living in Georgia then. He was on his way out of the country at the time, one step ahead of the law, with a few million dollars that didn't belong to him."

"I remember hearing something about it." Gabe's response seemed to be made out of habit rather than interest. She wondered if anything interested him. Her striptease certainly hadn't. She shuddered and tried not to think about what she'd done.

"His plane went down over the ocean. They recovered his body, but the money is still on the bottom of the Atlantic."

Gabe leaned back against the counter and slowly turned his head toward her. She found she couldn't meet his gaze.

"G. Dwayne had been playing it pretty straight until he married her," Ethan went on, "but Mrs. Snopes likes expensive cars and fancy clothes. He got greedy to feed her habits, and his fund-raising activities became so outrageous they eventually brought him down."

"Not the first televangelist to have that happen," Gabe observed.

Ethan's lips tightened. "Dwayne preached prosperity theology. 'Give that it may be given unto you.' Part with what you have, even if it's your last dollar, and you'll get a hundred dollars back. Snopes presented God as the almighty slot machine, and people fell for it big-time. He got Social Security checks, welfare money. There was a woman in South Carolina who was diabetic, and she sent Dwayne the money she needed for her insulin. Instead of sending it back, Dwayne read her letter on the air as an example for everyone to follow. It was a golden moment in televangelism."

Ethan's eyes flicked over Rachel as if she were a piece of garbage. "The camera caught Mrs. Snopes sitting in the front pew of the Temple of Salvation with her sequins flashing and tears of gratitude running through her rouge. Later, a reporter for the *Charlotte Observer* did some digging around and discovered the woman went into a diabetic coma and never recovered."

Rachel dropped her eyes. Her tears that day had been ones of shame and helplessness, but no one knew that. For every broadcast, she'd been required to sit in the first row all decked out in the teased hair, overdone makeup, and flashy clothes that had been Dwayne's idea of female beauty. When she'd first gotten married, she'd gone along with his wishes, but as she'd discovered Dwayne's corruption, she'd tried to withdraw. Her pregnancy had made that impossible.

When the corruption in Dwayne's ministry had become public, her husband had engaged in a series of emotional televised confessions in an attempt to save his skin. Using lots of references to Eve and Delilah, he talked about how he had been led from the path of righteousness by a weak and sinful woman. He was canny enough to take the blame himself, but his message was unmistakable. If it hadn't been for his wife's greed, he would never have strayed.

Not everyone had bought his act, but most had, and she'd lost count of the number of times in the past three years she'd been recognized and publicly berated. At first she'd tried to explain that their extravagant lifestyle had been Dwayne's choice, not hers, but no one had believed her, so she'd learned to keep quiet.

The door of the snack shop squeaked on its hinges, opening just far enough for one little boy to slip through and fly to his mother's side. She didn't want Edward to witness this, and she spoke sharply. "I told you to stay outside."

Edward hung his head and spoke so quietly she could barely hear him. "There was this — this big dog."

She doubted that, but she gave his shoulder a comforting squeeze anyway. At the same time, she regarded Ethan with all the fierceness of a mother wolf, silently warning him to watch what he said in front of her child.

Ethan stared at Edward. "I forgot you and Dwayne had a son."

"This is Edward," she said, pretending nothing was wrong. "Edward, say hello to Reverend Bonner."

"Hi." He didn't take his eyes off his sneakers. Then he addressed her in one of his very audible whispers. "Is he a charlotte town, too?"

She met Ethan's quizzical eyes. "He wants to know if you're a charlatan." Her voice hardened. "He's heard it about his father . . ."

For a moment Ethan looked taken aback, but then he recovered. "I'm not a charlatan, Edward."

"Reverend Bonner's the real thing, kiddo. Honest. God-fearing." She met Ethan's eyes. "A man who withholds judgment and is filled with compassion for the less fortunate."

Just like his brother, he didn't back down easily, and her attempt to shame him failed. "Don't even consider trying to settle here again, Mrs. Snopes. You're not wanted." He turned to Gabe. "I have a meeting, and I've got to get back to town. Let's have dinner together tonight."

Bonner tilted his head toward her. "What are you going to do with them?"

Ethan hesitated. "I'm sorry, Gabe. You know I'd do anything in the world for you, but I can't help you with this one. Salvation doesn't need Mrs. Snopes, and I won't be a party to bringing her back to town." He brushed his brother's arm, then headed for the door.

Gabe stiffened. "Ethan! Wait a minute." He shot out after him.

Edward looked up at her. "Nobody likes us, do they?"

She swallowed a lump in her throat. "We're the best, lamb chop, and anybody who can't figure that out isn't worth our time."

She heard a curse, and Gabe reappeared, a scowl twisting his lips. He planted his hands on his hips, and as he stared down at her, she grew conscious of his height. She was five feet seven, but he made her feel small and disturbingly defenseless.

"In all the years I've known my brother, this is the only time I've seen him turn anybody away."

"It's been my experience, Bonner, that even good Christians have a limit. For a lot of them, I seem to be it."

"I don't want you here!"

"Now there's a news flash."

His expression darkened. "This place isn't safe for a kid. He couldn't hang around here."

Was he weakening? She made up a quick lie. "I have a place to keep him."

Edward burrowed closer to her side.

"If I hired you, it would only be for a couple of days, just until I find someone else."

"Understood." She struggled to hide her excitement.

"All right," he snarled. "Eight o'clock tomorrow. And you'd better be ready to work your butt off."

"I can do that."

His scowl deepened. "It's not my responsibility to find you a place to stay."

"I have a place."

He regarded her suspiciously. "Where?"

"None of your business. I'm not helpless, Bonner, I just need a job."

The phone rang on the wall. He went over to answer it, and she listened to a one-sided conversation that dealt with a delivery problem. "I'll come in and straighten it out," Mr. Charm finally announced.

He hung up the phone, then crossed over to the door and held it open. He didn't do it as a courtesy, she knew, but only to get rid of her.

"I have to go into town. We'll talk about where you're going to stay when I get back."

"I told you it's taken care of."

"We'll talk when I get back," he snapped. "Wait for me over by the playground. And find something to do with your kid!"

He stalked out.

She had no intention of staying around long enough for him to find out that she was sleeping in her car, so she waited until he drove off then headed for her Impala. While Edward napped in the backseat, she washed herself, then laundered their dirty clothes in a small tributary of the French Broad River that ran through the grove. Afterward, she changed into her tattered jeans and an old melon-colored T-shirt. Edward woke up, and the two of them sang silly songs and told ancient knock-knock jokes while they hung their wet laundry on low branches near the car.

The late-afternoon shadows lengthened. She had no food left, and she couldn't postpone the trip into town any longer. With Edward at her side, she walked along the highway until they had left the drive-in behind, then she stuck out her thumb as a late-model Park Avenue approached.

It was driven by a retired couple from St. Petersburg who were summering in Salvation. They chatted pleasantly with her and were sweet to Edward. She asked them to drop her off at the Ingles grocery store on the edge of town, and they waved as they drove off. She was thankful they hadn't recognized her as the infamous Widow Snopes.

Her luck didn't hold, however. She'd only been in the grocery store for a few moments when she noticed one of the produce clerks staring at her. She concentrated on choosing a pear that wasn't overly bruised from the mark-down rack. Out of the corner of her eye, she saw a gray-haired woman whispering to her husband.

Rachel had changed so much that she wasn't recognized as often now as she had been in the first year after the scandal, but this was Salvation, and these people had seen her in person, not just on the television screen. Even without her teased hair and spindly high heels, they knew who she was. Swiftly she moved on.

In the bread aisle, a neatly dressed woman in her mid-forties with severely cut dyed black hair put down a pack of Thomas' English muffins and stared at Rachel as if she were looking at the devil.

"You." She spat out the word.

Rachel remembered Carol Dennis immediately. She had begun as a Temple volunteer and eventually worked her way to the top, ending up as one of the cadre of loyal followers who served as aides to Dwayne. Deeply religious, Carol had both adored and been intensely protective of him.

When his troubles had become public, Carol had never been able to accept the fact that a man who preached the Gospel as passionately as G. Dwayne Snopes was corrupt, so she shifted the blame for his downfall to Rachel.

She was almost unnaturally thin, with a sharp nose and pointed chin. Her eyes were as dark as her dyed hair, her skin flawless and pale. "I can't believe you've come back."

"It's a free country," Rachel snapped.

"How can you show your face here?"

Her defiance faded. She handed Edward a small loaf of whole-wheat bread. "Would you carry this for me?" She began to move on.

The woman noticed Edward, and her face softened. She stepped forward and bent toward him. "I haven't seen you since you were a baby. What a nice-looking young man you are. I'll bet you miss your daddy."

Edward had been accosted by strangers before, and he didn't like it. He ducked his head.

Rachel tried to get by, but Carol quickly angled her cart to block the aisle. "God tells us we should love the sinner and hate the sin, but it's difficult in your case."

"I'm sure you'll manage, Carol, a devout woman like yourself."

"You'll never know how many times I've prayed for you."

"Save your prayers for someone who wants them."

"You're not welcome here, Rachel. A lot of us gave our lives to the Temple. We believed, and we've suffered in ways you could never understand. Our memories are long, and if you think we'll stand by and let you flaunt yourself here, you're very wrong."

Rachel knew it was a mistake to reply, but she couldn't help defending herself. "I believed, too. None of you have ever understood that."

"You believed in yourself, in your own needs."

"You know nothing about me."

"If you showed any remorse, all of us could forgive you, but you still don't have any shame, do you, Rachel?"

"I have nothing to be ashamed about."

"He confessed his sins, but you never would. Your husband was a man of God, and you ruined him."

"Dwayne ruined himself." She pushed the cart out of the way, and nudged Edward forward.

Before she could get away, however, a teenage boy came slouching around the end of the aisle holding several bags of potato chips and a six-pack of Mountain Dew. He was slightly built, with an unkempt dirty-blond crew cut and three earrings. His jeans were baggy, and a rumpled blue shirt hung open over a black T-shirt. He came to a stop as he saw Rachel. For a moment his face was blank, and then his expression hardened with hostility.

"What's she doing here?"

"Rachel's come back to Salvation," Carol said coldly.

Rachel remembered that Carol was divorced and had a son, but she would never have recognized this boy as the quiet, conservative-looking child she vaguely recalled.

The teenager stared at her. He hardly looked like a model of religious devotion, and she couldn't understand such naked animosity.

She quickly turned away and discovered she was shaking as she headed into the next aisle. Before she'd gone far, she heard Carol's angry voice. "I'm not buying all that junk food for you."

"I'll buy it myself!"

"No, you won't. And you're not going out with those loser friends of yours tonight, either."

"We're just going to a movie, and you can't stop me."

"Don't you lie to me, Bobby! You had liquor on your breath the last time you came home. I know exactly what you and your friends are doing!"

"You don't know shit."

Edward looked up at Rachel, his eyes startled. "Is she that boy's mom?"

Rachel nodded and hurried him to the end of the aisle.

"Don't they love each other?"

"I'm sure they do. But they've got problems, pup."

As she finished her shopping, she was conscious of the attention she was attracting, which ranged from puzzled glances to condemning murmurs. Even though she'd expected animosity, the extent of it upset her. Three years might have passed, but the people of Salvation, North Carolina, hadn't forgiven a thing.

As she and Edward walked along the highway carrying their small supply of food, she tried to understand Bobby Dennis's reaction to her. He and his mother were clearly at odds, so she doubted that he was simply reflecting Carol's feelings. Besides, his antipathy had seemed more personal.

She stopped thinking about Bobby as she spotted a large grandpa car with Florida plates, the only kind she dared stick her thumb out for. A widow from Clearwater driving a maroon Crown Victoria stopped and took them back to the drive-in. As Rachel stepped out of the car, she turned her foot and the frail straps on the right sandal snapped. The sandals were beyond repair, and now she had only one pair of shoes left. Another loss.

Edward fell asleep just before nine o'clock. She sat barefoot on the trunk of the Impala with an old beach towel wrapped around her shoulders and gazed down at the crumpled magazine photo that had brought her back. She carefully unfolded it and, flicking on the flashlight she carried with her, looked down into the face of Gabe's older brother, Cal.

Although they bore a strong resemblance, Cal's rugged features had been softened by an almost goofy look of happiness, and she wondered if his wife, the attractive, rather scholarly-looking blond pictured smiling at his side, was responsible. They'd been photographed in Rachel's old house, a vast, overly ornate mansion on the other side of Salvation. It had been confiscated by the federal government to help cover Dwayne's unpaid taxes, and it had stood vacant until Cal had bought it and its contents when he was married.

The picture had been taken in Dwayne's former study, but it wasn't sentimentality that had made her rip it from the magazine. Instead, it was the object she'd spotted in the background of the photograph. Sitting on the bookcases directly behind Cal Bonner's head was a small, brass-bound leather chest, barely the size of half a loaf of bread.

Dwayne had bought the chest about three and a half years ago from a dealer who kept her husband's expensive purchases anonymous. Dwayne had coveted it because it had once belonged to John F. Kennedy — not that Dwayne had been a Kennedy fan, but he loved everything associated with the rich and famous. In the weeks before his death, as the legal net had tightened around him, she'd frequently seen Dwayne gazing at the chest.

One afternoon he'd called her from a landing strip north of town and, in a panicked voice, told her he was about to be arrested. "I — I thought I'd have more time," he'd said, "but they're coming to the house tonight, and I have to get out of the country. Rachel, I'm not ready! Bring Edward to me so I can say good-bye before I leave. I have to say good-bye to my son. You have to do this for me!"

She'd heard the desperation in his voice and knew he was afraid she wouldn't comply because of her bitterness over the way he'd ignored their child. Except for Edward's televised baptism, which had been the most watched program in the history of the Temple ministry, Dwayne had shown little interest in being a father.

Her disillusionment with her husband had started soon after they were married, but it wasn't until her pregnancy that she'd discovered the extent of his corruption. He'd justified his avarice by telling her he needed to let the world see the riches God bestowed on the faithful. Still, she wouldn't deny him what might be his last contact with his son.

"All right. I'll be there as soon as I can."

"And I want — I want to take something from home with me, as a reminder. Bring the Kennedy chest, too. And my Bible."

She understood about the Bible, which was a keepsake from his mother. But Rachel was no longer the naive Indiana country girl he'd married, and his request for the Kennedy chest made her instantly suspicious. At least five million dollars from the Temple ministry were unaccounted for, and it wasn't until she'd broken the small brass lock and assured herself the chest was empty that she did as he'd asked.

She'd sped along the mountain roads toward the landing strip with two-year-old Edward strapped into his car seat sucking on Horse's ear. Dwayne's mother's Bible lay on the seat next to her, and the small leather chest sat on the floor. By the time she'd arrived, however, it was too late to reach her husband.

Law enforcement had decided not to wait until nightfall to arrest him, and, acting on a tip, the local police and county sheriff had headed for the airfield. But Dwayne had spotted them approaching and taken off. Two deputies forced her out of the Mercedes and confiscated everything, even Edward's car seat. Afterward, one of them drove her home in a squad car.

It wasn't until the next morning that she received word that a plane crash had killed her husband. Not long after, she was evicted from the house with little more than the clothes on her back. It was her first lesson in exactly how unkind the world could be to the widow of a crooked televangelist.

She hadn't seen the Kennedy chest again, not until five days ago when she'd stumbled on the photograph of Cal Bonner and his wife in a *People* magazine that had been left at the Laundromat. For three years she'd wondered about that chest. When she'd broken the lock, she'd given the interior no more than a cursory examination. Later, she remembered how heavy it had been and wondered if it could have contained a false bottom. Or maybe a safe-deposit key lay concealed beneath the green felt lining.

As she drew the old beach towel tighter to ward off the night chill, she was filled with bitterness. Her son was sleeping in the backseat of a broken-down car after eating a peanut-butter sandwich and an overly ripe pear, yet five million dollars were missing. It was money that belonged to her.

Even after she paid off the last of Dwayne's creditors, there would be a few million left, and she intended to use it to buy security for her son. Instead of yachts and jewels, she dreamed of a small house in a safe neighborhood. She wanted to watch Edward eat decent food and wear clothing that wasn't threadbare. She'd send him to good schools and buy him a bicycle.

But she couldn't make any of those dreams come true without the goodwill of Gabriel Bonner. These past three years had taught her never to ignore reality, no matter how unpleasant, and she knew it might take her several weeks to get inside her old house so she could search for the chest. Until then, she needed to survive, which meant she had to keep her job.

The leaves above her rustled. She shivered and thought about how she had stripped herself naked in front of a stranger today. The churchgoing Indiana country girl she had once been couldn't have conceived of such an act, but being responsible for a child had forced her to leave her scruples behind, along with her innocence. Now she vowed to do whatever she must in order to keep Gabriel Bonner appeased.

CHAPTER
FOUR

Rachel had already cleared most of the weeds from the center of the lot by the time Gabe's truck came through the gate at seven forty-five the next morning. Her hair was secured back from her face with a piece of copper wire she'd found near the dumpster. She only hoped the worn seat of her jeans didn't give way.

With her sandals gone, she was forced to wear her only other shoes, a pair of clunky black men's oxfords one of her teenage coworkers had given her when she'd grown bored with the style. The shoes were comfortable, but too hot and heavy for summer weather. Still they were more practical for heavy work than her shabby little sandals had been, and she felt grateful to have them.

If Rachel thought her early-bird industriousness would please Gabe, she was immediately proven wrong. The truck came to a halt next to her, and he climbed out with the motor still running. "I told you to be here at eight."

"And I will be," she replied in her most cheerful voice, trying to forget how she'd stripped for him yesterday afternoon. "I've got fifteen minutes to go."

He wore a clean white T-shirt and faded jeans. He was freshly shaved, and his dark hair looked as if it might still be damp from his shower. For a few brief moments yesterday, she'd seen his mask slip, but now it was firmly back in place: bleak, harsh, unfeeling.

"I don't want you here when I'm not around."

All her good intentions to be respectful and compliant fled. "Relax, Bonner. Everything you own that's worth stealing is too big for me to carry."

"You heard me."

"And here I thought you were only cranky in the afternoon."

"It's pretty much a round-the-clock affair." His reply should have been humorous, but those emotionless silver eyes spoiled the effect. "Where did you stay last night?"

"With a friend. I do have a few left," she lied. In fact, Dwayne had forbidden any but the most superficial contacts with the people of Salvation.

He pulled a pair of yellow work gloves from his back pocket and tossed them at her. "Use these."

"Gosh, I'm touched." She clasped the gloves to her breast like beauty-queen roses and told herself not to say another word. Before the day was over, she had to ask him for an advance on her paycheck, and she couldn't afford to antagonize him. But he looked so remote as he slid back behind the wheel of his truck that she couldn't resist a small jab.

"Hey, Bonner. In lieu of Prozac, maybe some coffee would help your disposition. I'll be glad to make a pot for both of us."

"I'll make my own."

"Great. Bring me a cup when it's ready."

He slammed the door and left her standing in a cloud of dust as he drove toward the snack shop. *Butthead*. She shoved her sore hands into the gloves and bent to return to her task even though every muscle protested.

She couldn't remember ever being so tired. All she wanted to do was lie in the shade and sleep for a hundred years. It wasn't hard to figure out why she was exhausted: not enough sleep and too much worry. She thought longingly of the jolt of energy she got from a morning cup of coffee.

Coffee . . . It had been weeks since she'd had any. She loved everything about it: the taste, the smell, those beautiful pinwheels of beige and mocha when she stirred in the cream. She closed her eyes and, just for a moment, let herself feel it sliding over her tongue.

A blast of acid rock coming from the snack shop shattered her fantasy. She glanced toward the playground where Edward had emerged from beneath the concrete turtle. If Bonner was this upset because she'd come to work early, what would he do when he spotted Edward?

The moment she'd arrived that morning, she'd cleared the playground of broken glass and rusty can lids, anything that could harm a child, then set Edward to work throwing trash into a plastic garbage bag. She'd stowed away a supply of food and water, along with a beach towel for him to nap on, in the shrubbery that grew at the base of the giant screen. Then she'd suggested he play a game of "Where's Edward?"

"I'll bet you can't go all morning without letting Mr. Bonner see you."

"I can, too."

"Betcha can't."

"Bet I can."

She'd given him a kiss and left it at that. Sooner or later Bonner would spot him, and there'd be hell to pay. The idea that she had to hide her precious child away, as if he were something repellent, left her with another big black mark of resentment chalked up against Gabe Bonner. She wondered if he were this hostile to all children, or if he'd reserved his antipathy for hers.

An hour later Gabe threw a garbage bag at her and told her to pick up the trash out by the entrance so the place didn't look so bad from the highway. It was easier work than weeding, although she couldn't imagine he'd taken that into consideration, and she welcomed the change. After Gabe disappeared, Edward slipped around to join her, and the two of them were done in no time.

She returned to her weeding, but she'd barely started before a pair of paint-splattered work boots appeared in her peripheral vision. "I thought I told you to get that trash picked up out front."

She intended to respond politely, but her tongue had a will of its own. "Already done, *Kommandant*. Your slightest wish is my command."

His eyes narrowed. "Go inside and start cleaning out the ladies' room so I can paint in there."

"A promotion! And it's only my first day on the job."

He stared at her for a long, uncomfortable moment, during which she wished she could slap a gag in her mouth.

"Watch yourself, Rachel. Remember that I don't want you here."

Before she could reply, he walked away.

With a sideways glance to make certain Edward saw where she was going, she set off for the snack shop. A storage closet held the cleaning supplies she needed, but she was more interested in the pot of coffee sitting nearby. Unless Bonner was a big drinker, he seemed to have made enough for two, and she filled a styrofoam cup to the brim. She couldn't find any milk, and the coffee was strong enough to qualify for Super Fund cleanup, but she savored every sip as she carried it with her into the ladies' room.

The plumbing was old and filthy, but still usable. She decided to get the worst over with first and began cleaning the stalls, scraping up crusted muck whose origins didn't bear thinking about.

Before long, she heard the soft pat of sneakered feet coming up behind her. "Gross."

"You said it."

"I remember when we was rich."

"You were only two. You couldn't remember."

"Uh-huh. There was trains on the walls in my bedroom."

Rachel had put up the blue-and-white striped wallpaper herself, along with its border of colorful trains. The nursery and her bedroom were the only rooms in that awful house she'd been able to decorate herself, and she'd spent as much time in both of them as she could.

"I'm going back outside," Edward said.

"I don't blame you."

"He hasn't seen me yet."

"You're a slick one, buddy."

"Knock. Knock."

"Who's there."

"Madam."

She shot him a warning look. "Edddward . . ."

"Ma *darned* foot's stuck in the door." He giggled, stuck his head out to make certain Butthead wasn't around, and disappeared.

She smiled and returned to her work. It had been a long time since she'd heard her son laugh. He was enjoying his game of hide-and-seek, and being outside like this was good for him.

By one o'clock, she'd cleaned out the six stalls, as well as checked on Edward at least a dozen times, and she was so tired her head was spinning. A rough voice spoke from behind her.

"You're not going to do me a damned bit of good if you pass out again. Take a break."

She steadied herself on the metal partition as she straightened, then turned to see Bonner silhouetted in the doorway. "I will when I get tired. So far it hasn't happened."

"Yeah, right. There's a burger and some fries waiting for you in the snack shop. If you know what's good for you, you'll eat it." He strode out, and a moment later she heard the sound of his boots on the metal stairs that led to the projection room above the snack shop.

With a sense of anticipation, she quickly washed her hands and made her way to the snack shop where a McDonald's bag lay on the counter. For a moment she simply stood there and savored the tantalizing smells of All-American ambrosia. She'd been working since six that morning on an empty stomach, and she had to eat something, but not this. This was too precious.

Keeping an eye out for Bonner, she carried her valuable cargo toward the hiding place on the playground where Edward was waiting. "Surprise, pug. It's your lucky day."

"McDonald's!"

"Only the best."

She laughed as Edward tore into the bag and began stuffing himself with hamburger. As he ate, she scraped a thin layer of peanut butter from their hidden food stash on a piece of bread, folded it over, and raised it to her lips. She begrudged taking anything from their meager stash for herself. She had already failed her child in so many ways, and eating his food seemed like one more failure. Luckily, it didn't take much to keep her going.

"Want some fries?"

Her mouth watered. "No thanks. Fried food isn't good for women my age."

52

She took another bite of her sandwich and promised herself that once she found Dwayne's five million dollars, she would never again eat peanut butter.

Two hours later she had finished cleaning the ladies' rest room and was taking a paint scraper to the peeling metal doors when she heard a furious bellow.

"Rachel!"

What had she done now? Pinwheels of light spun in her head as she leaned down too quickly to lay the scraper on the floor. Instead of getting better, her dizziness was getting worse.

"Rachel! Get out here!"

She made her way to the door. For a moment the sun blinded her, but as her eyes adjusted to the light, she gave a muffled gasp.

Edward dangled from Bonner's fist by the scruff of his old orange T-shirt. His dusty black sneakers swung helplessly in the air, and his shirt bunched beneath his armpits, revealing his small, bony rib cage and the blue network of veins that ran just beneath his pale skin. Horse lay on the ground below his feet.

Bonner's skin was pale over the harsh ridge of his cheekbones. "I told you to keep him away from here."

She rushed forward, her exhaustion forgotten. "Put him down! You're scaring him!"

"You were warned. I told you not to bring him here. It's too dangerous." He set him to the ground.

Edward was free, but he stood frozen in place, once more the victim of a powerful adult force he could neither understand nor control. His helplessness cut her to the quick. She retrieved Horse, then scooped up her child and hugged him to her chest. The toes of his sneakers banged into her shins as she buried her cheek in his straight brown hair, which was still warm from the sun.

"What was I supposed to do with him?" she spat out.

"That wasn't my problem."

"Spoken like someone who's never had responsibility for a child!"

He went absolutely still. Seconds ticked by before his lips moved. "You're fired. Get out of here."

Edward began to cry as he wrapped his arms around her neck. "I'm sorry, Mommy. I tried not to let him see me, but he catched me."

Her heart pounded, and her legs felt like rubber. She wanted to rage at Bonner for frightening him, but that would only upset Edward more. And what was the use? One look at the blank canvas of Bonner's face told her his decision was final.

He pulled a wallet from his back pocket, peeled out several bills, and extended them toward her. "Take this."

She stared down at the money. She'd sacrificed everything for her child. Did she have to give up the last ounce of her pride, too?

Slowly she took the money and felt a little part of herself die.

Edward's chest heaved.

"Shh . . ." She brushed her lips over his hair. "It's not your fault."

"He seed me."

"Not for a whole day. He was so dumb it took him a whole day to find you. You did just fine."

Without a backward glance, she carried Edward to the playground where she gathered up their things. Blinking against the tears, she clutched her meager possessions in one hand and her son in the other. What kind of man would do something like this? Only one who had no feelings at all.

As she left the Pride of Carolina, she wanted to fall off the end of the world.

Gabriel Bonner, the man with no feelings, cried in his sleep that night. He jolted awake sometime around three in the morning to find a wet place on his pillow and the awful metallic taste of grief in his mouth.

He'd dreamed about them again tonight, Cherry and Jamie, his wife and son. But this time Cherry's beloved face kept changing into the thin, defiant face of Rachel Stone. And his son had held a bedraggled gray rabbit as he lay in his coffin.

He swung his legs over the side of the bed, and for a long time he did nothing but sit with his shoulders hunched and his face buried in his hands. Finally he pulled open the drawer in his bedside table and took out a Smith & Wesson .38.

The revolver felt warm and heavy in his hands. *Just do it. Put it in your mouth and pull the trigger.* He touched the barrel to his lips and closed his eyes. The cold steel felt like a lover's kiss, and he welcomed the click of it against his front teeth.

55

But he couldn't pull the trigger, and, at that moment, he hated his family for keeping him from the oblivion he craved. Any one of them — his father or mother, his two brothers — they would all put a dog out of its misery, but they wouldn't be able to bear it if he killed himself. Now their stubborn, unrelenting love kept him shackled to an intolerable world.

He shoved the gun back in the drawer and withdrew the framed photograph he also kept there. Cherry smiled back at him, his beautiful wife who'd loved him and laughed with him and been everything a man could want. And Jamie.

Gabe caressed the frame with his thumbs, and in his chest, his heart seeped. It wasn't blood that escaped — that had been shed long ago — but a thick, bile-like fluid that ran through veins that had become rivers of pain carrying a bottomless cargo of grief.

My son.

Everyone had told him his grief would be easier to bear after the first year, but they'd lied. It had been over two years now since his wife and son had been killed by a drunk running a red light, and the pain had grown worse.

He'd spent most of that time in Mexico, living on tequila and quaaludes. Then, four months ago, his brothers had come to get him. He'd sworn at Ethan and thrown a punch at Cal, but it hadn't done any good. They'd brought him back anyway, and when they'd dried him out, he had no feelings left. No feelings at all.

Until yesterday.

A vision of Rachel's thin, naked body swam before his eyes. She'd been all bones and desperation when she'd offered herself to him in exchange for a job. And he'd gotten hard. He still couldn't believe it had happened.

He'd seen one other woman naked since Cherry had died. She'd been a Mexican whore with a lush body and a sweet smile. He'd thought he could bury some small part of his anguish inside her, but it hadn't worked. Too many pills, too much booze, too much pain. He'd sent her away without touching her and drunk himself into a stupor.

He hadn't even thought about her again until yesterday. An experienced Mexican whore hadn't been able to make him respond, but Rachel Stone with her scrawny body and defiant eyes had somehow managed to penetrate the wall he'd built so solidly around himself.

He remembered the way Cherry used to curl in his arms after they'd made love and play with the hair on his chest. *I love your gentleness, Gabe. You're the most gentle man I've ever known.*

He wasn't gentle now. Gentleness had been burned out of him. He put the photograph back in the drawer and walked naked to the window where he stared out at the darkness.

Rachel Stone didn't know it, but getting fired was the best thing that could have happened to her.

CHAPTER
FIVE

"You can't do this!" Rachel exclaimed. "We're not hurting anyone."

The police officer, whose badge read *Armstrong*, ignored her and turned to the driver of the tow truck. "Go ahead, Dealy. Get this piece of junk out of here."

With a sense of unreality, Rachel watched the tow truck back up to her car. Nearly twenty-four hours had passed since Bonner had fired her. She'd felt so ill and exhausted that she hadn't been able to summon the energy to do anything but stay by the car. Half an hour earlier, a police officer driving by had spotted the reflection of the late-afternoon sun off the car's windshield and come to investigate.

The moment he saw her, she'd known she was in trouble. He'd swept his eyes over her and then spat. "Carol Dennis told me you'd come back to town. Not a smart thing to do, Miz Snopes."

She'd told him her last name was Stone — she'd legally reverted to her maiden name after Dwayne's death — but even though she'd shown him her driver's license, he'd refused to address her by anything but Snopes. He'd ordered her to move the Impala, and

58

when she'd told him it no longer ran, he'd called for a tow.

As she watched Dealy squeeze from the cab of his truck and lumber toward her rear bumper to attach the hook, she dropped Edward's hand and sprang forward to block the man's way. The skirt of her old blue chambray dress, cleaned now from the pounding she'd given it in the river, twisted around her legs. "Don't do this! Please. We're not harming anyone here."

He hesitated and looked over toward Armstrong.

But the wiry, straw-haired police officer with the creased face and small, unkind eyes, remained unmoved. "Get out of the way, Miz Snopes. This is private land, not a parking lot."

"I know that, but it won't be for long. Please. Can't you cut me a little slack?"

"Move aside, Miz Snopes, or I'll have you arrested for criminal trespass."

She saw that he was taking pleasure in her helplessness, and she knew she couldn't sway him. "My name is Stone."

Edward slipped his hand back in hers, and she watched Dealy fasten the hook to the rear of her car.

"You sure wasn't anxious to call yourself by anything but Snopes a few years back," Armstrong said. "Me and my wife was regulars at the Temple. Shelby even turned over an inheritance she got when her mother died so she could help out all those orphans. It wasn't much money, but it meant a lot to her, and now she can't seem to forget about the way she was cheated."

"I'm — I'm sorry about that, but surely you can see that my son and I haven't profited."

"Somebody did."

"Problem here, Jake?"

Her heart sank as she heard the soft, toneless voice she recognized only too well. Edward pressed against her side. She'd thought she'd seen the end of Bonner yesterday, and she wondered what new malevolence he was getting ready to inflict on her.

He took the scene in with those impassive silver eyes. She'd told him she was staying with a friend, but now he could see that she'd lied. He watched the Impala being hoisted and studied the meager pile of her belongings tossed out on the ground.

She hated having him look at her things. She didn't want him to see how little she had left.

Armstrong nodded a curt greeting. "Gabe. Seems the Widow Snopes here has been squatting on private land."

"Is that so?"

While Gabe watched, the officer once again began to question her. Now that he had an audience, his manner became even more overbearing. "You got a job, Miz Snopes?"

She refused to look at Gabe. Instead, she watched her Impala being towed away. "Not at the moment. And my name is Stone."

"No job, and no money from the looks of things." Armstrong rubbed his chin with the back of his hand. His skin was florid, she noticed, the complexion of a man who burned easily but was too stupid to stay out of the sun. "Maybe I should take you in for vagrancy. Now wouldn't that be a story for the newspapers. G. Dwayne Snopes's fancy wife arrested for vagrancy."

She could see him relishing the prospect. Edward pressed his cheek to her hip, and she patted him. "I'm not a vagrant."

"Sure looks that way to me. If you're not a vagrant, tell me how you're supporting that boy of yours."

A flutter of panic went through her, an urge to pick Edward up in her arms and run. A flicker in Armstrong's small, dark eyes told her he'd noticed her fear. "I have money," she said quickly.

"Sure you do," he drawled.

Without looking at Gabe, she dug her hand into the pocket of her dress and withdrew the money he'd given her, one hundred dollars.

Armstrong sauntered over and glanced down at what she held. "That won't hardly cover Dealy's towing fee. What're you planning to do then?"

"I'll get a job."

"Not in Salvation. People here don't appreciate anybody hidin' behind the Lord's name to make a fast buck. My wife wasn't the only one who lost a big chunk of her savings. You're foolin' yourself if you think anybody'll hire you."

"Then I'll go somewhere else."

"Dragging your kid with you, I suppose." A sly look came over his face. "Seems to me social services might have something to say about that."

She went rigid. He'd spotted her fear, and he knew where she was most vulnerable. Edward's free hand clutched her skirt, and she had to fight to keep her composure. "My son is just fine with me."

"Maybe, maybe not. I'll tell you what. You ride on into town with me, and I'll give the child-welfare people a call. We'll let them be the judge."

"This isn't any of your business!" She tightened her grip. "You're not taking me in."

"I do believe I am."

She backed away, bringing Edward with her. "No. I won't let you."

"Now, Miz Snopes, I suggest you don't add resistin' arrest to everything else."

An awful roaring sound surged through her head. "I haven't done anything wrong, and I won't let you do this!"

Edward made a soft sound of distress as Armstrong pulled a set of handcuffs from his belt. "It's up to you, Miz Snopes. You comin' willingly or not?"

She couldn't let him arrest her. She wouldn't, not when she knew they might take away her son. She hauled Edward up into her arms and braced herself to run.

Just then, Bonner stepped forward, his expression stony. "That won't be necessary, Jake. She's not a vagrant."

Her hands tightened around Edward's hips. He squirmed against her. Was this a trick?

Armstrong scowled, clearly unhappy with the interruption. "She's got no place to live, no money, and no job."

"She's not a vagrant," he repeated.

Armstrong switched the cuffs from one hand to the other. "Gabe, I know you was raised in Salvation, but you wasn't around when G. Dwayne ripped the heart right out of this town, not to mention most of the country. You'd best let me take care of this."

"I thought this was about Rachel being a vagrant, not about the past."

"Stay out of it, Gabe."

"She's got a job. She works for me."

"Since when?"

"Since yesterday morning."

Rachel's heart lodged in her throat as she watched the two men stare each other down. Bonner provided an imposing presence, and Armstrong finally turned away. Clearly unhappy about having his authority challenged, he slapped the handcuffs back on his belt.

"I'm gonna be checking up on you, Miz Snopes, and I'm warnin' you right now that you'd better watch your step. Your husband broke nearly every law on the books and got away with it, but believe me when I tell you that you ain't gonna be so lucky."

She watched him walk off, and only when he had disappeared did she release her grip on Edward and let him slide to the ground. Now that the crisis had passed, her body betrayed her. She took several uneven steps and slumped against the trunk of a maple to support herself. Although she knew she owed Bonner her gratitude, the words stuck in her throat.

"You told me you were staying with a friend," he said.

"I didn't want you to know we were living in the car."

"Get over to the drive-in right now." He stalked away.

Gabe was furious. If he hadn't interfered, she'd have run, and then Jake would have had the excuse he was looking for to arrest her. Now he wished he'd let it happen.

He heard her footsteps behind him as he strode back to the drive-in. The boy's voice carried on a current of air.

"Now, Mommy? Now are we gonna die?"

Pain sliced through him. He'd been numb inside, just the way he wanted it, but the two of them were cutting him open all over again.

He walked faster. She had no right to barge into his life like this when all he wanted was to be left alone. That's why he'd bought this damned drive-in in the first place. So he could go through the motions of living and still be left alone.

He made his way to his pickup, which sat in the sun next to the snack-shop door. The truck was unlocked and the windows rolled down. He jerked the door open and set the emergency brake, then turned to watch them approach.

As soon as she realized he was watching, her spine straightened, and she marched right toward him. But the boy was more cautious. He moved slower and slower, until he came to a stop.

She bent to reassure him, and her hair tumbled forward in a tangled flame curtain. A gust of wind shaped the worn fabric of her dress around her thin hips. Her legs looked frail in contrast to those big men's shoes she was wearing. Despite that, his groin stirred unexpectedly, adding to his sense of self-loathing.

He shot his head toward the truck. "Get in, boy. You stay here and keep out of trouble while I talk to your mother."

The boy's bottom lip began to tremble, and pain clawed away inside him. He remembered another little boy who'd sometimes lost control of his bottom lip, and for a terrible moment he thought he was going to collapse.

But Rachel wasn't collapsing. Despite his hostility and all that had happened, she stood squarely on her feet shooting him a dagger-sharp glare. "He's staying with me."

Her defiance was suddenly intolerable. She was alone and desperate. Didn't she understand her powerlessness? Didn't she understand she had nothing left?

Something dark and awful twisted inside him as he finally acknowledged the truth he'd been trying to ignore. Rachel Stone was tougher than he was.

"We can either have our conversation in private or in front of him. Your choice."

He watched her bite back the obscenities she wanted to throw in his face. Instead, she gave the boy a reassuring nod and a gentle prod toward the truck.

Jamie would have bounced onto the seat in one joyous motion, but her kid had a hard time pulling himself up. She'd said he was five, exactly the age Jamie had been when he'd died, but Jamie had been strong and tall, with glowing skin, laughing eyes, and a mind for mischief. Rachel's son was frail and timid.

His heart spilled bile, and he couldn't push away the ugly comparisons.

She shut the door of the truck and leaned into the window. Her breasts pressed against the side panel, and he couldn't look away. "Stay here, honey. I'll be back for you in a few minutes."

He wanted to weep at the apprehension on the boy's face, but that would mean more pain, so he distracted himself with malice. "Stop mollycoddling him, Rachel, and get inside."

Her spine straightened and her chin shot up. She was furious, but she didn't even glance in his direction. Instead, she swept into the snack shop as grandly as a queen, leaving him trailing in her wake.

Like a maggot, his malice ate away at the parts of him that were still healthy. She was beaten, but she wouldn't admit it, and that was unbearable. He needed to see her defeated. He needed to watch the last glimmer of hope fade from her eyes until her soul was as empty as his. He needed to stand by and watch her accept what he'd already discovered. Some things in life couldn't be survived.

He jerked the doors shut and threw the lock. "You're turning that boy into a sissy. Is that what you want? A sissy boy who's never going to leave your side?"

She spun on him. "What I do with my son is none of your concern."

"That's where you're wrong. Everything you do is my concern. Don't forget that I can put you in jail with one phone call."

"You bastard."

He felt an unfamiliar heat in his chest and knew that his malevolence had begun to char the borders of his heart. If he didn't leave her alone, his heart would burn away until nothing was left but a pile of ash. The idea tantalized him. "I want my money back."

"What?"

"You haven't earned it, and I want it back. Now." He didn't care about the money, and one chamber of his smoldering heart imploded. Good. That meant there were only three more to go.

She reached into the pocket of her dress and threw the small stack of bills at him. They fluttered to the ground like broken dreams. "I hope you choke on every penny."

"Pick that up."

She drew back her arm and slapped him as hard as she could.

What she lacked in muscle, she made up for in passion, and his head snapped to the side. The sting sent fresh blood pumping through his body, fresh blood he didn't want. It renewed his charred cells, undoing what he needed to accomplish and releasing a torrent of new pain.

"Take off your clothes." The words, born in the dark and empty place where his soul used to be, came unexpectedly. They sickened him, but he didn't take them back. All she had to do was show fear, and he would let her go. All she had to do was crumble.

But instead of crumbling, she was angry. "Go to hell."

Didn't she understand how isolated they were? She was locked inside a secluded building with a man who could overpower her in seconds. Why wasn't she afraid?

He realized he'd finally found a way to kill himself. If he took this any farther, he would die of spite. "Do what I say."

"Why?"

Where was her fear? He caught her by the shoulders and backed her against the wall, only to hear Cherry's voice whisper in his ear.

I love your gentleness, Gabe. You're the most gentle man I've ever known.

He knew that voice could tear him to pieces, and he blocked it out by pushing his hand under Rachel's dress and closing it around her inner thigh.

"What do you want from me?" Her anger had disappeared, and confusion had taken its place. He caught the faint fragrance of summer in her hair, sweet, enticing, full of life.

Tears that he would never shed pushed at the backs of his eyes. "Sex."

Her gaze met his, and her green eyes chilled him to the bone. "No. You don't."

"That just goes to show what you know." Despite everything, he was hard. Although his mind was dead to lust, his body didn't seem to have gotten the message. He pressed himself against her to prove how wrong she was and felt the sharp edges of her hipbones. God, she was thin. He pushed his hand higher and touched the nylon of her panties. Two days ago they'd been blue, he remembered. A frail wisp of blue nylon.

He was clammy with sweat. Beneath his callused palms, her skin felt as fragile as the membrane of an egg. He slipped his hand between her legs and cupped her.

"Do you give up?" He ground out the words, and only after they were spoken did he realize he'd made it sound as if this were some child's game they were playing.

He felt the faint tremor that passed through her body. "I'm not going to fight you. I don't care that much."

He still hadn't broken her. Instead, it was as if he'd done nothing more than give her another job. Pick up the trash. Clean the johns. Spread your legs so I can fuck you. Her acceptance made him furious, and he shoved her dress up to her waist.

"Damn it! Are you so stupid you don't know what I'm going to do to you?"

Her eyes bore into his without flinching. "Are you so stupid you haven't figured out yet that it doesn't matter?"

She robbed him of speech. His face contorted, and his breath grew ragged. At that moment, he looked the devil in the eye and saw his own reflection.

With a harsh exclamation, he pushed himself away from her. He caught a glimpse of pink nylon, then the soft whish of fabric as her skirt dropped back into place. All the fire in his body was gone.

He moved as far away from her as he could, over to the counter, and when he spoke, he couldn't summon more than a whisper. "Wait outside."

Other women would have run after they'd faced down the devil, but she didn't. She walked to the door, her head high, her posture erect.

"Take the money," he managed.

Even then he underestimated her. He expected her to tell him to go to hell and stalk out. But Rachel Snopes was stronger than false pride. Only after she had picked up every last bill did she walk away.

When the door shut behind her, he slouched against the counter and sat on the floor, his arms propped on his knees. He stared blindly ahead as the past two years unraveled in his head like an old black-and-white newsreel. Everything, he saw now, had led to today. The pills, the booze, the isolation.

Two years ago death had stolen his family, and today it had robbed him of his humanity. Now he wondered if it was too late to get it back.

CHAPTER
SIX

In Ethan Bonner's job, he was supposed to love everyone, yet he despised the woman who sat in the passenger seat of his Camry. As he turned out onto the highway from the drive-in entrance, he observed her scarecrow-thin body and hollow cheeks scrubbed free of the makeup that had once coated them. The wild auburn jumble of curls and tangles had nothing in common with the teased and tortured hair he recalled from three years earlier when the television cameras had shown her sitting beneath the Temple's famous floating pulpit.

Her appearance had once reminded him of a cross between Priscilla Presley during the Elvis years and an old-time country western singer. But instead of sequined clothing, she now wore a faded dress with one mismatched button. She looked both years younger and decades older than the woman he remembered. Only her small, regular features and the clean line of her profile remained the same.

He wondered exactly what had happened between her and Gabe. His resentment toward her deepened. Gabe had endured enough without being saddled with her problems, too.

A glance in the rearview mirror showed her little boy huddled amidst the meager pile of their possessions that were stacked on the backseat: an old suitcase, two blue plastic laundry baskets with broken handles, and a cardboard box held together with some tape.

The sight swamped him with both anger and guilt. Once again, he had fallen short. *You knew from the beginning I wasn't fit to be a minister, but would You listen? Not You. Not the Great Know-It-All. Well, I hope You're satisfied.*

A voice that sounded very much as if it belonged to Clint Eastwood echoed inside Ethan's head. *Quit your bellyaching, chump. You're the one who acted like a jerk two days ago and refused to help her. Don't put the blame on Me.*

Great! Just when Ethan had been hoping for a little compassion from Marion Cunningham, he got Eastwood. With a certain amount of resignation, he wondered why he was even surprised.

Ethan seldom got the God he wanted to hear. Right now, he'd wanted Mrs. Cunningham, the great "Happy Days" Mother God. It figured he'd get Eastwood instead. The Eastwood God was strict Old Testament. *You screwed up, punk, and now you're going to pay.*

God had been talking to Ethan for years. When he was a kid, the voice had come from Charlton Heston, which had been a major drag, since it was hard for a youngster to bare his soul to all that mighty Republican wrath. But as Ethan's understanding of the many facets of the power and wisdom of God had matured, Charlton had been stored away, along with the other

72

artifacts of his childhood, and replaced by images of three celebrities, all of them woefully inadequate to be divine representations.

If he had to hear voices, why couldn't they have come from more dignified people? Albert Schweitzer, for example? Or Mother Teresa? Why couldn't he get his inspiration from Martin Luther King or Mahatma Ghandi? Unfortunately, Ethan was a product of his culture, and he'd always liked movies and TV. Thus, he seemed to be stuck with pop icons.

"Is it too cold in here?" he asked, trying to overcome his animosity. "I can turn the air-conditioning down."

"Just fine, Rev."

Her cheeky manner set his teeth on edge, and he silently berated Gabe for getting him into this situation. But his brother had sounded so desperate on the phone when he'd called less than an hour ago that Ethan hadn't been able to refuse him.

When Ethan had arrived at the Pride of Carolina, he'd found the door of the snack shop locked and Rachel and her son sitting on the turtle in the playground. There was no sign of Gabe. He'd helped load up the pitiful pile of possessions that was stacked over by the riverbank, and now he was taking them to Heartache Mountain and Annie's cottage.

Rachel glanced over at him. "Why are you helping me?"

He remembered her as being shy, and her directness took him aback, just as it had two days earlier. "Gabe asked me to."

"He asked you two days ago, but you refused."

He said nothing. In some way he couldn't entirely define, he resented this woman even more than he'd resented G. Dwayne. Her husband had been an obvious crook, but she was a more subtle one.

She gave a wry laugh. "It's okay, Rev. I forgive you for hating my guts."

"I don't hate you. I don't hate anyone." He sounded stuffy and pompous.

"How noble."

Her disdain angered him. What right did she have to be condescending after she and her husband had destroyed so much with their greed?

None of the county's ministers had been able to compete with the Temple of Salvation's riches. They didn't have rhinestone-flecked choir robes or laser-enhanced worship services. The Temple had offered Las Vegas in the name of Jesus Christ, and many of the local church members couldn't resist the combination of show-business glitter and easy answers offered by G. Dwayne Snopes.

Unfortunately, as members fled their local congregations, they took their money with them, along with the funds that had always supported the county's good causes. Before long, an area drug program was abandoned, then the food pantry hours were cut back. But the biggest loss had been the county's small storefront medical clinic, an interdenominational venture that had been the pride of the local clergy. They had watched helplessly as the money their churches had spent helping the poor ended up in G. Dwayne

Snopes's bottomless pockets instead. And Rachel had been a big part of that.

He remembered the day he'd impulsively introduced himself to her as she was coming out of the bank. He'd told her about the clinic that was being forced to close and been encouraged by what he'd interpreted as a genuine look of concern behind her mascara-coated eyelashes.

"I'm sorry to hear that, Reverend Bonner."

"I'm not trying to assign blame," he'd said, "but the Temple of Salvation has taken so many members from our local congregations that the churches have had to abandon one worthy project after another."

She'd stiffened, and he could see that he'd made her defensive. "You can't blame what's happened on the Temple."

He should have been more tactful, but the large sapphires in her earlobes caught the sunlight, and he thought how even one of those stones could help keep the clinic open. "I'll admit that I'd like to see the Temple show a little more responsibility to the community."

"The Temple has pumped hundreds of thousands of dollars into this county."

"Into the business community, but not into philanthropy."

"You're obviously not a regular viewer, Reverend Bonner, or you'd know that the Temple does wonderful work. Orphanages throughout Africa depend on us."

Ethan had been trying to look into those orphanages, along with the rest of the Temple's finances, and he wouldn't let this pampered woman decked out in flashy jewelry and too-high heels get by with that one. "Tell me, Mrs. Snopes, am I the only one who wonders exactly how many of those millions of dollars your husband collects for orphans actually make their way to Africa?"

Her green eyes had turned into chips of ice, and he saw a flash of redhead's temper. "You shouldn't blame my husband because he has the energy and imagination to keep his pews filled on Sunday morning."

He couldn't hide his anger. "I won't turn my worship service into a lounge act for anyone."

If she'd responded sarcastically, maybe he could have forgotten about their encounter, but her voice had softened with something like sympathy. "Maybe that's where you're going wrong, Reverend Bonner. It's not *your* worship service. It belongs to God."

As she'd walked away, he had been forced to acknowledge the painful truth he didn't want to face. The grandiose success of the Temple merely highlighted his own shortcomings.

Although his sermons were thoughtful and delivered from the heart, they weren't dramatic. He'd never stirred his congregation to tears with the passion of his message. He couldn't heal the sick or make the crippled walk, and the walls of his church hadn't been bursting from overcrowding, even before G. Dwayne's arrival in Salvation.

Maybe that was why the dislike he felt for Rachel Snopes was so personal. She had held up a mirror that made him face what he didn't want to see — his utter lack of suitability to be a minister.

He turned off the highway onto the narrow road that led up Heartache Mountain to Annie's cottage. It was located less than a mile from the entrance of the drive-in.

Rachel pushed a tangled lock of hair behind her ear. "I'm sorry about your grandmother. Annie Glide was a feisty woman."

"You knew her?"

"Unfortunately. She had an aversion to Dwayne right from the beginning, and since she couldn't get past his bodyguards to give him a piece of her mind, she gave it to me instead."

"Annie was a woman of strong opinions."

"When did she die?"

"About five months ago. Her heart finally gave out. She had a good life, but we miss her."

"Has her house been empty since then?"

"Until recently. My secretary, Kristy Brown, has been living there for the past few weeks. The lease expired on her apartment before her new condo was ready, so she's staying here temporarily."

Rachel's forehead creased. "I'm sure she won't want two strangers moving in with her."

"It'll only be for a few nights," he said pointedly.

Rachel heard the unspoken message, but she ignored it. A few nights. She needed longer than that to find the Kennedy chest.

She thought of the unknown woman who was about to have a stranger and a small child move in with her.

And not just any stranger, but the town's most notorious citizen. Her head ached, and she surreptitiously pressed the fingertips of one hand to her temple.

Ethan swung wide to avoid a rut, and she banged her shoulder against the door. She glanced into the backseat to make certain Edward was all right and saw that he had a death grip on Horse. She remembered the grip Bonner'd had on her when he'd slipped his hand between her legs.

His cruelty had been deliberate and calculated, so why hadn't she been more frightened? She was no longer certain of anything, not her emotions, not even the unsettling combination of self-loathing and suffering she thought she'd seen in his eyes. She should be enraged by what had happened, but the strongest feeling she could conjure up at the moment was exhaustion.

They rounded the last bend, and the car stopped in front of a tin-roofed cottage with an overgrown garden on one side and a line of trees to the other. The house was obviously old, but it had a fresh coat of white paint, shiny dark-green shutters, and a stone chimney. Two wooden steps led to a porch, where a tattered wind sock flapped from the far corner.

With no warning at all, tears stung Rachel's eyes. This shabby old place seemed to her to be the very definition of the word *home*. It represented stability, roots, everything she wanted for her child.

Ethan unloaded their things on the porch, then opened the front door with his key and stood aside so she could enter. She drew in her breath. Late-afternoon sunlight streamed through the windows, turning the old wooden floors to butternut and casting a golden glow on the cozy stone fireplace. The furnishings were simple: brown wicker chairs with chintz cushions, a pine washstand topped by a sponge-painted lamp. An ancient pine-blanket chest served as a coffee table, and someone had filled a galvanized tin watering can with wildflowers and set it on top. It was beautiful.

"Annie collected junk, but my parents and I cleaned most of it out after she died. We kept it furnished so Gabe could move in here if he wanted, but the place had too many memories for him."

She began to ask what kind of memories, only to have him disappear through a doorway that led into a kitchen off to the left. He reappeared with a set of keys. "Gabe said to give you these."

As Rachel gazed at the keys, she recognized them for what they were, a sign of Gabe's guilt. Once again, she remembered the ugly scene between them. It was almost as if Gabe had been attacking himself instead of her. She shuddered inwardly as she wondered what other paths his course toward self-destruction might take.

With Edward trailing behind, she followed Ethan through the kitchen, which held a scarred pine farm table surrounded by four pressed-back oak chairs with cane seats. Simple muslin curtains draped the window, and a cupboard with punched tin doors stood opposite a white enamel Depression-era gas stove. As she inhaled the particular scent of old wood and generations of family meals, she wanted to weep.

Ethan led them out the back door and around the side of the cottage to an old single-car garage. One of the double set of doors dragged in the dirt as he pulled it open. She followed him inside and saw a battered red Ford Escort hatchback of indeterminate vintage.

"This belongs to my sister-in-law. She has a new car, but she won't let anybody get rid of this one. Gabe said you could drive it for a couple of days."

Rachel remembered the scholarly-looking blond in the *People* magazine photo. This wasn't her idea of the kind of car a woman like Dr. Jane Darlington Bonner would drive, but she wasn't going to argue with her good fortune. With a sense of shock, she realized that she'd been given everything she needed: a job, shelter, transportation. And she owed every bit of it to Gabe Bonner and his guilt.

The fact that he would also snatch all this away the moment his guilt faded wasn't lost on her, and she knew she would have to move quickly. Somehow she had to get her hands on the Kennedy chest soon.

"Hasn't it occurred to you that I may run off with your sister-in-law's car, and she'll never see it again?"

He gazed distastefully at the battered Escort and handed her the keys. "We couldn't be that lucky."

She watched him walk away, then heard his car start. Edward came up behind her.

"Is he really giving us that car?"

"We're just borrowing it." Despite its condition, she thought it was the most beautiful vehicle she'd ever seen.

Edward looked toward the house. He scratched the back of his calf with the opposite sneaker and watched a bluebird fly from an old magnolia and settle on the peak of the tin roof. His eyes were filled with yearning. "Do we really get to stay here?"

She thought about the mysterious Kristy Brown. "For a little while. A woman is already living here, and I'm not sure how she's going to like having the two of us move in with her, so we'll have to see what happens."

Edward scowled. "Do you think she'll be mean like him?"

No need to ask who *him* was. "Nobody could be mean like him." She gave his cheek a quick peck. "Let's go get our things and put them away." Hand in hand, they crossed the small stretch of grass toward the house.

In addition to the living room and old-fashioned kitchen, the cottage had three bedrooms, one of them a small room that held a narrow iron bed and an old black Singer sewing machine. She put Edward there, despite his protests that he wanted to sleep with her.

Bonner's comment about turning Edward into a sissy stung. He didn't understand about Edward's illness and the effect their chaotic lifestyle was having on her son. Still, she knew Edward was immature for his age, and she hoped having his own room, even if it were only for a few weeks, would give him a little self-confidence.

She chose the other unoccupied bedroom for herself. It was simply furnished with a maple bed, a wedding-ring quilt, an oak chest of drawers with carved wooden drawer pulls, and an oval braided rug fraying a bit on the edges. Edward came in to watch her put her things away.

She had just finished when she heard the front door open. She shut her eyes for a moment to gather her strength, then touched Edward's arm. "Stay here, sweetheart, until I have a chance to introduce us."

A small, rather stern-looking woman stood just inside the front door. She appeared to be a few years older than Rachel, maybe in her very early thirties. She was modestly dressed in a tan blouse buttoned to her throat and a straight brown skirt. She wore no makeup, and her dark-brown hair hung straight to just below her jawline.

As Rachel drew nearer, she saw that the woman wasn't really homely at all, merely a bit drab. She had small, regular features and trim legs, but there was a severity about her that overshadowed those attributes and made her seem older than her smooth complexion indicated.

"Hello," Rachel said. "You must be Miss Brown."

"I'm Kristy." The woman wasn't unfriendly. Rather, Rachel received the impression of deep reserve.

Rachel realized her palms were sweating. As she tried to surreptitiously wipe them on the legs of her jeans, her index finger caught in one of the tears. She snatched it out before she did any more damage. "I'm really sorry about this. Reverend Bonner kept saying you wouldn't mind having us stay here, but . . ."

"It's all right." As Kristy walked into the living room, she set the paper sack she'd been carrying on the pine-blanket chest, next to the watering can of wildflowers, and placed her rather matronly black purse on one of the brown wicker chairs.

"It's not all right. I know this is an awful imposition, but I don't seem to have anywhere else to go at the moment."

"I understand."

Rachel regarded her doubtfully. Kristy Brown couldn't be pleased with the prospect of housing the most hated woman in Salvation, but her expression gave little away. "You know who I am, don't you?"

"You're Dwayne Snopes's widow." She straightened the quilt that lay over the couch with an efficiency of motion that Rachel guessed was characteristic of everything she did. Rachel noticed that her hands were small and graceful, her neat oval fingernails covered with clear polish.

"Taking me in won't make you too popular in the community."

"I try to do what's right." Her words were sanctimonious, and she spoke them a bit stiffly. Still, something about her manner made them seem genuine.

"I took the unoccupied bedroom and put my son in the sewing room. I hope that's all right. We'll try to stay out of your way as much as possible."

"That's not necessary." She glanced around the room toward the kitchen. "Where's your little boy?"

She forced herself to turn toward the bedroom. "Edward, would you come out here? He's a little shy."

She hoped this explanation would keep Kristy from expecting too much from him.

Edward appeared in the doorway. He'd tucked Horse head-first into the waistband of his tan shorts, and he stared at the toes of his sneakers as if he'd done something wrong.

"Kristy, this is my son Edward. Edward, I'd like you to meet Miss Brown."

"Hi." He didn't look up.

To Rachel's annoyance, Kristy didn't say anything to ease his shyness but simply stared at him. This was going to be even worse than she'd thought. The last thing Edward needed around him was another hostile adult.

Edward finally lifted his eyes, apparently curious why he hadn't received a response.

Kristy's mouth curled into a full-fledged smile. "Hello, Edward. Pastor Ethan said you'd be here. I'm happy to meet you."

Edward smiled back.

Kristy picked up the sack from the blanket chest and walked over to him. "When I heard you'd be staying here, I brought you something. I hope you like it." Rachel watched Kristy kneel down until she and Edward were on eye level.

"You brought me a present?" Edward couldn't have sounded more surprised.

"Nothing fancy. I wasn't sure what you'd like." She handed him the sack. He opened it, and his eyes widened. "A book! A new book!" His features clouded. "Is it really for me?"

Rachel's heart felt as if it were breaking. There had been so much bad in Edward's life, he couldn't believe anything good was happening.

"Of course it's for you. It's called *Stellaluna*, and it's about a baby bat. Would you like me to read it?"

Edward nodded, and the two of them settled on the couch as Kristy began to read. As Rachel watched, a lump grew in her throat. He interrupted Kristy with questions, which she patiently answered, and as they continued reading, her plainness disappeared. She laughed at his chatter, her eyes sparkled, and she looked pretty.

Their interaction continued through the supper she insisted they share. Rachel ate sparingly, not willing to deprive Edward of even a bite of the chicken casserole he was devouring. With a feeling of pure pleasure, she watched the food disappear into his mouth.

After dinner, Rachel insisted on cleaning up, but Kristy wouldn't let her do it alone. While Edward sat on the front porch with his precious book, the two women worked in awkward silence.

Kristy finally broke it. "Have you thought about putting Edward in day care? There's an excellent facility at church, with a nursery school attached."

Rachel's cheeks burned. Edward needed to be around other children, and it would have done him so much good to be separated from her for a little bit. "I'm afraid I can't afford it right now."

Kristy hesitated. "It won't cost you anything. There's a scholarship I'm sure he'll qualify for."

"A scholarship?"

Kristy wouldn't quite meet her eyes. "Let me take him with me when I go to work tomorrow morning. I'll get it all straightened out."

There was no scholarship. This was charity, and more than anything, Rachel wanted to refuse. But she couldn't afford pride where her son was concerned. "Thank you," she said quietly. "I'd appreciate it."

The compassion she saw in Kristy's eyes filled her with shame.

That night, after Edward was asleep, she let herself out the back door and down the wooden steps. They creaked as she turned on the flashlight she'd remembered to take from the Impala's glove compartment before the car had been towed. Even though she was so tired that her legs felt boneless, there was something she needed to do before she could allow herself to sleep.

Keeping the beam low to the ground, she swept it along the line of trees behind the house until she found what she was looking for, a narrow path that curled into the woods. She walked toward it, picking out obstacles so she wouldn't trip.

A branch brushed her cheek, and a night bird cooed. Having been raised in the country, she liked being outside at night when she could be alone with the quiet and the clean, cool smells. Now, however, she could barely concentrate on putting one foot in front of the other.

Annie Glide's cottage was set high on Heartache Mountain, less than half a mile from Rachel's destination, but she had to stop several times to rest. In the end, it took her nearly half an hour to reach the notch. When she got there, she collapsed on a small outcrop of rock and looked down the other side of the mountain. Down toward the house where she had lived with G. Dwayne Snopes.

It sat brooding in the valley below, built on blood money and deception. The windows were dark now, and moonlight picked out the structure's shape but not its details. Still, Rachel didn't need light to remember how ugly it was, how overly grandiose and phony, just like Dwayne.

The garish monstrosity had been his idea of a Southern plantation. A pair of black wrought-iron gates decorated with gold praying hands blocked the bottom of the drive, while the exterior of the house held six massive white columns and a balcony decorated with ugly gold grillwork. The interior was filled with crypt-like black marble, ostentatious chandeliers, swags and tassels, mirrors and glitz, all of it capped off by a marble fountain in the foyer featuring colored lights and a Grecian maiden with showgirl breasts. She wondered if Cal Bonner and his wife possessed the good taste to remove the fountain, but then, she couldn't imagine anyone with good taste buying the awful house in the first place.

It was a steep descent into the valley, but one she'd made many times during the four years she'd lived there as she'd escaped the oppression of her marriage on her morning walks. The impatient part of her wanted to make that descent tonight, but she wasn't that foolhardy. Not only didn't she have the strength, but she also needed to be better prepared.

Soon. Soon, she would descend Heartache Mountain and claim what belonged to her son.

CHAPTER
SEVEN

After the incident in the snack shop, Rachel dreaded having to face Gabe again, but for the next few days, he did nothing more than bark out orders, then ignore her while he performed his own jobs. He spoke little, never met her eyes, and in general, reminded her of a man doing hard penance.

At night, she fell into a deep, dreamless sleep brought on by exhaustion. She had hoped the regular exercise would make her feel better, but the dizziness and weakness continued. On Friday afternoon while she was painting the interior of the ticket booth, she fainted.

Bonner's pickup turned into the drive from the highway just as she dragged herself back to her feet. Her heart thudded as his truck slowed. She tried to figure out how much he'd seen, but the inscrutable expression on his face gave her no clue. Grabbing her paintbrush, she scowled at him, as if he were interrupting her work, and he drove on.

Kristy volunteered to keep Edward on Saturday while Rachel worked, and Rachel gratefully accepted. At the same time, she knew she couldn't keep imposing on her housemate. If she were unlucky enough to still be in Salvation next Saturday, she would bring Edward along whether Bonner liked it or not.

Unfortunately, Rachel's plans to climb down the mountain and break into her old house the next evening after she'd tucked Edward in bed were thwarted by a torrential rainstorm. If only she could have driven, everything would be so much easier, but the locked gates made that impossible. On Monday, exactly one week since her car had broken down across from the Pride of Carolina, she promised herself she'd make the descent that night.

The day was cloudy, but dry, and by late morning, a few threads of sunlight had appeared. All morning, she'd been applying gray enamel paint to the metal walls of the rest-room stalls and thinking about how she would get into the house. The work wasn't hard, and, if it weren't for her dizziness and constant fatigue, even after her day of rest, she'd be enjoying it.

Leaning down, she used one hand to hold her blue chambray dress back as she dipped her paint roller in the pan. Painting in a dress was awkward, but she didn't have a choice. On Saturday, her jeans had finally given out in the seat, and they couldn't be patched.

"I brought you some lunch."

She spun around to see Bonner standing in the restroom doorway, a fast-food sack in his hand. She regarded him with suspicion. He'd stayed away from her since that nasty scene in the snack shop last Wednesday. Why had he sought her out now?

He scowled. "From now on I want you to bring a lunch. And stop working long enough to eat it."

90

She forced herself to meet his dead silver eyes straight on so he would know right away that his Jack the Raper performance hadn't intimidated her. "Who needs food? Your smile alone is enough to nourish me for weeks."

He ignored her jab and set the sack in one of the sinks. She waited for him to leave, but instead, he came over to inspect her work. "It'll take two coats," she said, doing her best to hide her wariness. "That old graffiti's hard to cover."

He nodded toward the door she'd just finished. "Make sure you keep the paint away from those new hinges. I don't want them binding up."

She set the roller in the paint pan and wiped her hands on the piece of terry cloth she was using as a rag. "I still don't see why you couldn't have chosen a nice egg-shell-white instead of this drab old gray." She didn't care about the color. She only cared about keeping her job and not letting him suspect for a moment how little energy she had left for even simple tasks.

"I like gray."

"Matches your personality. No, I take that back. Your personality is about ten shades darker than gray."

He didn't tense up. Instead, he leaned back against the unpainted side of the stall and studied her. "Tell you what, Rachel. I might consider giving you a raise one of these centuries if you start restricting yourself to four words when I talk to you. *Yes, sir. No, sir.*"

Let it go, her mind pleaded. *Don't bait him.* "It'd need to be an awfully big raise, Bonner. You're the best entertainment I've had since Dwayne. Now, if you don't mind, I have work to do, and you're a distraction."

He didn't budge. Instead, he openly studied her. "You get any scrawnier, you won't be able to pick up that paint roller."

"Yeah, well, don't worry about it, okay?" She bent down to pick up a rag, but her head began to swim, and she had to steady herself on the edge of the door.

He caught her arm. "Grab your lunch. I've just decided I'm going to watch you eat it."

She drew away. "I'm not hungry. I'll eat later."

He pushed the paint pan out of her way with the toe of his boot. "You'll eat now. Wash up."

She watched in frustration as he walked over to pick up the food sack. She'd planned to hide it in the back of the snack-shop refrigerator so she could save it for Edward, but she couldn't do that with him watching.

"I'll meet you at the playground," he said from the doorway. Then he disappeared.

She stomped over to the sink, where she scrubbed her hands and lower arms, splashing water on the paint-splattered skirt of her dress at the same time. Then she made her way to the playground.

He sat with his back propped against one of the jungle-gym bars and a can of Dr Pepper in his hand. One leg was stretched out, the other bent. He wore a Chicago Stars cap, along with a navy T-shirt tucked into jeans that had a small hole near the knee, but were still a thousand times better than the ones she'd had to throw out.

92

She found a place a few yards away next to the concrete turtle. He gave her the lunch sack. She noticed that his hands were scrubbed. Even the Band-Aid around his thumb was fresh. How did a man who worked so hard manage to keep himself so clean?

She placed the sack in the nest of her skirt, and pulled out a French fry. The smell was so delicious she had to resist cramming an entire fistful into her mouth. Instead, she took a nibble off the end and licked the salt from her lips.

He popped the top of his Dr Pepper, looked down at the can, and then over at her. "You deserve an apology for what I did the other day."

She was so surprised that she dropped one of the precious French fries in the grass. So that's what this cozy little lunch was about. His guilty conscience had finally caught up with him. It was nice to know he had a conscience.

He looked wary, and she suspected he was waiting for her to get all hysterical and go after him with both barrels. Well, she wouldn't give him that satisfaction. "Don't take this the wrong way, Bonner, but you were so pathetic that day I had to bite my tongue to keep from laughing."

"Is that so?"

She expected his scowl to deepen, but instead, he relaxed slightly against the bar of the jungle gym. "It was inexcusable. Nothing like that'll ever happen again." He paused, not quite meeting her eyes. "I'd been drinking."

She remembered the way his breath had fallen on her — clean, with no hint of alcohol. She still had the feeling his attack had more to do with his own demons than hers. "Yeah, well, maybe you should give it up. You acted like an ass."

"I know."

"The king of asses."

His gaze flicked back to her, and she actually thought she detected a spark of amusement in those hard silver eyes. Was that possible?

"You're going to make me grovel, aren't you?"

"Like a worm."

"Does anything put a cork in that mouth of yours?" His lips curved in something that almost resembled a smile, and she was so stunned it took her a moment to muster a response.

"Disrespect is part of my charm."

"Whoever told you that lied."

"Are you calling Billy Graham a liar?"

For a moment, the curl of his mouth grew more pronounced, but then the familiar scowl returned. Apparently his time for groveling was over. He gestured toward her with his Dr Pepper can. "Don't you have any jeans? Tell me, what kind of idiot does manual labor in a dress?"

Somebody who doesn't have anything else to wear, she thought. She wouldn't spend a penny on clothes for herself, not when Edward was growing out of his. "I love dresses, Bonner. They make me feel all cute and feminine."

"With those shoes?" He regarded her big black oxfords with distaste.

"What can I say? I'm a slave to fashion."

"Bull. Those old jeans of yours gave out, didn't they? Well, buy yourself some new ones. *I'll* buy you some new ones. Consider it a uniform."

He'd seen her swallow her pride again and again, but that had been for Edward. This was not. She made no effort to hide her scorn. "If *you* buy 'em, *you* wear 'em."

Several seconds ticked by while he seemed to take her measure. "You're tough, aren't you?"

"The toughest."

"So tough you don't even need food." His gaze moved to the food sack in her lap. "Are you going to eat those fries or just play with them?"

"I told you I wasn't hungry."

"That must explain why you look like a skeleton. You're anorexic, aren't you?"

"Poor people don't get anorexia." She pushed a second French fry in her mouth. It was so good she wanted to stuff the entire package in. At the same time, she felt guilty for robbing Edward of even part of a treat he'd enjoy so much.

"Kristy says you hardly eat anything."

It bothered her to discover that Kristy was reporting to Gabe behind her back. "She should mind her own business."

"So why don't you eat?"

"You're right. I'm anorexic. Now let's drop the subject, okay?"

"Poor people don't get anorexia."

She ignored him and savored another French fry.

"Try some of that hamburger."

"I'm vegetarian."

"You've been eating meat at Kristy's."

"What are you, the food police?"

"I don't get it. Unless . . ." He studied her with shrewd eyes. "That first day when you fainted, I gave you a cupcake, and you tried to pass it off to your kid."

She stiffened.

"That's what's going on, isn't it? You're giving your food to your kid."

"His name is Edward, and this heads the list of things that aren't any of your business."

He stared at her and shook his head. "You're acting crazy. You know that, don't you? Your boy's getting plenty to eat. You're the one who's starving to death."

"I'm not talking about this."

"Damn, Rachel. You're nutty as a fruitcake."

"I am not!"

"Then explain it to me."

"I don't have to explain anything. Besides, look who's talking. In case you haven't noticed, you crossed through that padded cell between normal and psychotic a good hundred miles back."

"That must be why we get along so well."

He spoke so pleasantly she nearly smiled. He took a sip of his Dr Pepper. She gazed beyond the far edge of the screen toward Heartache Mountain and remembered how much she'd loved these mountains when Dwayne had first brought her here. It used to be, when she'd gazed at the green vista out her bedroom window, she felt as if she were touching the face of God.

She looked over at Gabe and, for the briefest moment, she saw another human being instead of an enemy. She saw someone as lost as she and just as determined not to show it.

He rested the back of his head against the jungle-gym bar and gazed over at her. "Your boy . . . He's been eating a good dinner every night, hasn't he?"

Her feeling of kinship vanished. "Are we back to this again?"

"Just answer the question. Has he been eating a decent dinner?"

She nodded begrudgingly.

"Breakfast, too?" he asked.

"I guess."

"They have snacks at the day-care center and a big lunch. I'll bet either you or Kristy gives him another snack when he gets home."

But what about next month? she thought. Next year?

A chill passed through her. She was being pushed toward something dangerous.

"Rachel," he said quietly, "this business of starving yourself has to stop."

"You don't know what you're talking about!"

"Then explain it to me."

If he'd spoken harshly, everything would have been all right, but she had few defenses against that quiet, measured tone. She mustered the ones she could gather and went on the attack.

"I'm responsible for him, Bonner. Me! There's no one else. I'm the one who's responsible for his food, his clothes, the shots he gets at the doctor's office, everything!"

"Then maybe you should take better care of yourself."

Her eyes stung. "Don't you tell me what to do."

"The inmates at the asylum need to stick together."

His words, coupled with the clear understanding she saw in his eyes, took her breath away. She wanted to go after him again, but couldn't frame her thoughts. He was exposing something she should have examined long ago, but hadn't been able to face.

"I don't want to talk about this."

"Good. Eat instead."

Her fingers convulsed around the paper sack in her lap, and she made herself face the truth she didn't want to acknowledge.

No matter how much she deprived herself, she couldn't guarantee that Edward would be safe.

She experienced a surge of helplessness so powerful it nearly crushed her. She wanted to stockpile everything for him, not just food, but security and self-confidence, a healthy body, a decent education, a house to live in. And no amount of self-deprivation would do any of that. She could starve herself until she was a skeleton, but that still wouldn't guarantee that Edward's belly would stay full.

To her dismay, her eyes clouded, and then a tear slipped over her bottom lid and rolled down her cheek.

She couldn't bear having Bonner see her cry, and she regarded him fiercely. "Don't you dare say a word!"

He held up his hands in mock surrender and took a swig of Dr Pepper.

A long shudder passed through her. Bonner was right. Holding herself together these last few months had made her crazy as a loon. And only someone equally crazy could have seen the truth.

She looked her own insanity squarely in the eye. Edward had no one in the world but her, and she wasn't taking care of herself. By starving her body, she was making their already precarious existence that much more fragile.

She dashed at her eyes and grabbed the hamburger from the sack. "You're a son of a bitch!"

He slouched against the jungle-gym post and tilted the brim of his navy Chicago Stars cap over his eyes as if he were settling in for a nice long nap.

She stuffed the burger into her mouth, swallowing it along with her tears. "I don't know how you have the nerve to call me crazy." She stuffed in another bite, and the taste was so delicious she shivered. "What kind of moron opens a drive-in? In case you haven't noticed, Bonner, drive-ins have been dead for about thirty years. You'll be bankrupt by the end of the summer."

His lips barely moved beneath the brim of his cap. "Ask me if I care."

"I rest my case. You're a dozen times crazier than me."

"Keep eating."

She swiped at her damp eyes with the back of her hand, then took another bite. It was the most delicious hamburger she'd ever tasted. Globs of cheese stuck to the roof of her mouth, and the pickle made her saliva buds spurt. She spoke around a huge bite. "Why are you doing it?"

"Couldn't think of anything else to occupy my time."

She sucked a dab of ketchup from her finger. "Before you lost your mind, how did you make a living?"

"I was a hit man for the Mafia. Are you done crying yet?"

"I wasn't crying! And I wish you *were* a hit man because, if I had the money, I'd hire you right this minute to knock yourself off."

He tilted up the brim of his cap and regarded her levelly. "You just keep all that good, honest hatred coming at me, and we'll get along fine."

She ignored him and began eating the fries three at a time.

"So how'd you fall in with G. Dwayne?"

The question came out of nowhere — probably a diversion — but since he hadn't given her any real information about himself, she wasn't giving any in return. "I met him at a strip club where I was an exotic dancer."

"I've seen your body, Rachel, and unless you had a lot more flesh on your bones then, you couldn't buy chewing gum with what you'd earn as a stripper."

She tried to be offended, but she didn't have enough vanity left. "They don't like to be called strippers. I know because one of them lived across the hall from me a few years ago. She used to go to a tanning salon every day before she performed."

"You don't say."

"I'll bet you think exotic dancers tan in the nude, but they don't. They wear little thongs so they get really sharp white tan lines. She said it makes what they show off seem more forbidden."

"Tell me that's not admiration I hear in your voice."

"She made a good living, Bonner."

He snorted.

As her stomach began to fill, curiosity overcame her. "What did you used to do? Truth."

He shrugged. "It's no big secret. I was a vet."

"A veterinarian?"

"That's what I said, isn't it?" The belligerence was back.

She realized she was curious about him. Kristy had lived in Salvation all her life, and she must know some of Gabe's secrets. Rachel decided to ask her.

"You don't seem like the type a televangelist would fall for." He conducted his own bit of probing. "I'd have figured G. Dwayne would pick one of those pious church ladies."

"I was the most pious of them all." She didn't let a trace of her bitterness show. "I met Dwayne when I was a volunteer at his crusade in Indianapolis. He swept me off my feet. Believe it or not, I used to be a romantic."

"He was quite a bit older than you, wasn't he?"

"Eighteen years. The perfect father figure for an orphan."

He regarded her quizzically.

"I was raised by my grandmother on a farm in central Indiana. She was very devout. Her little rural church congregation had become her family, and they became mine, too. The religion was strict, but, unlike Dwayne's, it was honest."

"What happened to your parents?"

"My mother was a hippie; she didn't know who my father was."

"A hippie?"

"I was born on a commune in Oregon."

"You're kidding."

"I stayed with her for the first couple of years, but she was into drugs, and when I was three, she OD'd. Luckily for me, I was sent to my grandmother's." She smiled. "Gram was a simple lady. She believed in God, the United States of America, apple pie made from scratch, and G. Dwayne Snopes. She was so happy when I married him."

"She obviously didn't know him well."

"She thought he was a great man of God. Luckily, she died before she found out the truth." With the food gone and her stomach so full it ached, she turned to the shake, picking up a thick chocolate curl on the end of her straw and raising it to her mouth. So far, she'd offered all the information and received nothing in return. "Tell me. How does it feel to be the black sheep of your family?"

"What makes you think I'm the black sheep?" He actually sounded annoyed.

"Your parents are leaders of the community, your younger brother is Mr. Perfect, and your older brother's a multimillionaire jock. You, on the other hand, are a surly, bad-tempered, impoverished misfit who owns a broken-down drive-in and antagonizes small children."

"Who told you I was impoverished?"

She found it interesting this was the only part of her description of him he seemed inclined to challenge. "This place. Your mode of transportation. Those slave wages you're paying me. Maybe I'm missing something but I don't see any signs of big money around here."

"I pay you slave wages so you'll quit, Rachel, not because I can't afford more."

"Oh."

"And I like my pickup."

"So you're not poor?"

For a moment she didn't think he'd answer. Finally, he said, "I'm not poor."

"Exactly how not-poor are you?"

"Didn't your grandmother teach you it was rude to ask people questions like that?"

"You're not people, Bonner. I'm not even sure you're human."

"I've got better things to do than sit here and let you insult me." He snatched his empty Dr Pepper can from the sandy soil where he'd propped it and stood up. "Get to work."

As she watched him stalk away, she considered the possibility that she'd offended him. He definitely looked offended. With a satisfied smile, she returned to her chocolate shake.

Ethan stepped out of his office and followed the direction of childish squeals to the playground at the rear of the church where the children were waiting for their parents to pick them up. He told himself this was a good way to connect with the members of the community who weren't part of his congregation, but the truth was, he wanted to see Laura Delapino.

As he walked onto the playground, the Briggs twins abandoned their riding toys to run to his side.

"Guess what? Tyler Baxter barfed on the floor, and it got all over."

"Cool," Ethan replied.

"I almost barfed, too," Chelsey Briggs confessed, "but Mrs. Wells let me pass out straws."

Ethan laughed at the image that non sequitur conjured up. He loved kids, and for years he'd been looking forward to having a few of his own. Gabe's son, Jamie, had been the apple of his eye. Even after two years, it was hard for him to handle what had happened to his nephew and to Cherry, his sweet-tempered sister-in-law.

He'd almost left the ministry after their senseless deaths, but he'd gotten off easier than the rest of his family. The tragedy had pushed his parents into a midlife crisis that had nearly led to divorce, and Cal had shut out everything from his life except winning football games.

Luckily, after a brief separation, his parents' marriage had undergone a transformation that had left Jim and Lynn Bonner acting like lovebirds, as well as changing their lives. Right now the two of them were in South America, where his father was serving as a medical missionary while his mother set up a co-op to market the work of local artisans.

As for Cal, a genius physicist named Dr. Jane Darlington had come into his life, and now the family had another baby, eight-month-old Rosie, an impish blue-eyed darling who held all of them in the palm of her tiny little hand.

None of them, however, had gone through as tough a time as Gabe. Sometimes it was hard for Ethan to remember the gentle healer his brother had been. Throughout Ethan's childhood, there had always been an injured animal somewhere in the house: a bird with a broken wing in the kitchen, a stray dog to be nursed back to health in the garage, a baby skunk too young to survive on its own hidden away in Gabe's bedroom closet.

All his life, Gabe had wanted to be a vet, but he'd never planned on becoming a multimillionaire. His sudden wealth had amused everyone in the family, since Gabe was notoriously indifferent about money. It had happened accidentally.

His brother was insatiably curious, and he'd always liked to tinker. Several years after he'd opened his practice in rural Georgia, he'd developed a specialized orthopedic splint to use on one of the championship thoroughbreds he was treating for a local breeder. The splint had worked so well that it had quickly been adopted by the wealthy horse-racing community, and Gabe was making a fortune from the patent.

He had always been the most complex of the three brothers. While Cal was aggressive and confrontational, quick to anger and equally quick to forgive, Gabe kept his feelings to himself. Still, he'd been the first person Ethan had run to when he'd gotten into scrapes as a child. His quiet voice and slow, lazy movements could calm a troubled boy just as well as they soothed a frightened animal. But now his gentle, pensive brother had turned into a bitter, cynical man.

Ethan was distracted from his reverie by the arrival of Laura Delapino, the town's newest divorcée. She'd tossed a gauzy lime-green blouse over a black halter top, which she wore with a pair of tight white shorts. Her long fingernails were polished the same deep shade of red as the toenails visible through the straps of her silver sandals. Her breasts were lush, her legs long, her hair big and blond. She exuded sex, and he wanted some of it.

Men of God who secretly lust after trashy women! Live today on Oprah!

He groaned inwardly. He wasn't in the mood for this.

But it was no use. The Wise God knew a ratings hit when she saw one.

Tell us, Reverend Bonner — we're all friends here — why is it you're never interested in any of the nice women who live in this town?

Nice women bore me to tears.

They're supposed to bore you. You're a minister, remember? Why is it only our more flamboyant sisters who catch your eye?

106

Laura Delapino bent over to talk to her little girl, and he could see the outline of a pair of very lacy bikini underpants beneath those tight white shorts. A shaft of heat shot straight to his groin.

I'm talking to you, Mister, Oprah said.

Go away, he replied, which only made her mad.

Don't you start with Me! Next thing you'll be whining about how you're not cut out for the job and how the ministry is ruining your life.

He wanted Eastwood back.

Pay attention to Me, Ethan Bonner. It's time you found yourself a nice, decent woman and settled down.

Could you please shut up for a minute so I can enjoy the view? Laura's breasts strained against the cups of her halter top as she leaned forward to regard her daughter's artwork. Damn it! He wasn't meant to be celibate.

He remembered those wild years in his early twenties before he'd gotten the call. The beautiful, busty women; the nights of hot free sex — doing it every way he could think of. Oh, God . . .

Yes? Oprah replied.

He gave up. How could he enjoy Laura's body with the Greatest Talk-Show Host of them all listening in? As he turned away, he found himself wishing he could counsel teenagers to celibacy and preach on the sacredness of marriage vows without actually living those beliefs himself, but he wasn't made up that way.

He greeted Tracy Longben and Sarah Curtis, both of whom he'd grown up with, then he commiserated with Austin Longben over his broken wrist and admired

107

Taylor Curtis's pink sneakers. Out of the corner of his eye, he saw Edward Snopes standing off by himself.

Stone, he reminded himself, not Snopes. The boy's last name had been legally changed. Too bad Rachel hadn't done something about that first name. Why didn't she call him Eddie or Ted?

His conscience pinched him. The boy had been at the child-care center for three days, and Ethan hadn't once sought him out. It wasn't Edward's fault that he had dishonest parents, and Ethan had no excuse for ignoring him except misplaced anger.

He remembered the phone call he'd received from Carol Dennis the day before. His anger was nothing compared to hers. She was furious that he'd let Rachel stay in Annie's cottage, and he'd been too protective of Gabe to tell her it had been his brother's decision.

He'd tried to reason with her, gently reminding her they needed to be careful about passing judgment, even though he'd passed it long ago, but she wouldn't listen.

He didn't like crossing Carol. Although her brand of religion was more restrictive than his, she was a woman of deep faith, and she'd done the town a lot of good.

"If you let her stay in that cottage, Pastor," she'd said, "it will reflect on you, and I don't think you want that."

Even though she was right, her attitude had irritated him. "I guess I'll have to deal with that when it happens," he'd replied as mildly as he could manage.

Now he made himself walk over to Edward and smile. "Hey there, buddy. How'd your day go?"

"Okay."

The child gazed up at him with large brown eyes. He had a sprinkle of pale freckles across his nose. A cute kid. Ethan felt himself warming to him. "You made any friends yet?"

He didn't respond.

"It might take a while for the other kids to get used to having somebody new around, but sooner or later they'll warm up."

Edward looked up at him and blinked. "Do you think Kristy forgot to come and get me?"

"Kristy doesn't ever forget anything, Edward. She's the most reliable person you'll ever know."

Kristy overheard Ethan's words as she came up behind them. *Reliable*. That's all she meant to Ethan Bonner. Good old *reliable* Kristy Brown. *Kristy'll do it. Kristy'll take care of it.*

She sighed to herself. What did she expect? Did she think Ethan would look at her the way he'd been looking at Laura Delapino only a moment earlier? Not likely. Laura was flashy and perky, while Kristy was plain and uninteresting. She had her pride, though, and over the years she had learned to hide her painful shyness behind a brutal efficiency. Whatever needed to be done, she could do. Everything except win Ethan Bonner's heart.

Kristy had known Ethan nearly all her life, and he'd been attracted to flashy, easy women ever since eighth grade when Melodie Orr had gotten her braces off and discovered shrink-wrapped jeans. They used to make out every day after lunch next to the choir room.

"Kristy!"

Edward's face lit up as he spotted her, and warmth spread through her. She loved children. She could relax with them and be herself. She would have much preferred working in child care to her job as a church secretary, and she'd have quit years ago if she hadn't so desperately needed to stay close to Ethan Bonner. Since she couldn't be his lover, she'd settle into the role of his caretaker.

As she knelt down to admire the collage Edward had made that day, she thought about the fact that she'd loved Ethan for more than twenty years. She clearly remembered watching him through the window of her third-grade classroom when he went out for recess with the fourth-graders. He'd been just as dazzling then as he was now, the handsomest boy she'd ever seen. He'd always treated her kindly, but then he'd treated everyone that way. Even when he was a child, Ethan had been different from the others: more sensitive, less inclined to tease.

He hadn't been a pushover, though; his older brothers had taken care of that. She still remembered the day Ethan had fought D.J. Loebach, the junior high's worst bully, and given him a bloody nose. Afterward, though, Ethan had felt guilty and gone over to D.J.'s house with a couple of melting grape Popsicles to make peace. D.J. still liked to tell that story at deacons' meetings.

110

As she stood and took Edward's hand, she caught the whiff of a heavy, sensuous perfume. "Hey, Eth."

"Hi, Laura."

Laura flashed Kristy a friendly smile, and Kristy felt her heart curdle with envy. How could some women be so confident?

She thought of Rachel Stone and wondered where she got her courage. Despite all the horrible things people in town were saying about Rachel, Kristy liked her; she was even in awe of her. Kristy was certain she'd never have the courage to face people down the way Rachel was doing.

She'd heard about Rachel's encounter with Carol Dennis at the grocery store, and yesterday Rachel had stood up to Gary Prett at the pharmacy. The intensity of people's hostility upset Kristy. She didn't believe Rachel had been responsible for Dwayne Snopes's greed, and she couldn't understand people who called themselves Christians being so judgmental and vindictive.

She wondered what Rachel thought of her. Probably nothing at all. People only noticed Kristy when they wanted something done. Otherwise, she was white wallpaper.

"So Eth," Laura said, "why don't you come over tonight and let me throw a couple of steaks on the grill for us?" She rubbed her lips together as if she were smoothing out her lipstick.

For a fraction of a second Ethan's eyes lingered on her mouth, then he gave her the same open, friendly smile he gave the old women in the congregation. "Gosh, I'd love to, but I have to work on my sermon."

Laura persisted, but he managed to fend her off without too much difficulty. Kristy suspected he didn't trust himself to be alone with Laura.

Something painful twisted at her heart. Ethan always trusted himself to be alone with her.

CHAPTER
EIGHT

Rachel kept the beam of her flashlight low. As she neared the back of the house where she'd known so much misery, she bunched her hooded sweatshirt more tightly around her, warding off a chill that came as much from within as it did from the cool night breeze. The house was as dark as Dwayne Snopes's soul.

Even though the night was cloudy and visibility poor, she knew where she was going, and, with the few shards of gray moonlight that penetrated the clouds, she managed to navigate the curved path across the small stretch of overgrown lawn. The paint-spattered skirt of her dress caught on some shrubbery. As she freed it, she considered the fact that she would have to buy something else to wear soon, but her new resolution to take better care of herself didn't extend to luxuries like clothing, and she decided to postpone it.

She couldn't believe the difference having a full stomach made in the way she felt. It had been her turn to cook dinner tonight, and she'd eaten a full meal. Although she was still tired, the dizziness had vanished, and she felt stronger than she had in weeks.

The house loomed over her. She turned off her flashlight as she approached the back door. It led into a laundry room, and from there into the kitchen. She hoped Cal Bonner and his wife hadn't installed a security system. When she and Dwayne had lived here, their only problems had been with overly zealous fans, and the electronically controlled gates at the bottom of the drive had kept them at a distance.

She also hoped they hadn't changed the locks. Slipping her hand into the pocket of her sweatshirt, she pulled out a house key attached to a loop of coiled purple plastic that she used to slip over her wrist when she went on her walks up the mountain. This had been her spare key, the only one the police hadn't taken. She'd found it several weeks after she'd been evicted tucked into the pocket of this very same sweatshirt. If the key no longer worked, she would have to break one of the windows in the back.

But the key did work. The lock caught in the same stubborn place, then gave way when she pulled on it. A sense of unreality encompassed her as she stepped inside the mudroom. It smelled damp and unused, and the darkness was so thick she had to feel her way along the wall to the door. She pushed it open and stepped into the kitchen.

She'd always hated this room with its black marble floors, granite counters, and a crystal chandelier more suited to an opera hall than a kitchen hanging over the center work island. Dwayne's well-groomed appearance and polished manners camouflaged a man who'd been born poor and needed opulence surrounding him so he could feel important. He'd loved the house's garishness.

114

Even though it was dark, she knew the kitchen well enough that she could ease her way along the counters until she arrived at the entryway to the family room that stretched across the back. Even though the house was deserted, she moved as quietly as her heavy shoes allowed. Enough weak moonlight came through the sliding-glass doors for her to see that nothing had changed. The pit sofa and matching chairs still conjured up memories of an eighties bachelor pad. In the oppressive silence of the empty house, she crossed the room toward a back hallway and, with the aid of the flashlight, approached Dwayne's study.

The lofty room with its Gothic furnishings and heavy draperies had been Dwayne's idea of something that might be used by a member of the British royal family. A quick sweep of the flashlight revealed that the animal trophy heads were gone. So was the Kennedy chest.

Now what? She decided to risk turning on the green-shaded desk lamp and saw that the desk had been cleared of papers. There was a new telephone, a computer, and a silent fax machine. She gazed at the shelf where the Kennedy chest had been positioned in the photograph and saw only a pile of books.

Her heart sank. She began to search the room, but it didn't take her long to discover that the chest had disappeared.

She turned off the desk lamp, then slumped down on the couch where Cal Bonner and his wife had been photographed. Had she really thought this would be easy when nothing else had gone her way? Now she would have to search the rest of the house and hope that they'd simply moved the chest, not taken it away.

Using the flashlight to see, she made quick work of the living and dining rooms, then moved through the foyer and past the night-club fountain, which was mercifully unlit. The foyer rose two stories above her. The upstairs bedrooms opened onto a balcony surrounded by gilded wrought iron. As she mounted the curving staircase, she began to feel strangely disoriented, as if three years hadn't passed and Dwayne were still alive.

She'd met him when he was on his first crusade through the midwest. He'd been appearing in Indianapolis as part of an eighteen-city televised tour to expand his cable audience. Most of the members of her little church had agreed to be volunteer workers, and Rachel had been assigned to act as one of the backstage gofers, a task, she later learned, that was always given to the more attractive of the young female volunteers.

She was twenty at the time, and she hadn't been able to believe her luck when one of the crusade's staff members had assigned her to deliver a pile of preselected prayer cards to Dwayne. She was actually going to see the famous evangelist up close! Her hand had shaken as she'd knocked on the door of his dressing room.

"Come in."

She'd opened the door tentatively, just far enough to see G. Dwayne Snopes standing at the lighted mirror and running a silver-backed hairbrush through his thick blond hair, so attractively graying at the temples. He

116

smiled at her reflection, and she felt the full jolt of Snopes's charisma.

"Come on in, darlin'."

Her pulses pounded, and her palms went damp. She was giddy and overwhelmed. He turned, his smile grew wider, and she forgot to breathe.

She'd known the facts about Dwayne Snopes. He'd been a North Carolina tobacco broker when he'd gotten the call ten years ago and gone on the road as a traveling evangelist. Now he was thirty-seven, and, thanks to cable television, the fastest-rising evangelist in the country.

His magnetic speaking voice, bold good looks, winning smile, and charismatic personality were tailor-made for television. Women fell in love with him; men considered him one of the guys. The poor and the elderly, who made up the majority of his audience, believed him when he promised health, wealth, and happiness. And unlike the fallen televangelists of the eighties, everyone thought they could trust him.

How could you not trust a man who was so open about his own shortcomings? With a boyish earnestness, he confessed a weakness for alcohol, which he'd overcome ten years earlier when he'd gotten the call, and an attraction toward pretty women, which remained a struggle. By his own admission, his first marriage had ended because of his philandering, and he asked his television congregation to pray that he could continue putting his womanizing behind him. He combined Jimmy Swaggart's hellfire-and-damnation preaching with Jim Bakker's cozy God of love, abundance, and prosperity. In the world of Christian broadcasting, it was an unbeatable combination.

"Come on in, honey," he repeated. "I won't eat you. At least not till after we pray about it." His boyish mischieviousness immediately won her over.

She handed him the prayer cards. "I — I'm supposed to give you these."

He paid no attention to the prayer cards, only to her. "What's your name, darlin'?"

"Rachel. Rachel Stone."

He smiled. "God surely has blessed me today."

That was the beginning.

She didn't board the bus with the other members of her congregation that night. Instead, one of Dwayne's aides approached her grandmother with the news that the televangelist had received a message from God that Rachel was to accompany him as a helper on the rest of his tour.

Rachel's grandmother had been in frail health for some time, and because Rachel knew how much she needed her help, Rachel had refused a scholarship to Indiana University to stay home and take care of her. It had been difficult to satisfy her deep intellectual curiosity by taking only a few courses each semester at the local community college, but her grandmother meant everything to her, and she'd never resented the choice she'd made.

She'd told Dwayne's aide she couldn't travel with the crusade, not even for a short period of time, but her grandmother had overruled her. God's call could not be ignored.

118

During the next few weeks, Dwayne lavished attention on her, and she soaked up every drop. Each morning and evening, she knelt at his side as he prayed, so she was able to witness his unfaltering dedication to the business of saving souls. It would be years before she understood how complex the demons were that lurked beneath his faith.

She couldn't comprehend why he was attracted to her. She was a lean, leggy redhead, pretty in a well-scrubbed way, but she wasn't beautiful. He certainly didn't press her for sex, and when he asked her to marry him shortly before she was supposed to return home, she was stunned.

"Why me, Dwayne? You could have any woman you wanted."

"Because I love you, Rachel. I love your innocence. Your goodness. I need you at my side." The same tears that sometimes filled his eyes when he was preaching now glittered there. "You're going to keep me from straying from God's path. You're going to be my passport into heaven."

Rachel hadn't understood the ominous side to his words, the fact that he didn't believe he was saved and that he needed someone else to do it for him. Only during her pregnancy with Edward two years later did the last of the romantic scales fall from her eyes so she could see Dwayne exactly as he was.

Although his faith in God was deep and unshakable, he was a man of limited intellect with no interest in the finer points of theology. He knew his Bible, but he refused to acknowledge its contradictions or wrestle

119

with its complexities. Instead, he pulled verses out of context and twisted them to justify his actions.

He believed he was inherently wicked, but also that he was put on earth to save souls, and he never questioned the morality of his methods. His dubious fund-raising practices, his extravagant lifestyle, and his bogus faith healings were sanctioned by God.

His fame skyrocketed, and no one but Rachel understood that his public facade concealed a deeply held conviction that he was personally damned. He could save everyone but himself. That was to be her job, and in the end, he couldn't forgive her for not accomplishing it.

The beam of her flashlight settled on the door to the master bedroom. She had spent very little time in this room. Her eager sexuality had been a betrayal in Dwayne's eyes. He'd married her for her innocence. He wanted her, but he didn't want her to want him back. There were other women he could use to slake that thirst. Not many — he could sometimes hold Satan at bay for months at a time — but enough to damn him forever. She pushed away the unhappy memories and turned the knob.

With Cal Bonner and his wife living in Chapel Hill, the house was supposed to be empty, but the moment she stepped in the room she knew that wasn't true. She heard the creak of the bed, a rustle . . . With a hiss of alarm, she swung the flashlight around.

The beam of light caught the pale-silver eyes of Gabriel Bonner.

120

He was naked. The navy sheet rode low, revealing a taut abdomen and the blade of one muscular hip. His dark, too-long hair was rumpled, and stubble roughened his lean cheeks. He supported his weight on his forearm and stared directly into the beam of light.

"What do you want?" His voice was gruff from sleep, but his gaze was unflinching.

Why hadn't she realized he might be staying here? Ethan had told her Annie's cottage held too many memories for him. This house would have no memories at all, but she hadn't stopped to think that he might have moved in. Her reasoning powers had weakened along with her undernourished body.

She tried to come up with a lie that would explain why she had broken into the house. His eyes narrowed, as if he were trying to peer more deeply into the beam of light, and she realized the flashlight had blinded him. He couldn't see who his intruder was.

To her surprise, he turned toward the bedside clock and looked at its glowing face. "Damn it. I've only slept an hour."

She couldn't imagine what he was talking about. She took a step backward, but kept the light shining in his eyes as he swung his bare legs over the side of the bed. "You got a gun?"

She said nothing. He was definitely naked, she realized, although the beam of light was focused too high for her to make out any details.

"Go ahead and shoot me." He stared directly at her. She saw no fear in his eyes, nothing but emptiness, and she shivered. He didn't seem to care whether she was

121

armed or not, whether she shot him or left him alone. What sort of man had no fear of death?

"Come on! Do it. Either do it, or get the hell out of here."

The ferocity in his voice chilled her so that all she wanted to do was run. She snapped out the light, whirled around, and rushed into the hallway. Darkness enveloped her. She groped for the balcony rail and stumbled along it toward the stairs.

He caught her on the first step. "You son of a bitch." Grabbing her by the arm, he threw her against the wall.

Her side hit hard and then her head. Pain shot through her arm and hip, but the blow to her head dazed her just enough to dull its intensity. Her legs gave out, and sparks shot behind her eyelids as she slumped to the floor.

He fell on her. She felt bare skin and hard tendon, and then his hand tangled in her long hair as it curled on the carpet.

For a moment he froze, then he spat out a nasty curse and lurched to his feet. An instant later, light flooded the hallway from the eight-foot chandelier that hung above the foyer. Dazed, she looked up at him as he loomed over her and saw that she hadn't been mistaken. He was definitely naked. Even through those dizzying whirligigs that were scrambling her brain waves, she found her eyes drawn to the most naked part of him, and just when all her resources should have been focused on survival, she got distracted.

He was beautiful. Larger than Dwayne. Thicker. In her grogginess — it had to be grogginess — she wanted to touch.

Dwayne had never let her satisfy her sexual curiosity. Lusty pleasures were reserved for him, not for her. She was heaven's gatekeeper, designed for piety, not passion, and she'd never been permitted to caress him or do any of those things she fantasized about. She was suppose to lie quietly, praying for his salvation, while he rutted inside her.

Bonner knelt next to her, bending his near leg and spoiling the view. "How many?"

"One," she managed.

"Try to focus, Rachel. How many fingers am I holding up?"

Fingers? He was talking about *fingers?* She groaned. "Go away."

He left her side only to return a moment later with her flashlight. Once again, he knelt down, then flicked on the light, peeled open her lids, and shone the beam in her eyes. She tried to turn away.

"Hold still."

"Leave me alone."

He turned off the light. "Your pupils contracted. You don't seem to have a head injury."

"What do you know? You're a vet." A naked vet. She groaned again as she tried to sit upright.

He pushed her back. "Give yourself a minute. I want you fully recovered before I call the police and have you arrested."

"Bite me."

He gazed down at her, then sighed. "You need a serious attitude adjustment."

"Stuff it, Bonner. You're not going to have me arrested, and both of us know it, so just give it up."

"What makes you think I won't?"

"Because you don't *care* enough to call the police."

"You think I don't *care* that you've broken into this house in the middle of the night?"

"A little maybe, but not much. You don't care much about anything. Why is that, by the way?"

She wasn't surprised when he didn't answer. The world began to steady around her. "Look, would you mind putting some clothes on?"

He glanced down at himself as if he'd forgotten he was naked. Slowly he rose to his feet. "This bothers you?"

She gulped. "Not at all." Her gaze locked on that most amazing of all his body parts. Was it her imagination, or was it getting larger? She began to feel fuzzy again. Maybe she had a head injury after all. Except the fuzziness didn't seem to be in her head. It was in her legs. Her stomach. Her breasts.

"Rachel?"

"Um?"

"You're staring."

Her head shot up, and she could feel herself blushing. That made her mad. But she got even madder when she saw the faint twitch at the corner of his mouth and realized that something had finally struck Mr. Sourpuss's funny bone. Unfortunately, it was her.

124

She struggled into a sitting position. "Just get your clothes on, will you? You look revolting naked."

He splayed his hands on his hips. "You're the interloper! I was sound asleep when you broke into my bedroom. Now tell me what you're doing here."

She wobbled to her feet. "I've got to go."

"Sure you do."

"Really, Bonner. It's late, and I've had a swell time seeing you naked and all, but —"

"Move it." He steered her into his bedroom, and another crystal chandelier sprang to life as he hit the switch.

"Don't do that."

"Shut up." He pushed her down on the bed, which rested on a large dais befitting the king of the religious airwaves, then snatched up a pair of jeans from a straight-backed chair that had once been in her bedroom. She watched every motion as he thrust in first one leg and then the other. She didn't fail to note that he hadn't bothered with underwear. Dwayne had worn paisley silk boxers tailor-made in London. She barely repressed a sigh of regret as Bonner drew up the zipper. He might be a bastard, but he had one killer body.

The sizzle of sensual awareness she felt in his presence aggravated her. Her body had been dead to the world for so long. Why had it finally come alive now? And why with him?

She forced her attention away from him and took a quick survey of the room. The Kennedy chest was nowhere in sight, but the furniture was as dark and heavy as she remembered. Red velvet draperies decked out with black and gold tassels covered the windows. Although she'd never been in a whorehouse, she'd always believed this room would have fit right in.

The worst feature was the mirror surrounded by the red velvet canopy that hung over the bed. Since Dwayne had never brought other women here, and he'd kept the lights out when he had intercourse with her, she could only imagine what kind of kinky thrills that mirror had given him. Eventually she'd grown to suspect that he needed to see himself the moment he awakened to make certain God hadn't sent him to hell overnight.

"All right, Rachel. How 'bout you tell me what you're doing here?"

Some men, she decided, were better seen than heard. "It's late. Another time." He came over next to her, and a shiver passed through her as she gazed up into those implacable features. "I'm really not feeling well. I think I might have a head injury after all."

He brushed his hand over her face. "Your nose is cold. You're fine."

Now he had to turn into a comedian. "This is none of your business, you know."

"You want to run that one by me again?"

"This has to do with my past, and my past doesn't involve you."

"Stop stalling. I'm not letting you go till you tell me the truth."

"I was feeling nostalgic, that's all. I thought the house was empty."

He gestured with his thumb at the mirror mounted in the canopy over the bed. "Lots of good memories here?"

"This was Dwayne's room, not mine."

"Yours must have been next door."

She nodded and thought of the pretty sanctuary she'd made for herself in the adjoining room: the cherry furniture and braided rugs, the pale-blue walls with chalk-white trim. Only her old bedroom and the nursery didn't bear Dwayne's imprint.

"How did you get in?"

"The back door was unlocked."

"You're a liar. I locked it myself."

"I jimmied the lock with a hairpin."

"That hair of yours hasn't seen a pin in months."

"All right, Bonner. If you're so damned smart, how do you think I got in?"

"Jimmying locks works great in the movies, but it's not too practical in real life." He studied her, then, moving so swiftly she had no time to react, ran his hands down the sides of her body. It only took him a moment to find the key in the pocket of her sweatshirt.

He dangled it in front of her. "I think you had a key that you conveniently forgot to turn in when you were evicted."

"Give that back to me."

"Sure I will," he said sarcastically. "My brother loves having his house robbed."

"Do you really think there's anything in this house I'd want to steal?" She jerked her sweatshirt back up on her shoulder, then winced as a shaft of pain shot down her arm.

"What's wrong?"

"What do you mean, what's wrong? You threw me into a wall, you moron! My arm hurts!"

Guilt flickered across his face. "Damn it, I didn't know it was you."

"That's no excuse." She flinched again as he began moving surprisingly gentle hands along her arm, checking for injury.

"If I'd known it was you, I'd have thrown you over the balcony. Does this hurt?"

"Yes, it hurts!"

"Damn, you're a crybaby."

She lifted her foot and kicked him in the shin, but he was too close to do much damage.

Ignoring her, he released her arm. "It's probably just bruised, but you should have it X-rayed to be safe."

As if she had the money for an X-ray. "If it's still bothering me in a couple of days, I will."

"At least keep it in a sling."

"And get fired for not doing my job? No, thank you."

He took a deep breath, as if he were summoning the last ounce of his patience, and spoke in labored tones. "I won't fire you."

"Don't do me any favors!"

"You're impossible! I try to be a nice guy, and all I get is *mouth*."

Maybe it was that word *mouth*, but the image of the way he'd looked before he put on those jeans flashed

128

through her mind. She realized she was staring at him again, and he was staring back. She licked her dry lips.

His own lips parted as if he were about to say something, but then forgot what it was. He rubbed his thigh with the flat of his hand. She couldn't stand this sudden, inexplicable tension, and she pushed herself up from the bed, breaking the spell.

"Come on. I'll show you around."

"I live here. Why would I want you to show me around?"

"So you can learn something about the history of the house." And so she could get a look at the other rooms in hopes of finding the chest.

"It's not Mount Vernon."

"Come on, Bonner. I'm dying to see the house, and you don't have anything else to do."

She waited for him to tell her he could go back to sleep, but he didn't, and she remembered the remark he'd made earlier when he looked at the clock. "House tours in the middle of the night are good cures for insomnia."

"How do you know I have insomnia?"

So, she'd guessed right. "I'm psychic."

She moved toward Dwayne's walk-in closet, and before Bonner could protest, threw open the door. Her eyes slid across the neatly arranged shelves and half-empty rods. A few men's suits hung there. Were they Gabe's or his brother's? She saw some dark slacks and denim work shirts that definitely belonged to Gabe. Jeans were stacked on one shelf, T-shirts on another. No chest.

Bonner came up behind her, and before he could protest her invasion of his closet, she said, "Dwayne filled this place with designer suits, hundred-dollar silk ties, and more pairs of handmade shoes than anybody could wear in a lifetime. He always dressed up, even when he was lounging around the house. Not that he lounged much. He was a workaholic."

"I don't want to hurt your feelings, Rachel, but I don't give a damn about Dwayne."

Neither did she. "The tour only gets better."

She moved toward the hallway, then led him through the guest bedrooms, mentioning the names of famous politicians who'd stayed in each one. Some of what she told him was even true. He followed her, saying nothing, merely regarding her with a calculating look. He obviously knew she was up to something, but he didn't know what.

There were only two rooms left — her bedroom and the nursery — and she still hadn't spotted the chest. She approached the door to the nursery, but his hand shot out and covered hers before she could turn the knob.

"The tour's over."

"But this was Edward's nursery. I want to see it." She wanted to see her old bedroom, too.

"I'll drive you home."

"Later."

"Now."

"All right."

He seemed surprised that she gave in so easily. He hesitated, then nodded. "Let me put on some clothes."

"Take your time."

He turned away and disappeared into the bedroom. She spun around and began to push open the nursery door.

"I told you the tour was over," he said from behind her.

"You're being a total jerk! I have a lot of happy memories of this room, and I want to see it again."

"I'm so touched I'm getting tears in my eyes," he drawled. "Come on. You can help me get dressed." He shut the door before she could see inside and began steering her toward his bedroom.

"Don't bother. I'll walk home."

"Now who's being a jerk?"

It pained her to admit he was right, but it was frustrating to get so close and not be able to see the rest of the house. He closed the bedroom door after they were inside and headed into the walk-in closet.

She spotted the key lying on the bedside table where he'd left it, quickly slipped it into her pocket, then leaned against the bedpost. "Can I at least take a peek in my old room?"

He reappeared buttoning a denim shirt. "No. My sister-in-law uses it for her office when she stays here, and I don't think she'd appreciate you mucking around there."

"Who said anything about mucking around? I just want a peek."

"You can't have it." He picked up a pair of sweat socks from the floor and pushed his feet into them. As he put on his shoes, she glanced toward the far side of the room where the bathroom lay that linked this room with her old one.

"How often do your brother and sister-in-law show up here?"

He stood. "Not too often. Neither of them like the house very much."

"Why'd they buy it?"

"Privacy. They lived here for three months right after they were married, but they haven't spent much time here since. Cal was finishing out his contract with the Chicago Stars."

"What are they doing now?"

"He's started med school at UNC, and she's teaching there. One of these days, they'll renovate." He stood. "So why didn't you and G. Dwayne sleep in the same room?"

"He snored."

"Cut the bullshit, Rachel. Do you think you could do that? Do you think you could cut through the bullshit long enough for us to have an honest conversation, or have you been lying so long you've forgotten how to tell the truth?"

"I happen to be a very honest person!"

"Bull."

"We didn't sleep in the same room because he didn't want to be tempted."

"Tempted to do what?"

"What do you think?"

"You were his wife."

"His virgin bride."

"You've got a kid, Rachel."

"It's a miracle, considering . . ."

"I thought G. Dwayne was supposed to be a hound. Are you telling me he didn't like sex?"

"He loved sex. With hookers. His wife was supposed to stay pure."

"That's nuts."

"Yeah, well, so was Dwayne."

He chuckled just when she could have used a little sympathy.

"Come on, Bonner. I can't believe you're so mean you won't let me see Edward's nursery."

"Life's a bitch." He jerked his head toward the door. "Let's go."

It was useless to argue, especially since she had the key back and could return when she was certain the house was empty. She followed him into the garage, which held a long, dark-blue Mercedes and Gabe's dusty old black pickup.

She nodded toward the Mercedes. "Your brother's?"

"Mine."

"Jeez, you really are rich, aren't you?"

He grunted and climbed into the pickup. Moments later, they were heading down the drive through the praying-hands gates.

It was nearly two o'clock in the morning, the highway was deserted, and she was exhausted. She leaned her head against the seat and gave into a few precious moments of self-pity. She was no farther along now than she'd been when she'd first seen the magazine photo. She still had no idea if the chest was in the house, but at least she had her key back. How long would it be before Gabe realized she'd taken it?

"Damn!"

She lunged forward as he slammed on the brakes.

Blocking the narrow road that wound up Heartache Mountain to Annie's cottage, a glowing, geometric shape loomed nearly six feet tall. The sight was so unexpected and so obscene that her mind wouldn't immediately accept what it was. But the numbness didn't last forever, and her mind was finally forced to identify what it saw.

The smoldering remains of a wooden cross.

CHAPTER
NINE

An icy prickle slid down Rachel's spine. She whispered, "They've burned a cross to scare me away."

Gabe threw open the door of the truck and leaped out. In the glare of the headlights, Rachel watched him kick the cross down in a shower of sparks. Weak-kneed, she got out. Her hands felt clammy as she watched him take a shovel from the back of the truck and break apart the smoldering remains.

"I like it better when they welcome you to the neighborhood with a chocolate cake," she said faintly.

"This isn't anything to joke about." He began scooping up the charred pieces and moving them to the side of the road.

She bit down on her bottom lip. "I've got to joke, Bonner. The alternative doesn't bear thinking about."

His hands stilled on the shovel, and his expression was deeply troubled. When he spoke, his voice was soft and dark as the night that lay just outside the headlights. "How do you do it, Rachel? How do you keep going?"

She gripped her arms over her chest. Maybe it was the night and the shock of the cross burning, but the question didn't seem strange to her. "I don't think. And I don't rely on anybody but myself."

"God . . ." He shook his head and sighed.

"God's dead, Bonner." She gave a bitter laugh. "Haven't you figured that out yet?"

"Do you really believe that?"

Something snapped inside her. "I did everything right! I lived by the Word! I went to church twice a week, got down on my knees and prayed every morning and every evening. I cared for the sick, gave to the poor! I didn't screw over my neighbors, and all I got for my efforts was nothing."

"Maybe you have God mixed up with Santa Claus."

"Don't you preach to me! Don't you *dare* goddamn preach to me!"

She stood before him in the blue-white glare of the headlights with her fists knotted at her sides, and he thought he'd never seen anyone look so fierce and primitive. For a tall woman, she was almost delicate, with fragile bones and green eyes that seemed to devour her face. Her mouth was small and her lips as ripe as bruised fruit. Her tangled hair, lit from behind, formed a fiery pagan's halo around her face.

She should have appeared ridiculous. The ragged paint-smeared dress hung on her thin frame, and her big, cumbersome shoes looked obscene against such small, trim ankles. But she held herself with a ferocious dignity, and he was drawn to her by something so elemental — maybe the pain that lived in his bones — that he couldn't fight it any longer. He wanted her as he hadn't wanted anything except death since he'd lost his family.

He didn't remember moving, but the next thing he knew, she was in his arms and he felt her body beneath his palms. She was thin and frail, but not broken the way he was. He wanted to protect her and fuck her and comfort her and destroy her all at once. The chaos of his emotions coiled around his pain, deepening the agony.

She sank her fingers into the muscles of his upper arm, digging them in, hurting. He gripped her bottom and hauled her against him. He brushed his lips over hers. They were soft and sweet. He jerked his head back.

"I want you," he said.

Her head moved, and he realized she'd nodded. Her easy acquiescence infuriated him. He clasped her chin and hauled it up so that he was staring down into those tortured green eyes.

"Once again the noble Widow Snopes sacrifices herself for her child," he spat out. "Well, forget it."

She regarded him stonily as he released her. He grabbed the shovel and set to work clearing the road. He'd said he wouldn't do this to her again. After that dark night of his soul when he'd tried to destroy her, he'd promised himself he'd never touch her again.

"Maybe it wouldn't be a sacrifice."

He stopped moving. "What are you talking about?"

She shrugged. "That killer body of yours. I couldn't help but notice."

"Don't do this, Rachel. Don't keep trying to protect yourself by being a wiseass. Just say what you mean."

The bottom lip of that ripe little strawberry mouth trembled, but she was too tough to give into it. Her small breasts rose beneath the bodice of that awful dress as she took a breath. "Maybe I need to know what it's like to be with a man who isn't interested in having a saint in his bed."

So that was it.

"I'm twenty-seven years old, and I've only been with one man. He never even gave me an orgasm. Pretty funny, huh."

He didn't feel like laughing. Instead, he felt an illogical anger. "Now you want to go exploring, is that it? I'm supposed to be the guinea pig in your sexual development?"

Her redhead's temper sparked. "You're the one who came on to me, buster!"

"Momentary insanity."

He watched her marshal her forces to attack and wasn't surprised when she came up with her most obnoxious, simpery smile. "Gee, I hope not. As long as the room is dark and you don't talk, I could pretend you're someone else. It might be fun having my personal stud."

All the anger left him as abruptly as it had come. Good for her. She was a piece of work, determined not to give an inch, and for no reason he could think of beyond the fact that he hadn't hurt her after all, his mood lifted.

He tossed the shovel in the back of the truck. Later, he'd return and remove the charred wood. "Let's go."

Russ Scudder watched the headlights move away as Gabe Bonner's truck headed toward the Glide cottage.

"He was kissing her," Donny Bragelman said, shifting at his side.

"Yeah, I saw."

Both men sat in the grove of trees, thirty yards back from the road, too far to hear what Gabe and the Widow Snopes had been discussing, but close enough to have caught a few glimpses of what they were doing when they'd stepped in front of the headlights.

After Russ had set fire to the cross, he and Donny had hidden to watch it burn while they drank their second six-pack of the night. They'd just about been ready to leave when Gabe's truck had pulled up, and they'd had the satisfaction of seeing how upset Rachel Snopes had been.

"She's a slut," Russ said. "I knew she was a slut first time I met her."

He didn't know any such thing. In his days working security at the Temple, he'd mainly seen her with her kid. She'd always been nice to him, and he'd even liked her. But that was before it had all fallen apart.

At the beginning, everything had been great for Russ. The man who was in charge of security at the Temple had hired Russ to be his second-in-command. As Russ had guarded G. Dwayne and supervised building security, he'd felt as if he were finally doing something important, and the people of Salvation had stopped looking at him as if he was a loser.

But when G. Dwayne had fallen, he'd taken Russ down with him. Nobody would hire him because he'd been associated with the Temple, but Russ had family here, and he couldn't move away, so he was stuck. Eventually, his wife kicked him out — these days she barely even let him see his kid — and his life had turned to shit.

"Boy, I guess we showed her," Donny said.

Donny Bragelman was the only friend Russ had left, and he was a bigger loser than Russ. Donny had a habit of laughing at the wrong times and grabbing his crotch in public, but he had a regular job at the Amoco, and Russ could borrow money from him. He could also talk Donny into just about anything, including helping him with the cross tonight.

Russ wanted Rachel Snopes out of here, and he hoped the sight of that burned cross would scare her away. She'd been a big part of what had happened at the Temple, and he couldn't stand having her come back as if she hadn't done anything wrong, not after what had happened to Russ. The fact that Gabe Bonner had given her Russ's old job had been the final straw. For the last week, he hadn't been able to think of anything else.

Russ had gone to work for Gabe right after he'd bought the drive-in. It had been a shit job, and Gabe had been a prick to work for. He'd fired him after the first couple of weeks just because he'd been late a few times. Bastard.

140

"We sure showed her," Donny repeated, scratching his crotch. "Do you think that slut'll go away now that she knows nobody wants her here?"

"If she doesn't," Russ said, "she'll be sorry."

Three days later as Rachel applied a coat of royal-blue rust-resistant paint to the jungle gym, her gaze kept straying to the roof of the snack shop where Gabe was putting down tar paper. He'd taken off his shirt and wrapped a red bandanna around his forehead. His chest glistened with sweat and sun.

Her mouth felt dry as she observed the strong muscles of his back and arms: well-defined, tightly roped. She wanted to run her hands over them, sweat and all.

Maybe it was the food. Since she'd started eating well, her body had come alive again. That must be why she couldn't seem to get enough of looking at him. It was the food.

She dipped her brush in the paint can and decided to stop lying to herself. That dark embrace they'd shared in the road had changed something between them. Now the air was charged with sexual awareness whenever they were together. They did their best to avoid each other, but the awareness was still there.

She was hot, and she unfastened another button at the neck of her dark-green housedress. Kristy had found several boxes of old-fashioned housedresses stuck away in the sewing-room closet and passed them over to Rachel, who had gratefully accepted them. Accessorized with her clunky black oxfords, they looked

141

almost trendy, and she was delighted to replenish her meager wardrobe without spending a penny. Still, she couldn't help wondering what Annie Glide would think about the infamous Widow Snopes wearing her old dresses.

Right now, though, the dress felt as if it were suffocating her. Or maybe it was the sight of Gabe's muscles bunching as he moved a heavy roll of tar paper. He paused from his work, and her hands stilled on the paintbrush. She watched as he rubbed the back of his hand across his chest and looked over at her. He was too far away for her to see those eyes, but she felt as if they were stroking her body like silver smoke.

Her skin prickled. Both of them looked away.

With grim determination, she returned her attention to her work. For the rest of the afternoon, she forced herself to think less about lust and more about how she was going to get back into her old house and find the chest.

Rachel's hand stilled on the wooden spoon she'd been using to stir the pot of homemade marinara for tonight's dinner. She'd known it would be bad, but not this bad.

"They were killed instantly." Kristy looked up from the lettuce she'd been breaking into a pale-pink Tupperware bowl. "It was terrible."

Rachel's vision blurred as tears filled her eyes. No wonder Gabe was bitter.

"Jamie was only five," Kristy said unsteadily. "He was a perfect miniature of Gabe; the two of them were

142

inseparable. And Cherry was wonderful. Gabe hasn't been the same since."

For a moment it was hard for Rachel to breathe. She couldn't imagine the kind of pain Gabe was enduring, and she ached with pity for him. At the same time, some deep instinct warned her that pity had become his enemy.

"Anybody home?"

At the sound of Ethan Bonner's voice, Kristy dropped the paring knife. She drew in her breath, fumbled for the knife, and dropped it again.

Rachel was so shaken by what she had just learned that it took her a moment to register how strangely Kristy was behaving. Ethan was her boss, and she saw him nearly every day. Why was she so rattled?

Her housemate remained an enigma. Edward adored her, and the feeling was mutual, but Kristy was so reserved otherwise that Rachel didn't have a clear picture of the person beneath that plain, efficient exterior.

She still hadn't responded to Ethan's knock, so Rachel called out for him to come in. Out of the corner of her eye, she saw Kristy take a deep breath and turn back into the calm, reserved woman who did everything so well. It was as if the moment of surprise had never happened.

"We're just getting ready to eat, Ethan," Kristy said as he appeared in the kitchen doorway. "Would you like something?"

"Um. I shouldn't." He gave Rachel a chilly nod.

She took in his light-blue oxford shirt, which was neatly tucked into a pair of khaki trousers that bore a knife-sharp crease down the center. His blond hair was perfectly cut, neither too long nor too short, and with his height, those blue eyes, and his finely balanced features, he might have been a *GQ* model instead of a member of the clergy.

"I just stopped by to drop off material for the newsletter," he told Kristy. "You said you'd be putting it together in the morning, but I won't be in until two."

Kristy took the folder of papers he handed her and set it aside. "Wash up while we put the food on the table. Rachel's fixed a wonderful homemade marinara."

Ethan didn't bother with much more than a token protest, and they were soon seated. As he ate, he confined his remarks to Edward and Kristy. Edward gave a detailed account of his experience that day feeding Snuggles, the class guinea pig, and Rachel realized he had a relationship with Ethan that she knew nothing about. She was glad that Ethan hadn't projected his hostility toward her onto her son.

Kristy, she noticed, treated Ethan as if she were his mother, and he, a slightly backward ten-year-old. She chose his salad dressing, shook Parmesan on his spaghetti, and, in general, did everything for him except cut his food.

He, in turn, barely seemed to notice her attention, and he certainly didn't notice the hungry yearning in her eyes when she looked at him.

So, Rachel thought. That's the way it is.

144

Kristy refused to let him help clean up, something Rachel wouldn't have had any qualms about, and Ethan left soon after. Rachel sent Edward outside to catch fireflies while she and Kristy washed dishes.

As Rachel dried the plate Kristy handed her, she decided to meddle. "Have you known Ethan for long?"

"Nearly all my life."

"Um . . . And I'll bet you've been in love with him most of that time."

The bowl Kristy was holding slipped from her fingers and dropped to the linoleum floor, where it split into two precise pieces.

Rachel looked down. "Jeez. You even drop things neatly."

"Why did you say that? About Ethan? What did you mean?"

Rachel bent over to pick up the broken bowl. "Never mind. I'm too nosy, and your love life is none of my business."

"My love life." Kristy gave an unladylike snort and slapped the dishcloth into the sink. "As if I have one."

"So why don't you do something about it?"

"Do something?" Kristy took the broken pieces of bowl from Rachel and dropped them in the trash can under the sink.

"It's obvious you care about him."

Kristy was such a private person that Rachel expected her to deny it, but she didn't.

"It's not that simple. Ethan Bonner is the best-looking man in Salvation, maybe the entire state of

North Carolina, and he has a weakness for beautiful women in rhinestones and Spandex skirts."

"Put on some rhinestones and Spandex. At least he'd notice."

Kristy's delicately arched eyebrows shot up. "Me?"

"Why not?"

She actually sputtered. "Me? Me! You expect a — a woman like me — A — a church secretary . . . I'm — I'm plain."

"Says who?"

"I'd never do something like that. Never."

"All right."

She shook her head determinedly. "I'd look like an absolute fool."

Rachel propped one hip on the kitchen table. "You're not exactly dog meat, Kristy, despite your boring wardrobe." Rachel smiled and glanced down at her 1950s Sears and Roebuck housedress. "Not that I have room to cast stones."

"You don't think I'm dog meat?"

Kristy looked so hopeful that Rachel's heart went out to her. Maybe she finally had a way to repay this intelligent, insecure woman for her kindness. "Come on." She guided her into the living room, where she seated them both on the couch. "I definitely don't think you're dog meat. You have beautiful features. You're petite, which is something men seem to go for, not that I'd know anything about it. And you seem to have fairly nice breasts hidden away under that blouse, not that I'd know about that either."

"You really think I have breasts?"

146

Rachel couldn't hold back a smile. "I guess you're a better judge of that than I am. What I think, Kristy, is that you decided a long time ago that you weren't attractive, and you've never bothered to reassess yourself."

Kristy sagged back into the couch. Disbelief, hope, confusion played over her face. Rachel let her take her time, and while she waited, she gazed around at the simple, rustic living room and thought how much she liked it. The breeze coming in through the screen door smelled of pine, faintly overlaid with the sweet scent of honeysuckle. Outside she saw Edward chasing after a firefly, and she wondered if Gabe had ever sat here and watched his son do the same thing. The image was too painful, and she shook it off.

"So what should I do about it?" Kristy finally said.

"I don't know. Maybe a makeover?"

"Makeover?"

"Go to a good salon and have them do your hair and makeup. Visit a trendy little boutique for a wardrobe update."

For a moment she looked hopeful, and then her expression clouded. "What's the point. I could walk into Ethan's office stark-naked and he wouldn't notice."

"We can try that, too." Rachel smiled. "But let's do the makeover part first."

Kristy looked shocked, and then she laughed.

Rachel decided that she might as well go all the way. "One more thing. You have to stop fussing over him."

"What do you mean?"

"How can he look at you like a lover when you treat him as if you're his mother?"

"I do not!"

"You put the dressing on his salad!"

"Sometimes he forgets."

"Then let him forget. You baby him, Kristy. He won't die if he has to eat his salad plain."

"That's not fair. I work for him. Looking after him is my job."

"How many years have you done this job?"

"Eight. Ever since he took over as pastor."

"And you've done it well, right? Unless I miss my guess, you've been about the best secretary anyone could find. You can read his mind and predict what he wants even before he wants it."

She nodded.

"But what has it gotten you, other than a paycheck?"

Her mouth tightened with resentment. "Nothing. It hasn't gotten me anything. I don't even like the job. Lately I've been thinking I should go to Florida like my parents want. They went down there to retire, but they got bored, so they opened this little gift shop in Clearwater. They've been nagging at me to come down and help them run it."

"What do you want to do?"

"I want to work with children."

"Then do it."

Her resentment turned to frustration. "It's not that easy. At least this way I can be around him."

"Is that all you want your life to be about? Staying around Ethan Bonner?"

"You don't understand!"

"I might understand more than you think." She drew a deep breath. "Dwayne dressed me up like a hooker and expected me to behave like a saint. I tried to be everything he wanted, but it never was enough." Kristy placed a sympathetic hand on her knee. Rachel lowered her voice. "Instead of thinking about living for Ethan Bonner, maybe it's time you started to think about living for yourself."

Kristy's expression was an endearing combination of yearning and disappointment. "No makeover?"

"A makeover only if *you're* not happy with the way you are."

"I'm not." She sighed.

"Makeover, then. But do it for yourself, Kristy. Not for Ethan."

Kristy took a nibble on her bottom lip. "I guess that means no Spandex."

"Do you want to wear Spandex?"

"I'd look silly."

"You *do* want to!"

"I'll think about it. Not just that, but everything."

They smiled at each other, and Rachel realized that something had changed between them. Until tonight, they had been polite acquaintances. Now they were friends.

During the next few days, Rachel's body came back to life with a vengeance. She felt young and erotically charged. The late-June weather was beautiful, with low humidity and temperatures that only occasionally reached eighty, but she always felt as if she were burning up.

As she worked, she kept the buttons of her cotton housedresses unfastened at the throat and let the bodices fall open so the breeze could touch her skin. The damp, worn cotton molded to her breasts, defining their small, high shape in a way that made her feel voluptuous and sexy. She piled her hair on top of her head and fanned her thighs with her lifted skirts, trying to cool herself. And no matter what she did, she felt his eyes stroking her.

He'd look up from wherever he was working, wipe his hands on his jeans, and gaze at her. Her skin seemed to hum. It was crazy. She felt languid and tense at the same time.

Sometimes he'd bark out an order or a veiled insult, but she barely listened because her senses transformed whatever brusque words he was speaking into the ones he really meant.

I want you.

And she wanted him back. For sex, she told herself. Only for sex. Nothing more. No intimate entanglement, no exchange of feelings, only sex.

When her body grew so hot she feared it would burst into flame, she made herself think of other things: her growing friendship with Kristy, Edward's excitement as he told her about his day, and the Kennedy chest.

Each night she walked to the notch at the top of Heartache Mountain and gazed down at the house where she had once lived. She had to get inside so she could resume her search for the chest, but she couldn't take the chance that he'd be there. He hadn't said a word about the missing key, and, with the drive-in opening just two weeks away, she could only hope he'd forgotten about it. Surely he would have said something if he hadn't. She wanted to scream in frustration. If only he'd go away so she could get inside.

Nine days after the night she'd first broken into his brother's house, she finally got the opportunity she'd been waiting for.

He came up to her as she was fastening new chrome knobs to the storage cabinets in the snack shop. Even before she heard his footsteps, she caught the scent of pine and laundry detergent and wondered how someone who did manual labor always managed to smell so clean.

"Ethan and I have business to take care of. I'll be away for the rest of the afternoon, so lock up when you're done."

She nodded and her heart raced. While he was occupied with his brother, she could finally get into the house.

She finished her job in record time, then drove to Annie's cottage where she fetched the key from its hiding place in the back of her dresser drawer and set off down the mountain. By the time she reached the bottom, a light drizzle had started to fall.

The full skirt of the housedress she was wearing that day, a worn pink cotton printed with turquoise squiggles, grew damp, along with her heavy shoes and the tops of her socks. She took them off in the laundry room so she didn't leave any telltale tracks and proceeded barefoot up the stairs of the silent house.

She searched the nursery first, firmly repressing all those nostalgic pangs that made her want to curl up in the old rocker that still sat by the window and remember the feel of Edward's downy little head at her breast. When she didn't find the chest there, she headed for her former bedroom.

This room had changed more than any other, and as she gazed at the high-tech equipment positioned on a modern, L-shaped work station near the window, she wondered about Dr. Jane Darlington Bonner, Gabe's physicist sister-in-law. Was she as happy with her marriage as she'd looked in the magazine photo?

She made a quick search of the room's closet and bureau, but found nothing. The large bottom drawer set into one end of the work station was the only other place to look, but the idea of going through a stranger's desk seemed more an invasion of privacy than anything else she'd done. Still, she had to know, so she slid the drawer open, then drew in her breath as she saw the chest tucked inside.

She felt its contents shift as she took it out. Her breath quickened as she lifted the small hinge and saw a stack of multicolored computer diskettes lying inside. She withdrew them and placed them in the bottom drawer, then tucked the chest under her arm and rushed for the stairs. She felt light-headed with relief. As soon as she got the chest back to the cottage, she could search it, even take it apart if she had to.

Just as she hit the top step, Ethan Bonner pushed open the front door. She froze, but it was too late. He spotted her immediately.

His expression grew stony. "Adding larceny to your other sins?"

"Hi, Ethan. Gabe sent me over to pick this up."

"Did he?"

She forced herself to smile as she came down the steps, her feet bare and her damp skirt clammy against her legs. Nothing was going to make her give up this chest. "Don't ask me why he wants it. I'm just the hired help, and he doesn't tell me anything."

"Maybe he'd explain if I asked him."

"Oh, that's not necess —"

"Gabe!" Ethan tilted his head toward the front door, which he'd left open. "Come in here, will you?"

Panic rushed through her. "That's all right. I can talk to him when I get back to work." With a jaunty wave, she tucked the chest higher under her arm and made a dash across the cold marble floor for the back of the house.

Ethan caught her before she crossed the foyer and grabbed her by the arm with more force than was necessary for a man of God. "Not so fast."

Gabe appeared in the doorway. "Eth? What's going — Rachel?" For a moment, he stood frozen. Then he came inside and closed the door behind him. "I wondered when you were going to use that key."

"You gave her a key?" Ethan said.

153

"Not exactly. Let's just say I knew she had a spare."

He had set her up, and that made her furious. "If you knew I had it, why didn't you say something? And what are you doing here, anyway?"

The fact that she'd gone on the attack when she was clearly in the wrong seemed to rob Ethan of speech, but Gabe simply shrugged. "Cal said Ethan could take the dining-room table for the community room at church. We were loading it into the truck."

His eyes drifted downward over her damp pink dress, mud-splattered calves, and bare feet. She told herself it was the chill that turned her skin to gooseflesh. She regarded him accusingly. "You said you had *business*. This isn't *business*. This is moving furniture!"

Gabe said nothing, but Ethan had finally recovered. "I don't believe it. Are you actually going to stand there and let her attack you? *She's* the one who broke into the house!"

"Sometimes it's easier to give Rachel a chance to unwind before you try to talk to her," he said in his low, toneless voice.

"What's going on between you two?" Ethan's face grew redder. "Why are you even listening to her? She's a liar and a con artist."

"And those are her good points." Gabe gestured toward her feet. "Lose those sexy shoes of yours?"

"I didn't want to track mud."

"Considerate."

Ethan broke away and headed for the phone. "That's the box Jane uses to store her computer diskettes. I'm calling the police. There's been something strange about Rachel showing up here right from the beginning."

"Don't bother. I'll take care of her. Hand over the chest, Rachel."

"Stuff it."

He arched one dark eyebrow. "Take the truck, Eth. I've got the tarp over the table so it won't get wet."

"I'm not leaving. After everything you've been through you shouldn't have to put up with this, too. I'll take care of her."

Once again little brother had jumped in to shelter big brother. Rachel gave a snort of disgust.

Ethan heard and whirled to confront her, his expression indignant. "What?"

"Tragedy doesn't make people helpless," she pointed out. "Stop coddling him."

That seemed to shock even Gabe. He had never spoken to her about his losses, although he must have known Kristy would have said something to her by now.

Ethan's hostility had developed a cold edge. "What right do you have to comment on anything between my brother and me? Gabe, I don't understand this. I thought she was just working for you, but . . ."

"Go on, Eth."

"I can't do that."

"You have to. Remember you're on the town council, and, if you actually *witnessed* someone getting murdered, you'd need to report it."

"I don't think you should be alone with her," he said flatly.

"I won't be alone." Gabe gave her a thin smile. "I'll have Rachel's screams to keep me company."

CHAPTER
TEN

Ethan left the house reluctantly. Rachel realized that all she needed was a few minutes alone with the chest, a few minutes to look beneath the lining or find the secret compartment and she could go.

She wrapped her fingers more securely around the corners and tried to buy herself some time. "Your brother's a grouch. I guess it runs in the family."

He crossed his arms over his chest and leaned against one of the elaborate columns that led to the living room. "I'm surprised you didn't unbutton your dress and offer to take him on to keep him quiet."

"Everything happened too fast. I didn't have time to think of it."

He lifted an eyebrow and took a lazy step forward. "Hand it over."

Her heart felt as if it were moving toward her throat. "No way, Slick. This is mine. It was a present from my grandmother on my sixth birthday."

"Give it to me."

"She sold zucchinis in the broiling sun one entire summer so she could give this to me, and she made me swear always to keep it."

"We can do this easy or rough, it's up to you."

She swallowed hard. "Okay, you win. I'll give it to you. But first I need to dry myself off. I'm freezing." She edged away from him toward the family room.

He stepped in front of her, blocking the way. "Nice try."

With one swift movement, he pulled the chest from her arms.

Ignoring her gasp of dismay, he headed for the stairs. "Go ahead and dry off while I put this away. And I'll take that key when you're done."

"Stop it!" She couldn't let him do this, and she charged after him across the marble. "You're being a sadistic ass! Just let me look at it."

"Why?"

"Because I might have left something inside."

"Such as?"

She hesitated. "An old love letter from Dwayne."

He regarded her with disgust and turned back toward the stairs.

"Stop!"

He kept going.

"Wait!" She grabbed his arm, then wished she hadn't touched him, and quickly let go. "Okay, maybe Dwayne might have left something in it."

He paused with one foot on the bottom step. "Like what?"

"Like —" Her mind raced. "A lock of Edward's baby hair."

"You're going to have to do a lot better than that." He began to climb.

158

"All right! I'll tell you." She struggled to come up with another lie, but couldn't think of anything that would be even mildly convincing. She would either have to tell him the truth or let him take the chest away. It was no choice. She couldn't let the chest disappear again until she'd looked inside it, and she'd have to take the risk.

"Like the secret behind where he hid five million dollars."

That brought him up short. "Now we're getting somewhere."

She gazed up at him and worked hard to swallow. "The money's mine, Bonner. It's Edward's legacy. There are still some debts left, but the rest belongs to him. I earned every penny!"

"How do you figure?"

She got ready to give it to him — her smartest, sassiest, most wiseassed response. But then, just as the words were coming out, something happened inside her throat, and her voice broke. "Because I sold my soul for it," she whispered.

For a moment he didn't say anything. Then he tilted his head toward the top of the stairs. "I'll get you a robe. Your teeth are chattering."

Half an hour later, she sat across from him in the kitchen wearing nothing but her panties and his maroon terry-cloth robe as she stared down at the Kennedy chest. Her eyes were dry — she'd never cry in front of him again — but inside, she felt desolate.

"I was so sure." She shook her head, still unable to believe the chest held no clues. They had examined

159

every microscopic inch of it and found nothing: no secret compartment holding a safe-deposit key, no Swiss bank-account number etched into the wood beneath the lining, no map or microfilm or computer password.

She wanted to slam her fists against the table, but instead, she forced herself to think. "The county sheriff was there along with the Salvation police, so there was a lot of law enforcement. One of them must have looked in the chest when he confiscated it and found something. One of them must have it."

"That doesn't make sense." Gabe picked up her coffee mug and carried it to the sink, where he refilled it from the pot on the counter. "You told me you checked the box before you got into the car. You looked and didn't find anything, so why would they? Besides, if the sheriff or one of our local police had stumbled on that kind of cash, we'd have seen some evidence of it by now, and the only person in the community who's spent any big money has been Cal."

"Maybe he —"

"Forget it. Cal made millions while he was in the NFL. Besides, if he or Jane had found anything in that box, they wouldn't have kept it a secret."

He was right. She slumped back into the red-velvet banquette in the kitchen's eating alcove. In her day the alcove had been wallpapered with gruesome full-blown metallic roses on the verge of decay, but they were gone now, replaced with small yellow rosebuds. The wallpaper was so completely out of place that it could

160

only be some kind of private joke on the part of the current owners.

Gabe set the fresh mug of coffee in front of her and brushed her shoulder in a surprisingly gentle gesture. She wanted to tilt her cheek against the back of his hand, but he removed it before she could give in to the impulse. "Rachel, the odds are the money's at the bottom of the ocean."

She shook her head. "Dwayne had to leave the country too fast to handle any kind of complicated transaction. He couldn't possibly have taken that much money with him on such short notice."

Gabe sat across from her and set his arms on the table. Her eyes lingered there. His forearms were strong and deeply tanned, sprinkled with dark hair. "Tell me again everything he said that day."

She repeated the story, leaving out nothing. When she was done, she twisted her hands on the table. "I wanted to believe him when he told me he had to say good-bye to Edward, but I knew something was wrong. I suppose Dwayne loved Edward in an abstract way, but not in any way that counted. He was too self-centered."

"Then why didn't he just tell you to bring him the chest? Why did he bother asking you to bring Edward at all?"

"Because we were barely speaking at that point, and he knew that saying good-bye to his son was the one thing I couldn't refuse him." She cradled her coffee mug. "During my pregnancy with Edward, I finally came out of denial about what was going on at the

Temple, and I made up my mind to leave him. But when I told him, he went ballistic. Not out of sentiment, but because, in those days, I was popular with his electronic congregation." Her mouth twisted bitterly. "He said he'd take Edward away from me if I ever tried to leave. I had to stay where I was, go on television with him for every broadcast, and not give any sign I was unhappy. Otherwise, he told me he knew men who would testify that I'd seduced them, and he'd prove I was an unfit mother."

"Bastard."

"Not the way he saw it. He found scripture to justify it."

"You said he also told you to bring his Bible."

"It was his mother's. He was sentimental about —" She straightened, and her gaze locked with his. "Do you think the clue might be in the Bible?"

"I don't think there is a clue. The money's in the ocean."

"You're wrong! You don't understand how frantic he sounded on the phone that evening."

"He was about to be arrested, and he was getting ready to flee the country. That would make anybody frantic."

"Fine! Don't believe me." She sprang to her feet in frustration. She had to find that Bible. Locating the money was the only hope she had for the future, but he didn't care about that.

Her nose was beginning to run from too much emotion, and she sniffed as she stalked toward the

162

laundry room where her dress was tumbling in the dryer.

He spoke from behind her, his voice as gentle as the soft patter of rain outside. "Rachel. I'm on your side."

She wasn't prepared for his support, and she was so tired of fighting that it nearly undid her. She wanted to lean against him, if only for a moment, and let those sturdy shoulders bear some of the burden she carried. The temptation was so strong that it terrified her. The only person she could depend on was herself.

"You're all heart," she sneered, determined to put up a barrier between them that was so big he'd never cross it again.

But he didn't get angry. "I mean it."

"Thanks for nothing." She whirled on him. "Who are you kidding? After what happened to your family, you're so twisted inside that you can't even help yourself, let alone me."

The words were barely out before she caught her breath. What was happening to her? She hadn't meant to sound so cruel, and she felt a wave of dislike for the sharp-tongued woman she'd become.

He didn't respond. Instead, he turned away without a word.

Not even desperation was an excuse for the kind of nastiness she'd just administered. She stuck her hands in the front pockets of his robe and followed him into the kitchen. "Gabe, I'm sorry. I should never have lashed out at you like that."

"Forget it." He snatched his keys from the counter. "Get dressed and I'll take you home."

She came closer. "I don't mean to be a bitch. You were acting like a nice guy for a change, and I shouldn't have struck out like that. I really am sorry."

He didn't respond.

The dryer buzzer went off, and she knew there wasn't anything more she could say. He would either accept her apology or reject it.

She returned to the laundry room where she pulled out the pink dress. It was a dismal mass of wrinkles, testifying to its pre-permanent press origins, but since she had nothing else to wear, she pushed the door shut, slipped out of Gabe's robe, and stepped into it, wrinkles and all.

She had just pulled the dress over her arms when the door opened. She drew the bodice together and turned to him.

He looked hostile and unhappy: furrowed brow, tightly set lips, hands driven into the pockets of his jeans. "I just want to get one thing straight. I don't need anybody's pity, especially yours."

She dropped her gaze to her buttons, because it was easier than meeting his eyes, and began fastening them. "I don't pity you, exactly. You're too self-reliant for pity. But knowing that you lost your wife and son makes me feel sick."

He said nothing for a moment, but as she lifted her gaze, she saw that the tendons in his neck had relaxed. He pulled his hands from his pockets. His eyes drifted to her breasts, and she realized her fingers had stalled on the button there. She finished fastening it.

"What did you mean about Ethan coddling me?"

"Nothing. My mouth got away from me again."

"For God's sake, Rachel, could you just *try* to shoot straight with me for once!" He stalked away.

She frowned. He was as prickly as rusted barbed wire. She finished buttoning her dress as she followed him back to the kitchen, where he'd yanked on a Chicago Stars cap and was shoving on his sunglasses, obviously having forgotten that it was drizzling outside.

She walked over to him. Her full skirt brushed against the legs of his jeans, and she resisted the urge to curl her arm around his waist. "People talk to you as if they're afraid you're going to break apart at any minute. I don't think that's good for you; it keeps you from moving forward. You're a strong man. Everyone needs to remember that, including you."

"Strong!" He ripped off the sunglasses and sent them skittering across the counter. "You don't know anything about it." His cap hit the counter, then bounced to the floor.

She didn't back away. "You are, Gabe. You're tough."

"Don't confuse me with you!"

His footsteps punished the marble floor as he stalked past her and headed for the family room.

She'd been alone with pain too often herself to even think about letting him go. The family room was empty, but the sliding doors that led to the deck were open. As she walked toward them, she saw him standing outside clutching the railing as he stared up at Heartache Mountain.

The drizzle had changed to light rain, but he didn't seem to notice that he was getting wet. Beads of water glistened in his hair and darkened the shoulders of his T-shirt. She'd never seen anyone who looked lonelier, and she stepped out into the rain with him.

He gave no indication that he heard her coming up behind him, so that she wasn't quite prepared when he spoke. "I keep a gun by my bed, Rachel. And it's not there for protection."

"Oh, Gabe . . ."

Every part of her wanted to touch him and offer what comfort she could, but he seemed surrounded by an invisible barrier, one she was afraid to cross. Instead, she moved next to him and lay her arms over the wet railing. "Does it get any easier?"

"It was easier for a while. Then you showed up."

"I've made it more difficult for you?"

He hesitated. "I don't know anymore. But you've changed things."

"And you don't like that."

"Maybe I like it too much." He finally turned to her. "I guess these past couple of weeks have been a little better. You've been a distraction."

She gave him a weak smile. "I'm glad."

He scowled, but there wasn't any real anger behind it. "I didn't say you'd been a good distraction. Just a distraction."

"I understand." Rain soaked her dress, but it was warmer out here than inside the air-conditioned house, and she wasn't cold.

"I miss her all the time." His eyes searched her face, and his voice grew deeper, huskier. "So why do I want you so much that I ache with it?"

The rumble of distant thunder accompanied his words, almost seemed part of them. A tremor passed through her. "I think . . . I think we've been drawn together by desperation."

"I can't give you a damn thing except sex."

"Maybe that's exactly what I need from you."

"You don't mean that."

"You don't know what I mean." Being so close was suddenly overwhelming, and she turned her back to him. Crossing her arms over her chest, she moved to the other side of the deck. Overhead, the sky hung low, while mist clung to the mountains like a tattered gray prom dress.

"I had my womanhood stolen from me, Gabe. On my wedding night he gave me a lecture right from the nineteenth century on how my body was God's vessel, and he'd disturb it as little as possible. He made me lie there. He didn't touch my breasts or caress me. He just pushed himself inside me. It hurt like hell, and I started to cry, and the more I cried the happier that made him because it was proof of my virtue, proof that I wasn't carnal like him. But that wasn't true. I'd been fascinated by sex for as long as I could remember. So don't try to tell me what I want."

"All right. I won't."

The deep sympathy in his voice was too much for her. She turned and frowned at him. "I don't know why I'm talking to you about this, why I'm even *thinking* about having sex with you. Considering my luck with men, you're probably as big a dud in bed as he was."

One corner of his mouth lifted in a faint smile. "Could be."

She braced her hips against the railing. "Were you faithful to your wife?"

"Yes."

"Have you been with a lot of women?"

"No. I fell in love with her when I was fourteen."

He met her eyes, and she tried to understand what he was telling her. "Do you mean . . ."

"One woman, Rachel. There's only been one woman in my life."

"Not even anyone since she died?"

"A hooker in Mexico, but I sent her away as soon as she took off her clothes. You might be right about that dud thing."

She smiled, feeling strangely lighthearted. "Anybody else?"

He came toward her. "Nobody. And I think I've had my fill of questions for now."

"I've told you my entire sexual history, pathetic as it is. You could be a little more forthcoming."

"I haven't even thought much about sex since . . . for the last few years. At least not until you did your little striptease."

As he stopped in front of her, she tried not to let her embarrassment show. "I was desperate. I know I'm not much now, but I used to be pretty."

He touched her for the first time, picking up a lock of damp hair and hooking it behind her ear. "You're pretty, Rachel. Especially since you've started to eat. You've finally got some color in your cheeks."

She felt as if he were drinking in her face, and it flustered her. "Not to mention my cold nose. It's okay. You don't have to lie. All I'm saying is that I used to be fairly nice-looking."

"I was giving you a compliment."

"Which was the compliment part? The cold nose?"

"I didn't say a thing about a cold nose. You're the one. I —" He laughed. "You're the most maddening woman. I can't figure out why I like being with you."

"A thought for the day, Bonner. If the way you've been treating me is a mark of fondness, maybe you'd better take a fresh look at your interpersonal communication skills."

He smiled. "You're shivering."

"I'm cold," she lied.

"I guess I can take care of that." Once again, his hand went to her hair. He pushed his fingers through it on one side, then dropped his head and touched his lips to the corner of her jaw that he'd uncovered.

His body pressed against hers. She felt his lips on her cheek, and her arms wound around his waist, drawing him closer. Oh, yes . . . She absorbed the feel of him, the way the muscles in his back flexed beneath her palms, the heat from his chest against her chill breasts, his erection jammed against her. Just beneath the fragile layer of her skin, her pulses hammered.

His lips tugged her earlobe, and the sound of his breathing rasped in her ear. Her eyes drifted shut. She had so much at stake here. If she let this go farther, there would be no tender romance with him, only sex. Could she abandon the fantasy of a perfect love?

But then she realized she had abandoned that fantasy long ago. Somehow her life had grown too spartan for fantasies. She'd stripped her existence down to the bare essentials, not allowing herself even the smallest of luxuries. Would it be so terrible to grab something just for herself? Something that would give her pleasure?

He moved a few inches back, and his palms covered her breasts. As his warmth seeped into her skin, her uncertainty disappeared.

His thumbs brushed her nipples and his voice became a husky whisper in her ear. "I've been wanting to touch you here ever since I walked into the house and saw you standing there in this wet pink dress."

He scraped his thumbnails over the hard tips. She let out a sigh of pleasure. It felt so good. So perfect.

Back and forth his thumbnails went, abrading her through the wet pink cotton. Desire exploded inside her. Spirals of heat coursed through her blood, and she wanted more.

She touched him through his jeans, tentatively at first, then stroking him more aggressively, trying to discern his exact structure beneath the denim.

His breathing grew harsh. She wanted more. She reached for his zipper.

He stepped back as if she'd hurt him. His chest heaved, and he choked out his words. "Maybe we'd better slow down."

Only seconds earlier she'd been hot, but now a chill passed through her. She heard restraint in his voice, so familiar from her marriage, and he continued as he spoke again. "I don't want to rush you into anything you're not ready for."

That awful consideration. That horrible, stifling solicitude as if she weren't capable of making up her mind, as if she were breakable, untouchable, undefilable. Not a woman at all.

She'd spilled her guts to him, but he hadn't understood a thing.

"You're still new at this." He put more distance between them and ran the flat of his hand absentmindedly over his chest, as if he were smoothing his T-shirt. "Let's go inside."

She wanted to slug him and scream at him and burst into tears all at once. Why had she expected him to understand? She couldn't contain her hurt. "I'm not a virgin! And there's nothing you could do that'd be too raunchy for me, do you understand? Nothing that's too kinky! You've screwed this up, Bonner, and now you aren't ever going to touch me." Her anger boiled, then spilled over. "As a matter of fact, you can go to hell!"

She whirled around and shot down the slippery wooden steps to the lawn. It was wildly overgrown. Shrubbery hung over the flagstone path and grass tangled around her ankles as she fled.

"Rachel!"

She'd left her shoes in the laundry room, but she didn't care. She'd climb Heartache Mountain barefoot before she'd let another man treat her like she was some kind of sexually neutered icon.

Her hands knotted into fists at her side, and she realized she didn't want to run away at all. What she really wanted to do was go right back there and tell him what an insensitive, unfeeling, imperceptive ass he was!

She spun around and stalked toward the deck, only to see him doing his own war dance right toward her. As he approached, his teeth were clenched. "Don't you think you're overreacting just a little bit?"

She wanted to shout something really obscene at him, but she wasn't too effective with obscenity yet. A few more weeks in his company, though, and she could probably turn pro. "Stuff yourself."

In three long strides, he had her. He grabbed the front of her dress and began pulling open the top buttons. He looked annoyed, irritated, but not actually angry.

He peeled the dress apart. "You want kinky? I'll tell you about kinky. Do you know there are men in this world who get their kicks by bringing a woman right to the point of orgasm, and then, at the exact moment she comes, *strangling* her to death!"

He jerked the dress down, baring her to the waist as he trapped her arms in the fabric. Then he bent his head and bit her on the inner slope of one breast.

"Ow! That hurt!"

"Good. Any more trouble out of you, and I'll do it again."

His lips nuzzled her wet nipple, and her anger fled.

"Now where was I?" he asked.

She shuddered at the huskiness in his voice, the warmth of his breath on her cool skin. "Oh, Gabe . . . What if you screw this up again?"

172

"Then I guess you'll just have to keep after me till I get it right."

"I guess." She sighed and rested her cheek against his chest.

"In the meantime, you might be thinking about exactly how wide you can spread those legs because I intend to spend a long time between them."

She moaned. Maybe he'd gotten it right after all.

CHAPTER
ELEVEN

Just as she was starting to relax and think this might work out after all, he drew back again. "I know you're going to tear into me for this, but it strikes me that, for somebody who wants to be a wanton woman, you should look out for yourself better."

"What do you mean?"

"You've asked me a dozen questions since this got started, but not one of them had anything to do with whether or not I might have a condom on me."

He was right. She hadn't given a thought to birth control, probably because she'd never used it. It had taken her so long to get pregnant with Edward that she'd been afraid she was infertile.

"Do you have one? Stupid. Of course you don't. Why would you?" She jerked the dress back over her breasts and regarded him glumly. "Sex is so easy for some women. Why is it so hard for me?"

His knuckles brushed her cheekbone and he smiled. "Actually, I do."

"You do?"

He slipped his hand inside the collar of her dress and cupped her neck. "This past week the air between us has been hot enough to boil water, so I bought some on

Monday. And don't think everybody in town knows about it. I drove over to Brevard, so we could keep this between ourselves." He paused. "I wouldn't hurt you for the world, sweetheart."

The endearment felt like warm syrup poured right over her heart. His voice grew soft and gruff. "Now are you ready to settle down so we can enjoy this, or do we have to keep talking for another hundred years."

The unsteadiness inside her vanished. "I'm ready." She smiled. "Let's go inside."

He regarded her thoughtfully. "I don't think so. If you were a nice lady, I'd take you in the house. But a wanton woman like you doesn't need a bed." He slipped the dress back down over her shoulders and cupped her breasts.

The next thing she knew, they were kneeling in the wet grass and her dress had fallen down around her hips. Through the haze of her desire, she realized they hadn't kissed. She wanted to see what it would be like to engage in one of those dirty soul kisses with him. She leaned back far enough to gaze at his obstinate mouth, then tilted her head toward it and closed her eyes.

Her lips brushed his, but a strand of her hair was in the way. She reached up to push it aside, only to feel herself tumbling backward.

He sprawled next to her, slipped his hand under her full skirt, and ran his palm up the inside of her leg. A lock of wet, dark hair curled over his forehead. His white T-shirt had gone transparent from the rain, and she could see his flesh beneath. His fingers brushed over the silky crotch of her panties.

"You feel so good," he said.

She lay nearly naked in the high, wet grass, and she should have been cold, but she was on fire. She couldn't speak as he tortured her through the nylon, almost, but not quite, touching where she most wanted to be touched. He set one leg across her knee, holding it open, as if there were any need.

"Too many clothes," she managed, clutching a handful of wet cotton T-shirt in her fist.

"My thoughts exactly."

Even as they rose to their knees, he continued to cup her, rub her, so her legs remained parted and her breathing grew shallow and rapid. She jerked his T-shirt from his jeans and dragged the wet fabric up over his chest.

He pushed his finger beneath the leg opening of her panties and slipped it inside her.

She gasped and sagged against him.

"Don't move," he whispered.

He withdrew, circled, entered. Withdrew again. That torturous circling. Another entry.

"Oh, no . . ." she moaned.

He caught her earlobe between his lips and held her still like a great male animal keeping his mate in place while he took his pleasure.

She groped for the snap on his jeans, fumbled with the zipper, slipped her hand inside and caught him in her fist.

Now he was the one who gasped.

176

"Don't . . ." he moaned. He withdrew his finger and moved it forward. He rubbed.

"Don't . . ." she moaned, as she stroked him.

They shuddered together, each on the brink of a precipice neither was ready to tumble over.

He took his hand away.

She took her hand away.

They rose together, and he let her finish removing his clothes. They made a bed from her dress, his jeans and T-shirt. He threw her tiny yellow panties on top, then stepped back to gaze at her as she stood before him, the rain running in rivulets over her shoulders and past the sprinkle of freckles on her chest. It slid over her breasts and down her belly.

While he gazed at her, she looked her fill at him. His chest was muscular from hard work, his abdomen flat where it wasn't rippled with muscle. Rain matted the dark hair at his groin, making his erection even more prominent. She could no longer resist touching it.

"Take your time." He drew in his breath, and his voice rose slightly in pitch. "I'll give you all of five seconds."

He gave her longer, although not much, and then she found herself once again falling backward as he tumbled her onto the ragtag bed they'd made in the wet Carolina grass.

He spread her legs, and she knew that he was going to do something blissfully raunchy. She squeezed her eyes shut as he raised her knees. "Oh, Bonner . . . Please don't disappoint me."

"It's a good thing," he whispered against her inner thigh, "that I'm a man who does his best work under pressure."

"Ohhh . . ."

She hadn't expected that he would dawdle so much, taking his time as he parted her, studied her, touched here and there with the tip of his callused finger, brushed with his lips, his tongue . . . When she felt the first gentle suction, she began to sob.

He understood, and he didn't stop. She shattered within seconds.

As she recovered, she felt her eyes fill with tears. "Thanks, Bonner," she whispered.

"My pleasure."

He reached for the wallet that had fallen out of his jeans, but she caught his arm. "Not yet, okay?"

He groaned, but fell back. She liked that he was willing to let her take the lead, and now she was the one who dawdled, touched, and explored, satisfying years of curiosity.

With no warning, she found herself on her back while he grabbed his wallet and spoke in a strangled whisper. "I'm sorry, sweetheart. I know this is important to you, but believe me, you'll get a lot more enjoyment if you let me take over now."

"Okay." She smiled up at him.

He smiled back at her, but only briefly. She saw the exact moment when the shadow of remembrance came over his eyes, just as she watched him fight against it.

He shut his eyes, and she knew he was trying to forget that the woman who lay beneath him wasn't his

178

wife. She couldn't bear letting him pretend she was anyone else, so she brushed her fingertips across his lips, and said softly, "Don't go squirrely on me now, dude, or I'll have to throw you out and find a younger model."

His lids shot open. She grinned and took the condom from him. "I'll do this."

He grabbed it back. "No, you won't."

"Spoilsport."

"Hussy."

She'd erased the darkness from his eyes, and only seconds passed before he settled between her thighs.

He felt so good there. Heavy, but solid. Dampness had penetrated their makeshift bed, and the sodden grass squished beneath her back. She should have been uncomfortable, but she could have stayed like this for a thousand years, safe and sheltered beneath his strength with the warm summer rain falling on their bodies.

She had never imagined she could feel aroused and weepy at the same time. She pushed herself against him, needing more. He pushed back, but her body wasn't as willing to accommodate him as her mind.

"Sorry," she managed, wanting to burst into tears.

"It's been a long time for you," he replied, not sounding all that upset about it.

Once again he began his slow dallying. Even though his breathing was uneven and she could feel his tension, he didn't rush.

But she wasn't nearly as patient. It was his fault. He was too big; he was too . . . She arched against him and

179

writhed, really writhed, couldn't help herself because she had to . . . she simply had to . . .

"Easy . . . Easy . . ."

"No!" She pushed against him, doing her best to impale herself. Needing . . . wanting . . .

He reached between their bodies. What was he doing now? Idiot! Moron! Couldn't he stick with one thing at a time? Couldn't he —

She exploded into a million pieces at his touch, and he drove inside her.

Above them, the skies split open, drenching their naked bodies. She wrapped her legs around his and dug the heels of her hands into his shoulders, wanting him closer, even closer.

Rain pummeled his back as he thrust high and hard. She buried her head in the crook of his neck because she was drowning in the cloudburst, drowning in sensations so overpowering she didn't want the storm ever to end.

It went on forever and was still over too quickly. She lost herself once more, just as he came apart.

She held him and reveled in his rough shuddering. He was too big for her, too heavy, but she felt bereft when he finally eased his weight.

It was raining so hard they could barely see the house, and they both seemed to realize at the same time how embarrassing this lust in the rain was for two people who needed to keep some distance from each other. If they'd gone inside and found a bed, at least there would have been a certain dignity about it, but this backyard tussling in the rain spoke of a need so overwhelming that neither wanted to acknowledge it, certainly not with tender words.

He levered himself up, raised one knee, and glanced down at her. "Pretty good for a beginner."

She rolled to her side so that the ends of her hair dangled in the trampled grass. "Not quite as wild as I would have liked, but definitely adequate."

He arched one brow.

She gave him a cat's smile.

He smiled and stood, ridding himself of the condom, then leaned over to help her up. After scooping up their clothes, they walked naked back to the house. She began to shiver as the air-conditioning hit her. "If that big shower off the master bedroom is still working, I've got dibs."

"Be my guest."

Somehow she wasn't surprised when he joined her and showed her a whole new variation on the way a truly wanton woman could make love.

Gabe sat slumped on the side of the bed wearing only a pair of jeans. In the background, he heard the hum of Jane's hair dryer as Rachel tended to that untidy auburn tangle of hers.

He buried his head in his hands. He'd just lost another part of Cherry. Now he could no longer say that he'd only made love with one woman. That bond had been broken.

Maybe the worst part was how much he had loved being with Rachel. She was noisy and demanding, funny and passionate. And she'd made him forget the wife of his soul.

"Gabe?"

Rachel stood in the doorway that led from the bathroom to the master bedroom. His old T-shirt hung from her narrow shoulders, and his sister-in-law's jeans were too big for her hips. She'd used the rubber band he'd found to pull her hair into a ponytail, but damp auburn ringlets framed her small face. She didn't have on a speck of makeup, nothing to hide the sprinkle of freckles that dusted her nose, nothing to take away from the impact of those green eyes that saw too much.

"Gabe?"

He didn't want to talk to her now. He was too raw to engage in one of their sparring contests, and he didn't believe for a moment that lovemaking would have dulled the edges of Rachel's sharp tongue. Why couldn't she go away and leave him alone?

But she didn't go away. Instead she touched his shoulder and regarded him with such understanding that his throat tightened.

"It's all right, Gabe. I know you miss her, but you didn't do anything wrong."

His chest burned. Her compassion made him defenseless. Just seconds earlier he'd been dreading her waspish tongue, but now he would give anything to be hit by one of her wisecracks.

"Did Cherry ever lose her temper with you?"

Her name. Someone else had spoken her name. No one did anymore.

182

He knew his family and friends were trying to spare him, but he'd begun to feel as if she'd faded from everyone's memory except his own. Now the urge to talk about her was nearly irresistible.

"She . . . Cherry wasn't much of a fighter. She'd just get real quiet. That's how I knew I was in trouble with her."

Rachel nodded.

As he gazed at her, he felt as if he were glimpsing something rare, a generosity of spirit that was as much a part of her as a sassy mouth, and for a brief moment, he had the feeling that she understood something about him no one else did. But that was impossible. Rachel didn't know him at all, not like his parents, his brothers, the guys he grew up with.

She squeezed his shoulder, then bent down and pressed a kiss to his cheek. Her funny little rosebud mouth looked pink, as if she'd been nibbling a strawberry. "I want to go now."

He nodded slowly, got up, put on his shirt. He went through all the motions of getting dressed without once letting her see that he wanted her all over again.

That night, after Rachel had finished the dishes, she took Edward into town for ice cream. It had been months since she'd been able to treat him. When she'd been married to Dwayne, she'd paid little attention to money, but now she guarded every penny, and the ones she'd set aside for tonight were precious.

Edward bounced up and down as far as the Escort's seat belt would permit while he kept up a monologue on the relative merits of chocolate over vanilla. Rachel had invited Kristy to come along, but she'd declined. Maybe she sensed that Rachel needed time alone with her son. And time alone with her thoughts, too.

While Edward chattered on, the images of the afternoon burned in her mind: the rain, Gabe's body, her own abandon. She'd once imagined lovemaking could be like that, but she'd long ago given up hope that it would ever happen to her.

Just thinking about him made her body feel hot and restless. She lusted after him with an intensity that scared her, but she was also drawn to him in other ways. She was drawn to his darkness, his brutal honesty, and his grudging kindness. He didn't seem to realize that he was the only person in town who didn't judge her by her past.

Her mind began to toy with the edges of a fantasy in which Gabe was a less troubled man, but she pushed it away. She was too wise to fall in love with him, even in her imagination. He had too many shadows. And if those shadows ever lifted enough for him to fall in love again, it would be with a softer woman than Rachel, one who wasn't notorious, someone well-educated and well-bred, who didn't launch into verbal combat with him whenever she got the chance.

Once, she would never have considered having sex with a man she didn't intend to marry, but that dreamy-eyed girl was gone. She needed this joyous wickedness. And as long as she remembered that Gabe was for sex and nothing more, what was the harm? He would be her guilty pleasure, a small selfish indulgence she would permit herself to make life more bearable.

The ice-cream window built into one end of the caboose-shaped Petticoat Junction Cafe was doing a steady stream of business as she took Edward's hand and crossed the street. A thirtyish-looking woman holding a baby stiffened as she approached, then said something to a thin, dark-haired woman next to her. The woman turned, and Rachel saw that it was Carol Dennis.

Her lips moved, but Rachel was still too far away to hear what she was saying. Those around her could, however. Another head came up, and then another. Rachel heard a low buzz, like angry bees inside a wall. It lasted maybe five seconds, then stopped. Silence followed.

Her steps slowed and her heart pounded. For a moment nothing happened, and then Carol Dennis turned her back. Without a word, the young woman next to her did the same. A middle-aged couple followed, then an elderly pair. One by one, the people of Salvation gave her their backs. It was an old-fashioned shunning.

She wanted to run, but she couldn't do that. The breeze slapped the skirt of her navy cotton dress against her legs, and her hand tightened around Edward's as she drew him closer to the window. "What's it going to be?" she managed to ask him. "Chocolate or vanilla?"

He didn't say anything. She felt him lag, but she kept tugging him toward the window, refusing to show any weakness to these people. "I'll bet you'd rather have chocolate."

The young man standing behind the window had buzzed hair and a bad complexion. He stared at her, looking confused.

"Two small cones," she said. "One vanilla, one chocolate."

An older man appeared behind him. She remembered him as Don Brady, the cafe's owner, and a Temple supporter. He pushed the young clerk out of the way and regarded her with distaste. "Window's closed."

"You can't do that, Mr. Brady."

"For the likes of you, I can."

The wooden partition slammed down.

She felt sick, not for herself so much as for Edward. How could they do something like this in front of a child?

"Everybody hates us," he whispered at her side.

"Who cares about them?" she replied loudly. "This place has lousy ice cream anyway. I know where we can get something really good."

She pulled Edward away from all of them and headed back to the Escort, forcing herself to move slowly, so it wouldn't look as if she were running away. She opened the door for Edward, then leaned down to help him fasten his seat belt, but she was trembling so hard, she could barely hold it in place.

Something brushed her shoulder. She straightened and saw a chubby middle-aged woman in bright-green slacks and a white overblouse standing behind her. A green parrot pin perched on her collar and matching wooden earrings swung from beneath tightly curled salt-and-pepper hair. Her face was round, her features blunt, and she wore large glasses with flesh-colored frames that swooped down at the sides.

"Please, Mrs. Snopes. I need to speak to you."

Rachel expected to see hostility on the woman's face, but all she saw was worry. "I'm not Mrs. Snopes anymore."

The woman barely seemed to hear her. "I need you to heal my granddaughter."

Rachel was so taken aback she couldn't respond.

"Please, Mrs. Snopes. Her name is Emily. She's only four, and she has leukemia. For six months, she was in remission, but now . . ." Behind her glasses, the woman's eyes filled with tears. "I don't know what we'll do if we lose her."

This was a hundred times worse than the nightmare at the ice-cream window. "I — I'm sorry about your granddaughter, but there's nothing I can do."

"Just lay your hands on her."

"I'm not a faith healer."

"You can do it. I know you can. I used to see you on television, and I don't care what anyone says, I know you're a great woman of God. You're our last hope, Mrs. Snopes. Emily needs a miracle."

Rachel was sweating. Her navy dress stuck to her chest, and the collar felt as if it were choking her. "I — I'm not the person to give you a miracle."

If the woman had been hostile, it would have been so much easier to endure than the deep suffering that lined her face. "You are! I know you are!"

"Please . . . I'm sorry." She pulled away and hurried toward the other side of the car.

"At least pray for her," the woman said, looking lost and hopeless. "Pray for our baby girl."

Rachel gave a jerky nod. How could she tell this woman she never prayed now, that she had no faith left?

She sped blindly back to Heartache Mountain with her stomach twisted into a knot. Old memories came back to her of Dwayne's faith healing. She remembered a woman who'd had one leg longer than the other, and she could see Dwayne now, kneeling before her, grasping her longer leg at the shoe.

In the name of Jesus Christ, heal! Heal, I say!

And everyone watching on television saw the leg get shorter.

What they didn't see was the small action Dwayne had performed when he'd first knelt before her. As he'd lifted her longer leg, he'd surreptitiously slipped the back of her shoe down on her heel, and when he'd cried out to heaven, he'd simply pushed it back up. From the audience it looked as if her leg were getting shorter.

Rachel remembered exactly when her love for her husband had turned to contempt. It was the night she discovered that he wore a tiny radio transmitter in his ear during the healing services. One of his aides sat backstage and whispered the details of various illnesses audience members had noted on the cards they filled out before the broadcast. When Dwayne called out the names of people he'd never set eyes on, as well as precise facts about their illnesses, his fame as a faith healer had spread.

It had spread to a woman with wooden parrot earrings who somehow believed Dwayne Snopes's widow could heal her dying granddaughter.

Her fingers convulsed on the steering wheel. A short time earlier, she'd been daydreaming about making love with Gabe again, but reality had just hit her in the face. She had to get out of this town soon, or she'd go crazy. The chest was a dead end. She needed to find Dwayne's Bible and pray that it would tell her what she wanted to know.

Except she didn't pray anymore.

Edward's soft sigh drew her back. They'd pulled up in front of the cottage, and she realized she had forgotten about the ice cream. She regard him with dismay. "Oh, baby, I forgot. I'm sorry."

He stared straight ahead, not protesting, not saying anything, merely once again accepting the fact that life had handed him the short end of the stick.

"We'll go back."

"Don't have to. It's okay."

But it wasn't okay. She turned around and headed straight to the Ingles grocery store where she bought him a Dove Bar. He dropped the wrapper in a trash can by the front door, licked the chocolate, and they set off across the parking lot toward the Escort.

That was when she saw that all of its tires had been slashed.

CHAPTER
TWELVE

Rachel got up before six the next morning, even though she hadn't slept well. Barefoot and wearing her customary sleeping attire, a pair of panties and a man's work shirt she'd found in her closet, she padded into the kitchen.

As she put on a pot of coffee, she watched the buttery early-morning light splash through the back windows and make a crosshatched pattern on the scarred old farm table. Outside, dew sparkled in the grass, and the daylilies turned up their bright-orange trumpets. The pink crepe myrtle tree at the edge of the woods seemed blurred in the morning light, rather like a fanciful older woman in a feathery boa.

After the ugliness of last night, her eyes misted at the simple beauty around her. *Thank you, Annie Glide, for your magical cottage.*

If only this beautiful place could fix her troubles. She had no money to replace the Escort's tires, and she didn't know how she'd manage. Getting to work wouldn't be a problem. It was a long walk, but she could make it. But what about Edward? Last night Kristy had come to get them, and each day she took him to and from the day-care center, but she'd be moving soon, and then what?

Rachel had to find the Bible.

The morning was too precious to spoil with any more worry, especially when she knew she'd have plenty of time to do that later on in the day while she worked. The coffee was done, and she poured it into an old green mug that still bore the remnants of a Peter Rabbit decal, then carried it toward the front of the house.

This was her favorite time of the day, before Edward awakened, when everything was new and fresh. Sipping her coffee in the creaky wooden rocker on the front porch while the rest of the world slept was more precious to her than all of the luxuries of her old life with Dwayne. Then she could dream her new dreams, the little ones. A small backyard where Edward and his friends could play, maybe a garden, and a dog. She wanted him to have a pet.

She slipped the dead bolt on the front door with her free hand, turned the knob, and pushed open the screen. As she stepped out onto the porch and drew the clean mountain air into her lungs, a feeling of almost indescribable bliss came over her. No matter what else happened, she had this moment.

She turned toward the rocker, and her euphoria evaporated. Her mug clattered to the wooden floor, sending hot coffee splashing up onto her bare feet and legs, but she barely noticed. All she could see was the single crude word someone had painted in red on the front of the house, right between the windows.

Sinner.

Kristy came rushing out onto the front porch, her long cotton nightgown flapping around her legs. "What's wrong? I heard — Oh, no . . ."

"Bastards," Rachel hissed.

Kristy's hand flew to her throat. "It's so ugly. How could anyone in this town do something so ugly?"

"They hate me, and they don't want me here."

"I'm calling Gabe."

"No!"

But Kristy was already running inside.

The beautiful morning had turned into something obscene. Rachel cleaned up the spilled coffee with an old dish towel, as if spilled coffee was the worst outrage on the front porch. She was heading inside to get dressed when Gabe's pickup roared up the lane, tires spitting gravel. He parked it at a sharp angle and threw himself from the cab just as Kristy emerged from the front door in a seersucker robe.

Gabe looked as if he'd thrown on his clothes. His hair was rumpled and he'd stuffed bare feet into a pair of battered white sneakers. Only the day before they had been making love, but now he was regarding both of them with his take-no-prisoners look.

"Gabe, I'm so glad you're here," Kristy cried. "Look at this!"

But he'd already seen the ugly graffiti, and he glared at it as if the power of his vision could annihilate the image.

"You and I are paying Odell Hatcher a visit this morning, Rachel." His eyes stalled on the long expanse

192

of bare leg extending from beneath her shirt, and it took him a moment to recover. "I want the police patrolling up here."

"The town's turned mean," Kristy said softly. While Rachel stood silently, she told him about the tire slashing and what had happened at the Petticoat Junction Cafe. "It's as if Dwayne Snopes broke people's hearts, and the only way they can get back at him is to take it out on Rachel."

"The police won't care," Rachel said. "They want me gone just like everyone else."

"We'll see about that," he replied grimly.

"I don't want you gone," Kristy said.

"You should. I've been so selfish. I hadn't realized . . . This is going to spill over and affect both of you."

Kristy's eyes flashed. "As if I care."

"You just worry about yourself," Gabe said.

Before she could argue with them, the screen door creaked and Edward appeared. He held Horse at his side by one long ear and rubbed an eye with his fist. His faded blue two-piece pajamas were too short in the leg, and the decal of kick-boxing Dalmatians on the front was so cracked and faded Rachel felt ashamed of not doing a better job providing for him.

"I heard a mean voice."

She rushed to his side. "It's all right, sweetheart. It was just Mr. Bonner. We were talking."

Edward spotted Gabe. His mouth set in a mulish line. "He's too loud."

Rachel quickly turned him away. "Let's get dressed."

193

He let her take his hand without protest, but as she opened the screen door he muttered a word that she fervently hoped Gabe hadn't heard.

"Butthead."

By the time she and Edward were dressed, Gabe had disappeared, but as she entered the kitchen to help Edward with his breakfast, she caught sight of him on the front porch with a can of paint and a brush. She poured milk on Edward's cereal, then went out to him.

"You don't have to do that."

"Yes, I do." He'd covered the graffiti, but it still showed through. "It's going to take a second coat. I'll finish it up after work."

"I'll take care of it."

"No, you won't."

She knew she should insist, but she didn't have the stomach, and she suspected Gabe knew it. "Thanks."

Not long after, he poked his head in the house and told her to get in the truck. "We're going to see Odell Hatcher."

Twenty minutes later, they were seated in front of Salvation's chief of police. Rail-thin, with sparse, grizzled hair and a meat-hook nose, Hatcher regarded Rachel over the top of a pair of black plastic half glasses as he took down the information Gabe gave him.

"We'll look into it," he said when he was done. But she detected a glimmer of satisfaction in his eyes and guessed that he wouldn't extend himself more than he had to. Hatcher's wife had been a Temple member, something that had no doubt embarrassed him after the corruption was uncovered.

194

She decided it was time to go on the offensive. "Chief Hatcher, your department confiscated my car the day Dwayne ran off. There was a Bible inside, and I'd like to know what happened to it. It's a family piece, of no value to anyone, and I want to get it back."

"The car and everything in it went to cover Dwayne's debts."

"I realize that, but I still need to know where the Bible is now."

She could see that Hatcher didn't want to extend himself in even the smallest way; however, it was one thing to ignore the televangelist's widow, but quite another to do it with a member of Salvation's most prominent family watching.

"I'll check," he said with a grudging nod.

"Thank you."

Odell disappeared. Gabe got up and wandered over to the room's only window, which looked out onto a side street that boasted a dry cleaners and an auto-parts store.

He spoke from the window, his voice low and troubled. "You worry me, Rachel."

"Why?"

"You're reckless. You plunge into things without any thought to the consequences."

She wondered if he was talking about yesterday. So far, neither of them had alluded to what had happened.

"You're too impetuous, and it's dangerous. So far, no one has actually tried to harm you, but who knows how long that will last?"

"I won't be here long. Once I find the money, I'll leave Salvation so fast . . ."

"*If* you find the money."

"I will. And then I'm going as far from here as possible. Seattle, maybe. I'll buy a car that runs, and a pile of books and toys for Edward, and a little house that feels like a home. Then I'll —"

She stopped speaking as the police chief reentered the office and set an official-looking document in front of her. "Here's a list of everything we found in the car."

She gazed down at the neatly printed column of items: window scraper, registration papers, small chest, a lipstick. On it went, listing everything that had been in the car. She came to the end.

"Someone's made a mistake. There's no mention of the Bible."

"Then it wasn't in the car," Hatcher said.

"It was. I put it there myself."

"That was three years ago. People's memories are funny."

"There's nothing funny about my memory. I want to know what happened to that Bible!"

"I have no idea. It wasn't in the car or it would have been listed on this report." Hatcher regarded her with small, cold eyes. "Remember that you were under a lot of stress that day."

"This doesn't have anything to do with stress!" She wanted to scream at him. Instead, she took a deep breath to steady herself. "The chest that was in the car . . ." She pointed toward the report. "It ended up back at the house. How did that happen?"

196

"It was probably considered part of the household furnishings. The car was sold separately at auction."

"I put the chest and the Bible in the car at the same time. Someone in your department screwed up."

He didn't like that. "We'll increase patrols around the Glide cottage, Mrs. Snopes, but that won't change the way the town feels about having you back. Take my advice and find another place to live."

"She has as much right to live here as anyone else," Gabe said softly.

Hatcher pulled off his half glasses and tapped them on the desk. "I'm just stating the facts. You weren't around when Mrs. Snopes and her husband nearly tore this town apart. They didn't care who they took money from as long as they could feather their own nest. I know you've had a hard time lately, Gabe, and I can only guess you're not thinking straight. Otherwise, you'd be more careful in your choice of friends." The disrespectful way he regarded Rachel told her he believed Gabe was supporting her in exchange for sex. Since that was exactly what she'd proposed at one time, she supposed she shouldn't feel so offended.

"Maybe you'd better think about your family, Gabe," the chief went on. "I doubt your parents are going to be happy when they find out you've taken up with the Widow Snopes."

Gabe's lips barely moved. "Her name is Stone, and if she says the Bible was in the car, then it was there."

But Odell Hatcher wouldn't give an inch. He was a man who believed in bureaucracy, and if his paperwork said that something didn't exist, then it didn't exist.

Later that day as Rachel finished painting the last of the playground equipment, she took comfort in the support Gabe had given her, even though he believed she was on a wild-goose chase. She glanced across the lot where he and an electrician were installing floodlights. He seemed to sense her eyes on him because he looked up.

Her body tensed with awareness. At the same time, she wondered what the rules were now that their relationship had shifted so drastically. For the first time, she considered how difficult it would be to make even the simplest arrangement to be together.

When evening arrived, he announced that he was driving her home. She had no car, and she hadn't been looking forward to the long walk up Heartache Mountain, so she accepted gratefully. She'd worked hard that day. Not that she minded. She was beginning to believe she cared more about the drive-in than Gabe. She was certainly more excited about the opening.

As he started the truck, the tension that had been sizzling between them all day intensified. She lowered the window, and then realized the air-conditioning was already running.

"Heat getting to you?" He gave her a faintly wolfish look, but she was nervous now, and she pretended not to see it.

"It's been warm today."

"Hot's more like it."

His gentle pressure on her thigh encouraged her to slide closer, but she turned away and raised the window instead. He removed his hand.

198

She didn't want him to think she was being coy, especially when she wanted him so badly, and she knew she had to tell him. "Gabe, I started my period this morning."

He turned his head and regarded her blankly.

"My period," she repeated. When he looked no more comprehending, she remembered his professional background. "I'm in heat."

He gave a bark of laughter. "I know what it means, Rachel. I just can't figure out why you think I'd give a damn."

She hated herself for flushing. "I don't believe I'd be comfortable . . ."

"Sweetheart, if you're serious about being a hussy, you need to get rid of your hang-ups."

"I don't have any hang-ups. That's just hygiene."

"Bull. We're talkin' a major hang-up." He gave a dry chuckle at her expense and turned out onto the highway.

"Go ahead and laugh at me," she said grouchily. "At least this problem will go away. The other problem isn't so easy."

"What problem is that?"

She traced a thin streak of blue on the skirt of the tangerine-and-white checked dress she'd set aside for painting. "I just can't figure out how we're going to manage our — you know. Our fling?"

"Fling?" He sounded offended. "Is that what this is?"

They rounded a bend in the road, and she had to squint against the setting sun. "It's not an affair." She paused. "*Affair* is too serious. It's a fling, and the point is, I don't see how we're going to manage it."

"We won't have a bit of trouble."

"If you believe that, you haven't thought this through. I mean, we can't just take off in the middle of the day and . . . and . . ."

"Fling?"

She nodded.

"I don't see why not." He grabbed his sunglasses from the dash and shoved them on. She wondered if they were a defense against the glare or her.

"You're being deliberately obtuse."

"No. I just don't see the problem. Or are you still talking about that period thing?"

"No!" She jerked the visor down. "I'm talking generally. You think we're just going to *do it* in the middle of the day?"

"If we want to."

"Where would we go?"

"Anywhere we wanted. After what happened yesterday, I don't think either of us is too choosy."

He glanced over, and she saw her miniature reflection in the lenses of his sunglasses. She looked small, insignificant, capable of being blown apart by the next big wind. She turned away from the image.

"If the snack-shop counter doesn't appeal to you, we can drive to the house," he said.

"You don't understand anything."

"Then maybe you'd better explain it to me." He spoke like a man holding on to the last threads of his patience, and she had to choke out the words.

"You pay me by the hour."

"What does that have to do with anything?"

"What happens during the hour — the hours — we're . . . flinging?"

He regarded her warily. "This is a trick question, isn't it?"

"No."

"I don't know. Nothing happens."

"Something happens to my paycheck."

"This doesn't have anything to do with your paycheck."

She was going to have to spell it out. "Do you pay me for the hour we're flinging or not?"

He was clearly wary, and his answer tentative. "Yes?"

Her stomach sank. She turned away to gaze out the side window and whispered, "You jerk."

"No! I mean no! Of course I don't pay you."

"I'm barely making it as it is. I need every penny I can get! Yesterday afternoon cost me half a week's groceries."

There was a long silence. "I'm not going to win this one, am I?"

"Don't you see? Nothing can happen while we're working, even if we want it to, because you control my paycheck. And after work, I have a five-year-old to take care of. Our sexual relationship is doomed before it ever gets started."

"That's ridiculous, Rachel. And I'm not docking your pay for yesterday."

"Yes, you are!"

"Look. You're making a big deal out of nothing. If we want to make love, and the time is right, we'll make love. It doesn't have anything to do with paychecks."

He could pretend ignorance, but he knew exactly what she was talking about. At least he had the grace not to point out that she'd once offered him sex in exchange for the very paycheck they were arguing over.

He turned his attention back to the road, and nearly a mile slipped by before he spoke again. "You're really serious, aren't you? This is a problem for you."

"Yes."

"Okay. Then we'll both think about it and come up with a solution while you're having that period of yours." His hand settled on her thigh and he caressed her with his thumb. "Are you okay? After yesterday?"

He sounded so concerned, she smiled. "I'm terrific, Bonner. Top of the world."

"Good." He squeezed her knee.

"And yourself?"

His chuckle had a dry sound, as if it hadn't been used in a long time. "Couldn't be better."

"Glad to hear it." She glanced out the side window. "You just passed Heartache Mountain."

"I know."

"I thought you were taking me home."

"We'll get there." He slipped off his sunglasses.

They drove into Salvation, and, just as they were entering the downtown area, he pulled into Dealy's Garage. As he parked the truck in front, she spotted the Escort sitting off to the side.

202

"Oh, Gabe . . ." She threw open the door, rushed over to the car, and promptly burst into tears.

"Nothing like a new set of tires to stir a lady's heart," he said dryly as he came up behind her. He curled his hand around her waist and stroked her.

"It's w-wonderful. But I don't — I don't have enough m-money to pay you back."

"Did I ask you to pay me back?" He sounded faintly indignant. "Cal's insurance will cover it."

"Not all of it. Even rich people have deductibles. Dwayne had deductibles on all four of our cars."

Ignoring her, he grasped her upper arm and steered her toward the truck. "We'll come back and get it. We have something to do first."

As he pulled away from the garage, her feelings jumbled inside her as if they were being tossed around by a giant blender. He was gruff and kind, clueless about some things, wise about others, and she wanted him so badly her teeth ached.

He drove to the center of town and pulled into a parking space that sat directly in front of the Petticoat Junction Cafe.

"Come on. We're going to get ourselves some ice cream."

She caught his arm before he could open the door of the truck. The ice-cream window was enjoying a lively pre-dinnertime business, and she understood exactly what he intended to do. First the tires, and then this. It was too much. Her throat felt tight. "Thanks, Gabe, but I have to fight my own battles."

He wasn't impressed by her show of independence. His jaw set, and he glared at her. "Get your butt out of this truck right now. You're having ice cream if I have to hold your mouth open and shove it down your throat."

So much for his sensitivity. She didn't have much choice, so she pushed open the door. "This is my problem, and I can handle it myself."

His door banged behind him. "Like you're doing such a terrific job."

"I want a raise." She stomped toward the sidewalk. "If you can afford to throw money around on tires and ice cream, you can pay me something better than slave wages."

"Smile for the nice people."

She felt the stares of the adults around them: mothers with small children, a pair of highway workers in dirty T-shirts, a businesswoman with a cell phone pressed to her ear. Only a group of boys on skateboards seemed disinterested in the fact that the wicked Widow Snopes was treading on Salvation's holy turf.

Gabe approached the teenage girl standing behind the window. "Is the boss around?"

She chomped once on her gum and nodded.

"Go get him, will you?"

As they waited, Rachel noticed a clear plastic canister sitting by the window with a sign on it that said *Emily's Fund* and held a picture of a curly-haired toddler with a smiling scamp's face. The sign beneath asked for help paying the child's medical expenses as she fought leukemia. She thought of the woman with the parrot earrings.

You're our last hope, Mrs. Snopes. Emily needs a miracle.

For a moment, she had a hard time drawing in enough air to breathe. She concentrated on opening her purse, drawing out a precious five-dollar bill, and slipping it into the slot.

Don Brady's face appeared in the window. "Hey, Gabe, how's it —" He broke off as he spotted Rachel.

Gabe pretended not to notice that anything was wrong. "I was telling Rachel here that you make the best hot-fudge sundaes in town. How 'bout whippin' us up a couple of them. Large."

Don hesitated, and Rachel could see him trying to find a way out. He didn't want to serve her, but he wasn't prepared to defy one of the town's favorite sons.

"Uh . . . Sure, Gabe."

Minutes later, they walked away from the window with two large hot-fudge sundaes neither of them wanted to eat. As they headed back to Gabe's truck, they didn't think to look across the street. If they had, they might have have seen a small, wiry man smoking in the shadows and watching them.

Russ Scudder ground out his cigarette. Bonner must be fucking her, he decided. Otherwise, he wouldn't have replaced those tires so fast. That explained why Bonner had hired her. So he could fuck her.

Russ shoved his fists in his pockets and thought about his wife. He'd gone to see her yesterday, but she'd refused to talk to him. Jesus, he missed her. If only he had a job, he might be able to get her back, but

Rachel Snopes had taken the only job anyone in town had offered him.

He was glad he'd slashed her tires last night. He hadn't planned on doing it, but then he'd seen her car, and there was nobody around, and it had felt good. It had felt so good he'd gone up to the Glide cottage a few hours later with a can of spray paint and painted *Sinner* on the wall just like some Bible banger. Maybe now she'd get the idea that she wasn't wanted around here.

He thought old G. Dwayne might have liked what he'd done last night. Despite his Rolex watches and fancy suits, Dwayne had been a good ol' boy. He'd never meant anybody harm, and Russ knew for a fact that he prayed a lot and loved God and everything. It was Rachel had made him go bad. Dwayne wanted to keep her happy, so he'd dipped too deep into the Temple's bank account to buy her the things she nagged him for.

It was Rachel's greedy ways that had brought down the Temple and Dwayne Snopes. Her greed had brought down Russ, too, because if it weren't for her, he'd still be working security, still working the job that had made him feel like a man.

And now she was settling back into Salvation, just as if she hadn't done anything wrong. Now she was using Gabe the same way she'd used G. Dwayne, but the crazy son of a bitch was too stupid to see what she was doing.

Russ had tried to talk to his ex-wife about Rachel and how she was to blame for everything bad that had happened to him, but she didn't understand. She didn't understand how none of this was Russ's fault.

He needed a drink, and he turned toward Donny's place. A couple of drinks would settle him down. They'd make him forget that he had no job and that his wife had kicked him out and that he couldn't take care of his kid right.

"Is *he* going to be here?" Edward asked on Saturday morning as Rachel parked her precious Escort behind the snack shop.

No need to ask who *he* was. "Mr. Bonner's not as bad as we thought. He's given me a job and let us live in the cottage. He's also made sure I have a car to drive."

"Pastor Ethan got us the cottage and the car."

"Only because Mr. Bonner asked him to."

But Gabe remained Edward's enemy, and he refused to be swayed. On the other hand, he'd developed an unbending loyalty to Ethan, who apparently sought him out regularly at the day-care center. Rachel reminded herself she'd have to thank him for that, even if she choked on it.

Day care had been good for her son. He still hadn't made any close friends, but he was a little more talkative, a bit more demanding — although with Edward, that was relative. Twice now, when she'd told him it was bedtime, he'd said, "Do I have to?" For him, that was a major rebellion.

"Wait till you see the playground." She handed him a shopping bag filled with some toys to keep him occupied for the day, then picked up a sack that held their lunches and a few snacks. As they walked toward the playground, Horse dangling from his hand, she saw how much stronger he looked. His legs and arms were tanned, and there was a liveliness to his movements that she hadn't seen since his illness.

"The playground's all fixed up," she said. "And look. We added some picnic tables, so you'll have a place to sit and draw."

She'd bought him a new coloring set that included a sixty-four count box of crayons instead of a skimpy twenty-four, then she'd purchased new sneakers for him, as well as pajamas printed with race cars. When she'd let him pick out an inexpensive T-shirt, he'd bypassed the childish cartoon designs and chosen one that said *Macho Man*.

She glanced down at her own clothes. She cleaned the dirt and paint from her black oxfords every day, and they were holding up well. Thanks to Annie Glide's wardrobe of old housedresses, she hadn't needed to waste a penny on herself.

Just then, Gabe's pickup swooped into the lot accompanied by a wake of dust. Edward slipped behind the turtle where, she suspected, he intended to make himself as invisible as possible. She headed for the truck and watched Gabe step out, all lazy grace and boneless elegance.

Yesterday he'd given her the key to Cal's house so she could search for the Bible while he went out to dinner with Ethan. It hadn't been there, but she appreciated the fact that he'd trusted her enough to let her look.

His eyes caressed her as he came nearer, and she grew dizzy with the memory of how he'd felt inside her two days earlier.

"Good morning." His voice was deep and husky with sexual promise.

The breeze lifted the hem of her skirt so it brushed against his jeans. "Good morning yourself." Her tongue felt clumsy in her mouth.

He slipped his hand under her hair and curled it around the back of her neck. "No electrician today."

But they weren't alone, she was having her period, he didn't know about Edward, and he still controlled her paycheck. With a reluctant sigh, she drew away. "I can't afford you."

"Are we back to that again?"

"I'm afraid so."

He didn't say anything. He simply frowned at her paint-spattered orange dress and oxfords, which seemed to annoy him more each day. "You left those jeans of Jane's on the bed when you were looking for the Bible. Why didn't you keep them?"

"Because they weren't mine."

"I swear, I'm buying you some today."

She raised an eyebrow at him. "No jeans. Give me a raise instead."

"Forget it."

A good argument was just what she needed to distract herself, and she splayed a hand on her hip. "I'm working my butt off for you, Bonner. There's not a man in the world who would have done as much as I have for what you're paying, which, in case you've forgotten, is barely minimum wage."

"That's true," he replied agreeably. "You're the best bargain in town."

"I'm getting sweatshop wages!"

"That's why you're such a bargain. And don't forget that you're getting paid exactly what we agreed to."

A lot more, if she considered the fringe benefits of house and car. Still, at this rate, she'd never be able to set anything aside, and if she didn't find that Bible, she and Edward would be stuck in Salvation forever.

She still needed to tell him Edward was with her, but even though he was less inclined to snarl these days, she wasn't anxious to break the news. She stalled for a few seconds by dividing her ponytail in half and pulling it tight in the rubber band.

"I hope you don't mind, but I had to bring Edward with me today."

A wariness came over his expression. "I don't see him."

She tilted her head toward the playground. "He's hiding. He's afraid of you."

"I haven't done anything to him."

That was so patently untrue that she didn't bother contradicting him.

He glared at her. "I told you not to bring him here."

"It's Saturday, and there's noplace else for him to go."

"I thought Kristy was keeping him on Saturday."

"Out of the goodness of her heart, but I'm not imposing on her again. Besides, she'll be moving into her condo soon, and she has things to do."

He glanced toward the playground, but Edward remained hidden. Gabe's antagonism toward her son hurt. Couldn't he see how special Edward was? How could any intelligent person meet Edward and not fall in love with him?

"Fine," he snapped. "Just keep your eye on him so he doesn't get into anything."

"This is a drive-in, Gabe, not a china shop. There isn't much he can break."

Instead of replying, he headed for the back of the pickup where he grabbed a wooden spool of cable and stalked away.

His attitude toward Edward felt like a betrayal. If he cared about her, he should care about her son, too. If he —

She caught herself just in time. She was thinking about Gabe as if they had some future instead of remembering that her relationship with him had only two facets: he was her boss and he was her sex toy. That was all.

CHAPTER
THIRTEEN

I'm a fox.

I'm a fox.

I'm a fox.

Kristy pressed the palm of her hand to her chest, which was barely covered by a scoopy little ice-blue tank top tucked into a pair of white jeans so tight they would have showed her panty line if she weren't wearing something called a thong that didn't leave a panty line, but did give her a wedgie.

As she settled behind the neatly arranged desk in her office, her heart was beating so hard she could feel it in her throat, but she couldn't feel it beneath her palm because her breasts were in the way, monumental breasts pushed up to centerfold proportions by the Wonderbra that the saleslady at the boutique in Asheville told her she absolutely had to buy, along with several dozen other essentials that had eaten up a chunk of the savings she'd set aside to furnish the bedroom in her new condo.

She'd been building up her nerve for two weeks, ever since the night she'd told Rachel about her feelings for Ethan. In four days, she'd be moving into her condo. It was a time for new beginnings.

The breeze from the open window lifted a lock of her dark, baby-fine hair. It was cut short now and feathered. That's what the hairdresser had said: *We're feathering — feathering in a simple, yet important, sort of way.*

Now her simple, yet important, hair tickled her cheeks and brushed the nape of her neck. A few feathers flew over her eyebrows and into her eyes. Feathers flicked the sparkly one-karat cubic zirconia studs in her earlobes. Feathers, feathers, feathers, until she felt like a canary. It was so *untidy*.

When she'd walked into the cottage after her makeover yesterday and seen Rachel's jaw drop in amazement, she'd burst into tears.

Rachel, however, had burst out in delighted laughter. "Kristy, you look like a really stylish tramp! And I mean that in the very *best* way."

Rachel had hugged her and fussed over her and ordered her to lay out all her purchases: the clothes and underwear, the expensive new makeup, and the trillion-dollar-an-ounce exquisitely sultry perfume that had made Edward wrinkle his nose and tell Kristy she smelled like a mag'zine.

After admiring all Kristy's new purchases, Rachel had told her she was beautiful, then glared at her in that intimidating way she had. "You're doing this for yourself, aren't you, Kristy? You're doing it because *you* want to, not just because you're trying to catch the attention of that worthless Ethan Bonner."

"I'm doing this for myself," Kristy had repeated, even though both of them knew it was a lie. If she had

213

her way, she'd have her plain old long hair back, her plain old clothes, her plain old face scrubbed clean of everything but a little lipstick. If she were doing it for herself, she'd be invisible again, because she liked invisible. She craved invisible. She was *born* to be invisible.

But invisible wouldn't catch the attention of the dream-boat preacher.

Her blood froze as she heard his confident step in the hallway. The church office was closed on Mondays, so there was a lot of work they had to catch up on today. *Dear God, please let him be overcome with lust quickly because I don't know if I can carry this off for very long.*

"Morning." He breezed into the office. "Bring me the report from the mission committee, will you, so I can look it over? And let's see if we can get the July calendar finalized." He sailed past her desk and into his office without a glance.

Good old invisible Kristy Brown.

She snatched up her purse, pulled out the tiny flagon of perfume, and spritzed ten dollars' worth into her cleavage. She did a quick check of her appearance in the mirror of her new compact: light foundation, delicately arched eyebrows, thick, smoky-brown lashes, pale blush, and a crimson hooker's mouth.

Oh, dear. That mouth. But the makeup salesgirl had insisted and Kristy remembered what Rachel had said that morning. *One look at your mouth, Kristy, and Reverend Stud Man's going to be having some very naughty thoughts. Not that you care, since you bought that lipstick for yourself.*

Kristy collected the neatly arranged papers she needed, then promptly dropped them. As she bent to pick them up, she saw flashy magenta toenails peeking through the straps of a slim gold sandal, and she felt as if she were looking at someone else's foot.

I'm a fox. I'm a fox. I'm a foolish, feathered fox.

Ethan had his head bent over a curriculum catalog. Today he wore a white shirt with a narrow maroon stripe and navy slacks. His long tapered fingers played with the edges of the catalog, and she thought of those same fingers playing with the catch of her Wonderbra.

With her heart pounding, she set the mission committee's report on the desk, automatically straightened a pile of mail, then sat in her customary place opposite him. As she crossed her legs, the tight white jeans nearly cut off her circulation, but she ignored the discomfort.

Ethan studied the report. "I wish I knew how to light a fire under them. I want this year's Compassion Campaign to be our best yet, but the mission committee's most exciting idea so far is to put a financial thermometer poster in the narthex."

"Why don't we get the adult-education class involved in the planning? They're enthusiastic about mission."

Look up at me! Let me knock you out!

"Um. Good idea. Call Mary Lou and feel her out, will you?"

Feel me up, will you? That thought made her face turn red. She shifted and sent out a fresh cloud of perfume.

Ethan sniffed, but didn't look up.

She slid the July calendar across his desk. Surely he'd notice that she had six rings on that hand, seductive little gold and silver bangles that nestled together like lovers' hands.

He didn't notice. "We've got a conflict on the tenth. I have a synod meeting. Either we reschedule the Vacation Bible School picnic or they can have it without me."

She wanted to run from the office, but if she ran now, she'd never be able to do this again. She forced herself to her feet, then walked around the side of his desk until she stood next to him. "The children will be disappointed if you're not there. Why don't I have them shift the picnic to Thursday?"

He sneezed. She handed him a tissue from a box on the credenza, and he wiped his perfectly formed nose. "Isn't that the day we're inviting the parents in for lunch?"

"Not a problem." She pressed her hip closer to his side. "We'll move that earlier in the week."

"Okay." He tossed the tissue into the trash. "Make sure I'm there."

She couldn't take any more. Pointing to the calendar, she leaned down and popped one elevated breast right under his eyes. "The twenty-third will be the perfect day for the Friends of Jesus pageant."

Silence. A long, labored silence.

The muscles at the back of his elegant neck tightened. His lean fingers flattened on his desk, and her entire life seemed to flash before her eyes, all thirty boring years, as she waited for him to look up from her breast.

He slowly raised his head, moving inch by inch, but the power of speech seemed to have left him by the time his gaze reached her face. Finally, the muscles in his throat began to work as he swallowed. "Kristy?"

She told herself to pretend she was Rachel. What would Rachel do in this situation? She tilted up her chin and placed one trembling hand on her hip. "Yeah?" As the word came out, she nearly choked on it. She had never in her life answered anyone by saying *Yeah*.

He stared at her. "New . . . uh . . . New blouse — er — top?"

She nodded and tried to look bored, but it was difficult because this was the first time she could ever remember having Ethan Bonner's full attention. She began to perspire and hoped it didn't show.

He wasn't deliberately staring, she knew that. Rather, it seemed that he'd lost track of his eyes. He took in her hair, her makeup, her scarlet mouth, her breasts and clothes, back to her breasts.

He slowly began to recover. His eyebrows drew together, and there was a gruffness in his voice that didn't sound as if she'd maddened him with lust. "What've you done to yourself?"

She wanted to cry, but Rachel would kill her if she crumbled. "I — I was bored. It was t-time for a change."

"Change! You look like . . . like . . ." Once again, his eyes stalled on her breasts, then he drew a deep breath.

"You can wear whatever you like when you're not working, but that's not appropriate for the office."

"What's not appropriate?"

"Well, those jeans, for example . . ."

"You wear jeans to the office all the time. Billie Lake wears jeans when she subs for me."

"Yes, but . . . All right, yes, the jeans are fine. Of course, they're fine, but . . ." His eyes returned to her breasts. "Your . . . uh, lipstick is a little . . . Well, it's a little bright."

She was suddenly furious. He drooled over Laura Delapino with her crimson lipstick, but because she was good old reliable Kristy Brown, he only wanted to criticize. She couldn't imagine Rachel standing silently and letting a man do this do her.

"You don't like my lipstick," she said flatly.

"I didn't say that. It's not my place to like it or not. I just think for a church office . . ."

Rachel would never put up with this. Not in a million years. And neither would she.

"If you don't like it, you can fire me."

He seemed genuinely shocked. "Kristy!"

She had to get out of here before she started to cry.

"Now there's no need to get upset." He cleared his throat. "I'm sure once you have a chance to think this over . . ."

"I have, and I *quit!*"

She dashed from the office, feathers flying, then snatched up her purse and ran outside to her car where she promptly collapsed against the steering wheel and burst into tears. Had she really expected him to fall in love with her just because she'd cantilevered her breasts? She was still the same dull, pathetic woman who'd lived most of her life mooning over a man who would never in a million years moon back. Except now she was jobless, too.

Through her tears, she saw the back door fly open and Ethan come running out. She couldn't let him see her like this, a pathetic loser crying over her miserable life. She snatched her keys from her purse and shoved them in the ignition.

"Kristy!"

The engine roared to life. He ran toward her. She shot out of her parking space.

He rushed to the side of her car. "Stop it, Kristy! You're overreacting! Let's talk about this."

That was when she did the unthinkable. She rolled down the window, thrust out her hand, and gave Reverend Ethan Bonner the bird.

Two days had passed since Kristy had shown up at the church dressed like an upper-crust hooker, and Ethan still hadn't gotten over the shock. "Look at the way she's carrying on!" His glare took in thc Mountaineer's postage-stamp dance floor, where Kristy Brown was dancing with Andy Miels, who was nearly ten years her junior.

Her movements were a little self-conscious, but no one sitting at the bar's rustic pine tables seemed to notice.

Kristy had shown up at the Mountaineer in a tight black skirt that ended at mid-thigh and a clinging, deeply cut melon-colored top displaying a full set of breasts that no one had ever suspected she possessed. She'd accessorized the outfit with a glittery black-and-gold Y-necklace, the tip of which nestled at the top of her cleavage. Her fake diamond studs sparkled through the wisps of dark-brown hair that fluttered around her face as she danced.

Until Kristy had walked in, Ethan had been eating a hamburger and trying to extract information from Gabe about his relationship with the black widow. Last week when Ethan had caught Rachel trying to steal the chest that held Jane's computer disks, he'd wondered if his brother and Rachel might have something more going on than a work relationship. The possibility scared him to death. By now, Rachel had to know that Gabe was wealthy. He'd always been careless about finances, and she was the worst sort of opportunist. Every time she looked at him, she had to see a walking, talking cash machine.

But his probing into Gabe's private life had come to an abrupt end when Kristy arrived. "She came in here *alone!*" Ethan exclaimed. "She didn't even have the decency to bring a girlfriend." He glared at Kristy's dancing partner. "And I swear, Gabe, she used to baby-sit Andy Miels!"

"Doesn't look like either of them is thinking about that now," Gabe said.

Kristy was no stranger to the Mountaineer. Since the county was dry, local residents paid a minimal membership fee to belong to private "bottle clubs." The Mountaineer also had a small restaurant toward the

220

front that offered the best food in town and a lively bar in the back that frequently served as the town meeting place.

The Mountaineer was entirely respectable, and, over the years, Kristy had lunched here often and shared dinner in the quaint dining room with family or friends, but no one had ever seen her like this. Alone. In the bar. At night. And dressed like this.

Ethan could barely contain himself. "Do you know what she did Tuesday in the parking lot after she ran out on me? She gave me the old one-finger salute. Kristy Brown!"

"I believe you've already mentioned that," Gabe said. "Three times."

"She's moving into her condo this weekend. Don't you think that someone who's probably spent the day packing up boxes should be too tired to party?"

"She doesn't look real tired."

Kristy laughed at something Andy said and let him lead her back to the table he was sharing with a couple of his college buddies, who'd come to visit. They looked like a bunch of slackers to Ethan. Caps turned backward, earrings, scraggly goatees stuck to their chins like fraying Brillo pads.

Well-built slackers, though. Andy played football for North Carolina State, and the size of the others at the table made Ethan suspect they were his teammates.

"This is all Rachel Snopes's doing."

Gabe's fingers tightened around his glass of club soda. "Her name is Stone. Rachel Stone."

"She's turned Kristy into a — a slut."

"Watch it, Eth."

"Her clothes are so tight it's a wonder she can move. But she's moving all right. Look at that." Kristy had just propped her arms on the table and leaned forward to hear something one of the football players was saying. "She's — she's sticking herself right in their faces!"

"It's hard to believe you never noticed that chest until now."

"You didn't notice, either."

"I haven't worked with her nearly every day of my life for the past eight years."

Ethan's frustration boiled over. "It's a good thing she quit because otherwise I'd have had to fire her. How could I have my church secretary behaving like that?"

Gabe spoke mildly. "She doesn't dress much different from Laura Delapino or Amy Majors, and you seem to admire them."

"They're not Kristy, and I don't know why you're being so stupid about this. She was fine until the Widow Snopes moved in with her. It's obvious that corrupting Kristy is just one more part of Rachel's plan to upset this town."

"You think she has a *plan?*"

Ethan shrugged.

Gabe's voice dropped. "You listen to me, Eth. It's taking every resource Rachel has just to keep her head above water. She's been shunned, her tires have been slashed, Annie's cottage vandalized. Don't talk to me about her *plan* to upset this town."

222

He was right, but Ethan's flash of guilt disappeared as he watched Andy tilt his beer mug to Kristy's lips. He shot to his feet. "That's it! I'm getting her out of here."

From across the bar, Kristy watched Ethan storm toward her. He'd ironed his T-shirt again, she noticed. It was very old, vintage Grateful Dead, but one of his favorites, and he took good care of it.

Ethan's clothes were always neat. He'd even pressed his perfectly faded jeans. His blond hair was well-cut and combed into place, his eyes liquid blue. Once his mother told Kristy the Bonner family had a great, unspoken secret. Although no one ever said it aloud, they all loved Ethan the best.

Well, not Kristy. She didn't love him the best. He'd betrayed her, and now she was immune to that Gospel-preaching, God-speaking rat.

"Kristy, I'd like to talk to you."

"Shoot," she managed, just as sassy as anything Rachel would have come up with. For good measure, she added a head toss that sent her little feathers flying.

She wouldn't let him see how crushed she'd been by his attitude Tuesday morning. Afterward, she'd rushed back to the cottage and gathered up all her new clothes to throw them out. But then the sight of her reflection in the old cherry mirror over the dresser had stopped her.

As she'd gazed at herself, she finally understood what Rachel had been trying to tell her from the beginning. If she were going to do this, she had to do it for herself, not so she could catch a stuffy glamour boy of a preacher with the emotional maturity of a sixteen-year-old. That was when she'd decided she owed it to herself to give her new image a fair test trial and see how she liked it.

"I want to speak with you in private."

He wanted to lecture her. Without thinking, she picked up a napkin and began dabbing at water rings. It had taken all her courage to come in here alone tonight, and she wasn't up to being yelled at. She shook her head.

His voice grew harder. "Now, Kristy."

"No."

"Fuck off, asshole."

Andy's roommate had spoken, and Kristy stared at him, shocked. Nobody talked to Ethan like that. And then she remembered that Jason was from Charlotte and didn't know who Ethan was.

Andy punched his friend in the arm. "Uh — sorry about that, Pastor Ethan. Jason's not from around here."

Ethan gave them both a stare that threatened eternal damnation, then turned his Elmer Gantry eyes back on her. "Kristina, come with me immediately."

The jukebox launched into "You Don't Own Me."

Kristy's stomach curled with nervousness. She gathered up a crumpled cocktail napkin, cellophane from a package of cigarettes, and moved the beer pitcher closer to the center of the table so everyone could reach it more easily.

224

He leaned over and spoke so softly only she could hear. "If you don't do as I say, I'm going to pick you up and carry you out of here."

He didn't look like Pastor Ethan, everybody's friend, and belatedly Kristy remembered that he had a temper. He didn't display it often, and he was always remorseful afterward, but this wasn't *afterward*, this was *now*, and she decided not to take any chances.

Rising with as much dignity as she could muster, she nodded. "Very well. I suppose I can spare you a few minutes."

Ethan was not gracious in victory. "Darned right you can."

He took her arm in a firm grasp, but as she stepped forward, she found her nervousness easing. A fuzzy pink cloud had settled over her, bringing with it a feeling of well-being. She wasn't used to drinking, and although she'd barely finished two beers, she realized it had been enough to make her a bit giddy. It felt wonderful, and she decided that Ethan could preach at her all he wanted, and it wouldn't bother her one bit.

Ethan led her toward his car. As they approached, he used his free hand — the one that wasn't fastened to her arm — to pat the left pocket of his jeans. Not finding what he wanted, he tried the opposite one, then reached around to explore the back pockets.

He'd forgotten his keys again. They were undoubtedly lying on the table inside, which was why she always kept a spare set in her purse.

She automatically reached for it, then realized she wasn't carrying her old purse of many pockets, but a trendy little quilted number on a gold chain. She also remembered that Rachel had told her to stop mothering him.

"I left my keys inside." He held out his hand. "I need the spare set."

Good old reliable Kristy Brown. His absolute certainty that she would be carrying his spare keys — even though she no longer worked for him — poked a large hole in her fuzzy pink cloud, and she realized she wasn't nearly as drunk as she wanted to be. "That's unfortunate."

He released her arm. Giving her an irritated look, he hooked the purse by its chain and drew it off her shoulder. She watched in silence as he riffled through its contents.

"They're not here."

"I don't work for you anymore, remember? I don't have to carry around your keys."

"Of course you still work for —" He froze. Slowly his hand emerged from her purse holding a small square foil packet. "What is *this?*"

She was mortified. Her skin flushed, and that embarrassed her even more, until she realized it was too dark in the parking lot for him to see. She took a deep breath and struggled to speak calmly. "It's a condom, Ethan. I'm surprised you've never seen one."

"Of course I've seen one!"

"Then why are you asking?"

"Because I want to know what it's doing in your purse."

Her embarrassment faded, replaced by anger. "That's none of your business." She snatched it away from him, slipped it back into her purse, and returned the strap to her shoulder.

Two couples, one of whom belonged to Ethan's congregation, came out of the Mountaineer. Ethan grabbed her arm again and pulled her toward his car only to come to a stop as he remembered he couldn't get in. He glanced toward the couples, who were just beginning to move off the porch, and she knew he wanted to get away before he was spotted.

The Mountaineer was located on a quiet dead-end street between a children's boutique and a gift shop, both of which were dark for the night. Across the street was a small, wooded park with some picnic tables and play equipment. Ethan apparently decided the park was the closest escape because he turned her toward the street, and, with a none-too-gentle grip, led her there.

On nice days, local businesspeople ate their lunches on the picnic tables that were scattered underneath the trees. Using the light of the street lamp to keep from stumbling, Ethan led her to the most secluded of the tables.

"Sit down."

She didn't appreciate his bossy manner, so instead of sitting on the bench where he indicated, she stepped up on it and sat on the tabletop. He had no intention of relinquishing his authority by sitting below her, so he took a place at her side.

His legs were longer than hers, and they bent at a sharper angle. As she glanced over at him, she thought she saw him looking down her top, but when she heard the stuffy note in his voice as he spoke, she decided she'd been wrong.

"I'm your pastor, and the fact that a single woman in my congregation is carrying around a condom is very much my business."

Why was he acting like this? Ethan always respected people's choices, even if he didn't agree with them, and she'd heard his youth-group lectures on sexual responsibility. He vehemently preached abstinence, but he was also blunt about birth control and AIDS prevention.

"Every single woman in your congregation who's sexually active had better be carrying some of these around," she observed.

"What do you mean, sexually active? Who are you — I mean — But — How —"

Ethan Bonner, known for his sexual straight talk, was sputtering. He finally gathered himself together. "I didn't know there was a man in your life."

The last of her fuzzy pink cloud evaporated, and a sort of desperate boldness took its place. What, after all, did she have to lose? "How would you? You don't know anything about my life."

He seemed genuinely shocked. "We've known each other since elementary school. You're one of my oldest friends."

"Is that the way you see me?"

"Of course."

"You're right, I'm your friend." She swallowed, mustering her courage. "But you're not mine, Ethan.

Friends know things about each other, but you don't know anything about me."

"What do you mean? I know lots about you."

"Like what?"

"I know your parents, the house where you grew up. I know that you broke your arm two years ago. I know lots of things."

"A hundred people know *things*. But they don't know *me*. Who I am."

"You're a decent, hardworking Christian woman, that's who."

It was no use. She had tried to talk honestly to him, but he wouldn't hear. She began to stand on the bench. "I have to go."

"No!" He drew her back down. In the process, her breast brushed the side of his arm. He drew back as if he'd touched radioactive waste.

"Look, I'm — I'm not trying to offend you. Your sex life is your business, not mine, but, as your pastor, I'm here to advise you."

She hardly ever got angry, but that sparked her temper. "I'm not asking for advice, Ethan, because I've already made up my mind! That condom is in my purse because I'm making changes in my life, and I want to be ready for them."

"Sex before marriage is a sin." He didn't sound at all like himself. He shifted uneasily next to her, as if he realized he was being unbearably pompous. Once again, his gaze seemed to linger on her breasts. He looked away.

She spoke forcefully. "I believe it's a sin, too. But I also believe there's a hierarchy of sins. Don't try to tell me that murder and sexual molestation don't rank a lot higher on the list than a thirty-year-old unmarried woman finally deciding she's had enough of being a virgin."

She waited for him to express some surprise at her untouched state, but he didn't, and her spirits sank even lower as she realized he assumed she was a virgin.

"With whom do you intend to have it?"

"I don't know yet, but I'm looking. He obviously has to be unmarried and intelligent. And *sensitive*." She emphasized the last word, so that he'd understand this was a quality he'd never possess in a thousand years.

He bristled like a porcupine. "I can't believe you're ready to throw away a lifetime of propriety for a few carnal thrills."

He was sounding stuffier by the minute. "What's propriety gotten me? I have nothing that's important to me. No husband, no children. I don't even have a job I like."

"You don't like your job?" He sounded both hurt and mystified.

"No, Ethan. I don't like it."

"Why didn't you ever say anything?"

"Because I've been a wimp. It was safer for me to be depressed about my life than make changes."

"Then why did you stay all these years?"

That was one question she couldn't answer honestly. He probably knew anyway that she'd stayed because she was in love with him. "Fear of change. But I'm not afraid any longer."

"Rachel is responsible for this, isn't she?"

"Why do you dislike her so much?"

"Because she's taking advantage of Gabe."

Kristy didn't believe that at all, but Ethan was in no frame of mind to listen to reason. "You're right. Rachel *is* responsible because she's given me courage. I've never met a woman I admire more. She's living her life on the edge of catastrophe, but she never complains, and she works harder than anyone I know."

"Gabe's made it easy for her. He's given her a job and a car. He lets her stay in Annie's cottage and pays for Edward's day care."

"That's confidential. And Rachel has given Gabe a hundred times what he's given her. It's as if he's come alive since she's been here. He even laughs sometimes."

"His grieving has run its course, that's all. It has nothing to do with her. Nothing!"

Arguing about this with him was hopeless. For some reason, he was determined to be blind and stubborn when it came to Rachel.

His mouth set in a stubborn line. "I'd appreciate it if you'd at least give me the courtesy of two weeks' notice instead of leaving me in the lurch."

He had a point. Quitting like that hadn't been right, no matter what he'd done. She thought about how difficult it would be seeing him every day for the next two weeks. Still, she'd been doing it for eight years. What difference would another two weeks make? And it would be nice to have a paycheck while she looked for a new job. "All right. But only if you keep your nose out of my private life. And my wardrobe."

"I didn't mean to hurt your feelings, Kristy. It was the shock of seeing you look so different."

She rose from the table. "I'm chilly. I'm going back inside now."

"I wish you wouldn't do that."

"Forget the two weeks' notice."

"All right. Sorry. Go on in. You can sit with Gabe and me."

"No. I want to dance."

"I'll dance with you."

"That'll be a big treat." Obviously he thought the only way he could save her from sin was to force himself to dance with her.

"Why are you being so difficult?"

"Because I like it!" Her heart pounded. She was never rude, but she couldn't seem to help it, and the words kept rushing out. "Because I'm tired of twisting my own life in ten directions just to make things easier for other people."

"You mean easier for me."

"I don't want to talk any more."

She brushed past him and headed for the Mountaineer, even though all she wanted now was to go home and be alone.

As Ethan watched her disappear, guilt swamped him even as he told himself he had nothing to feel guilty for. "You have a wonderful life!" he called after her. "You have the respect of everyone in the community!"

"Well now, isn't that something cozy to cuddle up with on a cold winter night." As she shot the words back over her shoulder, she stepped into a pool of light from the street lamp. It defined her figure in a way that made his palms sweat.

The entire world had gone crazy, he decided. Right before his eyes, Kristy Brown had turned into a babe. As the light washed over her, her dark hair seemed to have fireflies dancing in it. She wasn't beautiful; her features were too ordinary for that. Although they were pretty, they were hardly exceptional. Instead, she was . . . sexy.

It bothered him to think of Kristy as sexy. There was something unnatural about it, like throwing lascivious glances at a sister. But ever since Tuesday morning he'd been thinking about those breasts.

Pig, Oprah said. *There's a lot more to Kristy Brown than big breasts.*

I know that! he shot back. It was the whole package: the small waist and rounded hips, the slender legs, that flighty hairstyle, and a new vulnerability — maybe that was the sexiest thing of all. Kristy no longer seemed so supremely competent, but like an ordinary person who had the same insecurities as everyone else.

He shoved his hands in the pockets of his jeans and tried to figure out why he was so upset by the changes in her. Because he was losing a darned good secretary, that was why.

Wrong, Oprah said. *You are so wrong.*

All right! There was too much truth in what Kristy had said tonight. He did regard her as one of his oldest friends, but until now, he hadn't realized how selfish that friendship had been.

She was right. Everything had been one-sided. He knew the events of her life, but nothing more. He didn't know how she spent her spare time, what made her happy, what made her sad. He tried to recall what she liked to eat, but all he could remember was the way she made sure there was always a supply of spicy brown mustard in the church refrigerator for his sandwiches.

When he thought of Kristy, he thought of a . . .

He flinched.

He thought of an efficient doormat. Always there, always willing to extend herself to help out. Never demanding anything for herself, only for others.

He stared off into the night. What a phony he was, calling himself a minister. This was one more example of his flawed character and why he needed to find another profession.

Kristy was a good person, a good *friend*, and he'd hurt her. That meant he had to make amends. And he only had two weeks to do it before she would disappear from his life.

CHAPTER
FOURTEEN

The next afternoon Gabe pried open the lid of the KFC bucket and extended it toward Rachel. They were sitting in their favorite place to take a lunch break, by the concrete turtle on the playground, with the big white screen looming above them offering shade from the midday sun.

Nine days had passed since that rainy afternoon they'd made love. The drive-in was opening a week from tonight, but instead of concentrating on that, all he'd been able to think about was having that sweet body underneath him again. Except she wasn't cooperating. First there'd been her hang-up about her period, something he was certain he could have overcome. But he hadn't pressed because he knew the money problem loomed in her mind, and he wanted her to realize how ridiculous that was.

His patience, however, had run out. There were only so many days he could spend watching those old cotton housedresses shape themselves around her body whenever a breeze swept through the lot, so he was making his move.

"You'll be glad to know I figured out the answer to our little dilemma."

"Which dilemma is that?" She pulled out a drumstick. He'd noticed she was partial to drumsticks. He, on the other hand, was partial to breasts, and, as he took one from the bucket, he enjoyed what he could see of hers peeking from the open buttons of today's ugly housedress, a red calico number he could swear he remembered Annie wearing when he'd been small enough to sit in her lap.

Rachel had pulled up the skirt and stretched her bare legs out in front of her. They were suntanned and lightly freckled. One knee sported an old scab, another a Band-Aid he'd affixed that morning after she'd ignored a scrape. Her calves seemed to get the worst of it. A bruise here, a scratch there. She worked too damned hard, but she wouldn't stick to the easier jobs he tried to give her, no matter how much he growled.

Her calves looked slim and feminine in contrast to the heavy white sweat socks collapsed around her ankles and those clunky black shoes. She kept them polished, he'd noticed, and he could only imagine the work it took to remove the paint and grime the shoes accumulated every day. At first he hadn't understood why she bothered, and then he realized that someone with only one pair of shoes had to take care of them.

He didn't like to think about Rachel slaving over those ugly shoes every night to keep them clean. He'd buy her a dozen pairs if he could, but she'd throw them right back in his face.

He cleared his throat. "The dilemma about your hourly salary and what you can do or not do during those hours."

"You're giving me a raise!"

"Hell no, I'm not giving you a raise."

He did his best not to smile at her look of disappointment. Although it wasn't easy, he was trying hard to keep her short of ready cash while he also made certain she had everything she really needed. The way she squeezed a dollar, he knew that if he gave her too much money, she'd save it up. And once she had enough, she'd leave town.

Sooner or later, she'd have to accept the fact that G. Dwayne hadn't left his five million dollars hidden away in Salvation, and then she'd no longer have a reason to stay. Gabe needed to make certain she couldn't afford to go. Not yet. Although he knew this town wasn't a good place for her, he also couldn't have her taking off until he was certain she had some way to stabilize her future. Her hold on survival was so very precarious, and somehow he had to make sure that she wouldn't ever be destitute again.

"I deserve a raise, and you know it."

Ignoring her, he said, "I don't know why I didn't think of this right away." He stretched out on his side in the grass, propped himself on one elbow, and took a bite of chicken he didn't want. "I've decided to put you on straight salary. That means that whether we fling or not, your paycheck won't be affected."

Her eyes lit up with dollar signs. "How much straight salary?"

He told her and waited for that little ripe strawberry mouth to bite his head off. Which it did.

237

"You are the stingiest, the most penny-pinching, tightfisted —"

"Look who's talking."

"I'm not rich like you. I have to pinch pennies."

"With a straight salary, you'll come out ahead. I'll still pay you overtime, but you won't be penalized if you have to take an hour off to run an errand. Or something." He paused and took another bite of chicken. "You should get down on your knees and thank me for my generosity."

"I should take a crowbar to your knees."

"Excuse me? I didn't quite catch that."

"Never mind."

He'd wanted to pull her into his arms right there. But he couldn't do it, not after the way it had been the first time between them. For all her talk about being a wanton woman, she deserved a bed this time, and not G. Dwayne's bed, either.

She deserved a date, too, although that didn't seem to have occurred to her. He wanted to take her out for a meal at a four-star restaurant just so he could watch her eat.

He loved doing that. Every day he came up with an excuse to feed her. He'd bring Egg McMuffins with him when he arrived in the morning and tell her he couldn't stand eating breakfast alone. Around noon, he'd announce that he was so hungry he couldn't concentrate until he had a bucket of KFC in front of him. In the middle of the afternoon, he'd haul out some fruit and cheese from the snack-bar refrigerator and make her take another break. If this kept up much

238

longer, he wouldn't be able to snap his jeans, but she was looking healthier by the day.

Her cheeks had filled out just enough so that her green eyes no longer seemed to be falling out of her face, and the bruises beneath her bottom lashes had disappeared. Her skin had taken on a healthy glow, and a few more freckles had popped out on her cheekbones. Her body was filling out a little, too. She'd never be plump, but she no longer looked quite so emaciated.

A shadow fell over him as he remembered how Cherry used to fret over her weight. He'd told her he'd still love her if she weighed three hundred pounds, but she'd counted calories anyway. He would have loved her fat or thin. He would have loved her crippled, old, shriveled. There was nothing that could have happened to her body that would have made him stop loving her. Not even death.

He tossed his half-eaten piece of chicken into the sack, leaned back into the grass, and threw his arm over his eyes as if he wanted to take a nap.

He felt her hand settle over his chest, and her voice was no longer angry. "Tell me about them, Gabe. Cherry and Jamie."

His skin prickled. It had happened again. She'd said their names. Even Ethan didn't do that anymore. His brother wanted to protect him, but Gabe was starting to feel as if they didn't exist in anyone's memory but his own.

The temptation to talk was almost overwhelming, but he held on to the few remnants of sanity he had left. He was crazy, but not crazy enough to have a cozy little chat about his dead wife's virtues with a woman he planned to make love to as soon as possible. Besides, he could just imagine what fodder Rachel and her sharp tongue would find in his memories.

The muscles in his shoulders flexed. He was lying to himself. Rachel would rip him apart for many things, but not his memories. Never that. Still, he resisted.

Her hand rested over his heart, and her soft breath fanned his cheek as she spoke with a tenderness he'd never heard. "Everybody else is too kind to point this out to you, Bonner, but you're in imminent danger of turning into one of those self-focused, self-pitying people nobody can stand." She gave him a gentle rub. "Not that you don't have plenty of reason for self-pity, and if you didn't still have so much of your life left, it might even be all right."

His blood churned, and a terrible anger rushed through him. She must have felt the constriction of his muscles because she laid her head on his chest to quiet him. A strand of her hair fell over his lips. He smelled her shampoo, and it reminded him both of sunshine and clean rain.

"Tell me how you met Cherry."

Her name again. His anger evaporated, and he felt an urgent need to talk about her, to make her real again. Still, it took him a while to manage the words. "A Sunday-school picnic."

He grunted as Rachel's sharp elbow dug into his stomach. Automatically lifting his arm, he opened his eyes.

240

She'd propped herself comfortably on his chest as if he were a lounge chair, and instead of giving him one of those pity-filled looks he'd grown accustomed to, she was smiling. "You were kids! Teenagers?"

"Not even. We were eleven, and she'd just moved to Salvation." He shifted into a half-sitting position, rearranging her elbow at the same time so it wasn't aimed directly at his diaphragm. "I was running around, not watching where I was going, and I spilled a glass of purple Kool-Aid on her."

"I'll bet she wasn't happy about that."

"She did the damnedest thing. She looked up at me and smiled and said, 'I know you're sorry.' Just like that. 'I know you're sorry.'"

Rachel laughed. "She sounds like a pushover."

He found himself laughing back. "She was. She always thought the best of people, and I can't tell you how many times that got her into trouble."

He lay back in the grassy shade of the giant movie screen, but this time he let the happy memories in. One after another, they came back to him.

A bee droned nearby. Crickets sawed away. Rachel's sun-scented hair blew across his lips.

His eyes grew heavy. He slept.

The next evening Rachel and Edward helped Kristy unpack. Kristy's new one-bedroom condo was small and charming, with a tiny patio and a compact kitchen complete with a skylight. The walls sparkled with fresh white paint and everything smelled new.

Her furniture had arrived from storage that day. It was mostly made up of the family pieces Kristy's parents hadn't wanted when they'd moved to Florida, and now Kristy was regarding all of it with displeasure.

Keeping her voice low, so no one but Rachel could hear, she said, "I know I don't have the money to replace this stuff, but it doesn't . . . I don't know. It doesn't fit me anymore." She gave a self-deprecating laugh. "Listen to me. Five days ago I got my hair cut and bought some new clothes. Now I think I'm a different person. I'm probably just feeling guilty about not moving to Florida like they want."

"This past week has been hard on you." Rachel placed the last of the glasses on a cupboard shelf that had already been lined with blue-and-lavender shelf paper. "And don't be depressed about the furniture. They're basic pieces. You can brighten them up with pillows, hang some museum posters. It'll look terrific when you're done."

"I suppose."

Edward strutted out of the bedroom. "We need a Phillips 'crewdriver to fix the bed. You got one?"

Kristy walked over to her small, neatly arranged tool kit, which sat open on the white counter that divided the galley kitchen from the condo's living area. "Try this."

With an air of self-importance that made Rachel smile, Edward took the screwdriver and swaggered off to join Ethan in the bedroom. Ethan Bonner might be at the top of Kristy's grudge list right now, but his generosity toward Edward made it hard for Rachel to hold on to her dislike. This was the first time her son had been given a chance to do real work with an adult male, and he was reveling in it.

Kristy glared toward the bedroom and hissed under her breath, "Ethan was awful Thursday night at the Mountaineer, but he's been acting as if nothing happened."

"I suspect he's having as hard a time forgetting about it as you are."

"Ha."

Rachel smiled and hugged her disgruntled friend. Tonight Kristy wore a bright-red T-shirt tucked into a pair of brand-new jeans. Her makeup had worn off, and she'd traded in her gold sandals for a pair of worn sneakers, so there was nothing overtly sexual about her dress, but Rachel had noticed the way Ethan's eyes had lingered on her anyway.

"I've wasted all these years mooning over an immature hypocrite, but I'm not doing it any longer!"

If Kristy got much louder, Ethan would hear her, but Rachel had interfered enough, and she didn't say anything.

"I saved most of my money while I was living at home, so I've got enough to go back to school. I only need a few classes to finish up my degree in early-childhood education, and I shouldn't have any trouble getting a job as a teacher's aide to help out with my mortgage payments until I'm finished."

"That's wonderful."

"I wish I'd done this years ago."

"Maybe you weren't ready until now."

"I guess." Kristy gave her a wistful smile. "It's nice, you know. For the first time in my life, I don't feel invisible."

Rachel suspected that came more from Kristy's mindset than her cosmetic changes, but she kept her opinion to herself.

Ethan appeared from the back bedroom with Edward at his side. "All done. Why don't Edward and I get started on that bookcase?"

"Thanks, but I'm not ready to put it up yet." Kristy spoke with a brusqueness that bordered on rudeness.

"All right. We can hook up the television."

"You've done enough, Ethan. Thanks anyway."

She couldn't have been more clearly dismissing him, but Ethan refused to take the hint and leave. "Come on, Edward. Let's see what we can do with that sticky bathroom door."

"The builder's sending someone to take care of it tomorrow. I don't really have anything else, Ethan. I'll see you at work tomorrow."

This was too direct to ignore, and as he returned the tools to the toolbox and made his way to the door, Rachel began to feel sorry for the gorgeous Pastor Bonner.

The windows were dark. Ever since the incident with the burning cross, Gabe had known that Rachel couldn't stay alone on Heartache Mountain. With Kristy gone, he was afraid for her.

He'd planned to get to the cottage earlier, but Ethan had stopped by, and Gabe had been forced to listen to

244

a lengthy monologue about how rude Kristy had been to him, then ignore some none-too-subtle hints that Rachel was after his money. That was definitely true, but not in the way Ethan meant. One thing had led to another, and now it was nearly midnight.

He parked the truck by the garage and sat there in the dark for a moment, his thoughts in turmoil. Talking about Cherry this afternoon with Rachel, even so briefly, had begun to ease something inside him. If only Rachel lived in the cottage by herself, moving in might not be so complicated. But he would also have to deal with her son, and just the thought of being around that pale, silent little boy made the blackness descend all over again.

The child was an innocent, and he'd tried to argue himself out of his feelings dozens of times, but he couldn't. Whenever he looked at Edward, he thought of Jamie, and how the worthier child had died.

He drew in a sharp breath. The thought was ugly. Unforgivable.

He pushed it away as he took his suitcase from the truck and headed toward the house. Even though the night was cloudy and none of the outside lights were on, he had no trouble making his way. He'd spent hundreds of nights at this cottage when he was a child.

How many times had he and Cal slipped through a back window after Annie had gone to bed so they could explore? Ethan had been too young to go with them, and he still complained about having missed out on some of Gabe and Cal's best adventures.

An owl hooted in the distance as Gabe came around the side of the house. His shoes made a soft swishing sound in the grass, and his keys jingled in his hand.

"Stay where you are!"

Rachel's shadow loomed on the front porch, tall and straight. His lips framed a wisecrack, but, as he made out his grandmother's old shotgun pointed at his chest, he decided being a smart-ass wasn't a good idea.

"I've got a gun, and I'm not afraid to use it!"

"It's me. Damn, Rachel. You sound like a bad detective movie."

She dropped the barrel of the shotgun. "Gabe? What are you doing out there? You scared the life out of me!"

"I came up here to defend you," he said dryly.

"It's the middle of the night."

"I planned to arrive earlier, but I ran into a little trouble with Ethan."

"Your brother is a moron."

"He's crazy about you, too." He stepped up on the porch and took the shotgun away from her with his free hand.

She reached inside the screen door to flick on the yellow porch light. His mouth went dry as he saw her standing there with bare feet, bare legs, and the same blue workshirt she'd been wearing the morning the house was vandalized. Her rumpled curls looked like ancient gold in the porch light.

"What's that?" she asked.

"As you can see, it's a suitcase. I'm moving in for a while."

"Did Kristy put you up to this?"

"No. Kristy's worried, but this is my idea. As long as she was living here, I never believed the danger to you would go beyond threats, but with her gone, you're more vulnerable."

He walked into the living room where he set down his suitcase and checked the shotgun. It wasn't loaded, so he gave it back. At the same time, he thought about the .38 he'd locked up before he left the house. Keeping a loaded gun next to his bed had suddenly seemed obscene. "Put that away."

"You don't think I can take care of myself, do you? Well, I can, so just hop back in that redneck truck of yours and go away."

He couldn't quite hold back a smile. She did that to him. "Save it, Rach. You've never been so glad to see anybody in your life, and you know it."

She made a face. "Are you really moving in?"

"I have enough trouble sleeping as it is without worrying about what's going on up here."

"I don't need a baby-sitter, but I guess I wouldn't mind a little company."

That, he knew, was the closest he'd get to an acknowledgment that she was worried. She disappeared to put the shotgun away, and he carried his suitcase down the back hallway to his grandmother's old bedroom, which was now empty of Kristy's things. As he gazed around at the old rough-hewn bed and the rocker in the corner, he remembered how scared he'd get at night when he was little. He used to sneak in here and crawl in with Annie. He could have climbed in with Cal, but he hadn't wanted his older brother to know that he was afraid. One time, though, he'd slipped in with his grandmother only to discover that his big brother was already there.

He heard Rachel behind him and turned. She looked rumpled and beautiful. The V-shaped crease in her cheek told him she'd been asleep when he'd driven up. He studied the shirt she was wearing more closely and felt vaguely irritated. "Don't you have anything else to sleep in?"

"What's wrong with this?"

"It's Cal's. If you need a shirt, you can wear one of mine." He tossed his suitcase on the bed, opened it, and yanked out a shirt that was clean, but marked here and there with various stains that hadn't come out in the laundry.

She took it from him and regarded it critically. "His is a lot nicer."

He glared at her.

She gave him an impish smile. "But yours looks more comfortable."

"Damn right it is."

She smiled again, and pleasure leached into some of the barren places inside him. He thought about how she managed to find amusement in the smallest things, even with her life hanging in shreds around her.

Her green eyes grew crafty, and he braced himself. She planted one hand on her hip, a gesture that hiked up her shirt a few more inches. She was killing him, and she didn't even know it. "If you expect me to cook, you have to buy all the food."

248

Rachel had more ways of holding on to her money than anyone he'd ever known, and he couldn't resist giving her a hard time. "Now why would I expect you to cook? I'm probably better at it than you are."

She thought about that. "You also eat a lot more, so it wouldn't be fair for me to spend my money on your food. Really, Gabe, you have the most enormous appetite I've ever seen. You're always eating."

Before he could figure out how to respond to that one, a small voice interrupted.

"Mommy?"

He whirled around and saw the boy standing there in the doorway. He was wearing a new pair of pajamas so big they had to be rolled at the cuff. Trust Rachel to protect her pennies by looking to the future.

She moved to his side as if the kid were burning up with fever, and when she bent over, he saw the edge of her panties. The boy gave him a brief, unfathomable look, then stared down at the floor. Gabe turned his back on them and busied himself unpacking.

"Come on, sweetie," Rachel said. "Let me tuck you back in."

"What's *he* doing here?"

She began moving him out of the room into the hallway. "It's Gabe's cottage. He can come here whenever he wants."

"It's Pastor Ethan's cottage."

"He and Gabe are brothers."

"Are not." Gabe heard them turning into Annie's old sewing room. The boy said something he couldn't quite make out, but it sounded like *behead* — a peculiar word for a five-year-old to know. The kid was strange, and Gabe knew he should feel sorry for him, but memories were swallowing him up.

Jamie in his pajamas fresh from his bath. That little whorl of dark, wet hair on the top of his head. The way he'd snuggle into Gabe's lap with his favorite book, sometimes falling asleep before they reached the end. Sitting there with a sleeping child heavy in his arms and one small, bare foot cupped in his hand . . .

"Do you have everything you need?"

He hadn't heard Rachel come back in. He blinked his eyes and shook his head. "No." The breath left his lungs in a shudder. "I need you."

She came to him at once, pressed her body against his, and he knew this waiting had been as hard on her as on him. He pushed his hands underneath the shirt she wore, his brother's shirt, and touched the soft skin beneath. But then she broke away. He felt a chill at her desertion, only to realize she was locking the door.

How many times had he or Cherry done that? Locked the bedroom door in that old Georgia farmhouse so Jamie wouldn't wander in? The pain came back.

Rachel cupped his jaw, and her soft whisper fell on his cheek like a prayer. "Stay with me, buddy. I need you, too."

She always seemed to understand. Once again, his hands found her warm flesh. She wiggled against him and began tugging at his clothes. She was demanding, impatient, and her clumsy eagerness aroused him to the

250

point where he could barely think. In moments he was naked except for one sock.

He had known Cherry's body as intimately as his own. Where she liked to be touched and how she wanted to be stroked. But Rachel was still a mystery.

He stripped his brother's shirt from her, being deliberately rough enough to tear a few buttons so she wouldn't be tempted to wear it again. Then he pushed her back on the bed.

She immediately rolled on top of him. "Who made you boss?"

He laughed and buried his mouth against her breast. She straddled his hips. She hadn't taken off her panties, and now she tortured him with them, lightly sliding the nylon back and forth, up and down, leaving a damp, silky trail.

When he couldn't stand it any longer, he curled his hands around her hips and brought her down hard against him. "Playtime's over, sweetheart."

She leaned forward, dragging her nipples across his chest. Her hair curled around her freckled shoulders, and, as a strand fell over his lips, the preacher's widow regarded him with devilish eyes. "Who says?"

He groaned, slipped his fingers inside her panties, and gave her a dose of her own medicine.

After that, both of them went a little crazy, and because they couldn't make any noise, their lust was all the more frenzied. She bit his chest, then sucked his tongue. He swatted her rear then kissed her until she was breathless. First one rolled on top, and then the other. She made him sit up, then impaled herself, not taking off the panties, merely pulling the crotch aside. Their passion was red-hot, visceral. Thrilling beyond belief. The very walls of the room oozed sex.

He hated it when he awakened in the night to find that she'd gone back to her own bed.

An idea tugged at the corner of his mind. Maybe he should marry her. It would keep her safe and out of trouble. And he wanted to be with her.

But he didn't love her, not like he'd loved Cherry. And he couldn't raise her son. Not now. Not ever.

For the rest of the night, sleep eluded him, and at dawn, he finally gave up and took a shower. He knew she was an early riser, but she still wasn't awake by the time he'd dressed. He smiled to himself. He'd worn her out.

The kitchen was quiet. He unlocked the back door and stepped outside. A wave of nostalgia hit him. He felt as if he'd taken a step back into his childhood.

Both he and Cal had been born when their parents were teenagers. His father had been in college, and then gone on to medical school, before he'd eventually set up practice in Salvation. His Bonner grandparents were well-to-do and embarrassed by their only son's forced marriage into the trashy Glide family, but Gabe and his brothers had loved their Glide grandmother, and they'd spent as much time on Heartache Mountain as their parents would allow.

He remembered running outside first thing in the morning, so eager to start the new day that Annie had to threaten him with her wooden spoon to get him to eat breakfast. As soon as he'd wolfed it down, he'd race back out to find the creatures that waited for him: squirrels and raccoons, skunks, possums, and the occasional black bear. Bears weren't as common now. The chestnut blight had wiped out their favorite feed, and the acorns that replaced them weren't nearly as reliable a food source.

He missed them. He missed working with animals. But he couldn't think about that now. He had a drive-in to run.

The thought depressed him. He moved down off the step and gazed toward the old garden. Last summer, his mother and Cal's wife Jane had tended it during the period when they'd both moved out on their husbands. It was overgrown again, although he could see where someone — Rachel, probably, since she didn't seem to know how to relax — had begun tidying it.

A shrill, high-pitched scream broke the morning stillness. It was coming from the front, and he shot around the side of the house, his heart pounding, thinking that this time it would be worse than painted graffiti.

He came to a dead stop as he saw the boy standing alone on the front porch, near the far end. He was still dressed in his pajamas and frozen in fear as he stared down at something that was blocked from Gabe's view.

Gabe ran forward and immediately spotted what had made Edward scream. A small snake coiled against the wall of the house.

He reached it in three swift strides. Shoving his hand through the railing, he snatched up the snake before it could slither away.

Rachel came flying out the front door. "Edward! What's wrong? What's —" She saw the snake hanging from Gabe's hand.

Gabe regarded the cowering child with impatience. "It's only a garter snake." He held the snake toward the boy. "See that yellow down its back? That's how you know it won't hurt you. Go on. You can touch it."

Edward shook his head and took a step backward.

"Go on," Gabe commanded. "I told you it won't hurt you."

Edward shrank farther back.

Rachel was at Edward's side in an instant, babying him as usual. "It's all right, sweetie. Garter snakes are friendly. There used to be lots of them on the farm where Mommy grew up."

She straightened and gave Gabe a look of cold fury. Reaching down, she snatched the snake from his hand and pitched it over the railing. "See. We'll let it go so it can find its family."

Gabe regarded her with reproach. She was never going to make a man out of the boy if she kept protecting him like this. Gabe had exposed Jamie to snakes when he was a toddler, making sure he could tell the good ones from the poisonous ones, and he'd loved touching them. The voice of reason told him there was a big difference between a child who'd grown up with snakes and one who hadn't, but his son was dead, and he couldn't listen to reason.

Edward curled against her. She patted his head. "How about some breakfast, Mr. Early Bird?"

254

He nodded against her belly, and Gabe could barely make out his words. "Pastor Ethan said I was s'posed to come to Sunday school today."

Rachel looked annoyed. "Maybe some other time."

He mentally cursed his brother for planting the idea in the boy's head. Ethan hadn't given a moment's thought to what Rachel would go through if she walked into a church service.

"That's what you said last Sunday," Edward complained.

"Let's open the new box of Cheerios."

"I want to go today."

Gabe couldn't stand listening to the kid argue. "Do what your mother says."

Rachel whirled on him. She began to speak, only to clamp her mouth shut and hustle her son inside.

Gabe avoided them both by taking a long walk in the woods until he found the place where he used to keep his animal sanctuary. He'd built some cages when he was around ten or eleven and used them to doctor whatever wounded animals either he or his friends happened to find. Looking back, he was surprised at how many he'd been able to save.

The memory brought him only sadness. Now he didn't even want to be around animals. He'd been able to heal so many living creatures, but he couldn't heal himself.

He wasn't ready to face either Rachel or the boy, so he headed into town, where he picked up coffee at McDonald's. Afterward, he made his way toward Ethan's church and parked in his accustomed place a block away. He'd been attending services the last few Sundays, always sitting in the back, coming in late and leaving early so he didn't have to talk to anyone.

Rachel had turned her back on God, but he'd never quite been able to do that. His faith wasn't strong like his brother's, and it hadn't helped him. But something was there, and he couldn't let it go.

Despite his recent irritation with Ethan, he liked hearing him preach. Ethan wasn't one of those irritatingly righteous men of God who thundered absolutes and acted as if they had the only pipeline to heaven. Ethan preached tolerance and forgiveness, justice and compassion — everything, Gabe realized, that Ethan wasn't showing to Rachel. His brother had never been a hypocrite, and Gabe couldn't understand it.

He glanced across the congregation and saw that he wasn't the only latecomer. Kristy Brown sneaked into a rear pew long after the Prayer of Confession. She wore a yellow dress with a very short skirt, and her expression practically dared people to make something of it. He smiled to himself. Like everyone else in Salvation, he'd never paid much attention to Kristy unless he'd needed something done. Now she'd become a force to be reckoned with.

After the service, he drove to Cal's house and called his brother to tell him he was moving out for a while. When Cal heard why, he exploded.

"You're moving in with the Widow Snopes? Ethan said you were tangled up with her, but I didn't believe him. Now you're living with her?"

256

"It's not like that," Gabe replied, even though that wasn't quite the truth. "She's become a target around here, and I think she's in danger."

"Then let Odell take care of it."

Gabe heard a soft little mouse-like squeal in the background, and realized it was coming from his niece. Rosie was a beautiful baby, full of mischief and already itching to try her wings. A small pain lodged in his chest.

"Look, Gabe, I've talked to Ethan. I know you've always had a weakness for wounded animals, but this wounded animal is a rattlesnake. Anybody who's been with you for five minutes can tell you're an easy mark when it comes to money, and — Hey!"

"Gabe?" His sister-in-law's voice cut in. Although Gabe had only been with Dr. Jane Darlington Bonner a few times, he had immediately taken to her. She was brainy, assertive, and decent, exactly what Cal needed after making a career out of youthful bimbos.

"Gabe, don't listen to him," Jane said. "Don't listen to Ethan either. I like the Widow Snopes."

Gabe felt duty-bound to point out the obvious. "That's nice to hear, but I don't believe you've ever met her, have you?"

"No," his sister-in-law replied in her no-nonsense voice. "But I lived in her awful house. When Cal and I were having all our trouble — I know it sounds silly, but whenever I was in her bedroom or the nursery, I'd feel this funny kinship with her. There was this wickedness about the rest of the house, and a goodness about those two rooms. I always thought it came from her."

He heard a bark of skeptical laughter from his brother in the background.

Gabe smiled. "Rachel's the farthest thing I can imagine from a saint, Jane. But you're right. She's a good person, and she's having a tough time. Try to keep big brother off my back for a while, will you?"

"I'll do my best. Good luck, Gabe."

He made some other calls, including one to Odell Hatcher, then packed up the perishables from the refrigerator and headed back to Heartache Mountain. It was mid-afternoon when he parked next to the garage. The cottage windows were open and the front door unlocked, but Rachel and the boy weren't inside.

He carried the groceries into the kitchen and unloaded them in the refrigerator. When he turned around, he saw the boy standing just inside the back door. He'd entered so quietly that Gabe hadn't heard him.

Gabe remembered the way Jamie had flown into their big old rambling North Georgia farmhouse, door slamming, sneakers banging, usually yelling at the top of his small lungs that he'd found a special earthworm or needed a broken toy repaired.

"Is your mother outside?"

The boy looked down at the floor.

"Please answer me, Edward," Gabe said quietly.

"Yes," the boy murmured.

"Yes, what?"

The boy's shoulders stiffened. He didn't lift his head.

The child definitely needed some toughening up, for his own sake. Gabe forced himself to speak quietly, patiently. "Look at me."

Slowly, Edward lifted his head.

"When you talk to me, Edward, I want you to say, 'Yes, sir' or 'No, sir.' 'Yes, ma'am' and 'No, ma'am' when you talk to your mother or Kristy or any lady. You're living in North Carolina now, and that's the way polite children speak around here. Do you understand?"

"Uh-huh."

"Edward . . ." Gabe's tone carried a soft warning note.

"My name's not Edward."

"That's what your mother calls you."

"She's allowed," he said sullenly. "Not you."

"What am I supposed to call you?"

The child hesitated and then muttered, "Chip."

"Chip?"

"Don't like Edward. Want everybody to call me Chip."

Gabe considered trying to explain to him that Chip Stone might not be the best choice of names, then abandoned the idea. He'd always been good with children, but not this one. This one was too strange.

"Edward, did you find the ball of string?"

The back door opened and Rachel came in. Her dirty hands and smudged nose indicated that she'd been working in the garden. Her gaze immediately flew to her son, as if she were afraid Gabe might have used thumbscrews on him when she wasn't looking. Her attitude made him feel guilty, and he didn't like that.

"Edward?"

The boy went over to the old cupboard, tugged open the left drawer with both hands, and pulled out the twine ball that had been there, in one form or another, for as long as Gabe could remember.

"Put it with the bucket I was using, would you?"

He nodded, then gave Gabe a wary glance. "Yes, ma'am."

Rachel regarded him quizzically. Edward let himself out the back door.

"Why'd you name him Edward?" Gabe asked, before she could start in on him about what had happened that morning with the garter snake.

"It was my grandfather's name. My grandmother made me promise to name my first son after him."

"Couldn't you call him Ed or something? Eddie? Nobody calls little kids Edward anymore."

"Excuse me. I seem to have forgotten . . . Exactly which part of this is your business?"

"All I'm saying is that he doesn't like his name. He told me I have to call him Chip."

Dark-green storm clouds gathered in her eyes. "Are you sure you're not the one who told him something was wrong with his name? Maybe *you* told him he should call himself Chip."

"No."

She stalked forward, finger pointed toward his chest like a pistol. "Leave my son alone." *Bang!* "And don't you dare interfere between us again the way you did this morning." *Bang! Bang!*

260

She'd never been one to mince words, and she kept after him. "What you did with that snake was cruel, and I won't allow it. If you try anything like that again, you can move right back out of here."

The fact that she was right made Gabe feel cornered. "In case you've forgotten, this is my house." It was his mother's. Close enough.

"I haven't forgotten anything."

A small flutter of movement in the periphery of his vision caught Gabe's attention. He looked past Rachel's shoulder toward the screen door and saw Edward standing there, taking in the argument.

Even through the screen, Gabe could sense his watchfulness, as if he were guarding his mother.

"I mean it, Gabe. Leave Edward alone."

He said nothing, merely looked past her toward the door. Edward realized he'd been spotted and disappeared from view.

The lines of strain at the corners of Rachel's mouth put Gabe out of the mood to argue with her. Instead, he wanted to pull her back to the bedroom and start all over again. He couldn't get enough of her. But they weren't alone . . .

He extracted the square of paper he'd stuck in his back pocket and unfolded it. It was his guilt offering for what had happened that morning, but she didn't have to know it. "Odell gave me the the names of everybody who was at the airstrip the night G. Dwayne escaped."

Her bad mood vanished. "Oh, Gabe, thank you!" She snatched the list from him and sat down at the kitchen table. "Is this right? There are only ten names on the list. It seemed as if there were a hundred men there that night."

"Four from the sheriff's office, and Salvation's entire police force. That's it."

Just as she started to study the list more closely, they heard a car approaching. He went into the living room ahead of her, then relaxed as he saw Kristy get out of her Honda. She was dressed to kill in khaki shorts and a slinky green top.

Rachel hurried to greet her. Edward raced around from the side and threw himself at Kristy. "You came back!"

"I told you I would." She bent down and kissed the top of his head. "I'm tired of working, so I came by to see if you want to go to the pig roast with me this afternoon."

"Wow! Can I, Mom? Can I?"

"Sure. But go clean up first."

Gabe wandered back to the kitchen and was pouring himself a cup of Rachel's pansy-assed coffee when the two women came in.

"But why would you want Dwayne's Bible? What do you —" Kristy broke off as she caught sight of him. He knew she'd been worried about Rachel being here alone, and he detected relief in her expression. "Hi, Gabe."

"Kristy."

"I want the Bible for Edward," Rachel said, without looking at him. "It's a family heirloom."

So, Gabe thought. She wasn't even going to tell Kristy the truth. He was the only one who knew.

Kristy sat down at the table and studied the list.

"One of these men had to have stolen it the night they confiscated my car." Rachel picked up the cup of coffee Gabe had just poured for himself and took a sip. He didn't know why, but it felt nice to be taken for granted. Rachel seemed to be the only person who expected anything from him these days.

Kristy regarded the list thoughtfully. "Not Pete Moore. He hasn't been inside a church in years."

Rachel leaned back against the sink and cradled the mug in both hands. "The person who took it might not have done it for religious reasons. He could very well have wanted it as a curiosity piece."

In the end, Kristy entirely eliminated six names and said the other four were highly unlikely, but Rachel refused to be discouraged. "I'll start with those, but if I don't discover anything, I'm talking to the rest."

The boy rushed into the kitchen. "I'm clean! Can we go, Kristy? Are they going to have a real pig there?"

As Rachel went over to check Edward's hands, Gabe picked up the coffee mug she'd abandoned and walked out onto the back porch. A few minutes later, he heard Kristy's car drive away.

Quiet once again settled over Heartache Mountain. He and Rachel would have the cottage to themselves for the rest of the afternoon. Heat rushed through his veins. God bless Kristy Brown.

He shut his eyes for a moment, ashamed of how much he wanted Rachel, because he didn't love her. He couldn't. That part of him no longer worked. But he loved being with her. She calmed something inside him.

The screen door banged behind him. He turned toward her, only to feel his anticipation fade as he saw the determined look in her eyes.

"Let's go, Gabe. We're going to find that Bible right now."

He got ready to argue, but then gave up. What was the use? Rachel's mind was made up.

CHAPTER
FIFTEEN

"Another waste of time," Gabe said as he closed the door of his truck.

The interior was hot, and the seat belt burned Rachel's fingers as she snapped it together over the skirt of the dress she'd been reserving for a special occasion, a square-neck yellow cotton printed with black-and-orange monarch butterflies. "We only have one more name to go."

"Let's eat instead. I could use a hamburger."

"I swear you have a tapeworm. We just ate an hour ago."

"I'm hungry again. Besides, checking up on Rick Nagel's going to be an even bigger waste of time than this was. The fact that he cheated off Kristy's geography test when she was in fifth grade doesn't mean he should be a suspect."

"I trust Kristy's instincts."

Gravel crunched beneath the tires as Gabe backed out of Warren Roy's short driveway. Rachel watched him flip on the air conditioner. At the same time, he gave her a look that combined both tolerance and irritation. He thought she was on a wild-goose chase, and he was probably right. The blank expressions on the faces of the first two men they'd visited had convinced her neither one had any idea what she was talking about. Still, the Bible had to be somewhere.

Something had been nagging at her ever since she'd first seen the list, and once again, she took out the paper to study the names. Bill Keck . . . Frank Keegan . . . Phil Dennis . . . Kirk DeMerchant . . . She hadn't known any of them.

Dennis. Her gaze shot back up the list. "Phil Dennis? Is he related to Carol?"

"Her brother-in-law. Why?"

She jabbed her finger at the paper. "He was there that night."

"Then you're out of luck. I heard he moved out west a couple of years ago, so if he took your Bible, it's long gone."

"Not if he gave it to Carol."

"Why would he do that?"

"She was loyal to Dwayne. She still believes in him, and that Bible would mean a lot to her. Maybe her brother-in-law knew that and took it."

"Or maybe not."

"You could be a little more encouraging, you know."

"This is as encouraging as I get."

His attitude was irritating, but at least he was sticking by her. She studied his profile with its hard planes and blunt angles and thought about telling him a knock-knock joke so she could watch his face soften when he smiled. A lassitude stole through her, a need for him that wasn't going away. She wanted to tell him to turn his truck around and head right back up

Heartache Mountain, but she couldn't do that, so she concentrated on folding the paper instead. "I want to see Carol next."

She waited for him to protest. Instead, he sighed. "You sure you don't want to get a hamburger?"

"If I eat another hamburger, I'll start to moo. Please, Gabe. Take me to Carol's house."

"I'll just bet she's another charter member of your fan club," he grumbled.

"Um." No need to tell him exactly how much Carol Dennis disliked her.

Carol lived in a white colonial tract house set on a rectangular lot fronted by two symmetrically planted young maples. Matching redwood planters filled with purple and pink petunias sat on each side of the front door, which was painted Williamsburg-blue and held a grapevine wreath decorated with yellow silk flowers. Rachel stepped ahead of Gabe and braced herself for what could only be an unpleasant interview, but before she could push the bell, the door opened and two teenage boys came out, followed by Bobby Dennis.

It had been nearly a month since she'd seen him with his mother at the grocery store, but as he caught sight of her, his face hardened with the same hostility. "What do you want?"

Gabe stiffened at her side.

"I'd like to speak with your mother," she said quickly.

He grabbed the cigarette the red-haired boy on his right had just lit, took a drag, and handed it back. "She's not here."

Rachel shuddered at the thought of Edward turning out like this. "Do you know when she'll be back?"

He shrugged, already bummed out on a life that had barely begun. "My mom don't tell me shit."

"Watch your mouth," Gabe said in a low, almost toneless voice that sent a shiver up Rachel's spine. Although he didn't do anything overtly threatening, he seemed to loom over the surly teenagers, and the Dennis boy began to study one of the petunia pots.

His red-haired friend, the one he'd taken the cigarette from, shifted nervously. "My mom and her are workin' at the pig roast today."

Gabe's lips barely moved. "You don't say."

The redhead's knobby Adam's apple wobbled in his throat. "We're goin' down there later. Do you want us to give her a message or something?"

Rachel decided to intercede before the poor kid swallowed his cigarette. "We'll find her. Thanks."

"Punks," Gabe said as they returned to the truck. The moment they were settled inside, he turned to her. "You are *not* going to that pig roast."

"You know, Bonner, finding this Bible is tough enough without having to drag you along every step of the way."

"The minute people set eyes on you, they're going to truss you up and stick you on the spit, right along with the pig."

"If you're going to be a wimp about it, you can just drop me off there. I'll get a ride home with Kristy."

He threw the truck into gear with a quick, irritated motion and backed out into the street. "We had that cottage all to ourselves this afternoon. Just the two of us. But are we taking advantage of it? Hell no."

"Stop acting like a horny teenager."

"I feel like a horny teenager."

"Yeah?" She smiled. "Me, too."

He stopped the truck in the middle of the street, leaned across the seat, and kissed her, a faint brush of the lips, sweet and fleeting. Ribbons of sensation unfurled inside her.

"Sure you don't want to change your mind about that pig roast?" He propped his elbow on the back of the seat and regarded her with an expression that was so mischievous it made her laugh.

"I definitely want to change my mind, but I'm not going to. Just one more stop, Gabe. I'll talk to Carol Dennis, and then we'll go back to the cottage."

"Why do I think it's not going to be that easy?" With an expression of resignation, he pointed the truck toward town.

The pig roast was being held in the athletic field attached to Memorial Park, the town's largest public space. The park itself contained green metal benches and neatly laid-out flower beds that bloomed with impatiens and marigolds. Beyond it, the athletic field baked in the midday sun with the only shade coming from the tents and canopies erected by the county's civic organizations, which used the annual pig roast to raise funds. The smell of charcoal and roasted meat permeated the air.

Almost immediately, Rachel spotted Ethan and Edward standing near a small pavilion where a bluegrass band played. Edward nibbled a cloud of pink cotton candy without taking his eyes from the musicians, but Ethan kept glancing toward a food tent about twenty feet away. Rachel followed his eyes and spotted Kristy listening to a sandy-haired man who seemed to be doing his best to impress her.

Ethan scowled. With his blond hair glimmering in the sun, he reminded Rachel of a morose young god. It served him right, she thought, for being so shallow.

As she and Gabe moved closer, she felt the stares of the people around her. Only the Florida retirees seemed oblivious to the fact that the notorious Widow Snopes had joined their ranks.

Edward turned toward her, just as if she were wearing a maternal homing device. "Mommy!"

He ran forward, sneakers flying, cotton candy dangling from one hand, Horse from the other. His sticky mouth turned up in a wide smile. He looked so happy, so healthy. Her eyes stung.

Thank you, God.

The prayer had been automatic, but she pushed it away as Edward charged into her legs. There was no God.

"Pastor Ethan bought me cotton candy!" Edward exclaimed, his attention focused so completely on her that he hadn't spotted Gabe, who was standing a few feet behind. "And Kristy got me a hot dog 'cause I almost cried when I saw the pig." His face fell. "I couldn't help it, Mommy. It's dead, and it had eyeball holes, and . . . They killed it and cooked it over the fire."

270

Another small loss of innocence on the path to adulthood. She wiped a ketchup smear from his cheek with her thumb. "That's why they call it a pig roast, partner."

He shook his head. "I won't ever eat a pig again."

She decided not to mention the probable contents of his hot dog.

"Kristy bought me a balloon, and it was red, but it broke, and —" Edward caught sight of Gabe and fell silent. She watched him draw Horse against his chest with the rabbit's hindquarters tucked under his chin. His withdrawal was almost palpable, and she remembered the ugly scene on the porch with the snake. Sometimes she thought she understood Gabe, but his callous behavior this morning had proven how little she knew him.

Ethan came up next to them, gave her a curt nod, then chatted with his brother, pointedly ignoring her. Apparently she wasn't the only one who felt ignored. She detected a small movement at her side and glanced down just in time to see Edward drop his cotton candy on Gabe's shoe.

Gabe jerked his foot back, but it was too late. He made an exclamation of disgust as a sticky pink mess covered the brown leather.

"It was an accident," she said quickly.

"I don't think so." He stared down at Edward, who stared at him in return. Resentment darkened her son's brown eyes, along with just enough five-year-old's cunning to tell her it hadn't been an accident at all.

271

He'd wanted Ethan to himself, and he blamed Gabe for taking his attention.

She reached into her old cloth purse for a tissue and found the toilet paper she was using instead to save money. She withdrew a neatly folded strip and handed it to him to clean his shoe.

Ethan touched her son's hair. "You've got to be careful with that stuff, Edward."

Edward looked from Gabe to Ethan. "My name's Chip."

Ethan smiled. "Chip?"

Edward nodded at the dirt.

Rachel darted a furious glance at Gabe. She didn't know how, but somehow this was his fault. "Don't be silly. Your name is Edward, and you should be proud of it. Remember what I told you about my grandfather? That was his name."

"Edward's stupid. Nobody has that name."

Ethan gave Edward's shoulder a comforting squeeze, then regarded his brother. "The volleyball game'll be starting soon. Let's play."

"You go on," Gabe said. "Rachel and I have someone we need to see."

Ethan wasn't pleased. "I really don't think that's a good idea."

"Don't worry about it, all right?"

A muscle ticked in Ethan's jaw. She knew he wanted to lash out at her, but overt hostility wasn't in his nature. He rubbed his knuckles over the top of Edward's head. "See you later, pal."

Edward looked deeply unhappy as Ethan moved away. He had been separated from the man he idolized, and his day was spoiled.

She took his hand. "I'm afraid your cotton candy's ruined. Do you want another one?"

Gabe jammed both hands into his pockets, and his scowl made it easy to read his mind. He thought she should be punishing Edward for deliberately dropping the cotton candy instead of rewarding him, but Gabe didn't understand everything her son had been through.

"No," he whispered.

Just then Kristy came up next to them. Her cheeks were flushed, and her eyes shone with an air of excitement. "You'll never believe this, but I have a date tonight. Mike Reedy asked me to go out to dinner with him. I've known him for years, but . . . I can't believe I said yes." Kristy had barely gotten her news out before her brow began to furrow as uncertainty poked into her excitement. "I probably shouldn't have. I'll be so nervous I won't be able to think of a thing to say."

Before Rachel could try to reassure her, Gabe wrapped his arm around her shoulders and gave her quick hug. "That's one of the best things about you, Kristy. Men like to talk, and you're a good listener."

"Really?"

"Mike's a great guy. The two of you'll have a good time. Just don't let him get too fresh on the first date."

Kristy stared up at him and then flushed. "As if anybody'd get fresh with me."

"Exactly the kind of attitude that can leave a woman barefoot and pregnant."

Kristy laughed, and the three of them chatted for a few more minutes before she excused herself to check out the church's white-elephant booth. Rachel noticed she'd waited until Ethan left to go over there.

"I want to go home now." Edward looked sulky and unhappy.

"Not quite yet, honey. There's someone I need to see first." She put herself between Gabe and Edward and began walking toward the concessions.

They passed the large charcoal grills the Rotary had set up to roast corn on the cob, then went by the Art Guild's popcorn concession.

"Gabe!" A thin, bushy-haired man who was soliciting funds for the Humane Society moved out from behind his table.

"Hello, Carl." Gabe walked toward him, but Rachel sensed he did it reluctantly. She and Edward followed.

Carl regarded her with curiosity but no particular hostility, so she knew he hadn't been associated with the Temple. The two men exchanged pleasantries, then Carl got to the point.

"We sure could use a vet at the shelter, Gabe. Last week we lost a two-year-old Doberman to bloat because Ted Hartley couldn't get over here in time from Brevard."

"Sorry about that, Carl, but I'm not licensed in North Carolina."

"I guess the Doberman wouldn't have cared too much about the paperwork."

274

Gabe shrugged. "I might not have been able to save him anyway."

"I know, but you'd have tried. We need a local vet. I always thought it was a shame you didn't come back to Salvation to practice."

Gabe deliberately changed the subject. "My drive-in's opening on Friday night. We're having fireworks and free admission. I hope you'll show up with your family."

"I'll be sure and do that."

They moved on, passing a table selling T-shirts for muscular dystrophy. The crowd jostled her, and she lost Edward's hand.

Someone bumped against her back, and she lurched into Gabe. He caught her arm as she righted herself. She glanced around, but saw nothing suspicious.

Edward stayed nearby, but he didn't take her hand again. It was as if he wanted to put as much distance as he could between Gabe and himself. Ahead, she saw a table covered with platters of baked goods, and, behind it, Carol Dennis unpacking a plate of iced brownies.

"There she is."

"I remember Carol when she was younger," Gabe said. "She was a sweet girl before she got so religious."

"Ironic, isn't it, what religion does to people?"

"I guess it's more ironic what people do to religion."

Carol looked up. Her hands stilled on the box of Saran Wrap she was holding, and Rachel saw all the old accusations form in her eyes. Rachel knew how unpleasant Carol could be and wished Edward weren't with her. At least he was lagging behind.

As she and Gabe moved nearer, Rachel decided everything about Carol was too sharp. The contrast between her pale skin and dyed black hair made her look brittle. Her cheekbones poked out at knifelike angles, her pointed chin lengthened an already long face, and her short, angular hairstyle was too severely cut to be flattering. She was thin and tense, as if all the softness had been leached out of her. Rachel remembered her sullen teenage son and felt a stab of pity for both of them.

"Hello, Carol."

"What are you doing here?"

"I needed to speak with you."

Carol glanced at Gabe, and Rachel sensed her uncertainty. She must feel compassion for him, but she wouldn't be able to forgive the way he was consorting with the enemy.

"I can't imagine what we need to talk about." Her expression grew less harsh as Edward came around from behind Rachel to stand at her side. "Hello there, Edward. Would you like a cookie? I think we have one to spare here."

She picked up a white plastic plate. Edward studied the contents, then selected a large sugar cookie dusted with red sprinkles. "Thank you."

Rachel took a deep breath and plunged in. "I'm looking for something that I think you might have."

"Oh?"

"Dwayne's Bible."

Surprise flickered across Carol's fox-sharp features, and then wariness took its place. Rachel felt a prickle of excitement.

"Why on earth would you think I'd have it?"

"Because I know you cared about Dwayne. I believe your brother-in-law took the Bible the night Dwayne was arrested and gave it to you."

"Are you accusing me of theft?"

Rachel knew she had to be careful. "No. I'm sure you took the Bible for safekeeping, and I appreciate that. But now I'd like it back."

"You're the last person who should have Dwayne's Bible."

She hesitated. "It's not for me. It's for Edward. He has nothing left that belonged to his father, and the Bible should be his." That part, at least, was true.

Rachel held her breath. Carol gazed down at Edward, whose mouth was rimmed with red sprinkles. Apparently he'd been won over by the cookie because he smiled at her.

Carol bit her lip. She didn't look at Rachel, only at Edward. "Yes. All right. I do have the Bible. The police would only have thrown it in the storage room, and I couldn't let that happen. They aren't always careful with things."

Rachel wanted to grab Gabe and spin him around until she was too dizzy to stand. Instead, she forced herself to speak calmly. "I'm grateful to you for taking care of it."

Carol spun on her. "I don't care about your gratitude. I did it for Dwayne, not for you."

"I understand." Rachel forced the words out. "I know Dwayne would have appreciated it."

Carol turned away, as if she couldn't stand being in Rachel's presence any longer.

"Maybe we could stop by your house later on." Rachel didn't want to press her too hard, but she was determined to get her hands on the Bible as soon as possible.

"No. I'll give it to Ethan."

"When will that be?"

She shouldn't have shown her eagerness because it gave Carol power over her, something she clearly liked. "I believe Monday is Ethan's day off. I'll bring it to the church office sometime Tuesday."

She couldn't stand to wait until Tuesday, and she began to protest only to have Gabe cut her off. "That'll be just fine, Carol. No hurry. I'll tell Ethan to expect you."

He caught Rachel's arm in a death grip and steered her into the crowd. "If you don't back off, you're never going to see that Bible."

She looked back to make sure Edward was following. "I can't stand that woman. She's deliberately torturing me."

"Another couple of days won't make any difference. Let's get something to eat."

"Don't you ever think about anything but your stomach?"

He slipped his thumb beneath the short sleeve of her monarch butterfly dress and stroked her upper arm.

"Every once in a while other parts of my body have been known to grab my attention."

Her skin broke out in goose bumps. At the same time, she found herself wishing he felt something more lasting toward her than sexual attraction. "Are you buying?"

He looked amused. "I'm buying."

She turned her head and glanced over her shoulder. "Come on, Edward. We're going to eat."

"I'm not hungry."

"You love watermelon. I'll get you a piece."

As they walked toward the food tents, Gabe heard the boy dragging his sneakers in the dirt. When he considered how much of Rachel's meager paycheck had gone toward buying those sneakers, he wanted to tell the child to pick up his feet, but he knew he was being unreasonable, and he kept silent.

They headed toward the center of the field, where several whole pigs roasted on spits above a large pit of glowing coals. Rachel wrinkled her nose. "I think I'll have corn on the cob instead."

"I thought you country girls were immune to being sentimental about animals."

"Not me. Besides, we raised soybeans."

He'd never been much of a fan of pig roasts himself, so he didn't give her a hard time. Before long, they were sitting at one end of a long picnic table with plates of buttered corn. He'd added a hot dog and coleslaw to his own meal in an attempt to get her to eat more, but she'd refused, and now he was stuck with food he didn't want.

"You sure you wouldn't like another hot dog, Edward? I haven't touched this one."

The boy shook his head and picked at the wedge of watermelon on his plate. Ever since they'd sat down, Gabe had watched him stealing glances at the next table where a man ate with his son, who looked to be around Edward's age. Edward gazed over at them again, and Rachel noticed.

"Is that boy in day care with you, Edward? You seem to know him."

"Uh-huh. His name is Kyle." Edward looked down at his watermelon. "And my name's Chip."

Over the top of Edward's head, Rachel gave Gabe an exasperated look. At the next table, the boy named Kyle and his father picked up their empty paper plates and disposed of them in one of the trash cans. Edward watched them carefully.

After the last paper cup had disappeared, the boy turned toward his father and raised his arms. His father smiled, swung him up, and set him over his shoulders.

An expression of such naked longing crossed Edward's face that Gabe winced. It was a simple thing . . . A father carrying his son on his shoulders. But Edward was too heavy for Rachel to carry that way. Too heavy for a mother to carry on her shoulders, but not a father.

Pick me up, Daddy! Pick me up so I can see!

Gabe looked away.

Rachel had witnessed the entire episode, and he saw her painful reaction as she took in one more thing in her life that she couldn't control. She opened her purse

280

to distract herself. "Edward, I think you're wearing more food than you've eaten. Let me clean you —"

Her hands grew still, then dipped inside and began to riffle through the contents. "Gabe, my wallet's gone!"

"Let me see." He took her purse and, looking inside, saw the orderly clutter of a pen, a grocery-store receipt, a folded wad of toilet paper, a small plastic action toy, and a tampon that was coming out of its wrapper. He could just guess how much she begrudged spending her precious money on tampons.

"Maybe you left it at home."

"No! It was in my purse when I gave you that tissue to wipe your shoe."

"Are you sure?"

"I'm positive." She looked stricken. "Do you remember when I fell against you? Someone bumped me hard. It must have happened then."

"How much money did you have in your wallet?"

"Forty-three dollars. Everything I had."

She looked so forsaken and bewildered that his heart turned over in his chest. He knew how strong she was, and he told himself she'd recover from this latest setback, but he also wondered how many times one human being could get knocked to her knees and keep climbing back up.

"Let me go check around over where it happened. Maybe it fell out of your purse when you were bumped and someone turned it in at one of the tables."

He could see she didn't believe that would happen. He didn't believe it himself. Her luck wasn't that good.

As they cleared their trash, Rachel tried to conceal how upset she was from Gabe. She desperately needed that forty-three dollars to make it through next week.

Edward lagged behind as they left the picnic tables. They had to pass the bake sale on their way, where Carol was still working, along with an older woman cheerfully dressed in red slacks and a short-sleeved blouse printed with red and yellow hibiscus. Rachel recognized her as the grandmother of Emily, the little girl with leukemia. Her heart sank as the woman spotted her.

"Mrs. Snopes!"

"What are you doing, Fran?" Carol frowned as the older woman shot out from behind the table and made her way to Rachel.

The woman's wooden parrot earrings bobbed as she smiled at Rachel, then turned her head toward Carol. "I've asked Mrs. Snopes to go to my daughter's house and pray over Emily."

"How could you do that?" Carol cried. "She's a charlatan."

"That's not true," Fran chided gently. "You know how desperately we need prayers. Only a miracle can save Emily."

"You won't get a miracle from her!" Carol's dark eyes bore into Rachel's, and her sharp features twisted with consternation. "Do you have any idea how much this family has suffered? How could you raise their hopes like this?"

Rachel began to deny that she'd done any such thing, but Carol wasn't finished. "How much are you

282

charging them? I'll bet you put a big price tag on your prayers."

"I don't have any prayers," Rachel replied honestly. She took a deep breath and gazed directly at Emily's grandmother. "I'm sorry I can't help you, but I'm no longer a believer."

"As if you ever were," Carol retorted.

But Fran merely smiled and regarded Rachel with deep compassion. "If you look into your heart, Mrs. Snopes, you'll know that's not true. Don't turn your back on us. My own prayers tell me that you can help Emily."

"But I can't!"

"You won't know until you've tried. Would you just go see her?"

"No. I won't give you false hopes."

"Pull out your checkbook, Fran," Carol said. "She'll change her mind."

For a woman who was supposed to be filled with the love of God, Carol's heart seemed to hold only bitterness. In Rachel's years at the Temple, she had seen many Carols, deeply religious men and women who were so judgmental and unyielding that all the joy had been snuffed from them.

Rachel was a good biblical scholar, and she understood what had happened to people like Carol. In their theology, everyone was inherently wicked, and only by being constantly on guard against the forces of evil could there be any hope for eternal life. For those like Carol, belief became a source of unending anxiety.

She'd seen those like Fran at the Temple, too — people who shone with an inner light. It never occurred to the Frans of the world to look for wickedness in others. They were too busy dispensing love, compassion, and forgiveness.

Ironically, Dwayne had been frustrated by Christians like Fran. He believed they lacked vigilance in the fight against the devil, and he feared for their souls.

"I'm sorry," she said, her voice husky with emotion. "I'm so sorry."

Gabe stepped forward. "Ladies, you'll have to excuse us, but we need to look for Rachel's wallet. She lost it a little earlier." He nodded at them and drew her away.

Rachel was grateful. She knew he didn't understand what had happened, but, once again, he had sensed her distress and intervened.

"I didn't realize you knew Fran Thayer," he said as they passed the charcoal pit.

"Is that her last name? She didn't tell me."

"What's going on?"

She explained.

"It wouldn't hurt you to go see her granddaughter," he said when she was done.

"It would be unconscionable. I'm not a hypocrite."

For a moment she thought he would argue with her, but he didn't. Instead, he gestured toward one of the tents. "It seems to me we were over there when you got bumped. Let me ask around."

He returned a few minutes later, and even before he spoke, she knew the news wasn't good. "Maybe somebody will turn it in to the police later," he said to console her.

She forced a smile they both knew was false. "Maybe."

He brushed his knuckles gently down the side of her jaw. "Let's go on back to the cottage. I think we've all had enough for today."

She nodded, and the three of them set off.

As they moved away, Russ Scudder stepped out from behind the lemonade concession. He waited until they had disappeared then pulled Rachel's wallet from inside the empty popcorn box he'd been carrying around and removed the money.

Forty-three dollars. Too bad there wasn't more. He stared at the wrinkled bills, tossed the wallet into the nearest trash can, then wandered toward the table the Humane Society had set up.

Earlier, Carl Painter had been asking people for donations, but Russ ignored the container decorated with a picture of a sad-eyed dog. Instead, he slipped the forty-three dollars into the plastic cylinder that sat next to it, the one marked *Emily's Fund*.

CHAPTER
SIXTEEN

That night, Rachel read Edward *Stellaluna* for the hundredth time. The beautifully illustrated story dealt with a baby bat separated from his mother and raised by birds with sleeping and eating habits different from his own. When she was done with the book, Edward took Horse's ear out of his mouth and looked up at her, his too-old eyes worried. "Stellaluna's mommy got in a accident, and then they didn't see each other for a long time."

"But they found each other at the end."

"I guess."

She knew her answer hadn't satisfied him. He had no father, no house, no extended family. He was just beginning to realize she was his only stability.

After she'd tucked him in, she went out to the kitchen and saw Gabe standing by the back door. He turned when he heard her, and she watched as his hand slid into his pocket. He withdrew several bills and gave them to her.

She counted out fifty dollars. "What's this?"

"A bonus. You've done a lot of work that isn't in your job description. It's only fair."

He was making up for the money that had been stolen from her purse and trying to save her pride at the same time. She looked down at the crisp bills and blinked. "Thanks," she managed.

"I'm going outside for a while. I'll be back soon."

He didn't invite her to go with him, and she didn't ask. Moments like this reminded her of how much there was that separated them.

Later, as she was just starting to get ready for bed, she heard him return. She finished undressing, then slipped into his old work shirt. After she'd washed her face and brushed her teeth, she went out to the kitchen where she found him crouched by a cardboard box sitting near the stove.

She walked over to investigate and saw that the box held a heating pad and a green plastic strawberry container lined with tissue. Inside lay a bedraggled baby sparrow.

On Tuesday, with the drive-in opening only three days away, Rachel was beginning to think they'd never be ready on time. She was excited about showing off the Pride of Carolina to the community. Having fireworks on opening night had been her idea, and she was making Gabe put up a row of colorful plastic flags near the entrance.

Unfortunately, Gabe didn't share her enthusiasm, and his lack of interest grew more apparent every day. At the same time, her affection for the old place grew. Looking at the fresh paint, sparkling new appliances, and weed-free lot gave her a feeling of accomplishment.

At three that afternoon, the snack-shop phone rang. She dropped the cloth she'd been using to wipe down the new popcorn machine and raced to answer it.

"I've got the Bible," Kristy said. "Carol's son just delivered it."

Rachel gave a sigh of relief. "I can't believe I'm finally going to have it. I'll pick it up tonight."

They chatted for a few minutes, and, as she hung up, Gabe walked in. She dashed around the end of the counter. "Kristy has the Bible!"

"Don't pin all your hopes on this."

She looked up into his unsmiling silver eyes and couldn't resist touching his cheek. "You worry too much, dude."

He smiled then, but only for a moment. She could tell he was getting ready to launch into another lecture, so she changed the subject. "How are things going with Tom?"

"He seems to know what he's doing."

Tom Bennett was the projectionist Gabe had hired. After the grand opening, Gabe planned to keep the drive-in open four nights a week. Tom lived in Brevard and would be commuting. Gabe was going to operate the ticket booth and work with Rachel in the snack shop during intermissions, along with a young woman named Kayla he'd hired to help out.

For some time Rachel had been puzzling over what to do with Edward when she had to start working at night, but in the end, her decision had been simple. She couldn't afford a sitter to stay with him very often, so most of the time he would have to come with her. She'd make a bed for him in Gabe's office next to the projection room and hope he'd fall sleep.

Gabe regarded her sternly. "Did you eat lunch today?"

"Every bite." As she gazed at his cranky, disagreeable expression, her mouth curled in a goofy smile. It had been a long time since anyone had looked out for her. Dwayne certainly hadn't, and by the time Rachel had entered her mid-teens, her grandmother's health had deteriorated to the point where Rachel had become her caretaker. But this grouchy, wounded man who only wanted to be left alone had appointed himself her guardian angel.

Her feelings were too much for her, and she walked back to the counter. "How's Tweety Bird doing?"

"Still alive."

"Good." He'd brought the baby sparrow to the drive-in with him so he could keep up with its frequent feedings. Earlier, she'd gone up to his office to ask him a question and seen his big frame bent over the box as he fed the small creature from the slanted tip of a straw. "Where did you say you found it?"

"Near the back porch. Usually you can locate the nest and put them back — it's an old wives' tale that birds are rejected by their mothers if they have a human scent on them. But I couldn't find a nest anywhere."

His expression grew even more irritable, as if the baby bird's continued survival displeased him, but she knew differently, and her smile widened.

"What are you so happy about?" he growled.

"I'm happy about you, Bonner." She couldn't resist touching him again, and she abandoned the rag she'd just picked up to go to him. He drew her closer. She laid her head against his chest and listened to the steady thump of his heart.

His thumbs rubbed her back through the soft cotton dress, and she felt his arousal pressed against her. "Let's get out of here, sweetheart, and go back to the cottage."

"We have too much to do. Besides, we just made love last night, or have you forgotten?"

"Yep. It's completely slipped my mind. You're going to have to remind me."

"I'll remind you tonight."

He smiled, but only for a moment before he dropped his head and kissed her.

This was no fleeting touch, but a full melding of their mouths that quickly grew hungry and demanding. His lips parted, and then her own. She felt his fingers tunneling through her hair. His tongue came into her mouth, and she reveled in the wildly erotic sensation of two people out of control.

The kiss deepened. He reached under her dress, pulled at her panties. She grabbed for the snap on his jeans.

There was a loud thump on the ceiling. They sprang back like guilty children, then realized Tom had merely dropped something in the projection room.

She grabbed the edge of the counter.

He took a long, unsteady breath. "I forgot we weren't alone."

Her delight bubbled to the surface. "You sure did. You got totally carried away by lust, Bonner. *Totally.*"

"I'm not the only one. And it's not funny. Having somebody walk in on the two of us is the last thing your reputation needs right now. It's bad enough that I'm living at the cottage with Kristy gone."

"Yeah-yeah." She regarded him mischievously. "That tongue thing . . . You did it on Saturday night, too. I like it."

He rolled his eyes, exasperated, but also amused.

"Do you know the last person I did anything like that with?"

"Not G. Dwayne I'll bet." He moved over to the coffeemaker, as if he didn't trust himself to stand so close to her. She saw the distinct bulge at the front of his jeans and felt a rush of womanly satisfaction.

"Are you kidding? He was a dry pecker."

"A *what?*"

"He used to give me these dry little pecking kisses that never quite made it to my mouth. No, the last time I kissed like that was my junior year in high school with Jeffrey Dillard in the Sunday-school storage closet. We'd both been eating Jolly Ranchers, so it was sweet in more ways than one."

"You haven't done any tongue kissing since your junior year of high school?"

"Pathetic, isn't it? I was afraid if I did I'd go to hell, which is one of the good things about the last few years of my life."

"How's that?"

"I don't worry about hell anymore. I've sort of developed a 'been there, done that' attitude."

"Rach . . ."

He looked so distressed she wanted to bite her tongue. Irreverence might help stave off her fear, but it upset him. "Lame joke, Bonner. Hey, you'd better get back to work before the boss catches you loafing. He's a real tightwad, and, if you're not careful, he'll dock your pay. Personally, I'm scared to death of him."

"Is that so?"

"The man has no pity, not to mention being stingy. Luckily, I'm smarter than he is, so I've figured a way to get a promotion."

"How's that?" He took a sip of coffee.

"I'm going to strip him naked and then lick him all over."

His lengthy coughing fit left her with a sense of satisfaction that carried her through the rest of the afternoon.

Edward crouched on his haunches, the heels of his hands braced on his knees, and gazed into the cardboard box. "It's not dead yet."

The kid's pessimistic attitude annoyed Gabe, but he tried not to show it. He returned the mixture of ground beef, egg yolk, and baby cereal he'd been using to feed the sparrow to the refrigerator. Edward had been hanging around the box all evening to watch, but he finally stood, pushed his rabbit headfirst into the elastic waistband of his shorts, and wandered into the living room.

292

Gabe stuck his head through the doorway. "Leave your mother alone for a while longer, okay?"

"I want to see her."

"Later."

The boy pulled the stuffed rabbit from his shorts, tucked it against his chest, and regarded Gabe resentfully.

Rachel had been holed up in her bedroom with G. Dwayne's Bible ever since Kristy had brought it over. If she'd found anything, the door would have blown open, but since it hadn't, he knew she was facing another disappointment. The least he could do was keep the boy occupied while she dealt with it.

Now he watched as the five-year-old ignored his instructions and tried to sidle inconspicuously toward the back hallway.

"I asked you to leave your mother alone."

"She said she'd read *Stellaluna* to me."

Gabe knew what he should do. He should get the book and read the story to the boy himself, but he couldn't do that. He simply could not let the child sit next to him while he read him that particular book.

One more time, Daddy. Read Stellaluna *one more time. Please.*

"The book's about a bat, right?"

Edward nodded. "A good bat. Not a scary bat."

"Let's go outside and see if we can spot one."

"A real bat?"

"Sure." Gabe led the way to the back door and held the screen open. "They should be out by now. They feed at night."

"That's all right. I got stuff to do here."

"Outside, Edward. Now."

The boy ducked reluctantly under his arm. "My name's Chip. You shouldn't come out here. You should stay with Tweety Bird so he don't die."

Gabe swallowed his impatience and followed the boy outside. "I've been taking care of birds since I was only a little older than you, so I guess I know what I'm doing." He recoiled from the harsh sound of his words and took a deep breath, trying to make amends. "When my brothers and I were boys, we'd find baby birds that had fallen out of their nests all the time. We didn't know then that you were supposed to put them back in, so we took them home. Sometimes they'd die, but sometimes we could save them."

As he remembered it, he was the one who'd done all of the saving. Cal's intentions were pure, but he'd get wrapped up shooting baskets or playing softball and forget to feed the bird. And Ethan had been too young for the responsibility.

"You told Mommy Pastor Ethan is your brother."

Gabe didn't miss the accusing note in Edward's voice, but he didn't let himself rise to it. "That's right."

"You don't look the same."

"He looks like our mother. My brother Cal and I look like our father."

"You don't act the same."

"People are different, even brothers." He picked up one of the tubular lawn chairs that leaned against the back of the cottage and unfolded it.

294

Edward dug the heel of his sneaker into the soft earth while he let the rabbit dangle at his side. "My brother's like me."

Gabe looked over at him. "Your brother?"

Edward's forehead puckered as he concentrated on his sneaker. "He's real strong, and he can beat up about a million people. His name is . . . Strongman. He never gets sick, and he always calls me Chip, not that other name."

"I think you're hurting your mother's feelings when you tell people not to call you Edward," he said quietly.

The boy didn't like that, and Gabe watched the play of emotions cross his face: unhappiness, doubt, stubbornness. "She's allowed to call me that. You're not."

Gabe picked up the other lawn chair and unfolded it. "Keep watching just above that ridge. There's a cave up there where a lot of bats live. You might be able to see some of them."

Edward tucked the rabbit next to him as he sat in the other chair. His feet didn't touch the ground, and his thin legs stuck out stiffly in front of him. Gabe felt the boy's tension, and it bothered him to be regarded as some sort of monster.

A few minutes ticked by. Jamie, with a five-year-old's impatience, would have jumped out of the chair after thirty seconds, but Rachel's son sat quietly, too afraid of Gabe to rebel. Gabe hated that fear, even though he couldn't seem to do anything about it.

The fireflies came out, and the last of the evening breeze died down. The boy didn't move. Gabe tried to

295

think of something to say, but it was the boy who finally spoke.

"I think that's a bat."

"No. It's a hawk."

The boy drew the rabbit into his lap and poked at a tiny hole in the seam with his index finger. "My mommy'll get mad if I stay out here too long."

"Watch the trees."

He stuffed the rabbit under his T-shirt and leaned back in the chair. It squeaked. He leaned forward and then back, making it squeak again. And again.

"Be quiet, Edward."

"I'm not Ed —"

"Chip, damn it!"

The boy crossed his arms over his lumpy chest.

Gabe sighed. "I'm sorry."

"I have to pee real bad."

Gabe gave up. "All right."

The lawn chair tilted as the boy jumped from it.

Just then, Rachel's voice drifted out of the back door. "Bedtime, Edward."

Gabe turned to see her standing inside the screen silhouetted against the kitchen light. She looked slim and beautiful, at once entirely herself, but at the same time, any one of a million mothers calling a child inside on that warm July night.

His mind shifted to Cherry, and he waited for the pain to hit him, but what he felt instead was melancholy. Maybe, if he didn't let himself think about Jamie, he might be able to live after all.

Edward ran for the back porch, and as soon as he reached his mother's side, he grabbed her skirt. "You told me not to say curses, didn't you, Mommy?"

"That's right. Curses are rude."

He glared at Gabe. "*He* said one. He said a curse."

Gabe regarded him with annoyance. The little tattletale.

Rachel herded the child inside without comment.

Gabe fed the baby sparrow again, doing his best not to touch him too much as he dispensed tiny dollops of food. Too much hand-feeding would accustom the bird to human contact and turn it into a pet, making it more difficult to release the creature back to the wild.

He wanted to be certain she'd had enough time to put the boy to bed, so he cleaned up the bird's nest by lining it with fresh tissue before he went into the living room. Through the front screen, he saw her sitting on the porch step with her arms propped on top of her bent knees. He stepped outside.

Rachel heard the screen door open behind her. The porch vibrated beneath her hips as he walked toward her. He lowered himself onto the step.

"You didn't find anything in the Bible, did you?"

She still hadn't managed to swallow her disappointment. "No. But a lot of text is underlined and there are marginal notes everywhere. I'm going through it page by page. I'm sure I'll find a clue somewhere."

"Nothing's easy for you, is it, Rach?"

She was tired and frustrated, and the energy that had carried her through the afternoon had vanished. There had been something deeply disturbing about reading those old, familiar verses again. She could sense them pulling at her, trying to draw her back toward something she could no longer accept.

Her eyes began to sting, but she fought against it. "Don't get sentimental on me, Bonner. I can handle just about anything but that."

He slipped his arm behind her and cupped her shoulder. "All right, sweetheart. I'll smack you around instead."

Sweetheart. He'd called her that twice today. Was she really his sweetheart?

She leaned against his shoulder and accepted the truth. She had fallen in love with him. She wanted to deny it, but it was no use.

What she felt was so different from her love for Dwayne. That had been an unhealthy combination of hero worship and a young girl looking for a father. This was a mature love, with her eyes wide open. She saw both Gabe's flaws and her own. And she also saw how destructive it would be to let herself fantasize about a future with a man who was still in love with his dead wife. Even more painful, a man who disliked her child.

The animosity between Gabe and Edward seemed to be getting worse, and she couldn't think of a way to make it better. She couldn't order Gabe to change his attitude or make him care about Edward.

She felt tired and defeated. He was right. Nothing ever came easy for her. "Try not to curse in front of Edward, will you?"

"It slipped out." He gazed at the dark line of trees that marked the edge of the front yard. "You know,

Rachel, he's a good kid and everything, but maybe you need to toughen him up a little."

"I'll enroll him in scowling lessons first thing tomorrow."

"I'm just saying . . . That rabbit he carries around all the time, for example. He's five years old. The other kids are probably making fun of him."

"He says he keeps it in his cubby when he's at school."

"Still. He's too old."

"Didn't Jamie have anything like that?"

His entire body stiffened, and she knew she had trod on forbidden ground. He could talk about his wife, but not his son.

"Not when he was five."

"Well, I'm sorry Edward's not macho enough for you, but the last few years have taken some of the spunk out of him. It didn't help that he spent a month in the hospital this spring."

"What was wrong with him?"

"Pneumonia." She traced a line of rickrack that edged the pocket of her dress. The depression that had been hanging over her ever since she'd realized the Bible wasn't ready to give up its secrets settled in deeper. "It took him forever to recover. At one point, I wasn't sure he'd make it. It was awful."

"I'm sorry."

The discussion of Edward had opened a gap between them. She knew Gabe wanted to close it as much as she did when he spoke. "Let's go to bed, Rachel."

She gazed into his eyes, and it didn't enter her mind to say no. He held out his hand and led her into the house.

Moonlight streamed over the old bed, touching the soft worn sheets with silver and gilding Rachel's hair as Gabe lay over her naked body. His need for her frightened him. He was a man of silence and solitude. These past few years had taught him that it was best for him to be alone, but she was changing that. She was pushing him toward something he didn't want to examine.

She twisted beneath him, legs spread, pressing herself against him. Her lovemaking was so unrestrained that he couldn't always control himself. Sometimes, he was afraid he'd hurt her.

Now he drew her arms above his head and manacled her wrists. He knew the feeling of helplessness would drive her wild, and, almost immediately, she began to moan.

Restraining her left him with only one hand to use. One hand to cup her breasts, one thumb to rub across the swollen tips. He substituted his mouth and moved his hand between her legs.

She was wet for him, slippery with desire. He caressed her, loving the woman's feel of her beneath his touch. How could he have forgotten this? How could he have let his pain destroy so much that was good?

Her short, breathy moans were loosening the limits of his control. She started to struggle against his restraint, but she wasn't putting anything into it, so he didn't let her go. Instead, he slid his finger inside her.

She gave a low, strangled scream.

He couldn't endure that sweet writhing any longer. He positioned himself, then entered in a deep, strong thrust.

"Yes," she gasped.

He covered her open mouth with his own. Their teeth scraped; their tongues mated. He took each of her wrists in one of his hands and drove into her, their arms extended.

She tilted her hips, then wrapped her legs around him. Moments later, she fell apart.

Nothing existed but this shuddering woman and the moonlight and the sweet-scented summer air blowing over their bodies from the open window. He found the forgetfulness he needed.

Afterward, he didn't want to move off her. The sheet tangled around their hips. He pressed his mouth against her neck, shut his eyes . . .

A small bundle of fury leaped on his back.

"Get off my mommy! Get off her!"

Something hard hit him on the head.

Little fists pounded at him, and fingernails scratched his neck. The room echoed with frantic cries. "*Stop it! Stop it!*"

Rachel had gone rigid beneath him. "Edward!"

Something much sturdier than five-year-old fists began to bang against the back of his head in hard, rhythmic whacks. Tears and panic clogged the child's voice. "You're hurting her! Stop hurting her!"

Gabe tried to deflect the blows, but his range of motion was limited. The boy was straddling his hips, and, if he rolled over, he'd reveal Rachel's nudity. How had he gotten in the room? He was certain Rachel had locked the door.

"Edward, don't!" Rachel grabbed for the sheet.

Gabe caught a small, flailing elbow. "I'm not hurting her, Edward."

A monumental blow, much harder than the rest, landed on the side of his head. "My name's not —"

"Chip!" Gabe gasped.

"I'll kill you!" the boy sobbed, then clobbered him again.

"Stop that right this minute, Edward Stone! Do you hear me!" Rachel had steel in her voice.

The boy slowly grew still.

She softened her tone. "Gabe isn't hurting me, Edward."

"Then what's he doing?"

For the first time since they'd met, Rachel seemed to be at a loss for words.

He turned his head and saw rumpled hair, along with red, tearstained cheeks. "I was kissing her, Ed . . . Chip."

A horrified expression came over the child's face. "Don't you *ever* do that again."

Gabe knew his weight was making it difficult for Rachel to breathe, but she spoke as soothingly as she could manage. "It's all right, Edward. I like it when Gabe kisses me."

"No, you *don't!*"

They clearly weren't getting anywhere, so Gabe spoke firmly. "Chip, I want you to go to the kitchen and get your mother a big glass of water. She's very thirsty."

The child gave him a mulish look.

"Please do what he says, Edward. I really need a drink of water."

The child reluctantly climbed off the bed, at the same time shooting Gabe a wordless tight-lipped warning that promised annihilation if he threatened his mother.

The moment he disappeared through the doorway, Gabe and Rachel leaped from the bed and began frantically grabbing for their clothes. Gabe yanked on his jeans. Rachel snatched up his T-shirt and jerked it over her head, then searched the floor for her panties. When she couldn't find them, she pulled on his briefs instead. It should have been funny, but all he cared about was being dressed before the boy returned.

He yanked up his zipper. "I thought you locked the door."

"No. I thought you did it."

The boy appeared in record time, running so quickly that water slopped over the sides of the blue plastic Bugs Bunny tumbler.

As Rachel moved forward to take it from him, she stumbled on something. Gabe looked down and recognized a copy of *Stellaluna* lying on the floor. It took him a moment to figure out why it was there, and then he realized this was what Edward had used to beat him over the head.

He'd been assaulted with a deadly book.

CHAPTER
SEVENTEEN

Rachel made a great play out of drinking the water. When she was done, she cupped the top of Edward's head. "Let's tuck you back in bed."

Gabe stepped forward. He knew this had to be settled before she shuffled him off. He eyed the small boy, remembering the fury of those young fists and, for a fleeting moment, he saw the child as he was and not as a shadow of someone else.

"Chip, I like your mother very much, and I'd never hurt her. I want you to remember that. If you see us touching each other again, you'll know it's because we want to touch and not because anything's wrong."

Edward gave his mother a look of disbelief. "How could you want to touch *him?*"

"I know it's hard for you to understand, especially since you and Gabe haven't been getting along very well, but I like being with him."

The boy regarded her mutinously. "If you got to touch somebody, *you touch me!*"

She smiled. "I love touching you. But I'm a grown-up woman, Edward, and sometimes I need to touch a grown-up man."

"Then you can touch Pastor Ethan."

Rachel had the nerve to laugh. "I don't think so, pug. Pastor Ethan is your friend, and Gabe is mine."

"They're *not* brothers, no matter what he says."

"Tomorrow when you see Pastor Ethan at school, why don't you ask him about it?"

Gabe noticed that his briefs were in imminent danger of sliding off Rachel's hips. "Come on, Chip. Let's give Tweety Bird one more feeding before you go back to bed."

But Edward was too smart to be bought off that easily. "How do I know you won't start kissing her again?"

"I will kiss her," he said firmly, "but only when your mother says it's okay."

"It's *not* okay!" Edward stomped toward the door. "And I'm going to tell Pastor Ethan on you!"

"Terrific," Gabe muttered. "That's just what we need."

Pastor Ethan, however, had troubles of his own. It was eleven o'clock in the morning, and not even half a cup of coffee remained in the pot he and Kristy shared.

It wasn't as if he didn't know how to make coffee. He made it for himself every morning at home. But this wasn't home. This was the office, and for the past eight years, Kristy had kept the pot full.

He snatched up the glass carafe, stormed past her desk, and made his way to the small kitchen just off the narthex, where he splashed water all over his new Gap polo. He stomped back into the office, pitched out the old grounds, threw some new in without counting the scoops, poured in the water, and punched the switch. There! That ought to show her!

Unfortunately, she was too busy humming an old Whitney Houston tune and tapping away at her computer to notice. He couldn't decide which was worse: the coffee, that cheerful humming, or the fact that she was wearing her old clothes to work.

Her shapeless khaki dress was driving him even crazier than the empty coffee pot. He'd seen it dozens of times before. It was roomy, comfortable, and utterly devoid of style. Where were the clothes he objected to? Those tight white jeans, the skimpy breast-hugging tops, those silly gold sandals?

And if she'd decided to turn herself back into the old Kristy, why hadn't she gone all the way? Why hadn't she tamed that little feathery haircut of hers and left her red lipstick in the drawer at home, along with that killer perfume that made him think of black lace and body heat?

As her hands flew over the keyboard of her computer, the tiny gold and silver rings on her fingers flashed in the sunlight that streamed in from the window behind her, while those fake diamond studs glimmered in her earlobes. His gaze fell on the bodice of her ugly khaki dress. If only he didn't know what nestled beneath it.

Think of other things, dear, Marion Cunningham advised in her sweet, understanding voice. *Concentrate on your sermon. I'm sure if you give it just a little more effort, it will be your best yet.*

He flinched. Why did the great Mother have to show up just when he was thinking about breasts?

The tapping stopped. Kristy rose from her desk, glanced over at him, and ducked out of the office to head for the rest room down the hall.

As soon as she got home, he knew she'd take off that ugly dress and slip into one of her new pairs of shorts and a top that showed off too much. And he wouldn't be there to see it because she'd made it more than clear that she didn't want him at her condo. No more home-cooked meals, no more dropping by to spill out his troubles about an unreasonable parishioner. Jeez, he missed her. He missed his friend.

He stared at her empty desk and thought about how she'd gone out to dinner with Mike Reedy again last night. That was twice now. On Saturday, Mike had taken her to a restaurant in Cashiers, and last night they'd eaten in the Mountaineer's dining room. Three people in the congregation had made sure he found out about it.

She wasn't back yet, and his skin grew clammy. He knew where she kept her purse. In the bottom left drawer, along with a small box of tissues and a first-aid kit. All his life, even during his wild days, he'd tried to behave honorably, and what he wanted to do wasn't honorable at all, but he couldn't seem to stop himself.

He shot across the office, jerked open the drawer, and pulled out her purse, the same little black number she'd taken to the Mountaineer last week when they'd had their disastrous conversation and she'd told him he wasn't her friend.

A real minister, someone who wasn't so flawed, someone with a true calling, would never do this. He flipped open the catch and looked inside. Wallet, comb, Tic Tacs, some makeup, car keys, a *Daily Word* devotional book. No condom.

He heard her footsteps, shoved the purse back in the drawer, and pulled out the first-aid kit.

"Is something wrong?"

A few minutes earlier, the expression of concern on her face would have lightened his mood, but not now. "Just a headache."

"Go sit down. I'll bring you some aspirin."

He handed her the first-aid kit and, for the first time all week, she started fussing over him, bringing him a glass of water, giving him the aspirin, asking if he'd gotten enough sleep last night. Unfortunately, her fussing didn't feel nearly as good as it should have because he couldn't remember a single time when she'd mentioned a headache and he'd brought her aspirin.

What had happened to that condom? Just the thought of her passing it over to Mike Reedy made him feel sick. Part of him knew he should be happy that she might have found someone, but not Mike Reedy, even though he'd always liked Mike and couldn't think of a single thing wrong with him, except that he shouldn't be making love with Kristy Brown.

After he'd swallowed the aspirin he didn't need, he gazed at her and wondered why it had taken him so long to notice how pretty she was. Not in a flashy way, even when she got dressed up, but in a quiet, sweet way.

"You know the drive-in's opening Friday night," he found himself saying.

"I just hope someone shows up. A lot of people in town are angry with Gabe for helping Rachel, and they're talking about a boycott." Kristy looked worried. "People can be so mean."

He spoke casually. "We both want to be at the drive-in on Friday night when it opens, so why don't I pick you up at eight?"

Kristy stared at him. "You want to go to the drive-in together?"

"Sure. How else are we going to show Gabe our support?"

The telephone rang on his desk. Kristy studied it for a moment before she finally picked it up. He soon realized she was talking to Patty Wells, the coordinator of the day-care center.

"Yes, Ethan's here. Of course. Send Edward right up, Patty."

She replaced the receiver and frowned. "He's been asking all morning to come talk to you. Patty tried to distract him, but he wouldn't give up. I hope nothing's wrong."

Both of them had been around Edward long enough to know that he never demanded anything, and they shared a wordless moment of concern.

Kristy returned to the outer office, and, a few minutes later, showed Edward in. She gave Ethan a worried look, one of a hundred they'd shared over the years when she'd ushered a troubled parishioner into his office. Then she retreated.

"You can shut the door if you want some privacy," Ethan said.

Edward hesitated and looked out at Kristy. Ethan knew how fond he was of her, and he was surprised when Edward pressed the door closed with both hands. Whatever was on his mind was obviously serious stuff.

Ethan had never liked the impersonality of talking across a desk, and he walked around to a small seating area near the window that held a couch and two comfortable chairs.

Edward climbed up onto the middle cushion of the couch and slid back into the seat, which made his legs stick out in front of him. He had a smear of red paint on the toe of one sneaker. Ethan had noticed how clean Rachel kept his worn clothes, which led him to believe the paint had come from that morning's art project.

Edward automatically reached out for something at his side, and, when he encountered only air, scratched his elbow. The stuffed rabbit, Ethan guessed.

"What's on your mind, Edward?"

"Gabe's a big liar. He says he's your brother."

Ethan began to correct him, but the deep unhappiness in the boy's expression made him hesitate. "Why do you think he's lying?"

"Because he's a butthead, and I hate him."

Ethan had been counseling troubled people for years, and he forced himself to detach so he could rephrase the boy's words. "Sounds like you don't like Gabe too much."

310

Edward shook his head vigorously. "My mommy shouldn't like him either."

Ditto to that, buddy. "I guess it upsets you that your mother likes him."

"I told her she can touch me instead, but she said she wants to touch a grown man, too."

I'll just bet she does. Especially a grown man with a hefty bank account and a casual attitude toward his money.

"I even said you'd let her touch *you*, Pastor Ethan, but she said you was my friend and Gabe was hers, and she said she wanted to kiss him and I had to stop hitting him."

Kissing him? Hitting him? It took a moment for Ethan to figure out which question to ask. "You were hitting Gabe?"

"I jumped on his back when he was kissing her, and I kept hitting him with *Stellaluna* till he let her go."

If he'd been hearing this story about anyone else, he would have been amused, but not about his brother. He knew he shouldn't ask, but he couldn't help it. "Where was Gabe when you jumped on his back?"

"Squishing my mommy."

"Squishing her?"

"You know. On top of her. Squishing her."

Damn.

Edward's brown eyes filled with tears. "He's a bad man, and I want you to make him go away, and I want you to let my mommy touch you instead."

Ethan pushed aside his own concerns and moved to the couch where he slipped his arm around the boy's shoulders. "It doesn't work that way with grown-ups," he said gently. "Your mom and Gabe are friends."

"He was squishing her!"

Ethan forced himself to speak evenly. "They're grown-ups, and that means they can squish each other if they want to. And Edward, that doesn't mean your mom doesn't love you just as much as always. You know that, don't you?"

The child thought it over. "I guess."

"You might not be getting along with Gabe right now, but he's really a good person."

"He's a butthead."

"He's had some bad things happen to him, and it makes him grouchy, but he's not bad."

"What bad things?"

Ethan hesitated, then decided the child should know the truth. "He had a wife and a little boy he loved very much. They died in an accident a while ago. He's still very sad about it."

Edward didn't say anything for a long time. Finally, he slid closer and let his head slump against Ethan's chest.

Ethan rubbed the boy's arm and thought about the mystery of God's ways. Here he was comforting the son of a man he'd despised and a woman he disliked, so why did he feel comforted himself?

"Gabe really is my brother," he said quietly. "I love him very much."

The child stiffened, but didn't draw away. "He's mean."

It was difficult for Ethan to fathom how his gentle brother could be unkind to this precious little boy. "I want you to think really hard. Isn't there anything nice Gabe has done for you?"

Edward began to shake his head, then stopped. "There's one thing."

"What's that?"

"He calls me Chip now."

Fifteen minutes later, Ethan was on the phone to Cal. Without breaking the confidentiality of his conversation with Edward, he let his oldest brother know they had big trouble on their hands.

"Giving out any free samples, bro?"

Rachel's head lifted as a deep male voice came from the doorway of the snack shop.

"Cal!" Gabe dropped the carton of buns he'd been carrying and shot out from behind the counter to greet the man who looked so very much like him. As the two slapped each other on the back, Rachel studied Cal Bonner and wonder what combination of genes had landed three lady-killers in the same family.

Unlike Ethan, Cal and Gabe's dark coloring and rough-hewed good looks clearly identified them as brothers. Gabe's hair was longer, his silvery-gray eyes lighter than Cal's, but both men were tall, lean, and muscular. Although she knew the ex-quarterback was the elder brother by almost two years, he looked younger. Maybe it was the general air of contentment he seemed to carry with him like an invisible football.

"You should have let me know you were coming," Gabe said.

"You didn't think I'd miss the grand opening tonight, did you?"

"It's just a drive-in, Cal."

His words stung. It wasn't just a drive-in to her. She wanted this old place to shine tonight.

All day, she'd been busy training Kayla, the young woman Gabe had hired to help out in the snack shop. She'd also been teaching Gabe the rudiments so he could help out during intermission. He caught on quickly, but she knew he was merely going through the motions. He should be healing animals, not serving up fast-food nachos.

"Want some coffee?" Gabe asked his brother. "Or ice cream. I'm getting to be a pro at making cones."

"No, thanks. Rosie started kicking up right after we left Asheville — she hates her car seat worse than poison — and I need to get back to the mausoleum to give Jane a hand."

Rachel didn't have to think hard to figure out what the mausoleum was.

Cal went on, his manner a shade too hearty. "I just stopped by to tell you Jane's decided to have a family brunch for you and Eth tomorrow around eleven to celebrate your new business. Think you can make it?"

"Sure."

"And Gabe, don't tell Jane I mentioned this, but if I were you, I'd eat something first. Knowing my wife, we'll probably be getting wheat-germ muffins and tofu casserole. You should see the garbage she feeds Rosie —

314

no sugar, no preservatives, nothing worth eating. Last week Jane caught me shaking out a few of my Lucky Charms on Rosie's high-chair tray, and she about took my head right off."

Gabe smiled. "I stand warned."

"This place looks terrific." Cal eyed the snack shop as if it were a four-star restaurant. "You sure have done a lot with it."

Rachel could barely conceal her disgust. He was as bad as Ethan. She might love this drive-in, but it was clearly wrong for Gabe. Why couldn't one of his brothers look him in the face and ask him exactly what he thought he was doing with his life?

For the first time, Cal noticed her. His smile faded before it had fully formed, and, even though they'd never met, she knew he'd figured out who she was.

"Rachel, this is my brother Cal. Cal, Rachel Stone."

Cal gave her a brusque nod. "Miz Snopes."

She smiled pleasantly. "Nice to meet you, Hal."

"It's Cal."

"Ah." She continued to smile.

Cal's mouth tightened, and she regretted her flippancy. This was clearly a man who thrived on battle, and she had thrown down the gauntlet.

After the incident with Cal, what was left of the afternoon went steadily downhill. Kayla dropped a huge jar of salsa, splattering it everywhere, one of the men setting up the fireworks display cut his hand badly enough to need stitches, and Gabe withdrew into himself. Later, when Rachel ran into town to pick up Edward, an old Chevy Lumina shot out from a side street and nearly hit her. As she laid on her horn, she glimpsed the hostile face of Bobby Dennis behind the wheel. Once again, she wondered how she could have sparked so much animosity in someone so young.

That night, Edward ran in and out of the snack shop as cars began to trickle into the lot. "I get to stay up as late as I want. Right, Mommy?"

"As late as you want." She smiled as she poured kernels into the popcorn machine. The fireworks display didn't start until dark, and she doubted if he'd stay awake for much of the goofy Jim Carrey crowd-pleaser that was the first feature.

A couple with several young children came through the door, their first customers, and she concentrated on helping Kayla fill the order. Not long after, a rowdy trio of teenagers walked in. One of them was Bobby Dennis. Rachel was waiting on an elderly man and his wife, so Kayla took care of them, but before they left, Rachel made a point of speaking. "I hope you enjoy the movies tonight."

He glared at her as if she'd cursed at him.

She shrugged. Whatever grudge this boy had against her, he wasn't going to give it up easily.

They did a steady stream of business, although not as much as she'd anticipated, and when the fireworks began, she glanced outside to see that the lot was barely half full. Since there wasn't much to do in Salvation on a Friday night, she knew a lot of people in town were making it clear that Gabe had to pay the consequences for hiring her.

Edward fell asleep not long after the Carrey movie began. His protest when she awakened him was unconvincing. As he leaned against her side while she helped him up the metal stairs, uneasiness over what she was doing to Gabe combined with worry about her own future. Dwayne's Bible hadn't revealed a single clue, and she was beginning to lose hope that it would. Maybe Gabe was right and the money had gone down in the plane with Dwayne.

She looked at her sleepy son. Gabe was making an effort to get along better with him. He'd taught Edward how to feed Tweety Bird without damaging the bird's soft beak and taken him on a walk in the woods near the cave where the bats lived, but Gabe's heart wasn't in it, and the atmosphere in the cottage grew more strained each day. She knew she had to do something soon.

Tom, the projectionist, smiled as she made her way through the projection room and tucked Edward into the sleeping bag she'd placed on the floor of Gabe's office. A boisterous man with a slew of grandchildren, he'd promised to let Rachel know if Edward woke up.

As she descended the stairs, she saw Gabe coming out of the snack shop. At the same time, a man she dimly recognized, although she couldn't immediately recall his identity, stepped from the shadows. "Doesn't look like you've got a full house tonight, Bonner."

Gabe shrugged. "Can't have a full house every night."

"Especially with the Widow Snopes working for you."

Gabe seemed to stiffen. "Why don't you mind your own business, Scudder?"

"Whatever you say." With a sneer, he walked away.

Russ Scudder. He'd lost a lot of hair since Rachel had last seen him and some weight, too. She remembered a more muscular man.

Gabe looked up as she came the rest of the way down the steps. "Russ used to work security at the Temple," she said.

"I know. I hired him to help out here, but I had to fire him after a couple of weeks. He wasn't reliable."

"He's right about what's happened. We should have had a bigger crowd. You're being punished because of me."

"It doesn't matter."

She knew it didn't, not to him, and that bothered her as much as the empty spaces. It should matter. "I wonder why he came tonight?"

"Probably needed a dark place to get drunk."

He moved off toward a car of noisy teenagers, and she returned to the snack shop to get ready for intermission. He reappeared to help out just as the first feature came to an end.

A line formed, but not a long enough one to give them trouble. Both of Gabe's brothers appeared to pick up food. Cal ordered two of everything, so she gathered that his wife was back in the car with their baby.

Ethan ordered double, too, but since Kayla was waiting on him, Rachel didn't notice. If she had, she might have been tempted to slip outside and see who he'd brought with him.

318

CHAPTER
EIGHTEEN

Ethan passed the tray of food to Kristy through the window of his car, then opened the door and slid behind the wheel. He immediately caught a hint of her perfume. Tonight it reminded him of black lace and a rumba, which was ridiculous because he'd never done a rumba in his life and didn't intend to.

He closed the car door. "They had those big chocolate-chip cookies, so I got a couple of them."

"That's fine." She spoke in the cool, polite voice she'd been using all evening, as if he were her boss, not her friend.

The tiny rings on her fingers glimmered from the flood-lights that had been turned on for intermission. He watched anxiously as she set the food between them and unwrapped her hot dog. He'd put mustard on it because that was how he liked his hot dogs, but the truth was, he didn't have any idea whether she liked mustard. They'd eaten a couple of thousand lunches together over the past eight years, but he couldn't seem to remember what she'd eaten at any of them, except he thought he recalled some salads.

"They didn't have any salad."

She regarded him quizzically. "Of course they didn't."

He felt like an idiot. "I wasn't sure whether you'd rather have regular mustard or spicy brown." He waited. "They had both kinds."

"This is fine."

"Maybe you like ketchup better?"

"It doesn't matter."

"And relish. Did you want relish?" He set his own hot dog down. "I can go back and get some."

"That's not necessary."

"Really? Because I don't mind." He had the door half open when she stopped him.

"Ethan, I hate hot dogs!"

"Oh." He closed the door and sank back into the seat, feeling foolish and depressed. On the drive-in screen, a clock, accompanied by marching sodas, ticked away the intermission time. He felt as if it were marking off the minutes of his life.

"I love chocolate-chip cookies, though."

He shook his head. "I've proved everything you threw at me the night at the Mountaineer, haven't I? I don't know anything about you."

"You know that I don't like hot dogs," she said gently.

She could have been bitchy, but she was being nice. It was one of so many good things about her. Why had it taken him so long to notice? He'd gone through most of his life barely thinking about Kristy Brown, and now he couldn't think about anybody else.

She wrapped her hot dog back up, returned it to the bag, and picked up a chocolate-chip cookie. Before she took a bite, she opened a paper napkin and spread it over the lap of her jeans. The jeans, along with her plain white blouse, had disappointed him. He supposed she'd decided to save her short skirts and tight tops for Mike Reedy.

He pulled the paper off his straw and punched it through the lid covering his large Cherry Coke. "So, I hear you and Mike are seeing each other." He tried to sound casual, as if the topic were of no more interest to him than last week's weather.

"He's a very nice person."

"Yeah, I guess." Tendrils of silky dark hair curled around her cheeks. He wanted to brush them back, and, for a moment, he imagined doing it with his lips.

She gazed at him. "What?"

"Nothing."

"Say it." She sounded impatient. "I know when you have something on your mind."

"It's just — Mike's a great guy, don't get me wrong, but — In high school, he was a little — I don't know. Maybe a little wild or something." For someone who was a pro at public speaking, he was making a mess of this.

"Wild? Mike?"

"Not now." He was starting to sweat. "No, it's like I said, he's a great guy, but he can be a little . . . spacey. You know. Distractible."

"So?"

"So." His throat was dry, and he took a sip of Cherry Coke. "I just thought you should know."

"I should know that he's distractible?"

"Yes."

"All right. Thanks for telling me." She bit into one side of the chocolate-chip cookie. Neat. No crumbs dribbled over the upholstery. He realized how much he liked Kristy's orderliness. Not just because she made things easier for him, but because his own interior world was so often chaotic, and she calmed him.

He wasn't calm now, however. That black-lace rumba perfume was getting to him, along with her neat white blouse buttoned all the way to the neck. Even as he told himself to change the subject, he plunged in again. "I mean, if he's driving or something, he might get . . . You know."

"Distracted?"

"Yes."

She set the cookie on her napkin, those seductive little finger rings glimmering. "Okay, Ethan. What's this about? All evening you've been acting strange."

She was right, so he didn't know why he was suddenly so angry with her. "Me? You're the one who decided to show up wearing jeans!" Only after the words had left his mouth did he realize how inappropriate they were.

"You're wearing jeans, too," she pointed out patiently. "Granted, you ironed yours, and I didn't, but —"

"That's not the point, and you know it."

"No, I don't know it. What are you trying to say?" She added the cookie to their growing pile of discarded food.

"Did you wear jeans the last time you went on a date with Mike?"

"No."

"Then why are you wearing them with me?"

"Because this isn't a date?"

"It's Friday night, and we're parked in the next-to-last row of the Pride of Carolina! I'd say that's a date, wouldn't you?"

Her eyes snapped, no longer gentle at all. "Excuse me? Are you telling me that, after all these years, the great Ethan Bonner finally asked me out on a date, and I didn't even *know* it?"

"Well, that's not my fault, is it? And what do you mean, *finally?*"

He heard a long labored sigh before she spoke. "Just what is it you want from me?"

How could he answer that? Should he say, "I want your friendship," or "I want the body you've been hiding away all these years"? No, definitely not that. This was Kristy, for pete's sake. Maybe he should just tell her she had no right to keep changing around on him, and he wanted things back the way they were, but that wasn't true. At the moment, he only knew one thing. "I don't want you sleeping with Mike Reedy."

"Who said I was?"

The fake diamond studs flashed in her earlobes. She was mad at him. Well, fine, he was mad at her, too, so what difference did the truth make? "I looked in your purse this week. The condom you had in there is gone."

"You looked in my purse? Mr. Honest Ethan?"

The fact that she seemed confused, rather than angry, took some of the wind out of his sails. "I apologize. It won't ever happen again. I was just —" He set aside his Coke. "I was just worried about you. You shouldn't be sleeping with Mike Reedy."

"Then who should I be sleeping with?"

"No one!"

She got all stiff and starchy. "I'm sorry, Ethan, but that's no longer an option for me."

"I sleep alone. I don't see why you can't, too!"

"Because I can't, that's all, not any longer. At least you have a seedy past to look back on. I don't even have that."

"It wasn't seedy! Well, maybe it was, but — Just wait for the right man, Kristy. Don't give yourself away cheaply. When the right man comes along, you'll know it."

"Maybe I know it right now."

"Mike Reedy isn't the right man!"

"How do you know that? You can't even remember that I hate hot dogs. You don't know when my birthday is or my favorite singer. How would you know who the right man is for me?"

"Your birthday is April eleventh."

"Sixteenth."

"See! I knew it was in April!"

She arched one fine eyebrow at him, then took such a deep breath he suspected she was counting to ten. "I took the condom out of my purse because I felt stupid carrying it around."

"So you and Mike haven't . . ."

"Not yet. But we might. I really like him."

"*Like* isn't good enough. You like me, too, but that doesn't mean you're going to have sex with me."

"Of course I'm not."

He felt a stab of disappointment. "Of course not."

"How could I? You're celibate."

Exactly what did she mean by that? That if he weren't celibate, she might consider it?

"And," she went on, "you're not attracted to me."

"That's not true. You're my —"

"Don't you say it!" Feathery tendrils flew and the fake diamond studs flashed. "Don't you dare say I'm your best friend, because I'm not!"

He felt as if she'd punched him. Much of his job involved counseling others. He understood the complexity of human behavior far more than most people, so why was he so clueless about her?

The clock on the screen ticked off its final minutes. He'd always been tenacious, but she'd somehow taken the fight out of him. He knew he was hurting her, even if he didn't understand exactly how, and the last thing he wanted was to hurt Kristy Brown.

"Kristy, what's happening to you?"

"Life is happening to me," she said softly. "Finally."

"What does that mean?"

Her silence lasted so long he didn't think she would answer, but she did. "It means I've finally stopped living in the past. I'm ready to move on with my life."

She looked over at him in a way that made him think she was engaged in some internal struggle. "It means I'm not going to be in love with you anymore, Ethan."

He felt as if a jolt of electricity had passed right through him, except he didn't know why he should be shocked. At some unconscious level, he supposed he'd known she was in love with him, but he hadn't let himself think about it.

She gave a soft, self-deprecating laugh that made him ache. "I've been so pathetic. All that wasted time. For eight years I sat at my desk, Little Miss Efficiency, bustling around to find your car keys and make sure you had milk in the refrigerator, and you never even noticed. I had so little regard for myself."

He had no idea what to say.

"Do you know what's really ironic?" There was no bitterness in her voice. She spoke calmly, almost as if she were talking about someone else. "I would have been the perfect woman for you, but you never noticed. And now it's too late."

"What do you mean, the perfect woman?" *And why was it too late?*

She regarded him sadly, as if his failure to understand disappointed her. "We have the same interests, similar backgrounds. I like looking after people, and you need looking after. We share the same religious beliefs." A slight shrug. "But none of that mattered because I wasn't hot enough for you."

"Hot enough! What kind of thing is that to say? Do you think that's all I look for in a woman?"

"Yes. And please don't patronize me. We've known each other too long."

He got mad. "Now I get it. That's what all of these changes have been about. The tight clothes, the new hairstyle, that damned perfume. You got yourself fixed up so I'd notice, didn't you? Well, I noticed, all right, and I hope you're happy about it."

The Wise God of Talk Shows clucked her tongue. *Ethan . . . Ethan . . . Ethan . . .*

Instead of retaliating as she should have, Kristy smiled.

"It's a good thing you did notice, or I'm not sure how long it would have taken me to come to my senses."

"What are you talking about?"

"It's so fundamental, Ethan. So trite. But I guess the simple truths are always like that, aren't they? Rachel warned me when this started that, if I wanted to make changes, I needed to make them for myself and not for you or anyone else. I pretended to agree with her, but I didn't really understand how right she was until that day I showed up for work all dressed to kill and you were so appalled with me."

"Kristy, I wasn't —"

She held up her hand. "It's okay, Ethan. I'm not upset about it any longer. I'm even grateful. Your rejection pushed me to do some things with my life I've needed to do all along."

"I didn't reject you! And I don't see how you can just instantly fall out of love with somebody you said you've loved for years." What was he doing? Was he trying to talk her into loving him?

"You're right. You can't." He felt a tiny spurt of hope, but it was quickly dashed as she went on. "Now I know that it hasn't been love. That needs to work two ways. What I've felt for you was infatuation, obsession. You've been my fatal attraction."

And now you are one boiled bunny, the Mighty Talk Show Host pointed out.

"I think you're giving up on us too easily," he heard himself saying.

"What are you talking about?"

"Our relationship."

"Ethan, we don't *have* a relationship."

"Yes, we do! How long have we known each other? Since — what, sixth grade?"

"I was in third grade. You were in fourth. Our classrooms were across the hall from each other."

He nodded, as if he'd known that, but the truth was, he didn't remember.

"You and Ricky Jenkins came plowing out of the door one day after school, and Ricky crashed into me." She began packing up their untouched food, her movements automatic. "I was carrying some books and a salt map of Mexico. I fell, the books went everywhere, Mexico cracked. I was so shy then. I hated for anyone to notice me, and, of course, I was mortified. Ricky ran right on, but you stopped and helped me pick everything up. When Ricky looked back and saw what you were doing, he yelled out, 'Don't touch her, Eth. You'll get cooties.' "

328

She looked over at him, and a small smile curled her lips. "I wanted to die when he said that, but you didn't pay any attention, even though some of the other boys had started to laugh. You took my arm and helped me get up, then you handed me my books and told me I could probably fix Mexico without too much trouble."

The clock on the screen had disappeared, and the second feature was about to begin. She folded her hands in her lap, as if that were the end of it, and he could feel her slipping away from him.

"Did you?"

"What?"

"Fix Mexico?"

She smiled. "I don't remember."

An ache filled him, a desire to make things better for the shy little girl Ricky Jenkins had knocked down. Ethan's hand seemed to have a will of its own as it slipped along the back of the seat and curved around the nape of her neck.

Her lips parted. Startled. The floodlights went out, plunging the lot into darkness.

He pushed the food sack out of the way, leaned forward, and kissed her. A pity kiss. A healing kiss. All better.

And then something inexplicable happened. As he felt those soft lips move beneath his own, the world split open and music exploded in his head, not Handel choruses or Puccini operas, but the raw shriek of dirty, sweaty, throbbing, feel-her-up, toss-her-down, come-on, come-on, *Come On Baaaaby!* rock 'n' roll.

His hands were all over her. Kneading her breasts, pulling at buttons, tugging at her bra clasp, delving into that sweet, plump flesh. And she wasn't resisting. Oh, no, she wasn't resisting at all. His lips found a small, puckered nipple offered up to him.

Her quick, efficient hands flew under his shirt, yanking it out of his neatly pressed jeans and playing feverish tracks on his back, while her breathy moans flamed his passion with fast, hot riffs.

He shoved his hand between her legs, cupping her through the denim. She pushed against him in a needy little bump and grind that took away his reason. He worked her zipper. She worked his.

The dirty backbeat of her tongue pulsed in his mouth, doing what he wanted to do. Had to do.

Skin. Soft, damp with perspiration. And then wetness. He sank into it with his fingers.

She had him in her hands, played a throbbing lick that pushed him to the edge of oblivion.

Where are You now? his mind screamed. *Why aren't You telling me to stop?* He waited for the Enforcer God, the Wise God, the Mother God, but he heard only silence.

"Stop," Kristy whispered.

His fingers were inside her body; her hand encircled him. "Stop," she said again.

But neither of them wanted to let the other go.

She shuddered, and he realized how close she was to falling over the edge. Her voice caught on a husky note. "You can't do this, Ethan."

Her dearness swept through him like a clean, cool breeze. She was worrying about him, as always. Never thinking about herself.

It had been a very long time, but he hadn't forgotten what to do. He drew her closer and moved his thumb . . . gentle circles. She gasped. He kissed her, and with all the tenderness in his heart, he let her fall.

Afterward, neither of them wanted to talk. They readjusted their clothes, moved apart, cleaned up his spilled Cherry Coke, pretended to watch the movie. He drove her home and wasn't surprised when she didn't ask him in, but as he opened the car door for her, he found himself inviting her to his sister-in-law's brunch the next day.

"No, thank you," she said politely.

"I'll pick you up a little before eleven."

"I won't be here."

"Yes," he replied firmly. "You will."

The phone rang as Rachel began to dry her hair from her morning shower. Gabe was in the backyard banging away at something, and Edward played on the front porch, so she wrapped the towel around her head and dashed to the kitchen to answer.

"May I speak with Rachel Snopes, please?" a woman said.

"This is Rachel *Stone* speaking."

A baby fussed in the background, and the woman's voice faded slightly. "It's all right, Rosie. I'm right here." Once again, she spoke directly into the receiver. "I'm sorry, Ms. Stone, but my daughter hasn't quite recovered from our car trip yesterday. We didn't get a chance to meet last night at the drive-in. I'm Jane Darlington Bonner, Cal's wife."

The woman's voice was businesslike, but not hostile. "Yes, Mrs. Bonner?"

"Please. Call me Jane. I'm having a family gathering in an hour or so. I apologize for the late notice — to be honest, I'm pretty much throwing the whole thing together at the last minute — but I'd like you and your son to come."

Rachel remembered Cal's visit to the snack shop yesterday afternoon. She'd been standing right there when he'd invited Gabe, and it would have been easy for him to include her in the invitation if he'd wanted to.

"Thank you, but it's probably not a good idea."

"You obviously met my husband yesterday." The lilt in her voice contained nothing but good humor.

"Yes."

"Come anyway."

Rachel smiled and felt herself warming to this woman she'd only seen in a magazine photograph. "It's not just your husband. Ethan's not too crazy about me, either."

"I know."

"And I very much doubt that Gabe wants me drawn any closer into his family circle. I think I'd better pass."

"I won't press, but I hope you change your mind. Cal and Ethan are two of the most pigheaded men on earth, but they mean well, and I'm dying to meet the notorious Widow Snopes."

Rachel found herself responding to the woman's gentle humor with a laugh. "Come up to the cottage anytime."

"I'll do that."

She had just hung up when Gabe walked in from the backyard. A trace of sawdust clung to his jeans, and he looked happier than he had in days.

She smiled at him. "What are you doing out there?"

"Building a little aviary. Tweety Bird's going to have to get acclimated to the outdoors before we can release him."

All this for one small, very common sparrow?

He walked over to the sink and turned on the water to wash his hands. "I asked Chip if he wanted to help, but he said no."

"Will you stop calling him that?"

"Not till he tells me to." He grabbed a paper towel and came over to give her a good-morning kiss. It was fleeting, but the casual intimacy made her remember last night's lovemaking. Now she laid her cheek against his chest and tried not to think about how soon this had to end.

His fingers captured a lock of her hair and looped it behind her ear. He kissed the place it had been, then stepped back. "We have to be at Cal and Jane's soon, and I still need to shower, so stop distracting me."

"We?"

"You know that I don't want you here alone."

Disappointment settled over her as she realized there was nothing personal in his invitation. He didn't want her drawn into his family; he was merely doing guard-dog duty. The bedroom was the only private place she occupied in Gabe's life, and he'd never promised her anything more.

"I don't think that's a good idea. I'd have a hard time eating with both your brothers shooting daggers at me."

"I haven't seen you run from a fight yet."

"Gabe, they hate my guts!"

"That's their problem. I have to go, and you're not staying here by yourself."

She concealed her hurt behind a smile. "All right. It might be fun to torture your odious brothers."

CHAPTER
NINETEEN

An hour later, they passed through black wrought-iron gates embellished with gold praying hands. Edward, who sat between Gabe and Rachel in the front seat of the truck, was subdued as he caught sight of the large white mansion. "Did I really live here, Mom?"

"You really did."

"It's big."

She started to say that it was ugly, too, but restrained herself. She tried not to make negative remarks to Edward about Dwayne and their life together.

Dr. Jane Darlington Bonner greeted them at the door, the baby in her arms and the spot of flour on her cheek making her look more like a Pillsbury Bake-off contestant than a world-renowned physicist. She had the classic good looks of someone who came from old money, but from a passing reference Gabe had made, Rachel knew her background was firmly middle-class. Her blond hair was pulled into a loose French braid, and she wore matching peach-colored shorts and top. Her stylish outfit made Rachel uncomfortably conscious of her own faded green-and-white-checked housedress and clunky black oxfords.

Jane, however, didn't seem to notice. She greeted Gabe with a kiss, then gave Rachel a welcoming smile. "I'm so glad you came. And you must be Edward."

"Chip," Gabe interjected to Rachel's annoyance. "Chip Stone."

Jane lifted one blond eyebrow in amusement. "I'm delighted to meet you, Chip. This is Rosie. She's been cranky ever since yesterday."

But Rosie didn't look cranky. As the nine-month-old baby caught sight of Edward, she gave a squeal of delight that revealed four tiny teeth. Her chubby legs began to pump and her bottom lip glimmered with baby drool as she reached out for him.

"She likes me," Edward said with wonder.

"It's a good thing," Jane replied, "because she doesn't like anybody else right now. Even her daddy can't do anything with her. Tell you what. Everybody's in the kitchen. I'll try putting her down on the floor, and maybe you could play with her. Would that be okay?"

Edward nodded eagerly. "She can even play with Horse."

Rachel had to give Jane credit. She barely blanched at the sight of the grimy, germ-ridden, one-eyed rabbit being thrust toward her bright-eyed, clean-smelling, blond-haired baby.

"Great idea."

She led them toward the kitchen, where Cal was pouring orange juice into a pitcher, while Ethan stood next to him uncorking a champagne bottle. Both men called out to Gabe before they noticed her, and then their expressions hardened simultaneously.

Gabe's hand settled protectively over the small of her back. He nodded at his brothers. "Cal. Eth."

"Anything else you want put out on the deck, Jane?" To Rachel's surprise, Kristy came in from the family room. "Hi, Rachel. Hey, Edward." She looked terrific in a loose-fitting plum-colored top and very tight white jeans. Little gold sandals sparkled on her feet. A shadow of uncertainty crossed Ethan's face as she appeared, but Kristy didn't seem to notice, and Rachel had the feeling she was deliberately avoiding looking at him.

While Edward played with Rosie on the black marble floor, and Cal sent Rachel hostile glances, Jane began thrusting various bowls, pitchers, and trays at everyone. "We're eating on the deck. It's one of the few places in this mausoleum where you can get comfortable." She realized what she had said and spun toward Rachel. "Oh, dear. I'm sorry. I've been around Cal so long I've forgotten how to watch my mouth."

"That's all right." Rachel smiled. "It *is* a mausoleum. Everybody knew that but Dwayne."

The stove timer went off, distracting Jane. Cal swept Rosie up from the kitchen floor, where she'd been happily chewing on Horse's grubby ear. She let out an ear-splitting shriek of protest and kicked her hard baby shoes, catching her father in the thigh.

His yelp amused Ethan. "Aim higher next time, Rosie Posie. That'll really get the old man's attention."

Edward retrieved his rabbit from the floor and handed it back to Rosie, who immediately quieted. They all moved through the family room to the deck.

As Rachel stepped outside, she remembered that rainy day a little more than two weeks ago when she and Gabe had first made love. Gabe must have remembered, too, because he turned his head to look at her, and something warm flickered in those cool silver eyes.

Contrary to Cal's warning, Jane didn't serve either wheat-germ muffins or tofu. Instead, they enjoyed a fragrant omelet casserole filled with chunks of mushrooms and tangy bits of apple, along with a fresh-fruit compote, blueberry coffee cake, and some wonderful mimosas.

While the adults gathered around the umbrella table, Edward sat next to the small mesh-sided play yard where Rosie was confined so she didn't get splinters from the deck. Rachel loved watching him as he dangled toys in front of her face, tickled her tummy, and made funny faces to entertain her.

It didn't take Rachel long to see how much Jane and Cal cared for each other. The former quarterback's expression, so unfriendly when he looked at Rachel, grew almost luminous whenever he gazed at his wife. They seemed to make excuses to touch each other: a brush of the hand here, a touch on the arm there, glances exchanged, smiles traded. And they both clearly adored their feisty blond-haired daughter.

But there were also some disturbing undercurrents at the table. Although she was accustomed to Ethan's dislike, Cal's hostility toward her had a colder edge to it, and she suspected he was even more protective of Gabe than his younger brother. To make matters worse, Ethan and Kristy seemed to be going out of their way not to look at each other, and Gabe was so tense she could almost hear him ping. She knew how difficult it was for him to be part of a family gathering when he no longer had a family of his own.

It was Cal who brought up the subject of the drive-in. "Can't believe what you've done with that place."

Ethan jumped in. "He took the biggest eyesore in the county and made it into something."

Both of them went on in falsely hearty tones, telling Gabe how great it was to have the drive-in open again and what a service he was rendering the community. Neither of them referred to Gabe's old life. It was as if his veterinary practice, along with his wife and son, had never existed. And the more they talked, the tenser Gabe became until Rachel couldn't stand it any longer.

"Gabe, tell them about Tweety Bird."

"Nothing much to tell."

"Tweety Bird's a baby sparrow that Gabe's been nursing back to health."

Gabe shrugged, and that small gesture was all his brothers needed to jump in and rescue him from a topic he might not want to discuss.

"That fireworks display went over really big last night. Rosie loved it, didn't she, Jane?"

Ethan nodded. "It was a great idea. And I know the families in this town are going to appreciate having a place to take their kids without spending a bundle."

Acting on pure instinct, Rachel leaned forward. "Gabe's building an aviary in back of the cottage to get the bird acclimated to the outdoors."

Gabe regarded her with irritation. "It's no big deal, Rachel."

Now she had all three Bonner brothers scowling at her. Only Jane and Kristy watched her with interest. "I think it is. Taking care of that scrawny little bird makes you happy. The drive-in doesn't."

"Tweety Bird isn't scrawny!" Edward exclaimed.

Gabe pushed himself abruptly back from the table. "Coffee's running low. I'll make a fresh pot." He disappeared through the patio doors.

Cal leaned back in his chair and stared at her with steely gray eyes. "Are you deliberately trying to make my brother unhappy?"

"Cal . . ."

He reacted to his wife's interjection with a small movement of his hand, wordlessly silencing her. Dr. Jane Darlington Bonner didn't look like the sort of woman who could be easily silenced, so Rachel sensed that her shrug of acceptance was voluntary. Maybe she had decided this confrontation was inevitable and that Rachel was tough enough to take him on.

"I've told Ethan the same thing I'm going to tell you," Rachel said. "Stop pampering him. Running the Pride of Carolina isn't what he should be doing with his life, and both of you need to stop acting as if he's

340

involved in something wonderful. Gabe's a vet, and that's what he needs to be doing."

"You think you know my brother better than his own family?" Cal said coldly.

"Yeah, I guess I do."

Gabe reappeared. "Coffee should be ready soon."

Ethan's gaze flickered from his older brother back to Gabe. "There's a ball in the garage. Let's throw it around while Mr. Quarterback cleans up the kitchen. You want to come with us, Edward?"

Edward took his time replying. "I want to, but if I do, Rosie's gonna cry 'cause she likes me so much, so I guess I'll stay here and play with her."

Rachel could see that her son's decision had won him the affection of Rosie's parents. Both of them smiled and told him he could go on, but Edward politely refused.

Ethan and Gabe stepped down off the deck. Rachel began to clear the table only to have Cal come up behind her and say softly, "Would you mind stepping into the study for a few minutes? I have something to show you."

Going off with him was the last thing she wanted to do, but Jane and Kristy had just disappeared into the kitchen, so there was no one to rescue her. She gave what she hoped looked like a careless shrug and followed him.

When they reached the study, he closed the door behind them. Through the window to her left, she saw the football fly, then Gabe ran into her field of vision to catch it.

Cal walked behind the desk that had once been Dwayne's and pulled open a drawer. "I have something here for you." He withdrew a slip of paper and extended it toward her. Even before her fingers closed around it, she knew that it was a check. She glanced down and drew in her breath.

It was made out to her in the amount of twenty-five thousand dollars.

Her voice croaked. "What's this?"

He settled into the chair and looked up at her. "A down payment on your future."

She stared at it, a sinking feeling in her stomach, knowing the answer to the question even before she asked it. "And what do you want in return?"

"I want you to leave Salvation and not contact my brother again." He paused. "You have responsibilities. A child to support. This'll make it easier."

"I see." A knot began to grow in her throat. She had come to Salvation to find a treasure, but she hadn't imagined this would be it. She swallowed hard, trying to make the knot loosen. "How long do I have?"

"I figure you'll need a little time to find a place to go, so I've postdated it. I'll expect you gone in ten days."

As she looked across the desk at him, she was surprised to see a flash of compassion in his eyes, and she hated him for it. She blinked hard. "Gabe laughs now. Not often, but sometimes. Did Ethan tell you that?"

"Reopening that drive-in has been good for him. He's finally starting to heal."

She wanted to argue with him, to tell him that *she* was the reason Gabe had begun to heal, but he wouldn't believe her. Besides, she didn't know if it was true. Maybe she didn't mean anything more to Gabe than a few hours of forgetfulness when they were in bed.

"Both Ethan and I believe that having you gone will speed up the process."

"If Gabe finds out about this, he'll be furious."

"That's why you're not going to say a word. Do you understand? If you even hint to him about this, the deal's off."

"Oh, yes. I definitely understand." She drew the check through her fingers. "Just tell me one thing. Exactly what do you think I'm doing to your brother that's so terrible?"

"I think you're taking advantage of him."

"How?"

His eyes narrowed. "Don't play games with me, lady, because I'll run you right over! Gabe's a rich man who's careless about his money. You want to take him for every penny he has, then set off for greener pastures."

"You know this for a fact?"

"Are you going to take the check or not?"

She gazed down at the check and wondered if the time would ever come when she could outrun her past. "Yes. Yes, I'm going to take it, Mr. Bonner. You bet your life I am."

She shoved the check into the pocket of her dress and turned toward the door, but his soft voice stopped her before she could leave.

"Mrs. Snopes, you won't like what happens if you try to screw me over on this."

Her fingers convulsed around the knob. "Believe me, Mr. Bonner, you're the last man on earth I'd screw."

She forced herself not to run from the room, but she was shaking by the time she reached the deck, where Jane and Kristy had abandoned their efforts to clean up and were sitting and talking.

The moment Jane saw Rachel, her expression grew wary. "What did he do?"

Rachel couldn't quite control the small quaver in her voice. "You'll have to ask him."

Jane rose and caught Rachel's hands in her own. "I'm sorry. The Bonners are — They're a family in every sense of the word. They'll fight the world for each other, but sometimes their loyalty blinds them."

The most Rachel could manage was a small nod.

"I'll try to talk to him again," Jane said.

"It won't do any good." She spotted Gabe's keys on the table, and she scooped them up. "I'm not feeling well. I'm sure Ethan won't mind driving Gabe back to the cottage. Come on, Edward, we have to go."

Edward protested Rachel's announcement, and Rosie fell apart when she realized she was losing her play companion. Her small face crumpled as Edward disengaged Horse from her hands. She reached out her arms for him or for the rabbit, Rachel wasn't sure which, and began to howl.

Edward gave her a clumsy pat on the head. "It's okay, Rosie. You're just having a bad day."

344

Rosie stopped crying, but her blue eyes brimmed with tears, and she regarded him with an expression so pitiful it could have melted stone.

Edward looked down at Horse. And then, to Rachel's astonishment, he handed the stuffed rabbit back to her.

Rosie clutched it to her tiny, heaving chest and gazed up at Edward with grateful eyes.

Rachel regarded her son with concern. "Are you sure about this, Edward?"

He hesitated for only a moment before he nodded. "I'm all grown-up now, Mom. Rosie needs Horse more than I do."

She smiled, squeezed his hand, and tried not to cry.

Gabe leaped out of Ethan's Camry before the car had even stopped and charged toward the front porch where Edward was constructing a lopsided log cabin from sticks he'd gathered. "Where's your mother?"

"I don't know. Inside, I guess." His gaze moved past Gabe to Ethan and Kristy, who were just getting out of the car.

Gabe began to walk toward the door only to stop as he saw the boy make a small gesture to the side, as if he were trying to pick up something that wasn't there. Then his arm fell back into his lap, and he gave a sigh that seemed to come from his toes.

Gabe wished he didn't understand the gesture. "You're missing that rabbit of yours, aren't you?"

Edward bent his head over his log cabin and scratched his knee.

"I heard you gave it to Rosie, but everybody'll understand if you want it back." He tried to contain the gruffness in his voice, but couldn't quite manage.

"Rosie won't understand."

"She's only a baby. She'll forget about it."

"Horse isn't the kind of thing a kid forgets about."

He spoke with such absolute certainty that Gabe knew there was no use arguing with him. In that way, he was exactly like his mother.

"Pastor Ethan! Kristy!" The boy smiled as they stepped up onto the porch. "You want to see my log cabin?" He was too young to sense the tension between them, but Gabe had felt it.

"You bet we do," Kristy said.

Gabe turned away and walked into the cottage. "Rachel?"

There was no answer. He made a quick search of the rooms, then found her outside where she was bent over a rogue tomato plant in the weedy garden.

She was wearing the orange dress she painted in. Sunlight dappled her hair and danced along those slender, golden-brown arms. Her feet were bare, and she'd buried her toes in the soft dirt. She looked timeless and sensual, made up of earth and fire, and he wanted to take her right there in that imperfect garden. He wanted to cover her body with his body, forget who he was, who she was. He wanted to go to her without a past or future, with no thoughts beyond this single moment.

She looked up. A light sheen of perspiration glistened along her cheekbones, and her lips parted in surprise. "I didn't hear you."

She gave no smile of greeting, no sign that she was glad to see him. "Why did you take off like that?" he snapped.

"I wasn't feeling well."

"You seem to be feeling fine now."

She didn't reply. Instead, she bent her head and began working a clump of chickweed free.

"If you wanted to leave, you should have told me. You know I don't like it when you're here by yourself."

"You can't be with me every minute. And why should you try?"

"What does that mean?"

"It means I'm not your responsibility."

The snippy note in her voice annoyed him. She was the one in the wrong, not him. He was doing everything he could to keep her safe, but she wouldn't cooperate. "You're my responsibility while you're under this roof," he found himself saying.

But she wasn't impressed by his bluster. "If you want to be useful, get a shovel and start digging a trench around those shrubs instead of growling at me."

"I'm not growling."

"Could have fooled me."

"Damn it, Rachel, you ran off without telling me! I didn't know what had happened. I was worried."

"Were you?" She cocked her head to the side and gave him a slow smile that melted his bones.

He determinedly shook off the spell she was weaving around him. "You don't have to look so pleased about it. I'm not exactly happy with you at the moment, and not just because of the way you ran off." He knew he should let it go at that, but he couldn't. "From now on, I'd appreciate it if you didn't try to psychoanalyze me in front of my family."

"Can't think of a better place to do it than around people who want you to get well."

"I *am* well! I mean it, Rachel. I don't want to hear any more negative remarks about the drive-in. Everything went great last night. You should be celebrating."

"Everything didn't go great. I love that drive-in, but you don't! And the day I'll celebrate is the day you go back to work as a vet."

"Why do you have to keep pushing me? Why can't you just let things be?"

"Because the way things are is tearing you apart."

"Yeah, well, that's not your problem."

"No, it's not, is it?"

He realized that he'd hurt her, but a squeal of laughter interrupted them before he could make amends. He turned automatically, and what he saw made the hair on the back of his neck prickle. Ethan was coming around the side of the house with Edward perched on his shoulders, Kristy lagging behind.

The boy looked as if someone had handed him a rainbow. His eyes sparkled, and his bangs flopped as Ethan jogged forward. Being carried around like this was exactly what Edward had been dreaming about at the pig roast when he'd watched his friend riding his father's shoulders, and Gabe wanted to feel good about what he saw, but instead, he was overwhelmed by a sense of utter wrongness.

He couldn't understand his reaction. This child had received so few breaks in life, and now Gabe was begrudging him this small, simple pleasure. He felt petty and mean-spirited, but he couldn't argue himself out of his feelings — he couldn't relinquish the absolute certainty that Edward Stone did not belong on his brother's shoulders.

Rachel had risen to her feet. But instead of enjoying her son's happiness or moving forward to greet Kristy, she stood absolutely still, her arms at her sides, as she watched Gabe.

He felt a chill as he realized she knew exactly what he was thinking. Somehow she could see into his head, and she knew how resentful he was. He wanted to explain, but how could he explain what he didn't understand himself? How could he justify the feelings he had toward this child she loved more than her own life?

He looked away, turning toward his brother instead. Unlike Rachel, he could trust Ethan not to judge him. "Thanks for dropping me off, Eth."

"No problem."

"Excuse me, will you? I have to get some bookkeeping done." He turned away, and, as he headed into the cottage, he tried not to look as if he were fleeing.

Rachel winced at the sound of the screen door banging. At the same time, she felt dizzy from the pain of what she'd seen in his eyes. Why couldn't he stop hating Edward? The resentment he hadn't been able to hide felt like a blow to her heart. She reeled from it as the frail hopes she'd been nurturing disintegrated around her.

Gabe's demons weren't going to let him go, she realized. And the love she craved for herself and her son would never materialize.

These past few years, she'd prided herself on being realistic, but she'd been hiding from the truth for weeks. His feelings weren't going to change, and every moment she stayed with him would only make their inevitable parting that much worse. There was no rosy future in sight for her. No passport to fortune hidden away in Dwayne's Bible. No eternal love. And no one but herself to care about Edward.

Her time in Salvation had finally run out.

They had a larger crowd at the drive-in on Saturday night, but Gabe seemed even more withdrawn and unhappy. Afterward, when he came to her bed, they didn't speak, and their passion seemed tainted.

On Sunday afternoon she watched through the bedroom window as he moved Tweety Bird into the aviary he'd built. This was what he needed to be doing, but if he ever figured that out, she wouldn't be around to see it.

The expression of bitter resentment she'd seen on Gabe's face yesterday when he'd gazed at Edward had finally forced her to take action. She'd called Kristy that morning and set her plan in motion. Now every moment had grown more precious. If only she could hate him for failing her, maybe it wouldn't be so

350

painful, but how could she hate a man whose greatest fault lay in his ability to love so absolutely?

She ran her thumbs over the bumpy cover of Dwayne's Bible. She'd read every marginal note and studied each underlined passage, but all she'd found was the age-old comfort of verses she thought she'd stopped believing in.

Resting the side of her head on the window frame, she gazed outside at the man with whom she'd so unwisely fallen in love. Now, while Edward was occupied on the front porch, she had to tell Gabe she was leaving.

The rickety back steps creaked beneath her feet as she stepped down into the yard. She watched Gabe make an adjustment to the aviary door latch with a pair of pliers while Tweety Bird's shrill cheeps kept him company. He looked up and smiled as he caught sight of her, sending her heart into a crazy little dance.

She drew a deep breath. "Gabe, I'm leaving."

"All right." He finished tinkering with the latch. "Give me a few minutes to put away my tools, and I'll come with you."

"No, that's not what I mean." *Don't do it!* her heart cried. *Don't say the words!* But her brain was wiser. "I — I'm leaving Salvation."

He grew absolutely still. In the magnolia behind him, a squirrel chattered away, while a crow cawed from its perch on the peak of the old tin roof. "What are you talking about?" He slowly rose, the pliers dangling forgotten in his hand.

"I talked to Kristy this morning. Her parents have been after her for months to move to Clearwater and help run their gift shop. I'm going to do it instead." She realized she was digging her fingernails into her palms, and she forced herself to relax. "Kristy says she'll feel better knowing I'm there to keep an eye on them, and they own a little apartment over the shop where Edward and I can live. Plus, all that Florida sunshine," she finished inanely.

There was a long pause. "I see." He glanced down at the pliers in his hand, but she had the feeling he didn't see them. "How much are they going to pay you?"

"About what you are — they can't afford much right now — but the business is going to grow. I'll make do, especially since I won't have rent." She thought of the check for twenty-five thousand dollars tucked away in her top dresser drawer, and her stomach clenched. "As soon as Edward starts school full-time, I'm going to try to get a scholarship and go back to college. I'll only be able to take a few courses at a time, but I want to study business and finance."

He shoved the pliers into the back pocket of his jeans, and his eyes had that old hard look in them. "I see. You have it all worked out, don't you?"

She nodded.

"No discussion? It didn't occurred to you that maybe we should talk this over before you made up your mind."

"Why?" She spoke gently because she had to make certain he knew she wasn't blaming him. "There isn't any future for us. We both know that."

352

But he was in no mood to be appeased. He stalked toward her, closing the distance between them with angry strides. "You're not going."

"Yes, I am."

He loomed over her, and she wondered if he was deliberately using his size to intimidate her. "You heard me. You're staying right here! Going to Florida is a harebrained idea. What kind of security would you have working for peanuts and relying on other people for the roof over your head?"

"That's what I do now," she pointed out.

For a moment he seemed taken aback, then he made a harsh gesture with his hand. "It's not the same thing at all. You have friends here."

"I also have enemies."

"That'll change once people get to know you and realize you're going to be part of the community."

"How can I be part of the community? There aren't any opportunities for me here."

"And you think there'll be opportunities for you working for an hourly wage in some cheap Florida gift shop?"

She turned away from him. "I'm sure it's not cheap, and I don't want to argue with you about this. I have to go."

"No."

"Please. Don't make it any harder." She walked over to the lawn chair and clutched it for support. The nylon webbing scratched her palm. "Kayla can run the snack shop. I'll work through next weekend, so she has time to get her bearings and you can find someone to help her."

"I don't give a damn about the snack shop!"

She wanted to point out how very true that was, but she held her tongue. In the aviary, Tweety Bird kept up his high-pitched cheeping. Who but Gabe would have gone to so much trouble to rescue a sparrow?

He jammed his hands into his pockets as if they'd become his enemies. "You're not going to Florida."

"I don't have any choice."

"Yes, you do." He paused and glared at her. The line of his jaw grew more stubborn. "We're going to get married."

Her heart skipped a beat, then began to hammer. She stared at him. "Married? What are you talking about?"

"Just what I said." He pulled his hands out of his pockets and stalked toward her, his expression belligerent. "We get along. There's no reason why we shouldn't get married."

"Gabe, you don't love me."

"I care a hell of a lot more about you than G. Dwayne ever did!"

He was breaking her heart. "I know you do. But I can't marry you."

"Give me one good reason."

"I already did. The best reason of all."

Something helpless flickered in his eyes. "What do you want from me?"

She wanted what he'd given Cherry and Jamie, but it would be cruel to say that. And what was the point? He

354

already understood. "Nothing more than you've already given me."

But he wouldn't be put off. "I can take care of you. Once we're married, you won't have to worry about where your next meal's coming from or what'll happen if you get sick." He paused. "You'll have security for Edward."

That wasn't fair. He knew she'd sell her soul for her son, and she fought back tears. At the same time she realized this was something they finally had to talk about. "You have to know that's the biggest reason I can't do this. There are different kinds of security. Spending his childhood with a man who dislikes him is worse for Edward than poverty." There. It was finally out in the open.

"I don't dislike him." But he wouldn't meet her eyes, and his voice lacked conviction.

"I'm being honest with you. Do the same for me."

With his back to her, he moved toward the aviary. "It's just going to take a little time, that's all. You want everything to happen instantly."

"You dislike him as much now as the day you first saw him." Her resentment bubbled over. "And it's so unfair. He can't help the fact that he's not Jamie."

He whirled around. "Don't you think I haven't told myself that a thousand times?" He drew a ragged breath, struggling for control. "Look, just give it some time and it'll work out. I know I've taken you by surprise, but once you think it over, you'll realize our getting married is the best thing."

She wanted to curl up in some dark corner and howl. Instead, she forced herself to stay where she was and finish this. "I'm not going to change my mind. I won't marry you. Kristy already called her parents, and they're going to send me two bus tickets. I'll work next weekend, and then Edward and I are leaving for Florida."

"*No!*"

Both of them jumped as Edward came running around the corner of the house, tears streaming down his face.

The bottom dropped out of her stomach. What had she done? She'd planned to break the news gently, not like this.

CHAPTER
TWENTY

"I don't want to go to Flor'da!" Tears streamed down Edward's flushed cheeks. He flailed his arms and stomped his feet. "We're going to *stay here! We're not* going! We're staying *here!*"

"Oh, sweetheart." She rushed to him and tried to put her arms around him, but he batted them away. For the first time since he'd been a toddler, he was caught in the throes of a full-fledged temper tantrum.

"We live here!" he screamed. "We live *right here*, and I'm *not* going!" He whirled toward Gabe. "This is all your fault! I *hate* you!"

Once again, she tried to embrace him. "Sweetheart, let me explain. Settle down so we can talk about this."

He sprang away and hurled himself at Gabe, hitting him in the knees. "This is *your* fault! *You're* making us go!"

Gabe regained his balance and caught Edward by the shoulders. "No! I don't want you to go! I'm not making you go."

Edward punched the side of his leg. "Yes, you are!"

Gabe caught his fists. "Calm down, Chip, and let your mother talk."

But Edward wouldn't be appeased. Once again he began to stomp his feet. "You *hate* me, and I know why!"

"I don't hate you."

"Yes, you do! You hate me because I'm not *strong*."

"Chip . . ." Gabe regarded Rachel helplessly, but she didn't know what to do any more than he did.

Edward jerked away and flew to Rachel's side. No longer yelling, he gulped for air between sobs. "Don't you . . . marry him, Mommy. You marry . . . Pastor Ethan!"

She squatted next to him, appalled that he'd overheard that part of their conversation. "Oh, Edward, I'm not going to marry anyone."

"Yes! Marry . . . Pastor Ethan. Then we . . . we can stay here."

"Pastor Ethan doesn't want to marry me, baby."

Once again she tried to embrace him, but he pushed away. "I'll *tell* him to!"

"You can't tell grown-ups something like that."

A wrenching sob. "Then marry . . . Rosie's daddy. I like him. He calls . . . me Chip and . . . he gave me a . . . head rub."

"Rosie's daddy is married to Rosie's mom. Edward, I'm not going to marry anybody."

Once again, Edward turned back to Gabe, but this time he didn't attack. His chest spasmed in hiccups of emotion. "If my mom . . . marries you, do we gets to . . . stay here?"

Gabe hesitated. "It's not that easy, Chip."

"You live here, don't you?"

"Now I do."

"You said you want to get married to her."

Gabe cast a helpless look in her direction. "Yes."

"Then I'll let you. But only if we get to *stay here*."

Edward was no longer the only one crying. Rachel felt as if she were being ripped apart. She knew she was doing the right thing, but there was no way she could explain it to him. "I can't," she managed.

Edward's head dropped. A tear splattered on the toe of his sneaker, and all the fight seemed to leave him. "I know it's because of me," he whispered. "You said you won't marry him because he don't like me."

How could she ever make him understand something so complex? "No, Edward," she said firmly. "It's not like that at all."

He regarded her with subtle rebuke, as if he knew she weren't being honest.

Gabe's interruption startled her. "Rachel, leave us alone for a few minutes, will you? Chip and I have to talk."

"I don't —"

"Please."

She'd never felt more helpless. Surely he wouldn't try to hurt Edward even more. No, he'd never do that. And the relationship between them couldn't get any worse. Still, she hesitated. And then she realized she had no idea how to handle the situation herself, so maybe she should let Gabe try. "Are you sure about this?"

"Yes. Go on."

She hesitated for a moment longer, but his implacable expression told her he wasn't going to change his mind, and the cowardly part of her needed to get away, just for a few minutes, so she could put herself back together again. Finally, she gave a reluctant nod and slowly rose to her feet. "All right, then."

Now that she'd agreed, she didn't know where to go. She couldn't bear the idea of being cooped up inside with nothing to do but pace from room to room. She turned toward the path into the woods instead, where she and Edward walked nearly every day, and prayed she was doing the right thing by leaving them alone.

Gabe watched Rachel until she disappeared into the trees, then he turned to the boy.

Edward regarded him warily.

Now that the time had come, Gabe couldn't think of anything to say, but every spark of decency he possessed told him he couldn't let this child be tortured by something that wasn't his fault. He made his way to the back step and sat down so he didn't tower over him.

Edward sniffed and rubbed his nose on the sleeve of his T-shirt.

Gabe hadn't planned to ask Rachel to marry him, but now that he'd said the words, he knew it was what he needed to do. What they needed to do. But the boy was standing in the way.

"Chip . . ." He cleared his throat. "I know things haven't been great between us, but you need to know that doesn't have anything to do with you. It's because of . . . because of things that happened to me a long time ago."

Edward stared at him. "When your little boy died."

He hadn't expected this, and the most he could manage was a shaky nod.

There was a silence, and then the boy spoke. "What was his name?"

Gabe drew a long, unsteady breath. "Jamie."

"Was he strong?"

"He was five, just like you, so he wasn't as strong as a grown-up."

"Was he stronger than me?"

"I don't know. He was a little bit bigger, so he might have been, but that's not important."

"Did you like him?"

"I loved him very much."

He took a cautious step forward. "Was you sad when Jamie died?"

His name! Gabe worked to find his voice. "Yes. I was very sad when Jamie died. I still am."

"Did you get mad at him like you get mad at me?"

Not ever in the same way, he thought. "Sometimes. When he did things wrong."

"Did he like you?"

Speech deserted him. He nodded.

Edward's arm moved. He glanced around, then his arm fell back to his side. The rabbit.

"Was he scared of you?"

"No." Gabe cleared his throat again. "No, he wasn't scared of me like you are. He knew I'd never hurt him. I won't hurt you, either."

He could see the boy framing another question, but the ones he'd already asked were slicing him open.

"Chip, I wish you hadn't overheard us talking, but since you did, you know that I want to marry your mom. She doesn't think it's a good idea, and I don't want you to give her a hard time about it. I'm going to try to change her mind, but she has to do what she thinks is right, and if she decides she won't marry me, it's not because of anything you've done. Do you understand what I'm trying to say? You haven't done anything wrong."

He should have saved his breath.

"She won't marry you because of me."

"Some of it has to do with you," he said slowly, "but not because it's your fault. Because of me. Your mother doesn't like the way I got off to a bad start with you. Because I wasn't nice. It's kept you and me from getting along too well. That's my fault, Chip, not yours. There's nothing wrong with you."

"I'm not strong like Jamie." Keeping his distance, he picked at a small scab on the back of his hand. "I wish Jamie could come play with me."

Out of nowhere, Gabe's eyes brimmed with tears. "I'm sure he'd have liked to do that."

"He could prob'ly beat me up." He sat down on the ground as if his legs could no longer support him.

"Jamie didn't fight too much. He liked to build things, just like you do." For the first time, Gabe thought of the similarities between the two boys, instead of the differences. They liked books, puzzles, and drawing. Both of them could entertain themselves for long periods of time.

"My daddy died in a plane crash."

"I know."

"He's in heaven right now taking care of Jamie."

The idea of G. Dwayne Snopes watching out for Jamie was too much for Gabe, but he didn't say anything.

"I wish my mommy would marry Pastor Ethan or Rosie's dad."

"Chip, I know you don't understand this, but I'd take it as a personal favor if you'd stop trying to marry your mother off to my brothers."

"My mommy won't marry you because me and you don't get along."

Gabe couldn't think of how to respond. He'd already told the boy it wasn't his fault. What more could he say?

"I don't want to go to Flor'da." Edward lifted his head to look at Gabe, but didn't quite meet his eyes. "If we got along, I bet she'd marry you, and we wouldn't have to go away."

"I don't know. Maybe. There are other problems that don't have anything to do with you. I just don't know."

A mulish expression came over Chip's tear-streaked face, and at that moment, he looked so much like Rachel, Gabe wanted to cry himself. "I do! I know!"

"Know what?"

"How to make her change her mind and marry you."

The boy looked so certain that, for a moment, Gabe was sucked in. "How?"

He began tugging up clumps of grass. "You could pretend."

"Pretend? I don't know what you mean."

More grass came up. "You could pretend you like me. Then my mommy would marry you, and we wouldn't have to go away."

"I — I don't think that would work."

His brown eyes filled with hurt. "Couldn't you even *pretend* to like me? It wouldn't have to be real."

Gabe forced himself to meet the boy's gaze and utter his lie with complete conviction. "I do like you."

"No." Edward shook his head. "But you could pretend. And I could pretend about you, too. If we pretended real good, my mommy would never know."

The boy's deadly earnestness was tearing Gabe apart. He looked down at the scuffed toes of his boots. "It's a little more complicated than that. There are other things —"

But Chip jumped to his feet, no longer listening. He'd said what he had to, and now he wanted to share the news. He dashed toward the path in the woods, calling out as he ran. "Mommy! Hey, Mommy!"

"I'm over here."

Gabe heard Rachel's voice, faint but still audible. He sat on the step and listened.

"Mommy, I got something to tell you!"

"What is it, Edward?"

"It's me and Gabe. We *like* each other now!"

Rachel dropped Edward off at child care on Monday morning, then sat in the parking lot gathering her courage. She knew what she had to do, but there was a big difference between knowing and doing. So many loose ends to tie up before she left.

She leaned her head against the Escort's window and made herself accept the fact that she and Edward would be getting on the bus and heading for Clearwater in a week. Misery settled over her, and her heart felt like a bleeding wound inside her chest. Watching Edward act as if he and Gabe had magically become friends was wrenching. All evening Edward had smiled at Gabe, this small, insincere crescent stretched across his teeth. At bedtime, she'd watched him gather his courage.

"Night, Gabe. I really like you a lot."

Gabe had flinched, then tried to cover it up. *"Thank you, Chip."*

She blamed Gabe, even as she knew he was doing his best not to hurt Edward. That made Gabe's helplessness all the more painful, and her decision to leave even more necessary.

When she'd tucked Edward in, she'd tried to talk to him about what was happening, but he'd only shaken his head.

"Me and Gabe like each other lots, so we don't have to go to Flor'da now."

One of the mothers came into the parking lot and glanced in Rachel's direction. She fumbled with the key in the ignition. One more week . . .

Oh, Gabe . . . Why can't you love my child for who he is? And why can't you come to peace with Cherry's ghost so you can love me, too?

She wanted to prop her head against the steering wheel and cry until she had no tears left, but if she gave in, she'd crumble into so many pieces she'd never be able to put herself back together again. And self-pity wouldn't change the facts. Her son wasn't going to grow up with a man who couldn't tolerate him. And she wouldn't live the rest of her life in another woman's shadow. Before she left, however, there was something she had to do.

The Escort shuddered as she pulled from the parking lot. She took a deep breath and set off down Wynn Road toward the small web of streets that made up the poorest part of Salvation. She turned onto Orchard, a narrow, potholed lane that curved sharply up the side of a hill. Tiny one-story homes with crumbling front steps perched on barren, untended yards. An old Chevy sat on blocks at the side of one house, a rusted boat trailer near another.

The small, mint-green house at the end of Orchard was tidier than most of the others. The porch was swept and the yard neat. A basket of ivy geraniums hung from a hook near the front door.

Rachel parked on the street and climbed the uneven front walk. As she stepped onto the porch, she heard the sound of a game show coming from the television inside. The cracked door buzzer didn't look operable, so she knocked instead.

A faded, but pretty, young woman appeared. Her short blond hair had a slightly brassy home-done look. She was small and thin, dressed in a cropped white sleeveless top and worn denim shorts that rode low on her narrow hips and showed her navel. She looked to be in her early thirties, but Rachel suspected she was younger. Something tired and wary in her expression made Rachel recognize a fellow traveler on life's bumpier highway. "Are you Emily's mother?"

When the woman nodded, Rachel introduced herself. "I'm Rachel Stone."

"Oh." She looked surprised. "My mother said you might stop by sometime, but I didn't believe her."

Rachel had dreaded this part of it. "It's not about that. Your mother . . . She's a lovely person, but . . ."

The woman smiled. "It's all right. She has a lot more faith in miracles than I do. I'm sorry if she's been bothering you, but her intentions are good."

"I know they are. I wish I could help that way, but I'm afraid I can't."

"Come in anyway. I could use some company." She pushed open the screen. "I'm Lisa."

"It's nice to meet you." Rachel stepped into a small living room overcrowded with a nubby beige sectional sofa, an old recliner, some end tables, and a television. The furniture was of good quality, but mismatched and worn in a way that made Rachel suspect the pieces came from Lisa's mother.

On the left, a section of counter separated the kitchen from the living area, with the pair of wooden shutters designed to divide off the space folded accordion-style against the wall. The beige Formica counter held the familiar clutter of canisters, toaster, a wicker basket spilling over with paperwork, two ripe bananas, and a lidless Russell Stover candy box filled with broken crayons. As Rachel gazed around at the plain, homey surroundings, she wondered when she'd be able to afford even this much.

Lisa turned off the television and gestured toward the recliner. "Would you like a Coke? Or maybe coffee?

Mom brought over some of her poppy-seed muffins yesterday."

"No, thanks."

Rachel settled in the recliner, and there was an awkward pause that neither of them quite knew how to bridge. Lisa swept up a copy of *Redbook* from the sofa and took a seat.

"How is your daughter?"

Lisa shrugged. "She's sleeping now. We thought her leukemia was in remission, but then she had a relapse. The doctors have done everything they can, so I brought her home."

Her eyes looked haunted, and Rachel understood what she wouldn't say. That she'd brought her daughter home to die.

Rachel bit her bottom lip and reached for her purse. From the very moment it had happened, she'd known what she had to do, and now the time had come. "I've brought something."

Rachel pulled out the check for twenty-five thousand dollars that Cal Bonner had given her and handed it over. "This is for you."

She watched the play of emotions ranging from confusion to disbelief cross Lisa's face.

Lisa's hand trembled. She blinked her eyes, as if she were having trouble focusing. "It's — it's made out to you. What is this?"

"I've endorsed it over to Emily's Fund. It's postdated a week from tomorrow, so you'll have to wait to deposit it."

Lisa studied the signature on the back, then gaped at Rachel. "But this is so much money. And I don't even know you. Why are you doing this?"

"Because I want you to have it."

"But . . ."

"Please. It means a lot to me." She smiled. "I do have one request, though. I'm leaving town next Monday, and, after I'm gone, I'd really appreciate it if you'd send Cal Bonner a note thanking him for his generosity."

"Of course I will. But . . ." Lisa retained the stunned look of someone who wasn't accustomed to hearing good news.

"He'll love knowing his money will be helping your daughter." Rachel allowed herself a moment of satisfaction. She would have fulfilled Cal's terms, so he couldn't ask for the money back. But he'd also know she'd gotten the best of him.

"Mommy . . ."

Lisa's shoulders straightened as a small, weary voice came from the back of the house. "Coming." She rose, the precious check clutched in her hand. "Would you like to meet Emily?"

If Lisa's mother had been present, Rachel would have made an excuse, but Lisa didn't seem to expect any miracle healing from her. "I'd love to."

Lisa tucked the check in her pocket, then led Rachel down the short hallway that opened between the living room and kitchen. They passed a bedroom on the right with a bathroom directly opposite, and then came to Emily's room.

Little girls in sunbonnets frolicked across the wallpaper and yellow eyelet curtains framed the room's single window. A bouquet of partially deflated helium balloons bobbed lethargically in one corner and get-well cards were propped on every surface. Many of them had begun to curl at the corners.

Rachel's eyes sought out the room's twin bed, where a pale little girl lay in wrinkled blue sheets. Her face was bloated, and dark bruises marred her arms. A few short wisps of fuzzy brown hair covered her small head like thistledown. She held a pink teddy bear and regarded Rachel out of luminous green eyes.

Lisa went to the side of her bed. "Want some juice, peanut?"

"Yes, please."

She fixed the pillow so Emily could sit up. "Apple or orange?"

"Apple."

Lisa straightened the top sheet. "This is Rachel. She's a friend, not a doctor. Maybe you'd like to show her Blinky while I get your juice. Rachel, this is Emily."

Rachel came forward as Lisa left the room. "Hi, Emily. Do you mind if I sit on your bed?"

She shook her head, and Rachel settled on the edge of the mattress. "I'll bet I know who Blinky is."

Emily glanced at her pink teddy bear and hugged it tighter.

Rachel gently touched the tip of the child's button nose. "I'll bet this is Blinky."

Emily smiled and shook her head.

370

"Oh, I've got it now." She touched Emily's ear. "This must be Blinky."

Emily giggled. "No."

They continued to play the game for a few more rounds until Rachel correctly identified the bear. The little girl was a born charmer, and it was heartbreaking to see the devastation the disease had wreaked on her.

Lisa came in with a yellow plastic mug, but just as Rachel began to get up from the side of the bed so she could give the juice to her daughter, the phone rang. Lisa extended the mug toward Rachel. "Would you mind?"

"Of course not."

As Lisa left, Rachel helped Emily sit the rest of the way up and brought the cup to her lips.

"I can do it myself."

"Of course you can. You're a big girl."

The child grasped the mug in both hands, took a sip, then gave it back.

"Can you drink a little more?"

Even that small effort had exhausted her, and Emily's eyelids drooped.

Rachel lay her back down and set the cup on the bedside table amidst a jungle of pill bottles. "I have a boy just a little older than you."

"Does he like to play outside?"

Rachel nodded and took the child's hand.

"I like to play outside, but I don't get to 'cause I have 'kemia."

"I know."

Old ways died hard, and, as Rachel gazed down into the little girl's small, pale face, she found herself once again berating the God she didn't believe in. *How could You do this? How could You let such a terrible thing happen to this beautiful child?*

From out of nowhere, Gabe's words came back to her. *Maybe you've got God mixed up with Santa Claus.*

Sitting next to this child who clung so desperately to life must have heightened her senses because the words struck her in a way they hadn't before. Something inside her grew still and calm, and, for the first time, she understood what Gabe had been trying to say. Her vision of God was a child's vision.

All her life she'd seen God as someone entirely separate from humans, an old man who arbitrarily dispensed good fortune and bad, all on some divine whim. No wonder she hadn't been able to love this God. Who could love a God so cruel and unfair?

God hadn't done this to Emily, she realized. Life had done it.

But even as she sat there, Dwayne's theology hammered at her. God was omnipotent. All-powerful. What did that mean to this dying child whose hand she held?

It came to her suddenly — the realization that she'd always thought of God's omnipotence in worldly terms. She'd compared it to the power of earthly rulers who had the mastery of life and death over their subjects. But God wasn't a tyrant, and at that moment, with Emily's small hand curled in hers, Rachel's entire vision of creation shifted.

God was omnipotent, she saw, not in the way of earthly kings, but in the same way that love was omnipotent. Love was the greatest power, and God's omnipotent power was the power of love.

Warmth stole through every part of her, moving out from her very center, and along with that warmth came a sense of ecstasy.

Dear God, fill this blessed child with the omnipotence of Your love.

"Your skin is hot."

The child's voice startled her. She blinked her eyes and her feeling of bliss faded. Only then did she realize how tightly she was gripping the little girl's hand, and she immediately let her go. "I'm sorry. I didn't mean to squeeze so tight."

As Rachel stood up, she realized her legs were trembling. She felt weak, as if she'd just run for miles. What had happened to her? She'd had a glimpse of something important, but she could no longer grasp exactly what it was.

"I want to sit up now."

"Let me see if it's all right with your mother."

The screen door banged, and a loud male voice rang out from the front of the house. "I know that car. Damn it, Lisa! What's *she* doing here?"

"Calm down. I —"

But he wasn't listening. Rachel heard a heavy tread in the hallway, then a man Rachel recognized as Russ Scudder filled the doorway of Emily's room.

"Hi, Daddy."

CHAPTER
TWENTY-ONE

Lisa pushed past Russ. "Emily, what are you doing sitting up?"

"I got hot."

Her hand flew to the child's brow. "You don't feel hot." She grabbed the thermometer from a glass on the bedside table and pushed it between Emily's lips. "Let's see if you're running a temperature."

Russ glared at Rachel, then moved toward his daughter. "Hey, puddin'."

"You said you'd come yesterday, Daddy." Emily spoke around the thermometer.

"Yeah, well, I was pretty busy. But I'm here now." As he sat on the side of the bed and took Emily's hand, he shot Rachel a venomous look.

"Rachel's got a little boy," Emily said. "Her hands is hot."

Russ's eyes grew fierce. "Get out of here."

"Stop it, Russ." Lisa stepped forward.

"I don't want her near Emily."

"This is my house now, and what you want doesn't matter."

"It's all right," Rachel said. "I have to go anyway. Good-bye, Emily. You take care of yourself."

Emily pulled the thermometer from her mouth. "Can your little boy come play with me?"

"We're going to be moving soon. I'm afraid he won't be around much longer."

Lisa tried to put the thermometer back in, but Emily shook her head. "Want to read a story. Want apple juice."

"What's going on?" Russ said. "You told me she's been too sick to sit up."

"I guess she's having a good day." Lisa walked over to Rachel. Taking her hand, she drew her into the hallway. "I'll never be able to thank you enough. That money's going to make a lot of difference."

Russ appeared behind them. "What money?"

"Rachel is giving us twenty-five thousand dollars for Emily's Fund."

"What?" He sounded as if he were choking.

"The check is from Cal Bonner," Rachel said. "It's his gift, not mine."

Lisa's expression indicated she didn't believe it, and Russ looked as if he'd been hit by a stun gun. Suddenly Rachel needed to get away from them both. "Good luck."

A small voice called out to her from the bedroom. "Bye, Rachel."

"Bye, sweetie."

She left the house and hurried to her car.

As Ethan pulled into the left lane of the interstate to pass a Ryder rental truck with two bicycles hanging off the rear, Kristy gazed at his calendar boy-profile. "I can't believe you're serious about this."

He slipped back into the right lane. "I'm just not cut out to be a pastor. I've known it for a long time, and I'm tired of fighting it. I'm planning to turn in my letter of resignation on Monday, as soon as we get back."

Kristy started to argue, then shut her mouth. What was the use? He'd dropped his bombshell just as they'd left Salvation. Now they were approaching Knoxville, and she'd been debating with him the whole time. Unfortunately, he showed no sign of changing his mind.

Ethan Bonner had been born to be a pastor. How could he not understand that? This was the worst mistake of his life, but no matter what she said, he wasn't going to listen.

"Could we please talk about something else?" he said.

It was already late, nearly evening on Friday. They'd be returning to Salvation after the conference's Sunday-morning prayer service and luncheon, which didn't give her much time to reason with him. "What will you do?"

"Counseling probably. Maybe I'll go back to school and get my Ph.D. in psychology. I don't know."

She played her trump card. "Your brothers are going to be so disappointed in you, not to mention your parents."

"We all have to live our own lives." They were approaching an exit ramp, and he pulled over. "I'm hungry. Let's get something to eat."

He knew as well as she did that the conference kicked off with a buffet dinner at seven, and her car trouble had already made them late. She hadn't wanted to spend too much time alone with him, so she'd planned to drive separately to Knoxville, but when she'd tried to start her normally reliable Honda, nothing had happened, and she'd been forced to go with him. "It's already six, and we really don't have time."

"Are you afraid somebody's going to give you an F on your report card if you're late?"

This sarcasm was new to him, one of several changes that had taken place since she'd told him she was quitting, and she didn't like it. "It's your conference, not mine. I wouldn't even be going if you hadn't nagged me into it."

Her two weeks' notice had been up nearly a week ago, but he'd bullied her into staying on the job through this weekend, and since her new position at the preschool in Brevard didn't start until Monday, she'd agreed. Now she wished she hadn't been such a pushover.

Being with him had grown even more painful since last Friday night at the Pride of Carolina. What had happened in the front seat of his car had destroyed her illusions that she might be getting over him. She still loved him, and she knew she always would, even though being around him this past week had felt like a ride on a runaway roller coaster.

He alternated between uncharacteristic bouts of snappishness and being so sweet and thoughtful that

377

she could barely hold back tears. When he wasn't snarling at her, he displayed an almost puppy-dog eagerness to please. She knew her accusation that he hadn't been a friend had stung him badly, and she only wished she could chalk his behavior up to an emotion other than guilt.

Sometimes she'd catch him watching her, and even her inexperienced eyes recognized the desire she saw there. It should have made her happy. Wasn't that what she'd wanted? But the knowledge only depressed her. She didn't want to be some babe he lusted after. She wanted to be his love.

She realized he'd passed the fast-food restaurants that sat near the freeway exit. "I thought you said you were hungry."

"I am." But he continued to drive down the two-lane country highway. Finally he slowed and made a left turn into the parking lot of a dingy diner that sat next to an eight-unit motel.

The diner's gravel lot contained mostly pickups. As he parked between two of them, she regarded the place with distaste. Its dirty mustard asphalt shingles and flickering neon beer signs hardly looked promising. "I think we should go back to the Hardee's."

"I like this place."

"It's not respectable."

"Good." He jerked the keys from the ignition and threw open the door.

It was going to be a long weekend if his mood didn't improve soon. Gruder Mathias, one of the town's retired clergy, was preaching for Ethan on Sunday, and Monday was his day off, so he wouldn't be in any hurry to get back.

With a sigh of resignation, she trailed after him to the entrance, which featured a pair of heavy wooden doors in a fake Mediterranean motif. She heard the whine of a country ballad even before they stepped inside.

A blast of air-conditioning plastered her tomato-red ribbed tank dress to her body. She smelled hot grease and stale beer. At the dimly lit bar, a group of ol' boys wearing gimme caps and muddy jeans sat drinking beer and smoking.

Since it was still relatively early, most of the tables were vacant, as were the brown vinyl booths. Dusty plastic vines that looked as if they'd been stapled to the paneled walls a decade earlier provided the decor, along with some framed health-department certificates that had to be forgeries.

Ethan steered her to a booth in the back. As soon as they were settled, the bartender, a no-neck bald-headed man, called over for their drink order. "What'll you have?"

"Coke," she replied, hesitating only a moment before she added, "In the can, please."

"I'll have scotch on the rocks."

Kristy gazed at Ethan in surprise. She'd never seen him drink strong liquor. He didn't even order margaritas in Mexican restaurants.

She had to remind herself that he was no longer her responsibility, so she bit her tongue.

One of the men at the bar turned to stare at her. Having men notice her was still new enough to make her uncomfortable, so she pretended not to notice.

The bartender brought over their drinks, then slapped down two laminated menus sticky with old condiments. "Jeannie'll be with you in a minute. Special tonight is fried catfish." He walked away.

Kristy poked the grubby menus out of the way with her little finger. Ignoring the empty glass of ice cubes, she wiped the rim of the can with her paper napkin before she took a drink. The Coke was warm, but at least it was sanitary.

The man at the bar continued to watch her. He was young, maybe in his mid-twenties, with a Miller Lite T-shirt and powerful biceps. She tugged nervously on one of her fake diamond studs. Her short tank dress was sexy, but not so trashy that it served as an open invitation, and she wished he'd look somewhere else.

Ethan took a sip of scotch and shot the man an accusing glare. "What do you think you're looking at?"

She gasped. "Ethan!"

The man at the bar shrugged. "Don't see no 'sold' sign on her."

"Maybe that's because you can't read."

Her eyes widened with dismay. Ethan, the dedicated pacifist, seemed to be spoiling for a fight with a brute who outweighed him by at least fifty pounds, all of it muscle.

The man at the bar uncoiled from the stool, and she swore she saw the light of anticipation in Ethan's blue eyes. Her mind raced. What would Rachel do?

She gulped and held up her hand toward the muscular man. "Please don't take offense. He hasn't been the same since he gave up the priesthood." It wasn't much of a lie, she thought.

But the bully didn't appear to be buying it. "He doesn't look like a priest."

"That's because he isn't anymore." She took a deep breath. "He's very protective of me. I'm . . . uh . . . Sister Kristina, his . . . sister."

"You're a nun?" His gaze slid to the scooped neck of her tank dress.

"Yes, I am. And God bless you."

"You don't look like a nun."

"My order doesn't wear habits."

"Aren't you at least supposed to wear crucifixes or something?"

She tugged on the delicate gold chain around her neck and withdrew the small gold cross that nestled between her breasts.

"Sorry, Sister." He shot another dark glance at Ethan, then he settled back on his stool.

Ethan regarded her with annoyance. "Just what in the Sam Hill do you think you're doing?"

"Keeping you out of a barroom fight!"

"Maybe I don't want to be kept out."

"Catfish!" she called over to the bartender. "We'll have the fried catfish. And bless you, too," she added belatedly.

Ethan rolled his eyes, but to her relief, he didn't pursue the subject. Instead, he pursued his scotch, and by the time an overly made-up, dark-haired waitress wearing cutoffs and a Garth Brooks T-shirt arrived with their food, he'd finished it.

"I'll have another scotch."

"Ethan, you're driving."

"Mind your own business, Sister Bernadine."

The waitress gave her a suspicious look. "I heard you earlier. I thought you said your name was Sister Kristina."

"Uh . . . Bernadine was my name before I went into the convent. Then I became Sister Kristina."

Ethan snorted.

The waitress turned to him. Ethan was as handsome as ever, and she was clearly interested. "So what's it like not bein' a priest anymore?"

He jerked his thumb toward Kristy. "Ask her."

"He's . . . Well, it hasn't been easy. Nothing's easy for people who turn their backs on their *true calling*." She twisted the cap off the ketchup bottle and cleaned the crusty rim with another paper napkin before she handed it to him. "They feel empty. Hollow. They try to fill that hollow with *liquor*, and the next thing you know, they're lonely alcoholics who've lost their looks."

The waitress brushed his shoulder with the tip of a frosted blue fingernail. "I don't think you'll have to worry about that, Father."

He gave her a lazy smile. "Thanks."

"Any time."

As the waitress sauntered toward the bar, Ethan openly enjoyed her swinging rear door. She returned with his scotch and departed with a smoky smile.

"Eat your dinner before it gets cold," Kristy snapped.

He sipped from his fresh drink. "What do you care whether my food's cold or not?"

"I don't."

"You're a liar." He glared at her so intently that she wanted to squirm. "You know what I think? I think you're still in love with me."

"And I think you're getting drunk." She willed herself not to flush. "You've never had a head for alcohol."

"So what if I am drunk?"

That made her angry. "You haven't turned in your resignation yet, Ethan Bonner! You're still an ordained minister."

"Not in my heart," he retorted angrily. "In my heart I've already resigned."

The words were barely out of his mouth before he winced. She watched as he went very still, almost as if he were listening to an internal voice speaking a message he didn't want to hear. Finally he muttered something she couldn't quite make out and picked up his fork to stab the catfish.

"It's already dead," she pointed out.

"Just pay attention to your own food and leave mine alone. Where's the salt?"

"Right next to you."

He reached for it, but, as angry as she was with him, she still loved him, and she couldn't watch him poison himself, so she whipped the salt shaker up before he could touch it and scrubbed at the corroded lid with another napkin, then thrust it at him. "Try not to touch anything."

His long fingers curled around the salt shaker at the same time his eyes curled around her. "You know what I want to touch, don't you?"

Her tongue wouldn't move.

"I want to touch you. Just like I did that night at the drive-in."

"I don't want to talk about it."

"I don't want to talk about it, either." He pushed aside his catfish, picked up his scotch, and gazed at her over the rim of the glass. "I want to do it."

She knocked over her Coke can, then scrambled to right it before it spilled all over the table. Her skin felt hot under her dress. "We . . . We have to be in Knoxville in half an hour."

"We're not going to make it. As a matter of fact, I don't care if we make any of the conference."

"But you've already paid the registration fee."

"So what?"

"Eth . . ."

"Let's get out of here."

He tossed down a few bills, grabbed her wrist, and pulled her outside. Her pulses raced. This was a new and dangerous Ethan she'd never seen.

He drew her down the stairs, and the next thing she knew, he was pressing her against the side of his Camry with his hips. "I can't stop thinking about that night."

He rubbed her bare shoulders with his thumbs, and she felt the heat from his body through the knit of her dress. A truck buzzed by.

"You care about me," he whispered. "Shouldn't I be the one you lose your virginity to instead of somebody you don't care about?"

"How . . . How do you know I haven't already lost it?"

"I just do."

Her conscience went to war with her desire for him. "It's not right."

He dipped his head and she felt his jaw move against her hair. "Why don't we lose our virginities together?"

"You're not a virgin."

"It's been so long since I've had sex that I feel like one."

"I don't . . . I don't believe it works that way."

"Sure it does." His lips touched her earlobe, and his scotch-soft breath brushed her cheek. "Yes or no. Your decision."

He was the snake, tempting her. He knew the way she felt about him, and it wasn't fair for him to deliberately manipulate her emotions like this.

"I don't love you anymore," she lied. "I never loved you. It was just infatuation."

His hands curved around the sides of her hips, and his thumbs brushed the tiny elastic ridge left by her skimpy panties. "You smell so good. I love the way you smell."

"I'm not wearing any perfume."

"I know."

She sighed. "Oh, Eth . . ."

"Yes or no?"

Anger exploded inside her, and she slapped away his hands. "Yes! Of course, yes! Because I'm weak and needy and I don't like you very much right now."

If she'd expected her outburst to slow him down, she was proven wrong.

"I can fix that." Within seconds, he had the car door unlocked and pushed her inside.

Instead of turning back out onto the highway, he simply swung the Camry across the gravel parking lot and into the narrow lane that led to the office of the EZ Sleep Motel.

"Oh, no . . ." She stared with dismay at the row of white wooden units with three large pines standing guard in front.

His voice held a pleading note she'd never heard before. "I can't wait any longer. I promise, Kristy, the next time it'll be champagne and satin sheets."

Without waiting for her to respond, he vaulted from the car and shot into the motel office. He was back within minutes. Again, he settled behind the wheel and drove to the end unit, where he parked crookedly, jumped out, and raced around to open her door.

The good Pastor Bonner hustled her inside like a teenager ready to score.

Ethan pushed the door shut behind them and let out a sigh of relief as he saw that the room was shabby, but clean. He knew there was no way on earth he could have kept her here if it had been dirty. And he wouldn't let her go. He simply couldn't stand this sense of separation between them any longer. He had to keep her here until he marked her for life.

The need to mark her was important, although he wouldn't do it with a hurtful bite or a marring bruise — that would be intolerable. But he wanted to do it with something indelible. He wanted a mark that would keep her by his side forever and make them best friends again. And the only way he could think of was to do it with sex.

No matter what she said, sex meant something to Kristy, or she wouldn't still be a virgin. Any man she had sex with would be important to her forever, and that's why it had to be him. Only him.

He searched for a less selfish reason to justify what he intended to do, and quickly found it. She was too precious for him to allow another man to ruin her. Kristy was unique, but everyone didn't understand that. What if her first lover didn't take care with her? What if he didn't understand how precious she was?

There were so many pitfalls awaiting her. Kristy was a nut about cleanliness, and that could make sex a problem for her. A man would have to be patient with her eccentricities, distract her with a little gentle teasing, a few deep kisses, until she forgot about hygiene and just enjoyed herself.

"This room is plenty clean," he pointed out.

"I didn't say it wasn't."

The idea that she might be disappointed made him defensive. "I know what you're thinking. Just because something's shabby doesn't mean it's dirty." He crossed to the bed and whipped down the spread and blanket to reveal a crisp white sheet. "See."

"Ethan, are you drunk?"

She looked so pretty standing there in that short red dress, with her eyes big and uncertain, that a lump formed in his throat. "I've got a nice buzz, but I'm not drunk. I know exactly what I'm doing, if that's what you're hinting at."

You don't have a clue what you're doing.

He ignored the voice, just as he'd been ignoring it ever since that night at the Pride of Carolina.

The old linoleum floor creaked beneath his feet as he moved to her side, drew her into his arms, and kissed her. He tasted spearmint, and he realized she'd popped a breath mint while he'd been registering for the room. As if she needed something artificial to disguise her own sweet taste.

Her body, warm and pliant, bent against him. He ran his hands up along her spine, then cupped her hips.

Her lips parted and her arms entwined his neck.

He stopped thinking as he lost himself in their kiss.

He had no idea how much time had passed before she drew away and looked deeply into his eyes. *I love you, Eth.*

Her lips didn't move, but he heard her as clearly as he heard God's voice. A sense of relief shot through him. Then she began to speak.

"This isn't right. I want to more than I ever wanted anything, but it's not right for you and it's not right for me. This isn't what God expects from us."

The words were soft, spoken from her heart, but he shut them out.

Listen to her, Ethan, Oprah admonished. *Listen to what she's saying.*

No. He refused to listen. He was a man, not a saint, and he was tired of letting God run his life. Instead, he slipped his hand beneath the hem of her dress and touched the soft skin beneath. "You were going to let Mike Reedy do this." He drew his hand upward, taking the dress with him until he reached her bra. Gently he squeezed her breast through the lace.

"Maybe."

"I don't care what you say. I'm a better friend to you than he is."

"Yes."

He traced his thumb over the soft swell that rose above the top of the bra. "Why would you let him make love to you, but not me?"

She was quiet for so long that he didn't think she'd answer. Then her fingers closed around his forearm. "Because I don't need commitment to have sex with Mike Reedy."

He froze. "Commitment?"

She stared at him with hungry eyes.

"Commitment? That's what you want from me?"

She nodded, looking miserable.

He waited for the panic to hit him, but it didn't happen. Commitment. What she really meant was *marriage*. He'd planned to get married someday, but that time had always been in the future. He withdrew his hand from beneath her dress.

"And I want love from you." Her throat worked as she swallowed. "Love even before the commitment."

He had to get something straight in his mind. "You don't want commitment from Mike?"

She shook her head.

"And you don't want love from him either?"

She shook it again.

"But you want it from me?"

She nodded.

He still didn't feel any panic. Instead, he was filled with a sense of exhilaration that came all the way from his toes. It was as if a huge burden had been lifted from his heart. *Of course.*

As clearly as if someone had snapped on the room's small television set, he heard a song — a *children's* song — along with a new voice echoing in his head.

As the song continued, a picture formed in his mind of all of Them combining into One: Eastwood, the Enforcer God; Oprah, the Counselor God; Marion Cunningham, the Mother God . . . They melded into a single new form.

The children's song ended, and the voice began to speak. *I love you just the way you are, Ethan. You're very special to Me. Through you, I shine the light of My love on all the world. You are My perfect creation. Just the way you are.*

And then, in Ethan's mind, this most wonderful God took off His formal suitcoat and slipped out of His stiff shoes. In a cozy sweater and sneakers, He sang His song of perfect love, telling all His children — every single one of them — that it was a beautiful day in His neighborhood.

At that moment, Ethan Bonner stopped fighting his destiny.

Kristy studied his expression, but, as well as she knew him, she couldn't tell what he was thinking. She only knew there would be no going back for her. She'd set aside her pride and spoken from her heart. If he didn't like it, that was his problem.

He took a deep breath. "Okay."

"Okay?"

"Yes." He gave a jerky nod. "Okay."

"Okay what?" She was bewildered.

"Love. Commitment. The whole thing." He grabbed the skirt of her dress and smoothed it back in place. "Kentucky."

"Kentucky? What are you talking about? Oh, Eth, you *are* drunk. I knew it!"

"I'm not drunk!" He spun her toward the door. "Come on. We're leaving right now."

The knowledge crushed her, and her throat constricted as she turned to face him. "You don't want me anymore."

He pulled her back into his arms. "Oh, baby, I want you so much I can't stand it. And I love you, too, so stop looking at me like that. I haven't been able to think about anything else since you walked into my office in those tight white jeans."

The small flame of hope that had started to burn inside her disappeared and she regarded him angrily. "You *love* me? Why don't you just say what you mean? You *lust* after me."

"That, too."

She'd always been able to read him so clearly, but now she felt as if she were in the presence of a stranger.

"I don't love you because of all the cosmetic changes you've made," he said. "I'm not that shallow. It's just that all those changes finally forced me to notice you and appreciate what's been right under my nose the whole time." He gazed at her as if he could see into her soul and wanted her to see into his. The flame of hope began to burn anew inside her.

His thumb settled in the hollow at the base of her neck. "You've been in my life for so long that I stopped thinking about you as someone who existed separately from me. You were just part of me. And then all these changes happened, and you decided to leave me, and I've been going crazy ever since."

"You have?" She felt delirious, entranced.

He smiled. "You don't have to look so happy about it." And then his forehead knitted, and a note of pleading sounded in his voice. "We can talk on the road. Come on, baby. Hurry. We really, really don't have any time to waste." He grabbed the doorknob with one hand, her shoulder with the other.

"Where are we going? Why are you in such a hurry?"

"We're going to Kentucky." He pulled her outside and hustled her toward his car. "It's not far to the border. There's no waiting period to get married, and we're getting married tonight, Kristy Brown, no matter what you say. And I'm not leaving the ministry, either!"

They'd reached his car. He was beginning to sound as if he were running out of breath, and he stopped by the passenger door to fill his lungs. "We'll do it all over again for our families when we get back. We can even pretend it's the first time, but we're getting married tonight because the two of us need to make love in the worst way, and it's not going to happen unless we say some permanent vows before God first." He froze. "You do want to get married, don't you?"

Happiness bubbled inside her. She smiled, then laughed. "Yes, I really do."

He squeezed his eyes shut. "Good. We'll work out the details on the way."

"What details?"

He pushed her into the car. "Where we're going to live. How many kids we're going to have. Who sleeps on what side of the bed. That sort of thing." He slammed the door, rushed around to the other side of the car, and climbed in. "I also should tell you the reason your car wouldn't start earlier was that I sneaked over to your condo and disconnected the battery cable so you'd have to ride with me. And I'm not sorry, so don't think you're going to get an apology!"

She didn't ask for one, and, within minutes, they were back on the road.

Bemused, Kristy spent the next ninety miles listening to the strangest lecture she'd ever heard. Ethan had always been a stickler regarding premarital counseling for the couples he wed, and now he tried to condense everything he knew into the time it took them to cross the Kentucky border and make the arrangements. He talked and talked and talked.

Kristy smiled and nodded.

They found a Pentecostal minister who agreed to marry them, but Ethan conducted the ceremony. He was the one who asked her to repeat the vows he recited, and he was the one who spoke his own vows in a deep, intense voice that came directly from his heart.

It was Kristy, however, who spotted the Holiday Inn not far from the outskirts of the Cumberland Falls Resort State Park.

They'd barely set their suitcases down before she tackled him, and he fell backward onto the king-sized mattress. She looked so eager, so excited, so thoroughly pleased with herself, that he laughed.

"Gotcha!" she said.

While he tried to catch his breath, she tore at the buttons on his shirt, then lunged for his belt buckle.

He gazed up into the beautiful, intent eyes of his virgin bride. "Let me know if I'm scaring you."

"Shut up and take off your pants."

That cracked them both up. But they didn't laugh for long; their mouths were too busy with hot, wet kisses. And since neither of them had the patience for slow disrobing, they were naked and groping each other within seconds.

"You're beautiful," she sighed as she stroked him. "Just the way I'd imagined."

He cupped the spill of her breasts and tried to find his voice. "You're even more than I imagined."

"Oh, Eth . . . That feels so good."

"You're telling me."

"I want you to do that a lot."

"Remind me if I forget."

She made a throaty moan as he ran his thumbs over her nipples.

"Do that again. Oh, yes . . ."

"Lie back, baby, and let me play with you."

She did as he asked. His caresses grew more intimate, and she sobbed in her passion. "Oh, Eth, I want to do everything." She moaned. "Yes. *That*. And I want . . . I want to *say* everything. Dirty words. I want to say dirty words. And dirty little phrases."

"Go ahead."

"I — I can't think of any."

He whispered a really good one in her ear.

Her eyes widened, and she climaxed beneath his hand.

Even though he was so hard he ached, he laughed because he was the only person in the world who knew her secret.

Kristy Brown Bonner was easy.

She calmed, but he was ready to explode. He longed to bury himself inside her, but, at the very last moment, he remembered something he'd forgotten to discuss in their hurried session of premarital counseling. He stroked her hair and noticed his hand was shaking from the effort it took to restrain himself. "Are we worried about getting you pregnant?"

"I don't think so." She regarded him searchingly. "Are we?"

He settled his weight between her thighs, kissed her, and thought of the babies they'd have. "No, we're definitely not."

She was tight and new and wet. He tried to take his time entering her, but she would have none of it. "*Now*, Eth . . . Please stop messing around. Oh, please . . . I want to remember this forever."

He drove home, and, as he fully possessed her, he gazed down into her eyes. They were filled with tears of love.

His own vision blurred, and the depth of his love for this woman brought the ancient words of that first couple to his mind. "Flesh of my flesh," he whispered. "Bone of my bone."

She caressed his hips with her palms and whispered back, "Flesh of my flesh. Bone of my bone."

They smiled. Their tears mingled. And when they came together, both of them knew that only God could have designed something so perfect.

CHAPTER
TWENTY-TWO

"Don't get too close, Chip."

"What are you doin'?"

Gabe gritted his teeth. "I'm tearing off the porch so I can build a deck here."

It was Saturday afternoon, and Gabe was supposed to be watching Chip. It was the first time Rachel had left him alone with the kid, but he knew she wouldn't have done it if she hadn't needed to run some mysterious errand in town. Gabe suspected that she was glad to find an excuse to get away from him. Ever since she'd made her announcement that she was leaving, she'd done her best to keep her distance.

He rammed the crowbar underneath one of the old rotted boards and shoved down on it. He was furious with her. Just because she couldn't have everything the way she wanted, she was deserting him. Deserting *them!* He'd thought she was tough, but she wasn't tough enough for this. Instead of sticking it out and trying to solve their problems, she was running.

"What's a deck?"

He regarded the child impatiently. Just as he'd gotten into the physically satisfying work of tearing off the back porch, Chip had abandoned the hole he was digging in the garden and come over to bother him.

"It'll be like the place where we ate outside when we went to Rosie's house last Saturday. Now step back so you don't get hurt."

"Why are you doing it?"

"Because I want to." He wasn't going to tell the kid he'd started the project because there wasn't much left to do at the drive-in these days, and he had to keep himself from going crazy.

Just walking into that ticket booth last night had dragged him down. It was only his second weekend in business, and he already hated every minute of it. He could have killed some time with Ethan if his brother hadn't taken off yesterday for a conference in Knoxville, and Cal was all wrapped up with his family, so Gabe had decided to keep himself busy by building this deck.

He told himself it would be a nice place for his parents and brothers to gather for summer cookouts. Legally, it was his mother's cottage, but since she and his father were still in South America doing their missionary work, he couldn't talk to her about his plan. She wouldn't mind, though. Nobody minded what he did, except for Rachel. She was the only one who ever criticized him.

She was going to leave after this weekend. He didn't know exactly when. He hadn't asked.

What the hell did she want from him? He'd done everything he could to help her. He'd even offered to marry her! Didn't she understand how hard that had been for him?

"Can I help?"

The boy still seemed to think that if he pretended to be Gabe's best friend, his mother would change her mind, but nothing was going to get her to do that. She was too stubborn, too damned pigheaded, and she thought everything was so simple, that he could just return to being a vet because she wanted him to. But it didn't work that way. That was the past, and he couldn't go back to it.

"You can help later, maybe." He shoved down on the crowbar. The old wood split and pieces flew. Chip jumped back, but not before a chunk nearly hit him.

Gabe threw down the crowbar. "I told you not to get so close!"

The boy made that futile reaching gesture for his rabbit. "You're scaring Tweety Bird."

It wasn't Tweety Bird who was scared, and both of them knew it. Gabe felt sick. He forced himself to speak calmly. "There's a couple of pieces of wood over there. Why don't you see if you can build something with them?"

"I don't got a hammer."

"Pretend."

"You got a real hammer. You don't pretend."

"That's because . . . Look in my toolbox. There's another hammer in there." He returned to work.

"I don't got any nails."

Gabe gave a vicious shove to the crowbar. The wood screamed as he pried up another floorboard. "You're not ready to use nails yet. Just pretend."

"You don't pretend."

Gabe fought to hold onto his temper. "I'm a grown-up."

"You don't pretend you *like* me." The boy banged the hammer against a short length of two-by-four Gabe had used earlier as a lever. "Mommy says we still got to go to Flor'da."

"I can't do anything about that," Gabe snapped, ignoring the child's first comment.

Chip began banging the wood with the hammer, hitting it again and again, not to accomplish anything, merely to make noise. "You can too do something. You're a grown-up."

"Yeah, well, just because I'm a grown-up doesn't mean I get to have things the way I want." The banging was getting on his nerves. "Take that wood over by the garden."

"I want to stay here."

"You're too close. It's dangerous."

"No, it's not."

"You heard me." Anger built inside him. Anger over everything he couldn't control. The death of his family. Rachel's desertion. The drive-in he hated. And this boy. This gentle little boy who stood like a roadblock in the path of the only peace Gabe had been able to find since he'd lost his wife and child. "*Stop that damned pounding!*"

"You said *damn!*" The boy slammed down the hammer. It caught the edge of the two-by-four. The board flew.

Gabe saw it coming, but he couldn't move quickly enough, and it hit him in the knee. "God damn it!" He lunged forward, grabbed Chip by the arm, and pulled him to his feet. "I told you to stop that!"

Instead of cowering, the boy defied him. "You *want* us to go to Flor'da! You didn't pretend! You said you would, but you didn't! You're a big damn *butthead!*"

Gabe drew back his arm and slapped the flat of his hand against the boy's rump.

For a few seconds neither of them moved.

Gradually, Gabe grew aware of the sting in his palm. He looked down at his hand as if it no longer belonged to him. "Jesus . . ." He dropped the boy's arm. His chest knotted.

You're so gentle, Gabe. The gentlest man I know.

Chip's face crumpled. His small chest shook, and he pulled back as if he were folding into himself.

Gabe fell down on one knee. "Oh, God . . . Chip . . . I'm sorry. I'm so sorry."

The child rubbed his elbow, even though it wasn't his elbow that hurt. He tilted his head to one side and caught his bottom lip between his teeth. It quivered. He didn't look at Gabe. He didn't look at anything. He just tried not to cry.

And in that moment Gabe finally saw the child as himself, instead of as a reflection of Jamie. He saw a brave little boy with flyaway brown hair, knobby elbows, and a small, quivering mouth. A gentle little boy who loved books and building things. A child who found contentment not in expensive toys or the latest video games, but in watching a baby sparrow grow stronger, in collecting pinecones and living with his mother on Heartache Mountain, in being carried around on a man's shoulders and pretending, if only for a moment, that he had a father.

How could he ever have mixed up Chip and Jamie in his mind, even for a moment? Jamie had been Jamie, uniquely his own person. And so was this vulnerable little boy he'd struck.

"Chip . . ."

The boy backed away.

"Chip, I lost my temper. I was mad at myself, and I took it out on you. It was wrong, and I want you to forgive me."

"Okay," Chip muttered, not forgiving him at all, just wanting to get away.

Gabe dropped his head and stared at the ground, but it was blurred. "I haven't hit anybody since I was a kid."

He and Cal used to beat up on Ethan. Not because Ethan had done anything, but because both of them had sensed he wasn't as tough as they were, and they'd been afraid for him. None of them had realized Gabe would prove to be the weakling.

"I promise . . ." He pushed the words out past the boulders in his throat. "I won't ever hit you again."

Chip backed away. "Me and my mommy are going to Flor'da. You don't have to pretend no more." With a muffled hiccup, he ran toward the house, leaving Gabe more alone than he'd ever been in his life.

Rachel locked the doors to Kristy's condo and put the spare keys in her purse, along with the bus tickets Kristy had left for her yesterday on the kitchen table before she and Ethan had taken off for their conference. As Rachel drove back to Heartache Mountain, she found herself memorizing every bend in the road, every grove of trees and patch of wildflowers. It was already Saturday, and she planned to leave Salvation on Monday. Staying any longer was simply too painful.

If she were going to move forward with her life, she knew she'd have to train herself to focus on the positive. After all, she wasn't leaving Salvation empty-handed. Edward was healthy again. She had Kristy's friendship. And for the rest of her life she'd have the memory of a man who had been almost wonderful.

Gabe was waiting for her on the front porch. She parked the Escort in the garage, and as she walked toward him, every limb of her body dragged with regret. If only it could have been different.

He sat on the top step, elbows balanced on splayed knees, his wrists hanging between them. He looked as dejected as she felt. "I have to talk to you," he said.

"What about?"

"About Chip." He looked up. "I hit him."

Her heart jumped into her throat. She flew up the steps, but he caught her before she reached the screen door.

"He's all right. I — I smacked him on the rump. I didn't hit him hard."

"And you think that makes it all right?"

"Of course not. He didn't do anything to deserve being hit. I never — I've never struck a child. It —" He stepped back from her, thrust his hand through his hair. "God, Rachel, I just lost it, and it happened. I told him I was sorry. I told him he hadn't done anything wrong. But he doesn't understand. How could he understand something like this?"

She stared at him. She'd been so wrong. Despite all the warning signs, she'd somehow convinced herself that Gabe wouldn't hurt Edward. But he had, and the fact that she should never have left them alone together made her the worst mother in the world.

She turned away and headed into the house. "Edward!"

He came out of the back hallway, looking small and anxious. She forced herself to smile at him. "Pack up, pardner. We're going to spend the next few nights at Kristy's. I'm even getting a sitter to stay with you so you don't have to go to the drive-in tonight."

She heard the screen door shut behind her and knew by the wary expression in Edward's eyes that Gabe had come in.

"Are we going to Flor'da now?" Edward asked.

"Soon. Not today."

Gabe came forward. "I told your mom what happened, Chip. She's pretty upset with me."

Why couldn't he just go away? Didn't he understand there was nothing he could say that would make this all right? Her hand trembled as she touched Edward's cheek. "No one has the right to hit you."

"Your mom's right."

Edward looked up at her. "Gabe got mad because I banged the hammer, and I wasn't s'pose to. Then I

404

called him the b-word." Edward dropped his voice to an anxious whisper. "Butthead."

Under other circumstances, it would have been funny, but not now. "Gabe still shouldn't have hit you, even though that was a rude thing for you to do, and you need to apologize."

Edward slipped closer to her side for courage and gave Gabe a resentful glare. "Sorry I called you *butthead*."

Gabe went down on one knee and regarded him with a directness he'd never displayed before. Now that it was too late, he could finally look her son in the eyes. "I forgive you, Chip. I just hope someday you can forgive me."

"I said I did."

"I know. But you didn't mean it, and I don't blame you."

Edward looked up at her. "If I mean it, do we still got to go to Flor'da?"

"Yes." She choked out the words. "Yes. We still have to go. Now run in your room, and pack up your things in the laundry basket."

He didn't argue any longer, and she knew he was anxious to get away from them both.

The moment he disappeared, Gabe turned to her. "Rach, something happened today. When I . . . It was — Chip didn't cry, but it was like he crumbled right in front of me. Not physically, but mentally."

"If you're trying to make things better, you're going about it the wrong way." She wouldn't let him watch her fall apart, so she turned away and headed for the kitchen, only to have him follow her.

"Just listen. I don't know if it was the shock of what I'd done, or . . . For the first time, I felt as if I were really seeing him. Only him. Not Jamie."

"Gabe, leave me alone, will you?"

"Rach . . ."

"Please. I'll meet you at the drive-in at six."

He didn't say anything, and, finally, she heard him walk away.

She packed up everything she and Edward owned and loaded it into the Escort. As she pulled away from Annie's cottage, she swallowed her tears. This small cottage had been a symbol of everything she'd dreamed about, and now she was leaving it behind.

At her side, Edward groped for Horse, and when he didn't find his old companion, chewed on his thumb instead.

Rachel called Lisa Scudder from Kristy's condo and got the name of a reliable high-school girl to watch Edward, then fixed him an early dinner from the leftovers she'd brought with her from the cottage. She was too upset to eat anything herself. By the time she'd changed into a clean dress, the sitter had arrived, and when she left, the two of them were safely tucked in front of Kristy's television.

Rachel would have given anything not to have to go to work that night. She didn't want to see Gabe, didn't want to think how he'd betrayed her trust, but she spotted him the moment she pulled into the drive-in. He stood in the middle of the lot with his fists clenched at his sides. There was something unnaturally still about his posture that alarmed her. She followed the direction of his gaze and drew in her breath.

The middle of the screen had been defaced with streaks of black paint like some giant abstract painting. She jumped out of the car. "What happened?"

Gabe's response was low and toneless. "Someone got in after we closed last night and wrecked the place. The snack shop, the rest rooms . . ." He finally looked at her, and his eyes seemed empty. "I've got to get out of here. I called Odell, and he's on his way. Just tell him I found it like this."

"But —"

He ignored her and headed for his truck. Moments later, it shot out of the lot, leaving nothing behind but a dusty trail.

She rushed over to the snack shop. The lock had been smashed and the door stood partially open. She looked inside and saw broken appliances littering the floor, along with spilled soft-drink syrup, melted ice cream, and cooking oil. She hurried to the rest rooms and found a sink partially ripped off one wall, rolls of paper towels stopping up the toilets, and broken ceiling tiles scattered over the floor.

Before she could inspect the projection room, Odell Hatcher arrived. He got out of his squad car along with a man she recognized as Jake Armstrong, the officer who'd tried to throw her into jail for vagrancy.

"Where's Gabe?" Odell asked.

"He was upset and he left. I'm sure he'll be back before long." She wasn't sure of anything. "He told me to tell you this is the way he found it."

Odell frowned. "He should have waited around. Don't you leave until I say it's all right, y'hear?"

"I wasn't planning to. Just let me call Kayla Miggs and tell her not to come in." Tom Bennett lived farther away, and he would have already left by now, so it was too late to contact him.

Odell let her make her call, then had her accompany him to inspect the damage and see if anything was missing.

The hundred dollars in change Gabe had left in the register was gone, along with the radio he liked to play when he worked, but she couldn't tell if anything else had been taken. As she stared at the desecration, she remembered Gabe's awful stillness. Would this send him back to that empty place he'd been dwelling in before she'd come to Salvation?

Tom appeared and, after he'd been filled in on what had happened, accompanied them to the projection room. The FM receiver that controlled the sound equipment had been flung to the floor, but the projector itself was too large for that, so the intruder had pounded it with something heavy, probably the folding metal chair that lay on the floor.

The destruction was so mindless that it gave Rachel the chills. She turned to Odell. "I have to block off the entrance before the customers start arriving. Tom can tell you better than I if anything's missing up here."

To her relief, he didn't protest, and she fled. But she had just descended the outside stairs when a white Range Rover roared into the lot. Her heart sank. Of all the people she didn't want to see right now, Gabe's big brother headed the list.

Cal jumped out and stalked toward her. "What's going on? And where's Gabe? Tim Mercer heard on his police radio there was trouble out here."

"Gabe's not here. I don't know where he went."

Cal caught sight of the drive-in screen. "What the hell happened?"

"Someone vandalized the place last night after we closed."

He cursed under his breath. "Any idea who did it?"

She shook her head.

Cal caught sight of Odell and rushed up the steps. She made her escape to the ticket booth.

As soon as she got there, she fastened the chain across the entrance, then dragged the sawhorse with the *Closed* sign into place. She'd painted that sawhorse herself. The same purple as the ticket booth.

When she was done, she stepped inside the ticket booth and stared out at the highway. Had it only been six weeks since she'd come to Salvation? Images began to flip through her mind like a music video of all that had happened.

A shadow fell over the doorway. "Odell wants to talk to you."

She whirled around and saw Jake Armstrong standing there, looking even more insolent than the day

409

he'd tried to arrest her. She felt a prickle of foreboding, then dismissed it. "All right."

Jake was standing too close to the door, forcing her to turn slightly so she could pass through without touching him. She'd barely taken three steps before she realized that the police chief, Cal, and Tom were all standing around her Escort, and the hatchback was open.

Her first thought was that they had no right to be poking around inside her car, but then she remembered the car belonged to Cal's wife. Still, she didn't like it. Her uneasiness increased, and she picked up her pace.

"Is there a problem?"

Cal turned to her, his expression vicious. "There's a big problem, lady. I guess you wanted a little revenge before you left town."

"Revenge? What are you talking about?"

Odell ambled around the hood of the car. In his hand, he held a crumpled white paper sack, the kind they used in the snack shop. It was smeared with what looked like melted chocolate ice cream. "We found the hundred dollars missing from the register. It was stuffed in this sack under the front seat of your car." He jerked his head toward the boxes in the backseat that were filled with her meager possessions. "Tom's small-screen TV was under one of those boxes and that radio you told us was missing."

Her heart kicked against her ribs. "But . . . I don't understand."

410

Tom looked hurt and confused. "It was the TV my wife gave me for my birthday. Remember I told you? So I could watch baseball while I was working."

Realization struck. They thought she was responsible. Her skin prickled with alarm. "Wait just a minute. I didn't do this! How could you even —"

"Save it for the judge," Cal snapped. He turned to Odell. "Since Gabe isn't around, I'm pressing charges."

She lurched forward, grabbed his arm. "Cal, you can't do this. I didn't steal these things."

"Then how did they get in the Escort?"

"I don't know. But I love this place. I could never destroy it like this."

She should have saved her breath. With a sense of unreality, she listened as Odell read her her rights. When he finished, Cal stared down at her, his gaze hard-eyed and condemning. "Jane liked you from the beginning," he said bitterly. "And you'd just about won over Ethan. He was starting to believe you really cared about Gabe. But all you've ever cared about was his bank account."

Her temper flared. "I could *have* his bank account if I wanted it, you idiot! He asked me to marry him."

"Liar." He ground out the words through clenched teeth. "So that's why you did it. Marriage is what you've had in mind from the beginning. You knew he was vulnerable right now, and you —"

"He's not *half* as vulnerable as you think!" she cried. "Damn you, Cal Bonner, you're —"

She gave a gasp of pain as Jake Armstrong grabbed her arms and wrenched them behind her. Before she could react, he'd snapped a pair of handcuffs on her wrists, securing them behind her in the same way dangerous criminals were restrained.

Cal frowned. For a moment she thought he was going to say something, but then Odell slapped his back. "I've got to hand it to you, Cal. I wouldn't have thought to look in her car."

She was going to cry. She blinked back her tears and stared at Cal. "I'll never forgive you for this."

For the first time he looked uncertain, then his expression hardened. "You deserve everything you get. I tried to make it easy for you with that check, but you got too greedy. By the way, I'll be stopping payment on it first thing Monday morning."

Jake Armstrong put his hand on top of her head and pushed her toward the backseat of the squad car more roughly than necessary. Her shackled wrists made the movement awkward, and she stumbled.

"Watch it." Cal caught her before she could fall and guided her into the backseat.

She jerked away from his touch. "I don't need your help!"

He ignored her and turned to Jake. "You be careful with her. I want her locked up, but I don't want anybody playing fast and loose. You got me?"

"I'll keep my eye on her," Odell said.

Cal began to move away.

Edward! What was going to happen to him? Kristy was gone and the sitter wasn't even sixteen.

"Cal!" Once again she had to swallow her pride because of her son. She drew a shaky breath and tried to speak calmly. "Edward is at Kristy's condo. He's with a sitter, but she's too young to take care of him for long, and Kristy's gone." Something inside her gave way, and her eyes brimmed with tears. "Please . . . He's going to be so scared."

He stared at her for a long moment, and then gave a brusque nod. "Jane and I'll take care of him."

Jake slammed the door and settled in the front seat next to Odell. As the squad car moved forward, she tried to absorb the fact that she was on her way to jail.

CHAPTER
TWENTY-THREE

It was starting to get dark, so Cal tucked Chip under his arm and hauled him like a sack of potatoes up the steps onto the deck. "You're getting too good with that football, buddy. You wore me out."

Chip giggled as Cal gave him a couple of extra bounces. Cal had hoped playing with the boy would take his own mind off what had happened a few hours earlier with his mother, but it wasn't working.

He looked up and saw Jane standing inside the French doors with Rosie in her arms, and he felt a jolt right in the middle of his chest. Sometimes it hit him that way — hard — the sight of these two females he loved more than anything in the world. There had been a time in his life when he hadn't wanted either one of them, and he never let himself forget that. The memory kept him humble.

Rosie was clutching that god-awful stuffed rabbit, and she started to kick and squeal as she caught sight of Chip. As soon as they were inside the French doors, Cal let the boy down, brushed Jane's lips with a quick kiss, and took Rosie from her.

The baby gave him a big grin, then blew a noisy raspberry, her newest trick. He smiled and wiped his face on her already damp T-shirt. Only then did he notice that Jane looked harried.

He lifted an inquisitive eyebrow. "I haven't been outside more than fifteen minutes."

She sighed. "Wait till you see our bathroom."

"The toilet paper again?"

"And the toothpaste. You didn't put the cap back on, and I wasn't fast enough."

As if she knew they were talking about her, Rosie gave him another drooly grin and clapped her hands in delight. For the first time he noticed that she smelled like Crest Tartar Control.

"Rosie's got a lot of mischief," Chip said with all the solemnity of an adult. "She's a handful."

Cal and Jane exchanged amused glances.

Rosie kicked again and held her arms out toward Chip, dropping the rabbit in the process. Cal set her on the floor, and she immediately threw herself at the boy's legs. He crouched and tickled her tummy, then looked up at Cal, his forehead puckered with worry.

"When's my mommy coming to get me?"

Cal stuck his hand in the pocket of his slacks and jingled the change. "Tell you what, buddy. How'd you like to have a sleepover right here?"

Jane looked at him with surprise, but he avoided her eyes.

"Is it okay with my mommy?"

"Sure it is. You can sleep in the room right next to Rosie's. Would you like that?"

"I guess." The worry marks didn't disappear from his forehead. "If Mommy says I can."

"It's fine with her."

Cal still hadn't figured out how he was going to break the news to the boy that his mother was in jail. He'd planned on having Ethan's help, but when he called the hotel in Knoxville where his brother was supposed to be staying, the desk said he wasn't registered. He'd asked for Kristy and heard the same thing, so they must have changed their plans. He'd ended up putting a message on his brother's home answering machine and hoping he'd check it.

He still needed to explain things to Jane, who was giving him one of those looks that said she knew something was going on, and he'd better come up with a few answers, especially since he'd led her to believe he was just bringing Chip by for a quick visit before they put Rosie to bed.

Cal leaned down to ruffle the boy's hair. "Keep an eye on Rosie for a few minutes, will you, buddy?"

"Sure."

The family room was gated off and childproofed, but they still couldn't leave her for long, and he didn't steer Jane any farther than the kitchen. He procrastinated by pulling her into his arms and nibbling her neck. She snuggled closer. It wouldn't take much to distract her, but he'd only be postponing the inevitable.

"Chip's spending the night with us," he said.

"I heard. What's going on?"

"Now don't get upset, but . . . We need to watch him for a while because Rachel's in jail."

"In jail!" Her head shot up, conking him in the chin. "My God, Cal, we have to do something." She tore

416

herself out of his arms and raced for her purse. "I'm going to her right now. I can't believe —"

"Honey . . ." He caught her arm, stroked it. "Stop for a minute. Rachel trashed the drive-in. She belongs in jail."

Jane stared at him. "What do you mean she trashed it?"

"Destroyed the kitchen, smashed some equipment, graffiti on the screen. The whole nine yards. Near as I can gather, she wanted Gabe to marry her, and, since he wouldn't do it, she decided to get even with him before she left town."

"Rachel wouldn't do that."

"I saw the drive-in and believe me, you're wrong. Odell found a pair of Greyhound bus tickets stuck in her purse. I guess this was her good-bye present to Gabe."

Jane sank down on one of the counter stools, then reached out and stroked her hand along his forearm. She liked to touch him. Even when they were arguing, she'd sometimes stroke him. "But it just doesn't add up. Why would she do something like that? She loves Gabe."

"She loves his bank account."

"That's not true. She cares for him. All you have to do is see the way she looks at him. You and Ethan are so protective of Gabe that you're blind where she's concerned."

"So are you, sweetheart, or you'd realize she's a money-grabbing opportunist."

Her soft stroking continued. "Don't you find it strange that a money-grabbing opportunist could be raising such a kindhearted little boy?"

"I didn't say she was a bad mother. The two don't necessarily go together."

He glanced into the family room to check on Rosie, but also to keep from meeting Jane's eyes because she'd managed to hit the nail right on the head about what was bothering him. A child didn't come any better than that little boy of hers, and Cal wasn't so blind he couldn't see how much she cared about him. He remembered the expression on her face when she'd cried out to him to take care of Chip. All the fight had gone right out of her, and she hadn't seemed to pose much of a danger to anyone.

Jane shook her beautiful brainy head. "This just doesn't seem right to me. How do you know she's guilty?"

Cal told her what they'd found in the Escort. As she listened, she got a stricken look around her eyes, and Cal's heart once again hardened against the Widow Snopes. He kissed Jane's fingertips. He didn't like it when anybody other than himself upset his wife.

"But how could I be so wrong about her? Gabe must be devastated. Still, I can't believe he'd have her thrown into jail."

Cal and Jane didn't keep secrets from each other, and he had to tell her what he'd done, but he wanted to wait until the kids were settled for the night. He was fairly certain they were going to have an argument about it, and from experience, he knew his best defense when his wife got upset was to get her naked as quickly as possible, something that would be a lot easier without a baby and five-year-old looking on.

"Come on, sweetheart. Let's go rescue Chip before Rosie wears him out."

The jail was small, with no separate quarters for men and women, and the loud complaints of a drunk echoed off the barren walls. Rachel paced the tiny confines of her cell and fought to suppress her panic, but it overwhelmed her. Fear for Edward. For herself. And fear that Gabe had fled again, just as he'd done after Cherry and Jamie died.

Gabe . . . She'd expected him to show up long before now. Surely he'd come back. At the very least, he wouldn't leave without saying good-bye to his brothers, and, when he discovered what had happened to her, he'd get her out of jail.

Maybe it was the night or the fact that she felt so alone, but she couldn't quite convince herself it would be that easy. The proof against her was damning, and there was no guarantee he'd believe her. She certainly had no explanation for how those things had ended up in the Escort.

It might be different if he loved her. Then he'd have to know in his heart she was innocent, wouldn't he? But he didn't love her, and now he might end up thinking as badly of her as everyone else in Salvation.

She bit her lip and concentrated on Edward, only to feel her heart race. His sense of security was so fragile, and once again, it was being destroyed. She wanted to believe that Cal would keep him safe, but she wasn't sure of anything anymore. For the first few hours she'd even let herself hope that Jane might intercede, but that hadn't happened.

She hugged herself against her fear and wondered how her life had come to this. She had no defense against Cal Bonner. He had money, reputation, the town's respect, and he'd let her rot in here if he thought it would protect his brother.

The outer door clanged, and she jumped as a man entered. She stiffened, expecting Jake Armstrong, who was on duty tonight. But the man wasn't Jake, and it took her a few moments to recognize Russ Scudder.

He had a cigarette hanging from his fingers as he came to a stop in front of her cell. It was nearly midnight, much too late for jailhouse visitors, and his presence gave her a chill.

"I asked Jake to let me in." He didn't meet her eyes. "Him and me . . . We go way back."

"What do you want?" She reminded herself that the cell was locked, but she still felt uneasy.

"It's —" He cleared his throat, took a drag from the cigarette. "I know I owe you, but your bail's high, and I'm a little short right now. That check you gave Lisa has to go into a special fund."

"I know." How could she tell him the check wouldn't be good if she didn't get on that bus on Monday?

"It was nice of you to give us that money."

She didn't know what to say or why he was here, so she kept silent.

"Emily's — She's doing better. Her white-cell count is way down. Nobody expected it." He finally looked at her. "Lisa's mom thinks you faith-healed her."

"I didn't."

"She's been getting better every day since you saw her."

"I'm glad. But it doesn't have anything to do with me."

"That's what I thought at first. But now I'm not so sure." His forehead puckered and he drew nervously on the cigarette. "It's happened so fast, and none of the doctors can explain why. She keeps saying you closed your eyes and your hands were hot when you touched her."

"The room was warm."

"I guess. Still . . ." He threw down the cigarette and ground it out. "I don't feel right about some things. My little girl . . ." He rubbed his nose with the back of his hand. "I'm not the best father in the world, but she means a lot to me, and you helped her." He pulled the cigarette pack from his shirt pocket and looked down at it. "I talked Jake into letting me come in here tonight because I wanted you to know that I'm sorry for some things, and that I owe you. Maybe there's somebody I can call who'll help you. All you have to do is let me know."

"There's nobody."

"If I had the money . . ." He put the cigarettes back into his pocket.

"It's all right. I don't expect you to bail me out."

"I mean, I would, but . . ."

421

"Thanks. I'm really glad about Emily."

He gave a stiff nod.

She had the sense he wanted to say more because he hesitated, but then he moved toward the door. As soon as he got there, however, he turned back to her. "I got something to tell you." He walked to her cell. "I did a couple of things I'm not proud of."

She listened as he told her that he was responsible for the burning cross, the slashed tires and graffiti on the front of the house, her stolen wallet. "I always liked Dwayne, and I liked the job I had at the Temple. It was the best work I ever had, and nothing's gone right for me since then." Once again, he reached for his cigarettes. "I worked for Bonner for a couple of weeks out at the drive-in, but he let me go. Then you showed up here, and when he hired you, a lot of stuff came together in my head that made me start resenting you. I guess I kind of thought that maybe I still owed something to Dwayne, too. But for whatever reasons, what I did wasn't right." He finally lit the cigarette, drawing the smoke deeply into his lungs.

"Are you the one who destroyed the drive-in?"

"No." He shook his head emphatically. "No. I don't know who did that."

"Why have you told me all this?"

He shrugged. "Lisa and Fran don't think too much of me anymore. But I still love my little girl, and I know I owe you."

She tried to take it in. If he'd made his confession at any other time, she'd be furious, but right now she didn't have energy to spare on Russ Scudder.

422

"All right. You've told me."

He didn't seem to expect any words of forgiveness, and she didn't utter them.

Later, as she sat in the dark on the small metal cot with her knees drawn up in front of her, she gave in to despair. Despite her tarnished reputation, despite all the evidence, Gabe had to believe her.

He had to.

The digital clock next to his bed read 4:28. Cal looked across the pillow at Jane curled up against him and knew that guilt had awakened him, along with worry about Gabe. Where was he?

Right after they'd tucked the children into bed, Cal had driven up to the cottage, even checked his parents' house in town, but he couldn't find any sign of his brother.

Cal still hadn't told Jane he was the one who'd pressed charges against Rachel. He'd kept finding excuses to postpone it, mainly because he hated her to be unhappy. Then they'd started to make love, and afterward they'd both drifted off. Still, keeping this from her wasn't right, and he resigned himself to breaking the news as soon as she woke up. No more excuses. No more postponements. He'd simply have to make her understand.

It wouldn't be easy. Jane didn't have any family, so she couldn't fully comprehend the bond he shared with his brothers. And she hadn't known Gabe long enough to realize what a soft touch he was. But Cal knew. And he'd guarded his brother as zealously as he guarded everyone he loved.

He thought of Rachel all alone in her jail cell and wondered if she was awake, too, worrying about her little boy. Why hadn't she considered that little boy before she'd struck out against Gabe?

He wanted to believe that she'd acted impulsively, without considering the effect her cruelty would have on a man who had finally been able to start a new life, but that didn't excuse her. She was one of those self-focused people who couldn't see any farther than her own needs and frustrations, and now she had to suffer the consequences. Satisfied that he was doing the right thing, Cal finally drifted off.

An hour later, he was jarred awake by the sound of door chimes, along with a furious pounding. Jane bolted upright next to him. "What's that?"

"Stay here." Cal was already out of bed. Grabbing a robe to cover his nakedness, he thrust his arms in the sleeves as he rushed out of the bedroom and down the stairs. When he reached the front door, he looked through the peephole. Relief rushed through him as he saw Gabe on the other side.

He threw open the door. "Where the hell have you been?"

Gabe looked terrible, red-eyed and exhausted, with stubble covering his jaw. "I can't find Rachel."

Cal stepped back to let him in. "You have a key. Why didn't you let yourself in?"

"I forgot. And I needed to talk to you." He shoved his hand through his hair. "Have you seen Rachel? She

424

was supposed to be staying at Kristy's condo, but nobody was there. I drove to the cottage. It's empty. Jesus, Cal, I can't find her anywhere. I'm afraid she's taken off."

"Cal, what's going on?"

Both of them looked up to see Jane coming down the stairs. She'd pulled on her pink nightshirt with a picture of Tinker Bell on the front. The fact that one of the most brilliant female physicists in the world had a fondness for cartoon nightwear usually made Cal smile, but not now. He wanted to keep her out of this.

Cal's uneasiness grew as Gabe rushed to the bottom of the stairs. His brother had always been a man who moved slowly — an easy walk, contained gestures. Now his movements were frantic. "I can't find Rachel. Like a fool, I walked out on her at the drive-in, and I haven't seen her since."

Jane looked confused. "She's in jail."

Gabe stared at her. "Jail?"

Jane touched his arm, her expression mirroring her concern. "I don't understand. Cal told me how Rachel vandalized the drive-in, and that you had her put in jail."

Seconds ticked by, then Gabe and Jane both turned to him, the motion so synchronized they might have been attached at the head.

He shifted uncomfortably. "I didn't actually say that it was Gabe, sweetheart. You just assumed . . ."

She was getting her squinty-eyed look, and he quickly turned to Gabe, keeping his voice calm and comforting as he spoke. "Rachel's the one who

425

destroyed the drive-in, Gabe. I'm sorry. We found the money from the register, along with some other things, hidden in the Escort. I knew you'd want Odell to press charges, so I did it for you."

Gabe's voice sounded as if it had been dragged over sandpaper. "You had Rachel thrown in jail?"

Cal pointed out the truth as gently as he could. "She broke the law."

The next thing he knew, he was flying across the foyer. As the back of his leg hit the rim of the Las Vegas fountain, he lost his balance and fell, ass-first, into the water.

Gabe watched the water splash over the edge of the fountain while he tried to suck enough air into his chest to breathe. Once he could do that, he was going to kill his brother.

Cal struggled to sit upright, his robe swimming around him. "She trashed your drive-in! She belongs in jail!"

Gabe erupted and shot toward the fountain, but before he could get there, Jane threw herself between them. "Stop it! This doesn't help Rachel."

"Help Rachel, my ass!" Cal exclaimed, wiping the water from his eyes. "Gabe's the one who needs help!"

Gabe shot around Jane and reached down to grab his brother by the collar of his robe. "It's *my* drive-in, you son of a bitch, not yours! And you didn't have any right!" He shoved him back into the water.

God . . . He'd broken out in a sweat. Rachel was in jail, and that might be Cal's fault, but it was his fault, too, because he'd run. At the time, all he could think about was getting away. He'd been too much of a coward to stay right there and deal with what had happened.

He had to get to her, and he spun toward the door only to freeze in his tracks at the sound of a small, familiar voice coming from the top of the stairs.

"Gabe?"

He looked up and saw Chip standing there in his Macho Man T-shirt and little white cotton briefs. A rooster tail of light-brown hair stuck up from the back of his head, and silvery tear streaks glistened on his cheeks.

"Gabe?" he whispered. "Where's my mommy?"

Gabe felt as if his heart were cracking open, but this time it didn't spill bile. This time it spilled fresh red blood, full of life and need and love. He took the stairs two at a time and swept the child up in his arms. "It's okay, buddy. I'm going to get her right now."

Brown eyes stared into his own. "I want my mommy."

"I know you do, son. I know."

He felt Chip trembling beneath his palms and knew he'd started to cry. To protect his privacy, he carried him into the guest room. There wasn't a comfortable chair, so he sat on the side of the bed and cradled him in his lap.

The little boy's tears were mostly silent ones. Gabe held him against his chest and stroked his hair. As much as he needed to get to Rachel, he had to take care of this first.

"Something bad's happened to my mommy, hasn't it?"

"There's been a misunderstanding, a big mix-up. Your mom's safe, but I think she might be scared, and I have to go get her."

"I'm scared, too."

"I know you are, son, but I'm going to bring your mom back to you real soon."

"Is she going to die?"

Gabe pressed his lips to the top of the child's head. "No, she's not going to die. She's going to be fine. Just scared, is all. And probably mad, too. Your mom can get real mad."

Chip nestled closer, and Gabe stroked the curve of his arm. It felt so good he wanted to cry himself.

"Why was Rosie's dad sitting in the fountain?"

"He . . . uh . . . slipped."

"Gabe?"

"Yes?"

The child's soft deep breath was a whisper in the night-quiet room. "I forgive you."

Tears stung Gabe's eyes. Chip had offered his forgiveness much too easily. The child wanted stability so badly he'd do anything to get it, even put aside the wrong Gabe had done to him.

"You don't have to. What I did was pretty bad. Maybe you need to think about it some more."

"Okay."

Gabe took the child's hand in his own and stroked the palm with his thumb.

428

The solid weight of the boy's head sank against his chest. "I thought about it," he whispered. "And I forgive you."

Gabe kissed his hair again, blinked, then eased back just far enough to gaze down into Chip's small face. "I have to go find your mom now. I know you're going to be scared until she gets back, so why don't we sneak into Rosie's room with some blankets and make a bed for you on the floor next to her crib. Would that make you feel better?"

Chip nodded, then wriggled out of Gabe's lap and grabbed his pillow. "I used to sleep in Rosie's room when I was a baby. Did you know that?"

Gabe smiled at him and picked up the comforter. "You don't say."

"Uh-huh. We have to be real quiet so we don't wake her up."

"Real quiet." With the comforter tucked under one arm, he took Chip's hand and walked out into the hallway.

"Gabe?"

"Yes?"

Chip stopped walking and gazed up at him, wide-eyed and earnest. "I wish Jamie could sleep in Rosie's room, too."

"Me too, son," Gabe whispered. "Me too."

Gabe would have torn Salvation apart to get Rachel out of jail, but, fortunately, as soon as he started pounding on the front door of Odell's house, the police chief woke up, so it wasn't necessary.

By seven o'clock, Gabe was pacing the floor of the main room of the police station, his eyes glued to the metal door that led to the jail. As soon as he got the chance, he was going to tear his brother apart.

But he knew he was shifting the blame away from where it belonged. If he hadn't run away, none of this would have happened.

When he'd left the drive-in, he'd driven across the county line and ended up at an all-night truck stop drinking lethal coffee and facing his demons. The hours had ticked by, and it was nearly dawn before he'd figured out that Rachel had been right all along. He'd been using the Pride of Carolina to hide out. Although he'd been existing, he hadn't really been living. He didn't have the guts.

The door opened, and Rachel appeared. She froze as she caught sight of him.

Her face was pale, her hair tangled, and her calico dress a mass of wrinkles. The big black shoes plunked down at the ends of her slender legs looked like concrete blocks, one more burden weighing her down. But it was her eyes that tore a hole in his chest. Big, sad, uncertain.

He shot across the room and gathered her into his arms. She shuddered, and, as she trembled against him, he thought of Chip, who'd done the same thing earlier. And then he didn't think of anything but holding tight to this feisty, stubborn sweetheart of a woman who'd pulled him back from the grave.

CHAPTER
TWENTY-FOUR

Rachel sagged against Gabe's chest. As she felt his arms wrap around her, she could barely speak. "Where's Edward?"

"With Cal and Jane." His hand stroked her hair. "He's fine."

"Cal —"

"Shh . . . Not now."

The police chief spoke from behind them. "We got evidence, y'know."

"No, you don't." Gabe drew away from her and drilled Odell with his gaze. "I put those things in the Escort myself, right before I drove off."

She sucked in her breath. He was lying. She could see it in his face.

"You?" Odell said.

"That's right. *Me*. Rachel didn't know a thing about it." The steely note in his voice dared Odell to contradict him, and the police chief didn't try. Gabe tightened his grip around her shoulders and steered her toward the door.

Daylight had broken, and, as she breathed in the clear air, she didn't think she'd ever smelled anything so beautiful. She realized Gabe was leading her toward

431

a Mercedes, parked in a space marked *Reserved for the Chief of Police*. It took her a moment to remember the car was his, since she'd never seen him drive anything but his pickup.

"What's this?"

He opened the door for her. "I wanted you to be comfortable."

She tried to smile, but it wobbled at the corners.

"Slide in," he said gently.

She did as he asked, and before long, they were traveling through Salvation's deserted streets, accompanied by the rich purr of a flawless German engine. As they reached the highway, he rested one hand over her thigh.

"I promised Chip I'd have you back in time for breakfast. You can stay in the car while I go inside and get him."

"You saw him?"

She waited for that stiff, distant look to settle over his face the way it always did whenever her son's name came up, but Gabe seemed more worried than aloof. "I didn't tell him you were in jail."

"What did you say?"

"Just that there was a mix-up, and I had to go get you. But he's a sensitive kid, and he picked up the fact that something was wrong."

"He's going to be imagining the worst."

"I made a bed for him so he could sleep on the floor next to Rosie's crib. That seemed to settle him down."

She stared at him. "You made a bed for him?"

Gabe looked over at her. "Just leave it alone for now, will you, Rach?"

432

She wanted to question him farther, but the hint of entreaty in his expression silenced her.

They drove another mile or so without speaking. She needed to tell him about Russ Scudder, but she was too tired, and he seemed preoccupied. With no warning, he pulled the car off onto the shoulder, slid down the driver's window, then gazed at her, looking so troubled she was alarmed.

"There's something you're not telling me, isn't there?"

"No," he replied. "I'm just trying to figure out how to go about this."

"Go about what?"

He leaned forward, slipped his fingers around her calf, and lifted it. "I know you've been through a lot, Rach, but I need something from you. I need it pretty bad."

Puzzled, she watched him draw off her shoe. Did he want to make love? But surely not here. It was fully daylight, and, although the traffic was thin, they were far from alone on the highway.

He pulled off her other shoe and feathered a gentle kiss over her lips. It felt good, more comforting than passionate, and she wished he'd keep kissing her like that, but he backed away, brushed the hair from her face, and gazed down at her with tender eyes.

"I know I'm a jerk. I know I'm insensitive and domineering and a couple dozen other things, but I can't look at you in these a minute longer." With a flick of the wrist, he hurled both of her shoes right out the window.

"Gabe!"

He threw the car into drive, and they shot back out onto the highway.

"What are you doing?" She turned in her seat and tried to catch sight of her precious shoes. "They're all I have!"

"Not for long."

"Gabe!"

Once again, that warm, comforting hand settled over her thigh. "Hush. Just hush, will you, sweetheart?"

She slumped back into the seat. Gabe had gone crazy. That was the only explanation. The destruction of the drive-in had pushed him right over the edge.

The inside of her head felt like a soggy loaf of bread, and she couldn't think. Later, she'd sort it out.

The praying-hands gates stood open for them. Gabe drove through and pulled the Mercedes to a stop in the center of the courtyard. One of her sweat socks had fallen off when he'd removed her shoe, and she bent to take off the other one, then opened her car door.

He looked over at her. "I told you I'd go in and get him."

"I'm not afraid of your brother."

"I didn't say you were."

"I'm going in."

She climbed the front steps barefoot. Her hair hadn't been near a comb since yesterday afternoon, and her calico dress was a road map of wrinkles, but she hadn't done anything wrong, and she wasn't going to hide from Cal Bonner.

434

Gabe came up next to her, as steady and solid as forever. Except Gabe wasn't forever. She would be leaving him behind tomorrow morning when she and Edward got on the bus.

The door was unlocked, and he gently steered her inside. Jane must have been watching for them because she immediately rushed into the foyer from the kitchen. She was dressed in a pair of jeans and a T-shirt. Her normally tidy hair was loose and her face clear of makeup.

"Rachel! Are you all right?"

"I'm fine. Just a little tired. Is Edward up yet?"

"Rosie just woke him." She caught Rachel's hands in her own. "I'm sorry. I didn't know what Cal had done until a few hours ago."

Rachel nodded, not knowing how to respond.

Just then, a baby's high-pitched squeal came from the top of the stairs followed by a little boy's belly laugh. She raised her head and looked toward the balcony in time to see Cal coming out of the nursery with Rosie and Horse tucked under one arm and her son under the other. He bounced both children and made a train noise, only to freeze as he saw the trio in the foyer below.

Edward lifted his head and spotted her. He was wearing the same navy shorts he'd had on when she'd left him with the sitter yesterday evening, but the blue T-shirt hanging so loosely from his shoulders must have come from Jane because it read *Physicists do it theoretically.* "Mommy!"

She wanted to run to him and squeeze him until all her fears went away, but that would only frighten him. "Hey, sleepyhead."

Cal lowered him to the carpet, and he came racing down the stairs, one hand on the banister, sneakers flying. "Gabe! You said she'd be back!" He ran across the hallway and hurled himself against her legs. "Guess what? Rosie pooed in her diaper and smelled up the whole room, and her dad called her Rosie Stink-O."

"Did he?"

"It was a big mess."

"I'll bet."

Rachel lifted her head and looked toward Cal, who was coming down the steps with his daughter tucked in the crook of his arm. He regarded her stonily.

"The coffee's ready in the kitchen," Jane said. "Let me see what I can scratch up for breakfast."

Rachel returned Cal's gaze for a moment, then took Edward's hand. "Thanks, Jane, but we need to go."

"But Mommy, Rosie's dad said I can have some of his Lucky Charms."

"Maybe another time."

"But I want some now. Can I? Please?" To her surprise, Edward turned to Gabe. Some of her son's wariness returned, and his voice grew smaller, his manner more cautious. "Please, Gabe?"

To her surprise Gabe reached out and rubbed his shoulder. It was a voluntary touch, and his voice held a note of tenderness that astonished her. "I think your mom's tired. How about if I buy you a box of Lucky Charms on the way home?"

She expected Edward to back off, but he didn't. Instead of pressing his case with her, he continued to speak to Gabe, and his wariness vanished. "But then I can't see Rosie put food in her hair. She does that, Gabe. Really . . . And I want to see it."

Gabe looked at her. "What do you say, Rachel?"

Rachel was so mystified by the change in their relationship that she didn't immediately reply, and Jane stepped in. "I know you're tired, Rachel, but you have to eat anyway. Let me fix you something before you go." With brisk determination, she swept her into the kitchen.

The men followed, silent and cautious. Edward, however, seemed unaware of the tension. He flew back and forth between Rosie, Gabe, and Cal, asking about Lucky Charms, Rosie's eating habits, and spinning an earnest story about his own babyhood when he swore a dinosaur had come to visit him in Rosie's room. The men were completely attentive to him, maybe because it kept them from having to deal with each other.

Rachel excused herself to use the powder room, where she freshened up as best she could, but with her bare feet and wrinkled old house dress, she looked like she should be traveling through Oklahoma with the Joad family instead of being entertained by the Bonners.

When she came out, Jane was opening a box of pancake mix, while Edward perched on a stool at the counter with a bowl of cereal and Cal fed oatmeal to Rosie, who was in her high chair. Gabe stood apart, leaning against the counter and cradling a dark-green coffee mug.

Jane glanced up from the box she was opening, then stared at Rachel's bare feet. "Did something happen to your shoes?"

Gabe glared at his brother and spoke before she could reply. "Odell confiscated them. She spent the night barefoot on that dirty concrete floor."

Jane shot Rachel a horrified look. Rachel lifted her eyebrow and, with a barely perceptible motion, shook her head. What was wrong with Gabe? That made his second lie this morning. Apparently he intended to make his brother suffer.

Jane bit her bottom lip and turned her attention to the pancake mix.

Cal immediately grew defensive. "I told them they had to take care of her, Gabe. Odell said he would." Rosie chose that moment to blow a happy raspberry, sending a shower of oatmeal at her father.

Edward piped up. "Rosie's mommy showed me her computer last night, and I got to see all these planets moving around, and she said they was part of the — uh —" He looked up at Jane and the familiar worried expression formed on his face. "I forgot."

She smiled. "The solar system."

"I remember."

Just then the front doorbell rang, and Cal jumped up to answer it. It was barely seven-thirty, too early for a casual caller, but as Cal's voice drifted into the kitchen from the foyer, Rachel soon realized the identity of the visitor.

"Where have you been?" she heard Cal say. "You were supposed to be in Knoxville, but the hotel said you weren't registered."

"Change in plans."

At the sound of Ethan's voice, Rachel regarded Jane glumly. "One more Mountie to Gabe's rescue. Aren't I just the lucky one?"

Gabe gave a mutter of disgust, slammed down his coffee mug, and headed toward the foyer as Ethan went on.

"We — I came back last night, but I didn't check my machine until half an hour ago. Kristy ran over to the jail as soon as she heard your message, and — Gabe!"

What had Kristy been doing at Ethan's so early in the morning? As Rachel pondered the implications, Jane gazed over at her, lines of worry etched in her smooth forehead. "I know you've been through a lot, Rachel, but for Gabe's sake, this really has to be settled."

"I suppose." Rachel took the wet paper towels Jane handed her and began cleaning up Rosie, who beamed at her. As the men's conversation continued in the hallway, Rachel planted a kiss on the baby's curls, then wiped up the tray. "Thanks for taking such good care of Edward. I was so worried about him."

"Of course you were. He's a wonderful little boy, smart as a whip. Cal and I adore him."

Jane stirred milk into a mug of coffee and gave it to her. Rachel took a seat on a counter stool just as the men appeared.

"Pastor Ethan!" Edward jumped down off his stool and began peppering Ethan with an account of his latest adventures. Ethan alternated between responding and throwing her unhappy looks that seemed to say he'd expected better from her.

Rosie began pounding on her high chair, demanding to be let down. While Jane filled another mug, Cal put his daughter on the floor. She immediately crawled over to Edward and pulled herself up on his legs.

He winced as her sharp little fingernails scratched his bare calf. "Rosie, you're a pain."

She clapped her hands, lost her balance, and fell back on her rump. Her face puckered, but before she could cry, Gabe scooped her up. It was the first time Rachel had seen him hold her, and from the surprise that flickered over his brothers' faces, she knew she wasn't the only one who'd noticed.

Gabe reached down and touched Edward's cheek. "How'd you like to watch TV while the grown-ups visit?"

"I don't like baby shows."

Jane abandoned her pancake mix and moved out from behind the counter. "Rosie's grandparents gave her a cartoon video for her birthday. It's still too old for her, but I bet you'll like it."

"Okay."

The two of them disappeared into the family room. Gabe set Rosie back down and put Horse in front of her. He eyed his brothers. "Since both of you are here, I think it's time we had a family meeting. I know you're tired, Rachel, but this has gone on long enough."

Rachel would rather have hidden in the bathroom than face such a biased jury, but she shrugged. "I haven't run from a fight yet, lover."

Ethan and Cal both stiffened. She gave herself a mental pat on the back. They were too easy.

Gabe regarded her with mild exasperation, then turned to his brothers. "All right. Here's the way it's going to be . . ."

Ethan cut him off. "Before you get started, you need to know how concerned Cal and I have been about the effect your relationship with Rachel's had on you." He paused. "Although Cal did go a little far last night."

"Yeah? Well, you weren't around to hold a prayer service!" Cal retorted.

Gabe exploded. "I'm not ten years old, for God's sake! And I damn well want to be able to fall asleep at night without worrying that one of you is going to have Rachel strung up while I'm not watching!" He shot his index finger at them. "She hasn't done one thing to either of you, but you've both treated her like dirt, and by damn, it's going to stop right now!"

Jane had returned to the kitchen. She patted Gabe's arm as she passed him, then went to stand beside her husband and stroke him.

Cal's jaw jutted. "This isn't about what she's done to us, and you know it. You're the one we're worried about!"

"Well, stop worrying!" Gabe shouted.

Rosie froze and blinked her eyes. Gabe drew a deep breath and dropped his voice. "Rachel's right. You're both like a couple of mother hens, and I can't stand it any longer."

Ethan said, "Look, Gabe . . . I have some experience here. I've done a lot of grief counseling, and you have to understand —"

"No! You're the one who has to understand. If either of you — either one of you ever hurts Rachel again — you're going to regret it. If you so much as frown at her, you'll have to deal with me. Do both of you understand?"

Cal shoved his hands in his pockets and looked uncomfortable. "I wasn't going to tell you this, but I don't seem to have a choice. You're not going to like hearing it, but you're blind where she's concerned, and you need to know the truth." He drew a breath. "I offered Rachel twenty-five thousand dollars to leave town, and she took it."

Jane sighed. "Oh, Cal . . ."

Gabe turned to Rachel and studied her silently for several seconds. Finally, he lifted one inquisitive eyebrow.

She shrugged, then nodded.

He gave her a faint smile. "Good for you."

This time Cal was the one who exploded. "What do you mean, good for her! She let herself be bought!"

At the angry sound of her father's voice, Rosie's face puckered. Cal gathered her up and kissed her, all the time looking like a summer storm cloud.

Gabe was accustomed to his older brother's blustering, and it didn't bother him a bit. "Rachel survives any way she can. It's a quality I'm just starting to learn from her."

Cal hadn't gotten the response he wanted, and, with Rosie tucked into the crook of his arm like a Super Bowl game ball, he gathered his forces for another attack. "How can you forget what she did at the drive-in?"

That sparked Gabe's temper all over again. "Tell me something, big brother. What would you do if you came home one night and found out I'd had Jane thrown into jail?"

Jane regarded him with interest while Cal's face reddened with outrage. "It's not the same thing at all. Jane's my wife!"

"Yeah, well, last week I asked Rachel to marry me."

"You did what?"

"You heard me."

Ethan and Cal stared at her. Earlier at the drive-in, she'd told Cal exactly this, but he hadn't believed her.

Rosie poked her tiny index finger in her father's mouth. Cal studied his brother and slowly withdrew her hand. "You're going to marry her?"

For the first time, Gabe seemed to lose some steam. "I don't know. She's still thinking about it."

This time when Cal confronted her, he seemed more confused than angry. "If he asked you to marry him, why did you trash the drive-in?"

She started to tell him she hadn't done it, but Gabe spoke first.

"Because Rachel's heart is bigger than her brain." He curled his hand around the back of her neck and rubbed the nape with his thumb. "She knew the drive-in wasn't good for me, but I wouldn't listen to her. Rachel is . . . She's pretty much a street fighter when it comes to people she cares about, and this was her own peculiar form of warfare."

For a moment she thought Gabe had decided to tell his third lie of the day, and then she realized he wasn't lying. He honestly thought she'd done it. The weasel! But just as she worked up a little righteous indignation, the gentle understanding she saw in his eyes took it right out of her. Even believing this, he was still on her side.

"Gabe! Gabe!" Edward squealed from the next room. "Gabe, you gotta see this!"

He hesitated, and she fully expected him to tell Edward to wait, but he surprised her. Spearing his brothers with another intimidating glare, he said, "Don't either of you go anywhere. I'll be right back." He turned to Jane. "Guard her from them, will you?"

"I'll do my best."

The moment he disappeared into the family room, Rachel rose from her stool. Both brothers watched her, their expressions bewildered. As Cal set Rosie down, Rachel reached inside herself for some well-deserved rage, only to find an uneasy jumble of frustration and a twisted sort of understanding. Love had a lot of faces to it, and she was looking at two of them right now. How wonderful it would be to go through life supported by these men, no matter how misguided they were.

She spoke quietly. "I don't really care whether you believe me or not, but, just to set the record straight,

Gabe's wrong. I'm not the one who vandalized the drive-in. That isn't to say I wouldn't have done it just for the reason he mentioned, but the fact is, I didn't think of it."

She went on, determined to clean the slate as best she could. "And Odell didn't take my shoes. Gabe threw them out the car window on the way over here."

When Cal spoke, his tone lacked its customary antagonism. "What does Gabe mean that he asked you to marry him, and you're thinking about it?"

"It means I told him no."

Ethan frowned. "You're not going to marry him?"

"You know I can't. Gabe's a soft touch. He cares about me, and that makes him protective. I guess it's a Bonner family trait." She cleared her throat, forced out the words. "Getting married is the only way he can think of to keep me out of trouble. But he doesn't love me."

"And you love him, don't you?" Ethan said gently.

"Yeah." She nodded. Tried to smile. "A lot."

To her dismay, her eyes filled with tears. "He thinks I'm tough, but I'm not tough enough to spend the rest of my life wanting what I can't have, and that's why I can't marry him."

Her toes tickled, and she looked down to see that Rosie had discovered them. Glad of the distraction, she dropped onto the black marble floor and sat cross-legged so the baby could crawl into her lap.

A sound came from Cal that was part sigh, part groan. "We screwed up big-time."

"*We!*" Ethan retorted, just as Gabe reappeared from the family room. "*I* wouldn't have had her thrown in jail! And I wouldn't have bribed her, either, Mr. Big Shot Billionaire!"

"I'm not a billionaire!" Cal exclaimed. "And if you had my kind of money, you would have done exactly the same thing!"

"Children, children," Jane admonished. And then, without warning, her hand flew to her mouth and she burst out in laughter. "Oh, my goodness!"

They all stared at her.

"I'm sorry, but it just hit me . . ." She calmed herself, then began laughing again.

Cal frowned. "What's wrong?"

"I — Oh, dear . . ." She whipped a tissue from a box on the counter and dabbed her eyes. "I forgot all about it till now. We got the strangest note in the mail yesterday afternoon. I was going to ask you what it meant, but then I started thinking about Bose-Einstein condensates. BEC atoms," she added, as if that explained it all, "and you brought Chip home with you, and it slipped my mind until now."

Cal regarded her with the patience of a man long accustomed to living with a woman obsessed with things like Bose-Einstein condensates. "What slipped your mind?"

Jane chuckled, then walked over to to a small pile of mail lying on the counter space next to the pantry. "This note. It's from Lisa Scudder. You remember. She's the mother of the little girl Emily who has leukemia. We made a contribution to her medical fund

446

last fall, but she acknowledged that months ago, so I was confused." Jane started laughing again, and all three Bonner brothers frowned. They clearly saw nothing funny about a child with leukemia.

Rachel, however, was very much afraid she understood the reason for Jane's sudden burst of merriment. Why hadn't Lisa waited as she'd asked?

She grabbed Rosie and hopped up from the floor. "I think it's time I got Edward home." She thrust the baby toward Ethan. "Gabe, would you mind driving —"

"*Sit!*" Jane commanded, pointing toward the floor.

Rachel accepted the inevitable and sat.

Rosie let out a squeal and reached for her. Ethan put her back down, and the baby promptly returned to Rachel's lap where she busied herself playing with the buttons on the front of Rachel's dress. In the meantime, Jane started laughing all over again, and Ethan couldn't stand it any longer.

"Really, Jane. If you saw how sick that little girl is, I don't think you'd be laughing."

Jane immediately sobered. "Oh, it's not that . . ." Another giggle slipped out, followed by more laughter. "It's just that Rachel . . . Oh, Rachel." She gasped for air. "We got a thank-you note from Lisa Scudder. Rachel gave Cal's blood money to Emily's Fund!"

All three men stared at her. Cal glared. "What are you talking about?"

"Your twenty-five thousand pieces of silver! Rachel didn't keep it. She gave it all away!"

Gabe looked down at Rachel. He seemed confused, like someone who'd just heard the earth was round instead of square. "You didn't keep *any* of it?"

"Cal really made me mad," Rachel explained.

"I see."

She retrieved her hair from Rosie's mouth. "I asked Lisa to wait until I left town before she sent the note. I guess she forgot." She gazed at Cal, who still had his head bent over the note. "The check's postdated. She can't deposit it until tomorrow."

Quiet fell over the group. One by one, they all looked at Cal.

He finally raised his head and shrugged. Then he turned to Gabe. "I don't know how you're going to do it, bro, but you'd better come up with a foolproof way to keep her off that Greyhound tomorrow." He jerked his head toward Rachel's bare feet. "That was a good start."

"I'm glad you approve," Gabe said dryly.

Cal turned toward the family room. "Hey, Chip! Could you come in here for a minute?"

Rachel jumped up with Rosie in her arms. "Cal Bonner, I swear, if you say anything to my son about . . ."

Edward appeared. "Yes?"

Rosie chose that moment to give Rachel a wet kiss on her chin. Rachel glowered at Cal and patted Rosie's diapered bottom. "Thank you, sweetheart."

Cal ruffled Edward's hair. "Chip, your mom and Gabe have some stuff they need to talk about. It's good stuff, not bad, so you don't have to worry. But the thing is, they need to be alone to do it, so do you think you could hang around here for a while longer? What do you say? The two of us can throw the football, and I'll bet Aunt Jane would love to boot up that computer of hers and show you a few more planets."

Aunt Jane? Rachel's eyebrows shot up. "I really don't think —"

"Great idea!" Ethan exclaimed. "What do you think, Chip?"

"Is it okay, Mommy?"

Only Rachel heard Gabe's soft whisper. "If you say no, my big brother's gonna beat you up."

She didn't want to be alone with Gabe and his Boy Scout's sense of duty. She needed honest love, not sacrifice. And after loving Cherry Bonner, how could he love someone as flawed as she was? She'd wanted so very much to protect herself from a long good-bye, but now it was being forced on her.

She glanced around the room, searching for an ally, but her most likely one now looked vague, as if she'd tumbled back into the world of subatomic particles. The little munchkin in Rachel's arms was adorable, but entirely useless in this situation. Her son had computers and football on his mind. And that left the Bonner brothers.

Her gaze flew from Cal's face to Ethan's and back again. What she saw there made her stomach sink. It had been bad enough to have these men regard her as Gabe's enemy, but now they seemed to have decided she was *good* for their brother. She shuddered as she contemplated where that might lead them.

"It's fine with your mother," Ethan said.

"She doesn't mind one bit if you stay here," Cal added.

Only Gabe paid any attention to her wishes. "It *is* all right, isn't it?"

She couldn't say no without looking like an ogre, so she nodded.

"Yippee!" he squealed. "Rosie, I get to stay!"

Rosie celebrated by slapping Rachel's cheeks with her small wet hands.

Gabe began to steer her toward the door, only to have Jane finally come out of her trance. "Rachel, would you like to borrow some shoes? I think I have a pair of sandals that —"

"She won't need them," Gabe said.

They reached the front door, and Cal shot forward. "Rachel?"

She stiffened, determined to throw every word of his sniveling apology right back in his face.

But instead of apologizing, he gave her a lady-killer grin that made her understand exactly how a brilliant woman like Jane could have fallen in love with someone so bullheaded.

"I know you hate my guts, and it'll probably take you a lifetime to forgive me, but . . ." He scratched his chin. "Could I please have Rosie back?"

CHAPTER
TWENTY-FIVE

Gabe turned off the shower in the cottage, grabbed a towel, and quickly dried himself. He couldn't blow this. No matter what, he had to knock some sense into that sweet stubborn head of hers. His life depended on it.

Wrapping the towel around his hips, he stepped out into the hallway. "Rach?"

No answer.

Panic raced through him. She'd suggested he take his shower first. What if she'd been trying to get rid of him so she could fetch Chip and leave town?

He flew down the hallway, poked his nose into Chip's bedroom and his own then into hers.

She hadn't gone anywhere. Instead, she'd fallen asleep on top of the quilt, her wrinkled dress bunched around her legs, grubby toes peeking out.

His shoulders slumped with relief. He smiled, got dressed, and spent much of the afternoon just sitting next to her bed and watching her sleep. It was the most beautiful sight he'd ever seen.

Three hours later, she finally stirred, but he wasn't there because he'd gone out to check on Tweety Bird. It was a good thing.

"Rach! Rachel, wake up! I need you!"

"We should have told them we got M-A-R-R-I-E-D." Kristy spelled out the word as she gazed across the interior of Jane's Range Rover at her new husband. "But they looked too frazzled to handle any more drama. I still can't believe Cal threw Rachel into jail."

"What I can't believe is that we offered to baby-sit these two little imps when we haven't even been M-A-R-R-I-E-D for a full day."

He glanced in the rearview mirror at Rosie and Chip. While Chip inspected a scab on his elbow, Rosie chewed contentedly on Horse's paw. They had borrowed the Range Rover because it was easier than moving Rosie's car seat. Now both children were sandy from their afternoon outing at the park.

"Cal and Jane have had them all morning," Kristy pointed out, "and we only took them for an hour."

He turned into the lane that led to the top of Heartache Mountain. "It's our honeymoon, for pete's sake. We should be making a baby of our own."

Kristy smiled. "I can't wait. But Cal and Jane needed a break. Today has been hard on everybody."

"Speaking of hard . . ."

"Ethan Bonner!"

"Don't you try to act all coy with me, Mrs. Bonner. I've seen your true colors."

"You want to see them again?"

He burst out laughing.

"Why'd you call Kristy 'Mrs. Bonner'?" Chip piped up from the backseat.

452

Ethan and Kristy exchanged guilty glances, then Ethan tilted his head toward the back while he kept his eyes on the road. "I'm glad you asked that, Chip. As a matter of fact, we want you to be the first to know . . . Kristy and I got married yesterday."

"You did?"

"Yep."

"That's good. Do you know there's lots of planets all over the place? And some of them are a trillion years old."

So much for the importance of marriage to a five-year-old.

Kristy started giggling all over again. Ethan smiled at her, and love spilled from his heart. How could he have been blind for so long?

They turned the final bend that led to the cottage, and both of them saw it at once. Kristy gasped. "The garage is on fire!"

Ethan shoved his foot on the accelerator, and the Range Rover shot toward the cottage. A shower of gravel flew up as he braked. Kristy threw open the door and jumped out.

He slammed on the emergency brake and shot Chip a quick, warning glance. "Stay right here! Don't move!"

Chip gave a frightened nod, and Ethan leaped out just in time to see Gabe and Rachel appear from the back of the cottage. While Gabe raced forward with the garden hose, Rachel rushed toward the outside faucet to turn it on.

Kristy was heading for the cottage. He followed her inside, and they whipped up several scatter rugs, then hurried back out with them.

As Gabe saw them coming, he thrust the hose at Rachel. "Keep the perimeter wet!" Ethan knew he was far more worried about the fire spreading to the cottage than the fate of the dilapidated old garage.

Gabe grabbed one of the rugs from Ethan. "You take the back. I'll take the front."

They separated, and began beating at several of the smaller brushfires. Ethan could have worked more efficiently if he'd been alone, but he kept looking around to make certain Kristy wasn't getting too close to the flames.

Luckily, the ground was still damp from the rain they'd had early Saturday morning, and they soon had the fire under control. Nothing was left of the garage except a smoldering pile of rubble, but the cottage was safe.

Kristy turned off the faucet and Rachel dropped the hose. Ethan came up to them. "What happened?"

Rachel pushed a strand of hair back from her face with her forearm. "I don't know. I was sleeping, then Gabe called me outside, and I saw the flames."

"You're soaked," Kristy said.

She was bedraggled, too, in a wrinkled calico housedress that looked as if it had been slept in and a pair of men's black rubber shower thongs.

"Look what I found in the weeds over there." Gabe appeared holding the red plastic gas can that was always kept in the garage.

454

"Anything left in it?" Ethan asked.

Gabe shook his head and threw the can down in disgust. "I don't care if I have to order twenty-four-hour surveillance. I'm getting to the bottom of this."

Rachel squeezed Kristy's hand. "It's a good thing the two of you stopped by. We would have had a hard time putting it out by ourselves."

"We came over to bring Chip back. We also have something to tell you." Kristy exchanged a conspiratorial smile with Ethan, and then her eyes widened. "Ethan, we forgot. We left the kids in the car."

"Kids?" Rachel moved toward the front of the cottage.

"We took Rosie, too," Ethan explained, as the rest of them followed. "Jane and Cal needed a break."

"What do you have to tell us?" Rachel asked.

Ethan smiled. "Maybe we'll let Chip break the news."

They rounded the cottage. Kristy drew in her breath, and then all of them froze.

The Range Rover was missing. And there was no sign of the children.

Bobby Dennis couldn't get enough air. He kept opening his mouth and trying to suck more in, but it was as if his lungs had shrunk. Both kids in the back were crying, and the boy wouldn't stop yelling at him.

"You let us out *right now*, or Gabe is going to shoot you with his gun! I mean it! He's got a million guns, and he'll shoot you, then cut you up with a knife!"

455

Bobby couldn't stand it anymore. "Shut up or you're going to make me wreck!"

The boy shut up, but the baby kept screaming. Bobby wanted to ditch the car and get away from them, but he couldn't because he'd left his Lumina behind miles ago. It was parked near the road that led up to Heartache Mountain.

Bobby'd been so wired he hadn't even seen the kids in the back when he'd jumped in the car. If he'd seen them, he sure as hell wouldn't have given in to the temptation to steal the Range Rover.

How had everything gotten so screwed up? It was Rachel Snopes's fault. If it wasn't for the Temple, his parents wouldn't have gotten divorced. Because of the Temple, his mom had gotten so religious that she'd driven his dad away.

Bobby still remembered how he used to have to go to services with her and listen to G. Dwayne Snopes preach, while his bitch of a wife sat there drinking in every word. G. Dwayne was dead, so Bobby couldn't get back at him, but after all these years, he'd finally gotten back at his wife.

Except everything was going wrong.

Even though he'd been drunk, he knew now that he never should have torn apart the drive-in. But when he'd come into the snack shop, she'd looked so happy working there it made him sick. It wasn't right she should be happy when his mom was bitching at him all the time, and his dad didn't call him anymore.

Him and Joey and Dave had been drinking Mountain Dew and vodka during the second movie.

Afterward, Bobby had wanted to party some more at this kid's house he knew, but Joey and Dave said they were tired. Buncha losers. Bobby'd gotten rid of them, had some more vodka, then gone back to the drive-in. Everybody had left, so he'd sneaked in and sorta gone crazy.

It wasn't till Saturday afternoon when he was driving around that he'd thought about the stuff he had locked in his trunk and started to worry about what he'd do if his mom or somebody found it. That's when he'd spotted Rachel's piece-of-shit Escort parked by those new condos. The street was quiet, nobody was around, and he'd been scared, so he'd hidden the stuff from his trunk under the boxes she had in the back. Today he'd heard she'd been arrested and put in jail. That made him feel good until he heard she'd got out right away.

He realized he was coming up too fast on the car ahead, and he swung into the left lane.

There was a pickup heading right toward him.

Adrenaline rushed through Bobby's veins. A horn blared, and, at the last moment, the pickup shot off the road, landing crookedly in a ditch.

"You're going too fast!" the boy cried from the backseat.

Bobby wiped the sweat out of his eyes with the shoulder of his T-shirt. "I told you to shut up!"

If only his mom hadn't found the weed in his closet this morning, she wouldn't have kicked him out of the house. She'd said it was for good, but he hadn't believed her until he'd gone back a couple of hours ago and seen a locksmith's truck parked in the drive. The truck had a sign on the side that said *24 Hour Service*.

He didn't know what to do. The last he'd heard, his dad was down in Jacksonville, so he decided to go there, but he didn't know if his dad would want him.

He'd drunk a couple of beers, smoked some weed, and as he was driving around, he'd passed the road that led up Heartache Mountain. He couldn't stand the fact that Rachel was out of jail and probably still all-smiley and everything. The next thing he knew, he'd ditched his Lumina in the trees and climbed through the woods.

He figured Gabe and Rachel would be cleaning up the drive-in, and he decided to burn the house while they were gone. But just as he'd sneaked the gasoline can from the garage, Gabe had stepped out on the back porch. Bobby wasn't crazy enough to burn the house when people were in it, so he'd thrown the gasoline on the garage instead.

When the fire had caught, he'd watched it for a minute and then started to go back through the woods to get his Lumina just as the Range Rover came up the road. Sixty thousand easy for a car like that.

After Pastor Ethan and Kristy Brown had jumped out, he'd gotten in and taken off. The damn kids in back hadn't made a sound till he was way down the highway. Now, all they were doing was making noise.

"If you let us out of the car, I won't tell Gabe what you did!"

Bobby punched the accelerator. "I'll let you out, okay! Just not yet. I got to get farther away."

"*Now!* You gotta let us out now! You're *scaring* Rosie!"

"Shut up! Just shut up, will you?"

The curve came at him too fast. He heard himself make this funny sound in his throat, and then he hit the brakes.

The boy screamed in the back.

The car began to fishtail, and Bobby's mom's face flickered in his head. *Mom!*

He lost control.

Rachel couldn't stop making whimpering sounds. *Please, God . . . Oh, please . . . Please . . .*

Gabe's knuckles were white on the Mercedes's steering wheel, his face gray beneath his tan. She knew he was thinking the same thing she was. What if they'd turned the wrong direction on the highway?

She told herself the police would find the children if she and Gabe couldn't. Kristy and Ethan had stayed behind to notify them. And the skid marks at the bottom of the lane had been distinct. Still . . . They'd already gone over ten miles. What if they'd guessed wrong? Or what if the bastard they were chasing had pulled off onto a side road?

She couldn't think about that. If she did, she'd start screaming.

Gabe sucked in his breath. "The car."

She saw it then. "Oh, God . . ."

The Range Rover was turned upside down in a ditch ahead to their right. Vehicles had stopped; people were clustered together. There were two patrol cars and an ambulance.

Oh, God . . . Please . . . Please, God . . .

The Mercedes's tires squealed, and a shower of gravel hit the undercarriage as Gabe pulled off the road. He jumped out of the car, and she ran after him, pebbles biting through the soles of the sandals Kristy had tossed at her. She heard him call out to the state trooper standing next to the ambulance.

"The children! Are the children all right?"

"Who are you?"

"I'm — I'm the boy's father."

The trooper jerked his head toward the stretcher. "They're stabilizing the kid now."

Rachel reached the stretcher just after Gabe did. But it wasn't Edward. They gazed down at Bobby Dennis.

Without a word, Gabe spun toward the car and bent over to look inside where one of the doors gaped open. He immediately straightened. "There were two small children with him. A five-year-old boy, and a baby girl."

The trooper grew immediately alert. "Are you saying this kid wasn't the only one in the car?"

Gabe offered a brusque explanation while she ran to look inside the Range Rover. The straps on Rosie's empty car seat dangled. Rachel looked frantically around and saw a white baby shoe in the weeds ten feet from the car.

"Gabe!"

He raced over to her.

"Look!" she cried. "Rosie's shoe." She squinted against the fading sun and spotted a tiny pink sock hanging in the weeds near a line of trees that marked the edge of a densely wooded area.

Gabe saw the sock at the same time she did. "Let's go."

Without waiting for the trooper, they moved into the woods together. Prickly bushes snagged at her skirt, but she paid no attention. *"Edward!"*

Gabe's voice boomed. "Chip! Call out if you can hear us!"

There was no response, and they forged deeper into the trees. Gabe's legs were longer than hers, and he quickly moved ahead. "Chip! Can you hear me?"

A low branch snared her shirt. She yanked it free, then looked up to see that Gabe had frozen in place.

"Chip? Is that you?"

Oh, God . . . She stopped in place and listened.

"Gabe?"

The voice was small and achingly familiar, coming from somewhere off to their left.

Gabe raced ahead, calling out. She rushed after him, her heart pounding.

The terrain sloped downward, and she slipped, then righted herself. Gabe disappeared. She followed the path he'd taken through a thicket of pines and came out in a clearing by a small creek.

That was when she saw them.

Edward sat huddled against the trunk of an old black gum tree some thirty yards away with Rosie curled in his lap.

"Chip!" Gabe's shoes pounded the ground as he flew across the clearing toward the children. Rosie had been quiet, but as soon as she saw him, she started to scream. Both children were dirty and tear-streaked. Edward's T-shirt was torn and one knee was scraped. In addition to her missing shoe and sock, Rosie's pink romper had a grease smear across the front. Gabe went down on his knee, snatched her up with one arm, and threw his other one around her son.

"Gabe!" Edward clutched at him.

A sob tore her throat as she ran forward.

Gabe thrust Rosie at her and pulled Edward to his chest, then pushed him away far enough to lift his eyelids. "Are you all right? Does it hurt anywhere?"

"My ears."

Gabe immediately turned Edward's head to look. "Your ears hurt?"

"Rosie's got a loud scream. It hurt my ears."

Gabe visibly relaxed. "Is that all? Anything else?"

Chip shook his head. "I was real scared. That boy was bad." He started to cry.

Gabe gave him a quick hug, thrust him at Rachel, and took Rosie to check her over.

Edward trembled in her arms and spoke against her belly. "Mommy, I was so scared. The car turned over, and I was afraid that bad boy would wake up and run off with us again, so I got Rosie out of her seat and carried her, but she was heavy, and she kept screaming 'cause she was scared, too, but finally she stopped."

Rachel spoke around her tears. "You were so brave."

Gabe, in the meantime, had quieted Rosie. Rachel looked up at him, and he nodded. "She's fine. We'll have them both checked, but I think they're all right.

Thank God they were buckled in when that car went over."

Thank you, God. Thank you.

Rosie rested her head against her uncle and brought her thumb to her mouth. Her little chest heaved as she took a few comforting sucks.

Edward reached out and patted her leg. "See, Rosie. I told you they'd find us."

Rachel kept her arm firmly wrapped around her son as they began to head across the clearing toward the highway, but they hadn't traveled more than a few yards before Rosie let out another shriek.

Edward winced. "See, Mommy. I told you she can really yell."

Gabe rubbed her back. "Hush, sweetheart . . ."

But Rosie wouldn't be hushed. She twisted her body, flung out her arms, and screamed.

Rachel followed the direction of her gaze and saw Horse lying at the base of the tree where they'd found the children. Rosie wanted her stuffed rabbit. "I'll get it."

She walked back to the tree, then came to a halt as she saw that the back seam had split open and the stuffing spilled out.

Shining, *sparkling* stuffing.

Gabe saw it at the same time she did. He hurried back to the tree and stared at the small pile of glittering stones. Most of them lay on the ground, a few clung to the rabbit's mangy gray fur.

Gabe let out his breath. "Diamonds."

She gazed numbly down at the sparkling stones. Dwayne had hidden his cache inside Edward's stuffed rabbit. The Kennedy chest and the Bible had merely been diversions so she wouldn't suspect the truth. When he'd begged her to bring their son to the airfield, it wasn't because he wanted to say good-bye, but because he'd known Edward would bring Horse along. Dwayne had wanted the diamonds, not his son.

At that moment, Rachel decided G. Dwayne Snopes was no longer Edward's father.

Gabe took her hand. "Looks like you finally found your fortune, Rach."

She poked at one of the stones with the toe of Kristy's sandal and knew he was wrong. These diamonds weren't her fortune. Her real fortune stood right in front of her, but she had no right to claim it.

CHAPTER
TWENTY-SIX

Rachel didn't get to take her shower until nearly ten o'clock that night after Edward had finally fallen asleep. She turned off the water and, as she dried herself, said one more prayer of thanksgiving that Edward and Rosie had both been given a clean bill of health by the doctors.

There had been so much to do since they'd recovered the children. Cal had locked up the diamonds for her in Dwayne's old safe, then all of them had spoken with the police. They'd also checked on Bobby Dennis, who was in the hospital, and Rachel had talked with Carol. Bobby's mother was badly shaken and very much in need of forgiveness. Rachel had given it without a moment's hesitation.

But she didn't want to think about Bobby now, so she concentrated on untangling her wet hair with Gabe's comb. She wasn't in any hurry. Right now, Gabe and his overdeveloped conscience were sitting out there waiting for her, and she knew that Mr. Eagle Scout had prepared himself to do the honorable thing. The comb caught on a snarl, and she tossed it down.

If she'd had her wish, she and Edward would have gone back to Kristy's condo for the night, but Edward and Gabe had refused to be separated. She still didn't entirely understand how the relationship between them had changed so drastically. It was ironic. What had once seemed like an insurmountable problem in her relationship with Gabe had disappeared, but an equally large barrier still stood in the way. Gabe didn't love her, and she couldn't live in Cherry's shadow.

She reached down to pick up the clean clothes Ethan and Kristy had brought her from the condo only to realize they weren't there. Wrapping a towel around herself, she cracked open the door. "Gabe? I need my clothes."

Silence.

She didn't want to walk out like this. "Gabe?"

"I'm in the living room."

"Where are my clothes?"

"I burned them."

"You did what?" She shot into the hallway. She felt defenseless enough without having to confront him wearing only a towel, so she stormed into his bedroom and pulled on one of his clean work shirts. After hurriedly buttoning it, she marched into the living room.

He looked as cozy as could be, slouched in a wicker armchair with his feet propped on the old pine-blanket chest that served as a coffee table, ankles crossed, and a can of Dr Pepper in his hand. "Want something to drink?"

She smelled the stench and spotted smoldering embers in the fireplace. "I want to know why you burned my clothes!"

466

"Don't talk so loud. You'll wake up Chip. And I burned your clothes because I couldn't stand looking at them another minute. You don't own one thing that's not butt-ugly, Rachel Stone. Except your panties. I like them."

He was acting as if he didn't have a care in the world. Where was the tense, difficult man she'd grown so used to? "Gabe, what's wrong with you? You had no right to do that."

"As your present and future employer, I have a lot of rights."

"Employer? The drive-in's closed, and I'm leaving tomorrow. You're not my employer any longer."

She saw by his stubborn expression that he wasn't going to make this easy on her.

"You refused to marry me," he said, "so I don't see any other way to go about it than to rehire you. I burned those bus tickets, by the way, along with your clothes."

"You didn't." She slumped down on the couch, all the wind knocked out of her. Did he think that just because he'd finally attached himself to her son, everything was all right? "How could you do that?"

For a moment he said nothing. Then he gave her a slow, calculating smile. "I know you too well, sweetheart. You're not going to keep those diamonds. That means it's time to cut a deal."

She regarded him warily.

He eyed her over the rim of his Dr Pepper, then sipped. As he lowered the can, he took his time studying her. His scrutiny made her fully conscious of the fact that she was completely naked beneath his shirt. She drew her legs closer together.

"I'm making some changes in my life," he said.

"Oh?"

"I'm going to get licensed in North Carolina and open up a practice right here in Salvation."

As upset as she was, she couldn't help but feel happy for him. "I'm glad. It's exactly what you should be doing."

"But I'm going to need some help."

"What kind of help?"

"Well . . . I have to hire a receptionist who can also pinch hit when I need surgical help."

"I already have a job in Florida," she pointed out. "And I'm not going to be your receptionist." Why did he have to belabor this? Didn't he understand how hard leaving him was for her?

"That's not the job I'm offering you," he said smugly. "Although if you'd volunteer to help out every once in a while, I'm sure I'd appreciate it. But no, what I'm thinking about for you is more in the way of a career than a job."

"A career? Doing what?"

"Things I need done."

"Such as?"

"Well . . ." He seemed to be thinking. "Laundry. I don't mind cooking and washing dishes, but I don't like laundry."

"You want me to do your laundry?"

"Among other things."

"Keep going."

"Answering the phone in the evenings. When I'm not working, I don't like to answer the phone. You'd have to do that. If it's somebody in my family, I'll talk. Otherwise, you take care of it."

"Doing laundry and answering the phone. This is supposed to be my new career?"

"And balancing my checkbook. I really hate that. I just can't get all worked up about tracking down every little penny."

"Gabe, you're a very wealthy man. You really need to look after your money better."

"That's what my brothers keep telling me, but I'm just not interested."

"Laundry, answering the phone, and balancing your checkbook. Is that it?"

"Pretty much. Except for one other thing."

"Which is?"

"Sex. That's the main part of your job."

"Sex?"

"It comes before everything else. Way before that checkbook."

"Having sex with you?"

"Yes."

"You want to *pay* me to have sex with you?"

"Plus laundry and the phone and —"

"You want to *pay* me! *This* is my new career! Being your full-time mistress and part-time housekeeper?"

"That mistress thing . . . It'd be nice. I kind of like the idea of having a mistress. But because of Chip and the fact this is a small town, we'd have to get married." He held up his hand. "Now I know you don't want to do that, so you wouldn't have to look at it as a real marriage right away. Instead, it could be purely a business deal . . ." His eyes narrowed. ". . . something a bean counter like yourself should appreciate." He straightened in the chair. "I need sex; you provide it. Strictly commerce."

"Oh, Gabe . . ."

"Before you get too indignant, we're talking a lot of money here."

Even though she knew she shouldn't, she couldn't help but ask. "How much?"

"The day we get married, I'll give you a cashier's check for . . ." He stopped, scratched his head. "How much do you want?"

"A million dollars," she snapped, angry with herself for even asking. But he was right. G. Dwayne's diamond stash could never be hers. She finally understood that.

"Okay. A million dollars."

She stared at him.

He shrugged. "I don't care that much about money, and you do. Plus, you'll have to spend a lot of time naked. It only seems fair."

She sank back into the cushions. The idea that a man this hopeless about his finances was allowed to roam free in the world was terrifying.

She felt as if she were hyperventilating. Just the fact that he *had* a million dollars was mind-boggling, let alone the notion that he wanted to give it to her. If only he were offering love instead, she'd snatch it up in a second.

He uncrossed his ankles and set his feet on the floor. "I know you had doubts about marriage because of the problem between Chip and me, but you might have noticed the problem has gone away."

She thought of the way Gabe and Edward had been with each other that evening. "I still don't understand quite how that happened. I know it wasn't just the kidnapping. I saw the way the two of you were behaving with each other this morning. How could something so serious go away so fast?"

"Have you ever hit that boy?"

"Of course not."

"Well, if you had, you wouldn't need to ask that question. And that's the other thing, Rachel. Besides the sex. I get an equal hand in raising Chip. We make decisions about him together." His voice grew deadly serious. "I'm not letting you take that boy away from me. I've lost one child, and I'm not going to lose another. If that means tearing up a hundred bus tickets and burning every stick of clothing you own, I'll do it."

"He's not your child."

"Yesterday morning he wasn't. Today he is."

She couldn't speak. Why was he making this so hard?

"You might have noticed that all the Bonners take kids pretty seriously."

She thought of the way Ethan and Cal treated Edward. As much as they had disliked her, they'd never shown him anything but kindness. And that morning Rosie had been passed from one adult to another, as if each person was responsible for her well-being. "I've noticed."

"Then it's a deal."

"Gabe, I barely survived one disastrous marriage, and I'm not going to put myself through that twice. If I ever marry again, it'll be for love."

His eyes crackled with indignation. "Do you seriously think you can sit there and tell me you don't love me, and I'm going to believe you? I'm not stupid, Rachel. Despite all your high-minded talk about being a wanton woman, you're as straitlaced as anybody I know, and if you didn't love me, there's no way you would have let me touch you, let alone spend some of the best nights of my life in your bed."

She thought seriously of punching him. Instead, she gritted her teeth. "It's not *my* love that's in question here."

He regarded her blankly.

She snatched one of the throw pillows from the couch and hurled it at him.

"Damn! You made me spill my Dr Pepper."

She jumped up. "I'm outta here."

He slammed down the can and jumped up, too. "You're not a reasonable woman, Rachel. Has anybody ever pointed that out to you?"

"Reasonable!" She was spitting mad. "Just because I won't be your charity case, you think I'm unreasonable?"

"Charity case? Is that what you think you are?"

"I *know* it. Ethan's not the only *saint* in the Bonner family."

"You think I'm a saint?" Instead of being annoyed, he looked rather pleased.

472

"Brother . . ." she muttered.

He pushed his index finger toward her. "I'm going to marry you, Rachel. So just get that through your head right now."

"Why would you want to marry me? You don't love me!"

"Says who?"

"Don't play games with me. It's too important." Her anger fled. She bit her lip. "Please, Gabe."

He went to her at once, and pulled her down on the couch next to him. "Why would I play games about something like this? Don't you think it's important to me, too?"

"Not the way it is to me. You care about me, but I need more. Can't you understand that?"

"Of course I can. Rachel, don't you know how I feel about you?"

"Not the way you felt about Cherry, that's for sure." She hated the sharp note she heard in her voice, hated herself for being jealous of a dead woman.

"My life with Cherry is over," he said quietly.

She gazed down at her hands. "I don't think it'll ever be over. And I can't live in competition."

"You aren't in competition with Cherry."

He didn't understand at all. She twisted her fingers and thought about walking from the room, but she had just enough fight left to give him one more chance. "Then tell me something bad about her."

"What do you mean?"

One part of her said to back off while her pride was still intact, but some things were more important than

473

pride. "You said I wasn't in competition with her, but I don't think that's true." She felt petty and miserable. She couldn't look at him, so she continued to gaze at her hands. "I need to hear something bad about her."

"This is silly."

"To you, maybe, but not to me."

"Rachel, why are you putting yourself through this?"

"There had to be something about her that wasn't wonderful. I mean . . . Did she snore?" She finally looked up and regarded him hopefully. "I don't snore."

He slipped his hand over her clenched ones. "Neither did she."

"Maybe she — I don't know. Put the newspaper in the trash before you had a chance to read it?"

"Once or twice, I guess."

She hated the compassion she saw in his expression, but she had to see this through. Her mind searched for something an almost-perfect woman might have done. "Did she ever . . . use your razor to shave her legs?"

"She didn't like the razors I used." He paused and regarded her pointedly. "Unlike you."

She began to feel desperate. Surely there was something. "I'm a very good cook."

If anything, his expression grew even more sympathetic. "She baked bread at least once a week."

The only time Rachel had tried to bake bread, she'd killed the yeast. "I hardly ever get traffic tickets."

He lifted one eyebrow.

She rushed on. "And sometimes people who are exceptionally kindhearted don't tell jokes well. They sort of screw up the punch line."

474

"You're reaching." He kissed her on the forehead, then let her go and sank back into the corner of the couch. "You really want to go through with this, don't you? Even though it doesn't have anything to do with you."

"She seems so perfect."

He took a deep breath. "All right, then. Listen up because I'm only going to say this once, so you'd better pay attention. I loved Cherry with all my heart, and now I feel the same way about you."

She exhaled a long, slow breath.

He said, "You might not have been able to save Dwayne's soul, but you sure saved mine. You pulled me out of all that self-pity I was caught in and turned my life upside down. I started to live again."

She could feel herself melting, and she moved toward him, but he held up his hand. "I'm not finished. You're the one who brought this up, so now you can listen. Cherry was . . . She was almost too good. She never lost her temper, and no matter how hard I tried, I couldn't get a bad word out of her about anybody, including people who were real creeps. Even if she was tired or not feeling well or Jamie had been acting up, she wouldn't snap or be grouchy, she'd just get quiet. She was so damned sweet."

"That makes me feel a lot better," she said dryly.

"Now here's the part I'm only going to say once." He drew a deep breath. "Sometimes living with Cherry was a little like living with Mother Teresa or somebody. She was so sweet, so reasonable, so damn *good*, that I didn't have a lot of room for error when it came to my own shortcomings."

Happiness unfolded inside her like a fan of rainbows. "Really?"

"Really."

"And with me?"

He smiled. "I have a *lot* of room for error."

She beamed at him.

"One other thing." He frowned. "Cherry used to hum. When she was cooking, cleaning, even reading a magazine, she'd hum. Sometimes it was okay, but other times, it kind of got on my nerves."

"Random humming can be annoying." Rachel found that she was starting to like Cherry Bonner.

"And the thing was . . . Because she always overlooked all my flaws, I could never get on her case about it."

"You poor thing." She bit her bottom lip. "Was she . . . I know I'm a jerk for asking, but . . . In bed?"

He began to look amused. "You're a mass of insecurities, aren't you?"

"Never mind. Forget I asked."

"It wouldn't be fair to Cherry if I held up a sex kitten like yourself as a standard for comparison."

Her eyes widened, and she smiled. "Really?"

He laughed.

She hurled herself across the couch, and his arms tightened around her as if he wouldn't ever let her go. His lips brushed her hair, and his voice grew gruff with emotion. "Cherry was the love of my boyhood, Rach.

You're the love of my manhood. And I do love you, with all my heart. Please don't leave me."

She couldn't respond because his mouth had settled over hers, and she lost herself in a kiss so shattering that nothing else existed.

When they drew apart, she found herself gazing into his eyes, and it was like looking into his soul. All the barriers between them were gone.

"Aren't you forgetting something?" he whispered.

She tilted her head in inquiry.

He brushed her lips. "Aren't you forgetting to say, 'I love you, too, Gabe'? What about that?"

She drew back, smiled into his eyes. "Is there any doubt?"

"You're not the only one who needs to hear the words."

"I love you, Gabe. All the way to the bottom of my soul."

He shuddered. "No more talk of leaving me?"

"No more."

"No more arguments about getting married?"

"Not a single one."

"You'll put up with my brothers?"

"Don't remind me."

"And Chip's going to belong to both of us?"

She nodded, unable for a moment to speak. Now that he'd set his heart to it, Gabe Bonner would be a better father to her son than Dwayne Snopes could ever have dreamed of being.

She stroked the stubborn line of his jaw, kissed him again. She wanted to laugh and sing and burst out in tears all at once. The emotions were too much, so she hid behind some gentle teasing. "Don't think I'm going to forget about that million dollars. You were right about me not keeping those diamonds, and you're not competent to handle your own money."

"You are?"

She nodded.

"You're right." He sighed. "Still, for a million dollars, a man has a right to expect something special." With no warning he swept her into his arms. As he carried her into his bedroom, one hand caressed her bare bottom. "Let me think . . . What kind of kinkiness would be worth a million dollars?"

A dozen ideas skipped through her mind.

"First I'm going to strip you naked." His throaty whisper made her shiver. "Then I'm going to stretch you out on that bed and love every single part of you."

A soft moan slipped through her lips.

"And Rach? Chip's out like a light, so we've got all the time in the world. I'll be going about it real slow."

She struggled for air.

He set her on her feet, then locked the bedroom door. He returned to her at once, and his fingers brushed her collarbone as he unbuttoned the shirt. He dipped his head to her neck and nipped the skin with his teeth. The shirt slid to the ground. He nuzzled and nibbled and worked his way from one delicious spot to another.

When she couldn't stand it, she began pulling at his clothing, and she didn't stop until he was naked.

478

His body. She drank in the sight of those ridges of muscle, the lines between tanned and lighter skin, the patch of dark hair on his chest and at his groin. She cupped him, feeling the heavy weight there, the tensile strength, loving the sound of his irregular breathing.

They fell back on the bed and discovered neither of them had the patience for slowness. She needed his heavy weight on top of her, anchoring her to this bed, this house, this town — binding the two of them together forever. And he needed it too.

Only when he was buried deep inside her did they slow. She wrapped her legs around his, loving the feeling of being completely open for him, of being possessed by him.

His gray eyes gazed down into hers. "I love you, Rachel."

She lifted the hand she'd curled around his hip and brought it to the nape of his neck, sheltering him as she smiled her own love back before she whispered the words she knew he wanted to hear. "I love you, Gabe."

He moved inside her, and their passion built, but neither looked away. They kept their eyes locked, unwilling to give in to the primal instinct that craved privacy at this moment of deepest vulnerability.

He didn't drop his head to the crook of her neck, but kept it above her, staring down. She didn't turn her cheek into the pillow but gazed upward.

The boldness of allowing another person, even one so deeply loved, to have such an open conduit into the other's soul intensified every movement.

Green eyes swallowed silver. Silver devoured green.

"Oh, Rach . . ."
"My love . . ."
Eyes open, they came together in a melding of souls.

Epilogue

"I don't know what's wrong with me. I just can't seem to make up my mind." Rachel caught her lip between her teeth, the perfect picture of an indecisive female except for the faintly diabolic glimmer in her eyes. "You were right, Ethan. I should have listened to you. The couch did fit better by the window."

Ethan exchanged a long-suffering look with his oldest brother. "Let's move it back to the window, Cal."

Gabe watched from the doorway with a great deal of amusement as his brothers hoisted the heavy couch until it was once again beneath the cottage's front window. He loved watching Rachel torture his brothers. She made Ethan fetch and carry for her, and when Cal visited, she developed an insatiable need to have all the new furniture they'd bought for the cottage rearranged.

She held the biggest grudge against Cal, so, even though he was around less frequently, he got the worst of it. She'd conned him into going to school with Chip last fall as his show-and-tell project, and she made him sign a ton of autographs for every kid she met. She still loved to save money, so she'd also made him agree to give future free medical care to Chip and the other children she and Gabe had, to all of Ethan and Kristy's children, and to herself, as long as she didn't have to take her clothes off. Cal had the nerve to argue with her about the last part.

No matter what Rachel demanded from his brothers, Gabe acted dumb, as if he didn't know what was going on. It drove them crazy, but they never complained because they still felt so guilty about the hard time they'd given her. As penance, they did as she asked, and she rewarded them by asking for even more.

Just this morning Gabe had inquired exactly how much longer she thought she could stretch this thing out, and she'd said she figured she could get another six months from it, but he doubted it. She didn't have a real killer instinct, and his brothers could be charming bastards when they set their minds to it. For a long time now, she'd been running more on mischief than retribution.

Cal finished positioning his end of the couch and shot Gabe an irritated look. "Tell me one more time, Rach. Why is it that lazy lug you married can't help move your furniture?"

Rachel reached down to stroke Snoozer, their calico cat. "Now, Cal, you know that Gabe has a trick back. I just don't think it's wise for him to aggravate it."

Cal muttered something under his breath that sounded like "Trick back, my ass."

Rachel pretended she didn't hear, while Gabe tried to support his beloved wife by looking like someone who might actually *have* a trick back.

As he lounged in the doorway, he realized that, after a year of marriage, he hadn't come close to getting tired of watching her. For the cookout they were having today, she wore tailored walking shorts with a silk maternity top, both of them the same blue as the hyacinths that had come up this spring in front of the cottage. A pair of small diamond earrings dangling from thin European wires glimmered through her auburn curls, which were cut shorter now, but were still a little disheveled, the way he liked. He'd bought her bigger diamond earrings, but she'd made him exchange them, saying this size suited her just fine.

What he most enjoyed about her appearance today — and most days, for that matter — were her shoes, a slim pair of silver sandals with a tiny wedged heel. He loved those sandals. He loved all the shoes he bought for her.

"Cal, that armchair . . . I hate to ask, but you're always so sweet about helping me. Would you mind moving it nearer the fireplace?"

"Not at all." Gabe could almost hear Cal's teeth grinding as he hoisted the chair across the room.

"Perfect." Rachel beamed at him.

Cal looked hopeful. "Really?"

"No, you're right. It's not perfect at all. Maybe by the couch?"

At that moment, the back door slammed and Jane shot past them on her way to the bathroom. Cal glanced at his watch and sighed. "Right on schedule."

"Three pregnant women and one bathroom." Ethan shook his head. "Not a pretty sight. I hope you get the expansion to the cottage finished soon, Gabe."

"It should be done before winter."

Unlike everyone else, his parents had fallen in love with Rachel the moment they'd met her, and his mother had deeded the cottage to them as a wedding present. Even though they had the money to buy a much more luxurious home, they both loved living on top of Heartache Mountain, and they didn't even consider moving. They needed more room, however, so they were building an airy two-story extension off the back that was designed to stay true to the cottage's rustic architecture, while giving them the additional space they needed.

Despite the construction mess, Rachel had wanted to throw a family cookout to celebrate Gabe's formal adoption of Chip. It was a big deal to everybody in the family except Chip and Gabe. They'd adopted each other a year ago on the night Rachel'd been put in jail.

"At least we only have one of our wives throwing up this time," Ethan said. "Remember when we were all here on Christmas Eve, and Rachel and Kristy were both at it."

Cal shuddered. "It's not something any of us is likely to forget."

To avoid the construction rubble, they'd set up the picnic area near Rachel's garden, which was in bloom from the rosebushes they'd planted, and now Kristy called in through the side window. "Rachel, come out here. You have to see Rosie's new trick."

"I'll be right there." She patted Cal's back. "We can finish this later."

The cat followed as Rachel waddled toward the door. Rachel had her weight thrown back on her heels and her big belly leading. Gabe felt a surge of primitive male pride knowing he'd done that to her. In another month, the baby would be born, and none of them could wait.

The moment Rachel disappeared, Cal and Ethan collapsed on the couch they'd moved to four separate locations. Gabe took pity and brought them each a beer. Then he settled in the armchair he suspected he'd have to wrestle back to its original position as soon as his brothers left and lifted his own bottle. "Here's to the three luckiest men on earth."

His brothers smiled, and, for a while, they just sat there sipping their beers and thinking about how lucky they really were. Cal had finished his first year of medical school at UNC, and he and Jane were enjoying living in Chapel Hill. The architects had completed the plans for the renovation that would turn the mausoleum into a spacious contemporary. It would be their permanent home when Cal finished his residency and came back to join their father's practice.

Ethan seemed to have finally found peace in his role as a minister, although he griped about the series of church secretaries he'd gone through in a futile attempt to replace Kristy, who refused to leave her job teaching preschool to come back to work for him. And Rachel . . .

Chip dashed in, followed by Sammy, his year-old black Lab. Sammy dashed over to Gabe, while Chip ran to Cal. "Rosie's a pain."

"What'd she do now, pal?" Cal gave Gabe's son a quick hug. From the back of the house, the wheel on the hamster cage squeaked.

"Crashed my fort right after I got it built."

"You don't have to put up with that," Cal said. "Tell her *no*. Or build your fort out front where she can't get to you."

Chip regarded him with reproach. "She was helping, and she didn't mean to."

Cal rolled his eyes. "One of these days you and your Uncle Cal are going to have to have a long talk about dealing with women."

Chip wandered over to Gabe, crawled up on his lap, and settled in. At six, he'd started to shoot up, and, before long, his feet would brush the floor, but he still liked being in Gabe's lap. Chip's beloved Lab collapsed across Gabe's foot. "You know what I think's gonna happen, Dad?"

Gabe brushed the top of his head with a kiss. "What's that, son?"

Chip gave a sigh of resignation. "I think when me and Rosie grow up, we're gonna prob'ly get married, just like you and Mom did."

The men didn't laugh at his pronouncement. All of them had come to respect the mysterious bond that had formed between the two children, even though none of them quite understood it.

"Sometimes a man's got to do what a man's got to do," Cal observed.

Chip nodded. "That's what I was thinking."

They did laugh then.

A huge Rosie-howl came from the side yard. Sammy lifted his head from Gabe's foot, and Chip sighed. "I better go. She's got Grandma and Grandpa wrapped around her little finger."

The men waited until Chip and his dog had disappeared, then grinned at each other. Cal shook his head. "That boy is spooky. Six going on thirty."

Ethan smiled. "I just hope the three new ones turn out half as terrific as those two."

Gabe glanced through the back window. Shadow, a collie mix he'd adopted a few months ago, lay patiently on the ground and let Rosie climb on him. Chip approached his parents. His Grandpa Bonner felt his bicep, while his grandmother reached over and ruffled his hair.

He was glad to have his parents back from South America, not only for his own sake, but for Chip's. The Bonner family had taken his son right to its collective heart, along with his mother. Chip also had friends now, and he'd done well in kindergarten. Gabe was so proud of him.

Jane, looking healthy, if a little green, came back through the living room. Tasha, an older cat Gabe had rescued from the shelter, waddled after her. Jane was nearing the end of her second month of pregnancy and was delirious with happiness when she wasn't throwing up.

Cal started to rise, but she waved him back down. "I'm fine. Visit with your brothers."

They exchanged smiles, and Cal patted her rear.

Gabe thought about how much he loved doing that. Not patting Jane's rear, of course, but Rachel's. Being able to pat a woman's rear whenever you wanted was one of the best things about being married, although nobody ever told you that.

"I spoke with Carol Dennis yesterday," Ethan said.

Gabe and Cal exchanged grim looks. The memory of the day Bobby Dennis had jeopardized their children's lives was something they'd never forget. Nor would Ethan and Kristy. They were still beating themselves up for having left the children alone in the car, even though nobody blamed them for it.

It had taken six months for Bobby to recover from his injuries, but the car accident had turned out to be a blessing in disguise for the kid. He'd been clean and sober for the past year, and he and Carol had gotten the counseling they so desperately needed.

Gabe suspected their relationship would always be difficult, but, according to Ethan, they were finally communicating. Bobby had also stopped blaming Rachel for his problems, which was a good thing, because if Gabe had still believed the kid was a threat to her, he'd have run him out of town, counseling or not.

"Carol said Bobby's planning on starting college in August. He actually finished high school with some decent grades."

488

Cal shook his head. "I still can't believe the way Rachel kept visiting him in the hospital. That woman's got more heart than sense. You know what people are saying about that, don't you? That if Rachel hadn't visited him, he wouldn't —"

Gabe groaned. "Don't say it."

"That reminds me." Ethan glanced out the window at Kristy, who was holding Rosie's hand against her belly so she could feel the baby move. He smiled, then returned his attention to the discussion at hand. "I'm going to need some help from you with Rachel. Brenda Meers is taking a long time recovering from her pneumonia, and I want Rachel to visit her."

"Here we go again." Cal stretched out his legs and looked amused.

Gabe thought he and Ethan had an understanding about this, and he regarded his brother with exasperation. "Eth, I told you last time that I'm not getting in the middle of this. You're Rachel's pastor, and you'll have to talk to her yourself."

The men sipped their beer and thought about how tough that might be.

"How long do you think she's going to keep fighting this thing?" Cal finally asked.

"I'd give her another forty years," Gabe replied.

Ethan held up his hand. "I'm not the bad guy here. I don't know whether she heals people or not, but the fact is, a lot of them seem to get better after she sits with them for a while."

The injured animals got better, too. Gabe was always making excuses to get her to handle the ones under his care. He didn't understand how it happened. He only knew that they seemed to heal faster after she'd touched them.

"A faith healer in denial." Since Cal wasn't the one who had to deal with Rachel, he continued to look amused. "Nobody in this town has a bad word to say against her since Emily's miracle. And when Bobby Dennis recovered from that spinal injury after the doctors said he'd be paralyzed . . ."

"People love her," Ethan observed. "It's ironic. G. Dwayne told everybody he could heal, but he couldn't. Rachel insists she can't, and she can."

"We don't know that for a fact," Gabe pointed out. "It could all be coincidence. Just do what you've done before, Eth. Tell Rachel that Brenda's sick and could use some cheering up. As long as you don't mention healing, you know she won't turn you down."

"Isn't she getting suspicious about all these sick calls I keep sending her out on?"

"She's so wrapped up in Chip, and the renovations on the cottage, and the new baby, and her classes, and making plans for the money she got from selling G. Dwayne's diamond stash that I don't think she has time to get suspicious." She was wrapped up in him, too, but Gabe didn't mention that because he didn't want to brag in front of his brothers. Not that Cal and Ethan didn't have plenty of room to brag themselves.

Rachel loved the finance courses she was taking at the local community college, although she pretended she was doing it only because he was so hopeless about

490

money. If she left it up to him, she said, they'd end up in the poorhouse.

Just to give her a hard time, he'd pointed out that she'd never have to worry about the poorhouse if she'd hung on to some of G. Dwayne's fortune instead of using it for her pet charity after she'd paid his debts, but she paid no attention. She and Ethan were working together to establish a statewide foundation that would help single mothers get on their feet by providing decent child care while they took classes and started new jobs. Rachel had backed into the perfect career for herself.

She's also helped the community by setting up a group to run the Pride of Carolina on a nonprofit basis. The drive-in had become the most popular spot in town on summer weekends.

"It's hard to believe . . . Just over a year ago, everybody in Salvation hated her guts. Now she's a local heroine." Cal spoke with a great deal of pride for a man who'd been one of her chief persecutors.

Rachel had Snoozer in her arms as she stuck her head up to the screen. "Everybody's getting hungry, Gabe. How about starting the grill?"

The men ambled out to the backyard where their parents sat together on an old quilt with Rosie perched between them and the dogs reclining nearby. Ethan moved over to Kristy, and she cuddled up to him. Cal wrapped his arm around Jane, then reached over to pat her uneasy stomach.

Gabe simply stood there, taking in the sight of these people he loved so much. Rachel set a stack of paper plates on the picnic table and looked up at him. He smiled at her, and she smiled back, their thoughts perfectly matched.

I love you, Gabe.

I love you, Rach.

Chip charged forward. Gabe knew what he wanted, and he reached out his arms.

A moment later, Chip was settled on his shoulders, his hands clasped across his father's forehead, legs dangling over his chest.

Rachel started to cry.

She did this sometimes at family gatherings when her happiness got to be too much for her. They were all used to it. They liked to tease her about it. They'd tease her about it today. Soon . . . Maybe after lunch . . .

But for now, Cal needed to clear his throat. Jane sniffed. Ethan had a little cough. Kristy wiped her eyes. His mother handed a tissue to his father.

Gabe's heart swelled. Life was good on Heartache Mountain.

He threw back his head and laughed.

The Cinderella Moment

Gemma Fox

While off to seek her fortune, Cass meets Prince Charming in a carriage — a railway carriage, that is. That chance conversation, and apparent good luck of finding a mobile phone, turns her whole life upside down. But what if Prince Charming turns out to be the Big Bad Wolf after all?

A summer job in Brighton, an ex-husband who makes pumpkins look bright and a very unlikely pair who double as fairy godmothers, when not on the pull or drinking themselves into a stupor, take Cass on an adventure which is almost more nightmare than fairytale. So when midnight strikes, will everything vanish, or will the real Prince Charming be revealed?

ISBN 0-7531-7666-1 (hb)
ISBN 0-7531-7667-X (pb)

A Question of Love

Isabel Wolff

Sometimes the questions you ask yourself are the hardest ones to answer . . .

Laura Quick is an unlikely candidate to present a quirky new quiz show. But her boss, Tom, sees that her quick-wittedness and knack for general knowledge make her the ideal choice and offers her the chance of a lifetime.

When old flame Luke turns up out of the blue, Laura's sisters think it's time for her to move on and lay to rest the memory of her husband, Nick. But dating Luke again is a step back in time — and may spell trouble. Luke is every bit as charismatic as when he broke her heart. But this time around he's got a 6-year-old daughter in tow — as well as an ex-wife whose behaviour is a little extreme.

As Laura questions whether to gamble everything on a past love, she must also face up to the unexpected truth about Nick and the life she thought she once knew . . .

ISBN 0-7531-7652-1 **(hb)**
ISBN 0-7531-7653-X **(pb)**

Just Like Heaven

Marc Levy

Now a major Hollywood film

What do you do when you find a strange girl in your closet — and she can disappear and reappear at whim? What if she tells you she is lying in a coma on the other side of town? Should you have her see a psychologist or should you consult one yourself? Or do you take a chance and believe in her?

This is the dilemma Arthur, a young San Francisco architect, must face when he discovers Lauren in his apartment. Arthur is the only man who can share Lauren's secret, the only one who can see her, hear her and talk to her when no one else so much as senses her presence. So when doctors prepare to end Lauren's physical care — which would destroy the magical bond she and Arthur cherish — he must find a way to save her. For, after all, it is only her love that can save him.

ISBN 0-7531-7678-5 (hb)
ISBN 0-7531-7679-3 (pb)

Babyville

Jane Green

Meet Julia, a wildly successful television producer who appears to have the picture-perfect life. But beneath the surface, things are not as perfect as they seem. Stuck in a loveless relationship with her boyfriend, Mark, Julia thinks a baby is the answer . . . but she may want a baby more than she wants her boyfriend.

Maeve, on the other hand, is allergic to commitment. A feisty, red-haired, high-power career girl, she breaks out in a rash every time she passes a buggy. But when her no-strings-attached nightlife leads to an unexpected pregnancy, her reaction may be just as unexpected . . .

And then there's Samantha — happily married and eager to be the perfect mother. But baby George brings only exhaustion, extra pounds and marital strife to her once tidy life. Is having an affair with a friend's incredibly sexy husband the answer?

ISBN 0-7531-7616-5 (hb)
ISBN 0-7531-7617-3 (pb)

Lessons in Duck Shooting

Jayne Buxton

Ally James's life is in dire need of a makeover. Juggling the demands of a neurotic boss, the sudden appearance of her ex-husband's latest arm candy and the endless whirl of school runs seems to have become a mammoth effort of late. And watching The Little Mermaid with her kids is probably the closest she has come to an exciting date in years. So when her best friend bullies her into a dating seminar, Ally finds herself reluctantly giving in. American relationship guru Marina Boyd claims that all you need is some shrewd self-marketing and a steady stream of trial men — or, to use her term, duck decoys — and you're on a sure-fire road to Mr Right.

Ally's not so sure, though. Can packaging and promoting possibly be the same as dating and falling in love? Ally is about to find out . . .

ISBN 0-7531-7634-3 (hb)
ISBN 0-7531-7635-1 (pb)

ISIS publish a wide range of books in large print, from fiction to biography. Any suggestions for books you would like to see in large print or audio are always welcome. Please send to the Editorial Department at:

ISIS Publishing Limited
7 Centremead
Osney Mead
Oxford OX2 0ES

A full list of titles is available free of charge from:

Ulverscroft Large Print Books Limited

(UK)
The Green
Bradgate Road, Anstey
Leicester LE7 7FU
Tel: (0116) 236 4325

(Australia)
P.O. Box 314
St Leonards
NSW 1590
Tel: (02) 9436 2622

(USA)
P.O. Box 1230
West Seneca
N.Y. 14224-1230
Tel: (716) 674 4270

(Canada)
P.O. Box 80038
Burlington
Ontario L7L 6B1
Tel: (905) 637 8734

(New Zealand)
P.O. Box 456
Feilding
Tel: (06) 323 6828

Details of ISIS complete and unabridged audio books are also available from these offices. Alternatively, contact your local library for details of their collection of ISIS large print and unabridged audio books.